AFTER THE BALL

Max Allan put his arm around India's waist and drew his cape round them both. Close-pressed to one another they walked toward her cottage.

They came to the steps and he turned her in his cape until she was facing him in the darkness.

Her mouth was almost on a level with his and he only had to bend his head a little as she lifted her face to take his kiss. She felt she must repay him for such joy and so she clasped his golden head and tried to kiss him as he kissed her.

"I have never seen a girl like you," he was trembling and his voice was deep and low. "Will you still let me kiss you when I come home?"

"Yes," said India, "I will. But never another so long as I live."

INDIA ALLAN

Elizabeth Boatwright Coker

BANTAM BOOKS • LONDON

TORONTO • NEW YORK

INDIA ALLAN

A Bantam Book / published by arrangement with
Mockingbird Books

PRINTING HISTORY

Dutton edition published October 1953
Bantam edition / September 1977

ISBN 0–553–10526–4

Published simultaneously in the United States and Canada

Bantam Books are published by Bantam Books, Inc. Its trade-
mark, consisting of the words "Bantam Books" and the por-
trayal of a bantam, is registered in the United States Patent
Office and in other countries. Marca Registrada. Bantam
Books, Inc., 666 Fifth Avenue, New York, New York 10019.

PRINTED IN THE UNITED STATES OF AMERICA

This story is for a lovely lady
RIETTA BOATWRIGHT

CONTENTS

PROLOGUE

*Charleston,
March 31, 1850*

PROLOGUE

MR. HURLEY, the barber, walked slowly along the pink brick wall with iron spikes across the top and stopped by the iron gate wrought in a pattern of scrolls and fans which had always intrigued him for what it had never let him see of the secluded St. Julien garden. He breathed deep of the fresh salt smell from the bay as a particularly brisk gust of wind freaked around the corner from the Battery and set the tall palmettos inside the cloistered garden to rustling their fronds restlessly.

Mr. Hurley had never been inside the St. Julien house so this was an occasion of rare excitement. Houses were Hr. Hurley's infatuation. Many came to be shaved or clipped in his shop on Broad Street just to hear the big red Irishman talk about the dwelling places of the high and mighty. From his lips scandal dripped succulently, he being able to describe everything down to the last tassel on a telltale cushion. For Mr. Hurley had memorized the houses of Charleston so well that even in the night in his own hot little rooms on St. Michael's Alley he could, aided by a bit of laudanum, whisk himself lustily into canopied four-posters of heroic proportions; waltz with the grace of a dancing master in Mrs. King's octagonal drawing room at one of her annual balls during Race Week; lean arrogantly against the marble mantel brought from Italy by Mrs. Joel Poinsett; or hasten down the secret stairs of the Horry mansion, from the study to the street, and find his round little love waiting underneath a black magnolia in the moonless dark.

Mr. Hurley lifted the heavy tail of the polished brass lizard and let the striking part fall gently so as not to make too loud a knock against the iron gate. Almost

3

at once the gate opened—the Negro must have been standing, waiting, on the other side. Mr. Hurley followed the man up a short walk to a handsome flight of half round marble steps from which a fanlighted door opened into the bow of a hall which ran through the house to another door. The house, of small dark English brick, was a parallelogram with bows on the north and east sides, a bowed piazza on the west, and a long broad piazza on the south. Mr. Hurley shivered with pleasure. This was different from most of the single and double houses of the city with their aloof sides to the street and their proudly façaded fronts facing little narrow walled gardens. The hall was wide and cool and the only pattern on the carefully worked paneled walls was the fretted shadow of a live-oak branch thrown through the leaded-glass fan from a gnarled old tree outside. He had heard of the stairway which had been hung ninety years earlier by trained men fetched at Hector St. Julien's expense from England, and here it was, before his very eyes, springing like a living thing unsupported from each floor to the next, giving a peculiarly graceful and airy effect to the flagged hall which might otherwise have seemed too formal and severe.

"Come on," said the Negro, purposely omitting the "sir."

Mr. Hurley shrugged his shoulders and impudently stepped into the dining room which opened from the hall, letting his small green Irish eyes gorge their fill. As he turned to ascend the stairs he saw that the Negro was trying to decide whether or not he had better come back down and count the silver.

"Where to?" Mr. Hurley asked roughly.

The Negro led the way to the second-floor landing lighted by a triple window. Mr. Hurley made as though to stop at the arched double doors leading into the drawing room but the expression on the Negro's face changed his mind so, sighing, he went on up to the third floor. Through the oval window in this hall he could see a white sea bird smooth as porcelain winging softly past. Suddenly he realized that he had not heard a sound in the entire house.

"Who is dead?" he asked.

"In here," said the Negro.

Mr. Hurley entered a paneled bedroom painted a muted rose, looking rosier with the afternoon sun streaming in through the windowpanes onto a flowered Aubusson rug.

"Here the barber, Miss Rachel."

A strange-looking woman was sitting in a chair by a mantel carved with a group of shepherds in the center panel and sunbursts on either side. She drew her thick light brows together as the big Irishman brushed too close to a delicate Sheraton table by the door causing an etched hurricane candle shade to tinkle dangerously against the old waxed wood.

"Excuse me, mam, I'm Mr. Hurley, the barber."

The strange lady inclined her head slightly and picking up a blue Dresden bell in trembling fingers rang hysterically until a door opened and a handsome six-foot-high Negro woman in a smart city dress of purple challis trimmed all around with green silk tassels came leading a small girl by the hand.

Mr. Hurley caught his breath; but not at the bizarre Negro woman. It was the child he saw; only the child. She had the most wonderful hair he had ever come across. Coal-black and soft as soot, it hung about her slender waist like a guardian. His thick freckled fingers tingled just to touch it.

"Where would you like the child to sit?" the lady asked.

"Is it her hair I have come to cut?"

"Miss Rachel, before God let me beg you one more time not to cut India's hair. She hasn't been all that sick and Mr. Guy will be killing mad." The Negro woman's slanting eyes looked at Mr. Hurley as though he were an odd bit of furniture from the servants' quarters pulled in there by mistake.

"Mr. Hurley," a petulant note crept into the lady's voice, "doesn't the hair sap the strength of a child who has had a long sickness?"

Mr. Hurley knew that the healthy hair of the obviously well child did not sap her strength but for the life of him he could not miss this opportunity:

"Indeed, mam, I can see by her pale cheeks and liverish eyes that it will be necessary to cut the child's hair immediately."

The lady turned her chair to the fire so that she need not see. Mr. Hurley busied himself opening his bag and getting out a pair of long shears. He ran his finger down the blades to make sure they were sharp. The Negro woman, muttering loudly, spread a cotton sack on the floor to protect the rug and the child sat in a fragile gilt chair with her back to the long oval mirror in the far corner of the room.

An electric shock passed through Mr. Hurley as he gingerly picked up the hair by the child's temple and severed it with one quick incisive snap. The child sat motionless, staring at the shepherds marching across the fire-bright mantel, her dark gray eyes hard as stones. Awareness of the child as a person was not in Mr. Hurley as slowly at first and then in a frenzy he grasped handfuls of hair and hacked it off, letting it drop in black pools on the snowy cotton cloth around his stubby feet. Finally he lifted the last long tress and with a cry cut it apart from the little head.

"My God, what large ears!" the Negro said.

"I have finished, mam. Do you want the hair?" Mr. Hurley's voice was thick and he bumped hard against the gilt chair.

"No," said the lady.

"May I have it?"

"If you wish."

He squatted on the floor, pushed the pliant slippery mass, that was tangling now like floss, into his bag and hastened from the room. Down the curving stairs he ran, never even pausing for an instant to explore the drawing room which was open and empty, its mirrors catching the last of the sunrays like static lightning in their frigid depths.

The Negro man was waiting when he reached the first-floor hall, holding open the opposite door from the one in which he had entered. Out onto the southern piazza Mr. Hurley flew, hugging his bag close to his chest. He stumbled going down the steps, and the walk through the garden, sweet with fragrant olive and hyacinths, to the other entrance under a little dome-shaped pavilion seemed endless with the contemptuous black man close on his heels.

Once again outside the high wrought-iron fence he could not resist the temptation to plunge his hand into the bag and fasten his thick fingers in the soft hair. Had the child been beautiful or ugly? Her he had not even noticed and yet he held a part of her in his hands. India, the Negro woman had named her. India St. Julien.

As soon as the dreadful man was gone India sprang from the gilt chair and rushed over to her mother.

"May I get the pony this minute, Mama?"

Rachel St. Julien snatched her daughter close crushing the shorn head into her breast. "Oh, my precious little Norman," she cried wildly, "tomorrow. Tomorrow surely. But not today. Just stay with Mama today, my little darling."

"No, you promised I could have the pony today. You always say tomorrow and I will have it today. You wait and see; and when I get my pony I will ride up down every street in Charleston and speak to people whether they are nice or not."

The Negro woman followed her nurseling, leaving Rachel St. Julien crying softly in her cheerful bedroom.

"Why does she treat me as though I were sick all the time, Duchess? Why can't she let me be like other little girls? She promised me a pony if I would let my hair be cut. Make her not persuade Papa against the pony, Duchess. Make her."

"Don't worry, you'll get the pony. Mr. Guy is going to be killing mad when he sees what she has done to you this time."

"But why does she act so strange, Duchess?"

"Haven't you gone every day of your eight years with her to put flowers on the three graves in the cemetery?"

"Oh, you mean my brothers?"

"That's right."

"But they were drowned in the hurricane when I was just a baby. That's no reason not to let me do anything."

"Reason for your mother."

"Come with me into the drawing room to see myself, Duchess. Do I look like a boy? A really truly boy?"

"You look just like the oldest boy, Norman, only not nearly so beautiful. His eyes were blue and soft, yours are as wild as a sea gull's."

"Was he a nice boy?"

"The favorite. Wait till your papa sees you. Norman could ride better than any of the little boys in Charleston. He'll get you your pony today."

On the second floor the upper hall lost its length because there was a card room at the south end of it, opening on the upper gallery through a wide door with beautifully carved side lights. The paneled drawing room extending across the whole western end of the house had a handsomely ornamented ceiling of plaster worked in garlands of roses with two elaborate crystal chandeliers which made, when the hundreds of candles were lighted, living fire in the huge Venetian mirrors filling each panel of the side walls. The woodwork was painted a soft green and the delicate gold-silk-covered gilt furniture imported from France, gave a courtly atmosphere of city formality.

From the mirrors India could see herself reflected endlessly. What if her ears did stick out a little. She didn't care. They made her look like a real boy. A dark boy with bright eyes. She clapped her hands, spinning around to see the back, the side, the front of her head.

Duchess, sometimes called The Duchess, sat down on the longest gold sofa, opened a silver box on a round Chippendale piecrust table and selected one of Guy's expensive Havanas, bit off the end with her carefully filed teeth, and settled back comfortably, blowing the fragrant smoke in a thick cloud around her long narrow head topped with a big knob of oiled jetty hair.

"You look like a little prince," she said in her deep husky way. "When I was in the Governor's house in Barbados he had a boy your age who refused to let anyone cut his curls. They were yellow and hung below his fat waist. He was very unattractive. Always pinching me on the titty when his mother was present and I couldn't pinch him back."

"Oh, Duchess, did you ever truly pinch a governor's son?"

"Many times, but I made sure no one could hear him scream."

"I'm glad you are my nurse now. Aren't you?"

"I like you very well but I don't like being anybody's servant. When Mr. Guy came visiting the Governor he took a fancy to me and bought me as a gift for Miss Rachel. I was very anxious to come to America and I became very fond of Norman. I wanted him to grow into a man."

"Tell me about Norman."

Neither of them was aware when Guy St. Julien came in or knew how long he had been watching from the doorway. Guy St. Julien was a thin pointed-looking man with a high forehead sharply peaked with black hair. His nose was long and slightly hooked and his eyes gray and uneasy. He was forty-four but he looked older and already let his shoulders droop tiredly.

"Duchess, Duchess, what have you let her do to the child?"

"You can see for yourself. She's trying to pretend that India is Norman," Duchess said, sifting an ash into the palm of her hand.

"I am India. I don't want to be anybody else." India burst into tears and ran and caught Guy around his waist. "Please, please, she promised I could have the pony today. Please, Papa, please. I am so tired of never seeing anybody but Duchess and Mama."

Guy put his narrow hand on India's cropped hair which gleamed sootily and felt as tender as a blackbird's breast. He let his fingers caress her cheek, looking into the cloudy gray eyes tear-shining under the straight black brows.

"Like a little Greek boy," he said to her; "my little Greek boy. Did you know that through my mother, Helen Turnbull, you are truly of Greek descent? That you should be proud of. Always proud! Duchess, do you know where Norman's riding clothes were stored?"

"In her wardrobe. But you'd better not upset Miss

Rachel by dressing India in his breeches. Lately she has been singing that lullaby about the buzzards and the butterflies every night when I finally get her into bed. What difference does India's hair make? It will grow back by January."

"Go fetch Norman's clothes and put them on India. In here. In this very room and I will have Siah bring my horse. Would you like to ride behind me all the way to Uncle Alston's, my darling? He has your pony ready. It's been waiting for two years now."

The boy's clothes fit India perfectly and Duchess looked pleased when the arrow-straight child with the short black hair strutted admiringly up and down in front of all the mirrors.

"Shall I show Mama?" she asked.

"She'll see," Duchess answered.

Guy was in the saddle already when Duchess and India reached the courtyard; he lifted her up behind him and seated her on his cape, which he had folded up and placed on the horse's loins for a pillion. India had to sit there astride and hold onto his belt. She called good-by to her mama who had come out onto the upper southern gallery with her long light hair hanging loose and wild; but Rachel came running down from the gallery by the outside stairs with India's hair ribbon—she handed it to Guy and told him to take good care of their child. Then she put her hand in the nurse's, like a child herself, and let herself be guided back into the house.

As Guy and India rode out onto the Battery, the bells of all the churches in the city unexpectedly started tolling; drums began to beat on every square and a large group of horsemen came galloping from King Street. Guy's horse fretted and curvetted excitedly so he dismounted and led him to the sidewalk. India sat high and proud on the big gelding watching the horses clatter past striking sparks from the cobblestones, with their steel-shod hoofs, their riders shouting over and over, "John Calhoun is dead! John C. Calhoun is dead!"

Her father clutched at her ankle as if to support himself. "The South, the poor South!" he whispered. He was so stiff and blue about the mouth, that India grew afraid. By now people were streaming from the big fine houses and out of alleys, and in no time the gardens along the sea wall were packed and jammed with wailing folk of every kind.

The sun was setting under a gold and crimson banner with long lilac and rose streamers of clouds trailing across the whole sky and over the water Fort Sumter caught the last of the glow, lighting up suddenly like a burning brand. Reflections of the glorious color were on all the faces, and India couldn't for the life of her understand why everybody was weeping or why the bells sounded so sad when everything was still so beautiful.

PART ONE

The Meeting
White Sulphur Springs,
July, 1858

Wade Hampton, Preston Hampton, the Pickens, Franklin Moses, Calbraith Butler and Martin Gary were real people. The rest of the main characters are definitely fictional.

CHAPTER I

FROM THE MOMENT India took hold of the high stepping hackney pony and cantered him easily, so like Norman would have done, around the star-shaped flower beds of her Uncle Alston's garden, Guy tried to give her all of Charleston for her fancying.

Rachel lost all identity for him. India, loosed from all restraint, fascinated him with her high spirits and her vitality and he followed her worshipfully, sometimes letting days pass without entering Rachel's room. This neglect coming on top of the shock of India's clipped head undid Rachael completely and she died quietly in her sleep one windy January night.

India was not slow realizing her new power, and though everyone agreed that she was a charming child and other children flocked to play at her house where there were no rules, the more observant also agreed that she was very spoiled and that this was all her father's fault. Guy St. Julien had been proud of his boys but this girl-child with her fearless eyes, smooth glowing cheeks, and swift feet was a plaything. He bought her toys, animals, hats, dresses from London and Paris, and spent as much time with her as his failing health and brilliant law practice allowed, showing off her accomplishments to every visitor.

Each morning he took her for a canter about the city. Dressed in Norman's breeches, always riding astride, she became something to watch for as she trotted along the shady streets on the hackney. Hamlet had style and speed, a shiny arched neck and delicate high-action clean-boned legs that could make stride for stride with Guy's big Eclipse gelding. They rode wherever India's fancy flew: to joke with the old Negro women selling croker sacks of tiny rice birds in open stalls near the market where tame buzzards flapped up and down ludicrously; down by the bay to listen to the sad rhythmic chanteys of the weary Negro boatmen rowing bales of cotton in from the Up Country; along South Battery

15

where neat Maumas walked the little children; on the wharves to hail steamers from New York and Liverpool; Broad Street where, near St. Michael's, Mr. Hurley would be waiting and come running with a sack of benne candy for her tiny pockets; out to the Washington Race Course to see the horses train.

She talked and laughed with everybody who interested her. She was wild and gay but she was such a pretty thing with so sweet a smile and light feet and whenever she misbehaved was always so sorry that it usually ended with her father trying to make her happy again to comfort her. Some of her playmates complained that she was bossy but these she would soon wheedle into doing her way by making them think they, rather than she, had started the game.

One day when she was ten her father's Aunt Childs, hearing she was in bed with a spell of dengue fever, came to call.

"Here Miss Turnbull," the Negro butler, whose name was Beverly, announced to India who promptly stuck out a coated tongue at the old lady bringing a sack of peppermint drops to her. Fixing India with her sharp black eyes, in her wonderful voice inherited from the Greek mother, she discoursed on sin and on the judgment to come, ending with: "India, why don't you pray to God to make you better so he won't whirl you away in a hurricane as he did your poor little brothers?"

She was answered with, "Oh, dear Aunt Childs, I do but he only makes me badder and badder."

Her education was scant. In the Misses Johnson's School For Young Ladies and Gentlemen she excelled at shinny and stingaree with the boys, accomplishing little in composition or the arts of needlework and china painting though she had a mockingbird facility in mimicking the sounds of a foreign language and could chatter in French and German with a happy disregard for moods and tenses.

Only in her dancing class was she the star pupil. Wearing the soft slippers and long white cotton stockings considered necessary for dancing, India was guided around the room by M. Tootet's aloof finger tips, outwardly calm, inwardly on fire. Even the prim toe points and bowing of the slow minuet could transport her into a more delicious world. Not a Charleston world. When India danced she was no longer a St. Julien and an Episcopalian and a pupil in Miss Johnson's school. She was a pagan Greek maid dancing on the slopes of Hymettus against the tall black cedars that sang with the sea wind from the Aegean Gulf.

When she was thirteen her father took her to the races, and watching a spectacular filly of Colonel Hampton's named Flossie Fisher capture one of the big purses, flying over the hurdles like a homing pigeon, she *must* have Flossie Fisher for her own.

"If you can ride her." Guy gave in, as he always gave in to India.

After that, astride or sidesaddle, India spent most of her time on horseback. Her obsession became so violent that even Guy agreed with his outraged Aunt Childs that India must be sent away from Flossie Fisher to a young ladies' academy.

The Duchess selected dresses and hats suitable for a princess; packed India's trunks; then shortly unpacked them as various institutions in Baltimore, Philadelphia, Richmond, and Winston-Salem agreed that India was better off at home with Flossie and Papa in Charleston than upsetting their entire plan of finishing gentle females into proper Southern ladies.

By the time she was sixteen she had become startlingly beautiful and Guy proudly presented her at the St. Cecilia. But after that the young gentlemen came flocking so eagerly that Guy, alarmed lest one of them take her fancy, whisked her away to New Orleans to divert her with Mardi Gras.

That year his cousin Erica Beauregard was one of the queens and she invited India to attend her court. Here the soft-voiced Orleanians found her frankness irresistibly different from the usual belles who wooed and whispered with their fans. But her New Orleans triumph ended abruptly after she overzealously tried to do away with a frisky mouse sharing her room in the fashionable hotel in the Vieux Carré, and burned the hotel to ashes,

intending merely to singe the portiere up which the
mouse had run.

A lawyer friend of Guy's saw to it that India's name
did not appear in the *Picayune* but Erica decided that a
sweet young creole could quite ably fill India's place in
her court, so from New Orleans Guy and India and
The Duchess journeyed to White Sulphur Springs for
the spring and summer season, settling comfortably in
one of the elegantly furnished cottages in the newly
built Carolina Row.

CHAPTER II

THE SUMMER of 1858 was the gayest in a hundred
years at the White Sulphur. The new hotel had been
built and there were almost three thousand people at
the resort brought together for pleasure, health, mate-
hunting, and political ambition. Despite the echoes of
pistol shots from the firing range where young blooded
males from North and South were polishing their marks-
manship to defend whatever honor they might be called
upon to unstain in the not too distant future—be it
States' Rights, John Brown's Body, the railroad to the
West, the caning of a senator, their sister's bathing costume, or the length of their horse's trot—they still paraded in fashionable clothes to and from the spring
twice a day while the German band played stirring
marches under the old oaks and locusts on the smooth
green sward; bowed courteously to each other in the
lancers and held each other too close while the Viennese
orchestra played haunting waltzes for the sealing of
their fate each balmy night.

The sixteenth of July had been set aside for the formal grand opening of the new ballroom and on the
fifteenth all the conversation in the noisy crowded dining room and the long new parlor was of tomorrow!
Wade Hampton's Hunt—the picnic in the meadow following—the wonderful, wonderful ball that would be
the highlight of the whole summer.

During the siesta hour after dinner, in front of the main hotel, all was abustle. The assistant manager was sitting at a table under a locust tree, the register book open before him trying to get rid of the people who had arrived on the midday stagecoaches. There wasn't any room for them here, the place was packed to the doors. There wasn't a cot or a pallet or a blanket or a bench or a row of three chairs that did not have its nightly occupant. The manager was a thin reddish man with a bald head and large ears. His face was livid, and any manners he had superimposed on his none too genial nature had long evaporated on this unusually hot July afternoon. He exhorted the weary travel-bruised people to go to boardinghouses within a mile or so of the Springs—they could attend the opening ball tomorrow night from there. He begged them to go on to Lewisburg nine miles west; to the Blue Sulphur Springs, twenty-two miles west where there were always plenty of rooms: to the Warm, the Sweet, the Salt. There they could wait their turn and he would accommodate them when he could. Reservations! What did that matter! The certain thing now was, they would have to get on away from here. None of them had come in their own carriages. He knew quality from quantity and quantity had got to be very annoying.

He was annoyed in any event. All day he had been besieged with people demanding to be moved to more elite quarters—Baltimore Row or Virginia Row or the new Carolina Row; ones who resented being so near the kitchen; the pleasant, smiling people who tipped enormously and who had to be turned out of the best cottages when the Southerners who owned them swept through the gates in huge creaking coaches and claimed their feathered nests; the dispossessed who had to exchange Paradise Row for Flea Row and were squalling and howling; Mr. Dabney Lagrone who had threatened to cane him for having pulled his imported four-horse carriage with the solid silver mountings out under a tree to make room in the shelter for the six-horse scarlet coach of the Carolina nabob said to be arriving around sunset with an entourage rivaling an Eastern potentate's.

India was sitting under an ancient oak in front of their cottage watching the hullabaloo of the incoming visitors. Even in the deep shade the heat was dry and stifling. She idly kicked at a green lizard showing her his coral blanket, and the silver rowels attached to her black satin *français* boots tinkled like little bells. Where could Preston Hampton be? He had especially told her to be ready at three o'clock. How she hated waiting for anybody; even a Hampton.

Peering into the dust rising in pinky clouds from the turnpike, she saw a caravan going out of the narrow neck toward the junction of the Warm and the Sweet Springs roads. It was probably the incense-burning Virginia editor who had called Wade Hampton "haughty" in the parlor at the tea party yesterday; or the spiteful West Point major who, after watching Hampton kill a running deer with one of the new Colt revolvers at one hundred and thirty-eight yards, he himself having missed the animal with a shotgun at fifty yards, had named him "arrogant"; or that dreadful loose-lipped Mr. Edmund Ruffin whom Hampton had publicly called a "troublemaking fool" for his seditious articles, sent from the Springs to Mr. Barnwell Rhett's Charleston *Mercury*, boring at the foundations of the nation, capitalizing the little events of the Springs summer that had a curious way of playing into his hands as though he himself had just pulled them out of the hat; or the red-haired widow from Texas who had arrived this morning with twelve trunks full of Paris gowns and promptly fainted on hearing that the rich widower, the catch of the country, had married frail faraway Up Country Mary McDuffie only a short month before!

Whoever was leaving would not be missed. There would be dozens of fancy widows and argumentative gentlemen left. This summer the young men were in the majority. If only, India sighed, if only *one* of them could interest her.

Preston Hampton almost did. But not quite, he being just her age and far too docile to her every whim. Why didn't he come? It was so tiresome sitting alone. All the ladies were in siesta and the only men about were either lying on the grass under the old trees down by the springhouse reading the papers that had come on the noon stage, or hidden back up the hill at a "tiger" playing cards and gambling.

Getting to her feet she started over to the dark grove where the Colonnade, three privately owned Greek temples of aristocracy, was set apart from the rest of the resort. Her bottle-green riding habit with its tight-fitting jacket and cleverly divided draperied skirt revealed an arresting combination of slenderness and sinuous grace. The black English high silk hat, softly shining as her hair, was held on by a French veil of green gauze faintly shadowing the sudden whiteness of her skin. The white piqué collar at her throat fastened with a thin black bow emphasized her oval face. Her mouth was rather large but she had full bright red lips and a good nose. But it was her dark gray eyes that gave her a wildwood beauty. Challenging and mischievous under straight black brows, they might have belonged to the original Nike of Samothrace or any creature poised for victorious flight. There was something quite unreined about India, almost wayward; yet the hands with fine long fingers lightly holding a pair of chamois gloves were the sensitive steadfast hands of the born lady.

Climbing up the graveled path to the first house in the Colonnade, the most costly residence in the whole resort, she saw Wade Hampton lying in a barrel-stave hammock strongly reinforced to sway his enormous bulk.

"Are you asleep, Mr. Wade?"

"If I had been, you would have waked me. Why, India! I thought you and Preston had gone up the mountain to catch first sight of the nabob so that Turner Ashby and I could ride to the foot of the mountain with an escort to meet him."

"Flossie cast a shoe yesterday. Perhaps the blacksmith hasn't finished with her yet. It's cool here on your porch. May I ride along with the hunt tomorrow?"

"Heavens, no."

Wade Hampton swung his muscular legs to the floor looking admiringly at India. Physically more powerful than his biggest African field hand, he was the despair of his London tailor who tried to cram his wide square shoulders into fine broadcloth coats and to bind his sinewy neck in stiffly starched fashionable stocks. For at forty he was so male as to be almost frightening. But India loved his leonine features that somehow blended together with an Olympian handsomeness, his nose straight and long, his jaw and brow wide, and his steady eyes brilliant and gray blue.

"Papa says I may."

"Papa is not Master of this hunt; I am. The course is too hard for you."

"Not on Flossie. Preston showed me the way you were planning to run it and I cleared every barrier yesterday without a trick."

"Even if you ride you haven't a chance to come in ahead."

"I left Bay Monarch far behind yesterday."

"Mr. Rose from Pennsylvania will win or Maximilian Allan."

"Who is Maximilian Allan?"

"Don't you know?"

"No. He can't be important. I'm sure I can win."

"He is important. He plants thousands of cotton acres in the Up Country and he is arriving today from the Sweet Springs, bringing his mare which won the Maryland Cup this year. While I don't say Flossie isn't as good a jumper, nobody can outride Max Allan, not even I. Besides, Turner Ashby would be offended. I refused to let his sister ride with us and she's the finest horsewoman in Virginia."

"You've never seen me let Flossie all the way out. I know I can get to the kill first. I know it."

The big man looked at the vibrant, enthusiastic young girl and his throat tightened. So tender and so impatient to run away with life, she reminded him of the bride of his youth. He could never have refused her a pleasure. Never.

"If you'll wager me a hat, just like the one you're wearing, made to fit my big head, that you will lead Max Allan to the kill," he said, striving to be light, "perhaps I'll let you come along."

"You mean you will! Oh—you darling! What will you give me if I surprise you and win?"

"A bale of cotton. But you will have to hide your hair and wear young Wade's riding breeches. He isn't going. Can you ride astride?"

"Yes—yes—yes—oh, here comes Preston at last."

Preston was another big Hampton with a poet's face and wrestler's body. At sixteen he was as tall as his father and muscled like a full-grown man. He was riding Bay Monarch, one of the giant Monarch hunters bred at Millwood for bone and heart enough to carry the Hampton men who were all huge and heavy and all horsemen. Bay Monarch was fussing now as Preston jerked his head away from nuzzling the pretty little mare trotting by his iron side.

"I can, Preston! He says I can!" India ran down the steps and Hampton lifted her gently into the black velvet sidesaddle embroidered at the corners with red silk roses and valley lilies of real pearls that Guy had had made in Spain for her sixteenth birthday.

CHAPTER III

"LET'S MAKE THE CIRCLE," India said to Preston, trotting off down the gravel path past Latrobe's pink brick Baltimore Row where a group of small boys waiting for the Cake Man were being drilled by Charley Bonaparte who, with a little crimson undress cap on his head, a toy saber at his thigh, stopped shouting at his troops, shouting instead: "Preston's got a sweetheart!"

Preston, blushing, kicked Bay Monarch into an extended trot, but India touched her high hat with her whip in mock salute and pulling Flossie up sharp made her rear and walk six paces forward on her clean hind legs. The children ran screaming—all but Charles Joseph who brandished his saber swearing in true Little Corporal terms at India.

Flossie didn't seem to relish the swearing so, waving at the grandmother, Betsy Patterson Bonaparte, who had come out onto the porch to see what the racket

was about, India leaned forward and cantered after Bay
Monarch past Paradise Row, Carolina Row, Mr. Hen-
derson's house where Presidents stayed, Alabama Row,
Louisiana Row; turned a right angle by the bowling alley full of young men in blue swallow-tailed coats and
fawn trousers waiting for the young girls from the South
in floppy flat leghorn hats and soft, too long muslins and
the young girls from the North in smart small hats and
crisp crinolined taffeta to come forth from their naps
and promenade about the grounds down to the springhouse. Together now Flossie and Bay Monarch slowed
to an easy pace past Wolf's Row and the two white
cottages well back on the hillside to the right of the
spring where resplendently albeit none too cleanly at-
tired gentlemen called the cards at loo and whist and
faro. As they neared the pavilion over the bubbling
spring they saw it deserted except for the wild-eyed Edmund Ruffin sitting at the entrance muttering his hate
the Union.

The road up the mountain was singularly beautiful.
Tall, dark spruce, pine, and arborvitae soaking up the
hot sun gave off a pungent sharpness. A breeze raised a
fine reddish dust from the bone-dry clay road toward
pale blue sky. India heard at each hoof stroke the
brittle sound of the baked ruts as they broke, flying outwards like exploding gunpowder.

"Are you sure the hunt will be run where we rode
yesterday?"

"Yes. You can see the meadow from here where the
barriers are; to the right, in the fold of the mountain, is
the uphill run that turns back again into the same meadow. I don't think you ought to insist on coming, India.
Suppose you get hurt?"

"Flossie won't let me get hurt. You know I couldn't
bear sitting in a carriage with a lot of giggly girls, seeing
you flying past on Bay Monarch."

"You've got to learn to sit back someday like a proper lady. If war does come with the North I'll ride with
the cavalry and you will have to stay at Millwood with
the aunties. Kiss me."

He rode close, and a kind of a quiver passed over
his sweet young face as he put an arm about her shoul-

ders and suddenly kissed her veiled cheek vehemently.

Bay Monarch blew on Flossie's neck but the mare backed her ears and nipped him on his tender nose. India was kinder. She let Preston hold her a full minute just in case there *might,* there truly *might,* be a war and he lie dead on some far battlefield.

This kind of kissing satisfied Preston, making him feel very much a man and most protective toward India who was riding one of the hottest thoroughbreds in the country with a light rein and complete control.

The horses were sweating when they reached the summit which, as all summits, lay lonely in the burning sun. Preston lifted India down, taking the horses some way off and tying them to a thick cedar to let them cool off in its heavy shade.

Wandering along the edge of the cliff, India looked down at the resort, hearing the thin tones of a horn in the German band beginning its afternoon concert on the lawn. Around lay the countryside green with summer, sparkling with the ribbon of Howard's Creek watering the upland cradle. Outside again the road from the Sweet curved and twisted around the mountain with shadows drifting upon it from the great summer clouds that rose over the green-crested Alleghenies beyond.

Sitting down on a grassy slope near the edge she pulled up her thick green skirt letting the breeze blow over her hot legs and ankles, listening to the low hum of insects busy above the pine-needled ground, picked up a few brown needles that she could reach without moving more than her hand and began to chew them, savoring the sharp resiny taste. Thinking: I wonder if he will be handsome and gay, this nabob; or like the one who came with such a noise from Edgefield in the Up Country two years ago. How we dressed ourselves up to parade before him in the dining room and what a horror to find him over fifty, wearing a wig and having large false teeth. And lovely Lucy Holcombe from Texas who was just eighteen actually married him! How could she? But I guess she must have been so bored that anybody as rich and politically powerful as he was exciting to her.

Looking up she noticed a hawk hanging overhead.
With a flowing movement of its wings it was floating
in the air. Suddenly it stopped as if recollecting the dullness of existing, then, swooped a time or two at nothing
before darting away swiftly across the sky.

Preston came and sat beside her doubling himself
up on the soft ground and hugging his big knees. India lay back lazily against the mountainside, fitting her
body into the needled slope as though the warm earth
were a lover shaped to her comforting. She felt the sun
burn her cheek; the breeze loosed a strand of her sooty
hair. She felt the air on her neck, in the hollow of her
throat.

"Preston, why did Lucy Holcombe marry that old
Senator—Mr. Pickens?"

"She wanted to go to all the courts of Europe and
let them see how beautiful she was."

Far away to the left a wood dove began her plaintive
lateday calling. India listened, then began to think that
owing to the slender lonesome song the air was becoming stuffier, hotter, and stiller.

"We won't be able to see the coach from here," she
cried, jumping to her feet, looking down and seeing
everything exactly the same as she had seen it a few
minutes before—the resort, the valley, the creek, the
road winding—the only difference being a Dearborn
wagon stopped at the foot of the mountain.

Just then Flossie whinnied and from the road below
the cliff where they were standing a horse answered,
the neigh rising into a shrill sharply-broken quaver.

"That could be Lovely Lulu! Look—behind the wagon—gracious! More wagons piled with luggage, a calash, a buggy, a gig—and—it's the Allans all right for
there's the scarlet coach! Can you make it straight
down the side of the mountain? Let's get a good look at
them before we report to Papa."

Down the steep wooded hillside they dropped, the
horses putting their feet carefully so that they would
not slip, feeling the slippery pine needles screaking under their steel-shod hoofs, loosening shards of rock that
went scattering down before them like warning bullets.
They went slowly. The path was narrow and the young

conifers swung dry heavily scented branches against them. There were no sunrays here and the air was cool. In a clump of arborvitae just above the place where the mountain dipped into the road, Preston halted and dismounted.

India heard the creaking and the low talking and the clinking of harness. She smelled the many horses and the polish the Negroes were rubbing on the scarlet coach and the wood-smoky smell of a small fire over which a pot of water was boiling for someone's bathing. She was amazed at the number of Negroes and vehicles assembled. Several outriders were wiping down fat saddle horses and sprucing up their own identical plum-colored jackets; brown maids in bright blue dresses with high mitered tignons on their trim round heads dusted the seats of the gig, the open calash, and the buggy in which they were to ride; jacketed serving men wiped dust from the Dearborn wagons piled high with trunks and bags and boxes; two outstandingly tall Negroes in finely tailored gray livery covered with gold braid and buttons carefully polished the body of the coach itself which was painted scarlet with gold rococo trim. At each corner of the coach gilt cherubs, freshly bathed, hailed the passing scene. The doors were emblazoned with an ornate coat of arms; the plate-glass windows sparkled like rock crystal and the inside upholstery—the bit that India could see—was soft, tufted dove-gray satin. A youngish woman was seated in the coach boredly fanning herself with a guinea-feather fan tied at the end with purple tassels. From the front she was rather pretty but when she turned her head in the direction of the little fire she looked like a fish. A mackerel perhaps or a roe shad. She had pale red hair and pink damask skin that illy matched the flamboyant crimson of the equipage.

The lady was beckoning now with her fan to one of the tall liveried men who, India guessed, must be the coachman and footman, they were so elegant. The taller opened the door and the lady handed him a robe of scarlet velvet, decorated with two rows of gray-colored woolen fringe, which he tossed decoratively over the box on which he was to sit in all his highness.

"Let's ride over by the fire and see what they're up to, then we can cut back to the path and be at Papa's in five minutes," Preston whispered, remounting Bay Monarch.

They rode on a long slanting rising stretch of road that ran across the lower face of the mountain and the grade was so steep as they neared the bottom that Preston again dismounted and led the gelding so that Fossie could balance herself against him if she slipped. They were trying to be terribly quiet and every sound was magnified to their excited senses. A blue jay flew across their path with a cheerful cry that sounded as loud as a hag's scream; squirrels barked at each other in the trees; far away to the left the wood dove continued to wail gently; a covey of partridges startled by the horses' hoofs rose up, and with their soft "trrrrr" flew away and settled in a clump of mountain laurel across the road; grasshoppers, crickets, chipmunks, and tree frogs struck up their squeaking monotonous music in the underbrush.

It was just then that the path ended and they were, without warning, near the group by the little fire. At first India noticed only the six magnificent bays shining like polished satin in silver-studded harness scrubbed to an unbelievable brightness. Flossie saw them too and whickered nervously. India patted her neck whispering, "Hush, girl; hush, pretty!"

Flossie tossed her head flicking a bit of foam from her mouth on to India's knee. The strange champing horses had excited her and she backed against a wooden van parked beneath a sycamore tree. As her hindquarters touched the iron wheel, a horse inside started kicking—blat—boom—bump—against the closed tail gate. Flossie jumped as though every hoofbeat had been purposely directed at her rump and rushed into the clearing where the little fire smoked, almost running over a half-naked man who jumped agilely aside but caught her bridle jerking her cruelly to a sudden stop.

"What in the devil are you trying to do? Run me down?"

India felt her foot tremble in the stirrup but her

hands were firm on the reins and she held Flossie steady, answering him coolly, "The horse in the van frightened her. I was just—just—oh—just passing by."

She tried to look not interested but she couldn't look any way except completely curious.

The young man had laughing topaz-colored eyes set in a narrow pale-brown face and golden hair brushed sidewise over his forehead and behind his ears. His face indicated that he would be tall and lean but he was not tall; only, she guessed, a little taller than she. A streak of sunlight reached down on his broad smooth chest and strong round arms making them appear freshly washed with some golden gloss.

"My shirt, Chance." He let go the bridle and stepped away as the six-foot-six Negro of the coach appeared with a fine newly ironed ruffled shirt. Putting out his arms for the Negro to slip the shirt on them, he saw that she was still staring at him so he lifted a thick gold eyebrow ever so little and bowed exaggeratedly low, saying:

"If the lady will permit—"

She saw the powerful muscles of his back as he bowed and the columnar beauty of his thick tanned neck. Then realizing that she was just sitting there like a fool staring at a strange man completely stripped to the waist, she kicked Flossie in the side and crouching forward put the mare with a fierce drive at the rock wall dividing the forest from the highroad. Flossie delightedly jumped into a quick gallop, gaily whisked her tail at the six high-headed, interested coach horses and drew up both her front legs and her back ones in the very act of leaping and cleared the rock wall like a springing cat.

"Bravo!" the stranger shouted enthusiastically. But India didn't hear him for the pounding of Bay Monarch's big hoofs on the clay road behind her mare.

CHAPTER IV

ON THE PORCH of the Hampton house three men lingered over a silver bowl of frosted mint juleps called a Hail Storm. Shadows from the old oak were lengthening across the graveled paths and a sudden breeze filled the air with the fragrance of a thousand roses.

Wade Hampton shook the long ash off his cigar and beamed on his guests—Guy St. Julien and handsome Governor Manning of South Carolina.

Guy's restless eyes had calmed a bit with his third julep. They were cloudy eyes and his parched, high-bred face might have been eighty years old. He had been a wiry, tight brown man but was now a dry, flaccid yellow one looking to have some incurable sickness or unease. His thin hands immovable on the frosted silver goblet, Guy listened to the cultured voice of John Manning.

"What the average Low Countryman can't realize is that the true Midas is now Up Country cotton. If Barney Rhett only lived in Edgefield this rabid talk of Secession would soon die down. It's his outrageous *Mercury* that keeps the whole state so stirred up."

"What about our sea island cotton?" Guy smiled at the two Up Countrymen and downed his julep.

"Henry, another julep for Mr. Guy!" Hampton rocked happily in his special hammock. "Upland cotton gives the magic touch to more pocketbooks than your sea island cotton and rice, Louisiana's sugar, Virginia's tobacco, or all three put together. The Chestnuts, Mannings, Hamptons, Allans, and so forth, have built far finer houses than you see in Charleston. We have handsomer silver and pictures, more of us go to college, and travel the word over for amusement —all on Up Country cotton."

"Now—Wade, you exaggerate."

"No, he doesn't, Mr. St. Julien. It's the old story of quantity turning the tables on quality," Governor Manning said.

"And he doesn't mean people," Hampton put in hurriedly. "The world has gone mad about the cheap cotton goods made by the new machines in Liverpool and the cheap cotton laces of Lyons. My shoemaker's wife in her inexpensive cottons will soon put in as good an appearance as Mrs. Hampton in her Paris frocks. That is—if you Low Countrymen don't secede us into the poorhouse."

"I don't think it's that simple, Wade," Guy said, "there's too much hate behind it. All Northerners resent you planters waving your whips over black backs and enjoying the good life despite your sinful ways. They think you enjoy and abuse the advantages of wealth and luxury."

"You're speaking of the Abolitionists, not of the North as a whole."

"Haven't you noticed the definite coolness shown you by many of your old friends from above the Mason-Dixon Line this summer? I have. Judge Howie hasn't been to call on me a single time and last year we drank our daily glass of brandy together and solved the country's problems quite simply," Guy said. "I can't understand his behavior, of all people. He's a Democrat as am I. Our interests certainly should be identical."

"What we need is a strictly Southern party to protect our interests. The Democratic Party now is divided on every practical issue—tariff, internal improvements, slave property, and the right of secession." Governor Manning waved to Henry to fetch him another julep.

"We must all unite behind Buchanan. At least he is on our side." Guy leaned his head back staring dreamily up through the green light sifting from the long tree branches. "But you're right, Wade. Industry is the ultimate answer. I wish I had invested some of my money in Northern mills."

"I wish I were orator enough to persuade the North to value cotton properly and what it can be made into as England does. North and South then could work together for their mutual benefit and you'd hear' no further talk of freeing slaves. Not so long as raw material can be furnished so cheap with slave labor."

"That was a damn good speech you made in the

Senate in the spring, Wade, about not reopening the slave trade. You got an ovation. Why not make one along these lines this fall?" Governor Manning said.

"My feelings were aroused over that."

"Aren't they over this?"

"No; this has to do with money."

"You don't like money, Wade?" Guy widened his misty eyes. Hampton laughed a little and Governor Manning said lightly,

"Why, Mr. St. Julien, he has Henry follow him with a bag of money everywhere he goes to count out the dollars and pay the bills. Wade won't touch the filthy stuff with his own hands."

"I still think slavery is the keystone of the arch." Guy spoke quickly, coming to Hampton's rescue.

"Of course it is," Hampton said, "for on that the cotton, sugar, rice, and tobacco planters all stand or fall. So much of our wealth is invested in the slaves who harvest our crops that we'd be ruined if it were suddenly swept away. Take Maximilian Allan for example, the young fellow I'm waiting for—"

"Is that Cantelou Allan's son?" Guy asked.

"Yes, did you know Cantelou?"

"We were at Princeton together but no particular friends. He married my wife's cousin—Emmy Shepherd. What's the boy like?" Guy carefully replaced his glass on the banister and spread his veined hands.

"As daring and hot as his father," Hampton said. "He's a godson of Senator McDuffie, Mrs. Hampton's father. Graduated from Princeton himself in June and is touring the springs with his sister. He plans to sail for the Orient in the autumn, stopping to visit the Pickens in St. Petersburg somewhere along the way. Miss Emmy runs the plantation waiting for her young stallion to calm down a bit. They are among the wealthiest folk in the country but would be ruined overnight if their slaves were freed. All they have is land and Negroes."

"In other words—cotton," said Governor Manning.

"That's right."

"I'd like to meet the boy. Emmy was a gorgeous girl. I never heard whether she and Cantelou were happy or not."

"She was burned and scarred dreadfully shortly after the marriage," Hampton picked up his frosty drink. "I don't think Cantelou ever appreciated Miss Emmy properly. He was thrown from a horse and killed on a back street in Columbia when Max was a tiny boy. Miss Emmy let the fancy woman he had been supporting come to the funeral and even gave her a black Chantilly lace veil to wear when she saw the cheap bit of gauze the creature brought."

"Ah—that proves your point. If Northern looms had been to Lyons and learned to make lace from Upland cotton, who could have told the true widow from the false?" Guy said, slowly getting up from his rocking chair.

CHAPTER V

AT EVERY DEER HUNT in White Sulphur Wade Hampton rode the biggest hunter in his stable, wore the highest silk beaver that could be imported from England, the brightest pink hunting coat strongly sewed by his London tailor, and he always was master, a splendid symbol of the Walter Scott drama surging around him. Sitting erect, the seams of his coat straining to burst from the huge bulging of his stupendous muscles, with the hat low on his thick curly chestnut hair, he looked like an unbound Prometheus joyfully sharing his gifts with the earth people.

As the impresario of the hunt—and today was *the* day of the whole season at the White—he had planned every detail even to the spot chosen for the climactic killing of the deer. Hunting of any kind was the delight of his life; from dove shooting in a planted field to knife fighting with a full-grown bear alone on a craggy mountainside, it was always the most important moment in the world when he had made the kill. He had enjoyed other things too, especially in his earlier years, but now at forty with a new bride, three almost grown children, the largest bank account in the South, beautiful homes, thousands of slaves, acres,

blooded horses, he had only two passions: cotton planting and hunting. If asked he would admit surely that
he loved hunting best.

The elements that went into a day of hunting such
as today shared many of the complicated and delicate
elements of a battle. The forces must be mustered, the
lay of the land reconnoitered, the adversary appreciated and maneuvered into such an untenable position
that victory would be won when and where he, the
Master, desired it. Such a performance could be anything from a boring fiasco to a thrilling pageant of
heroic proportions. There was never any sure predict-
ing. In the gathering of the men and materials for today's drama, however, Wade Hampton proved himself a
true strategist. Always between the making of his enormous crops, he had been fascinated as a boy with the
pleasant trifles of summer life around the pavilions of the
White; and this year he had given as much thought to
this particular festive day as he had to his last political
campaign when he was elected a state senator from
Richland County.

So he rode out very early into the center of the
green in the gray morning light. It was going to be a
perfect day for hunting. Fog lay white as milk over the
resort but it was already growing thinner and the sunlight was sifting through. And dripping with dew there
shone, through the white haze, the rusty roads and pale
fences and groves of dark green trees. Glimpses of blue
smoke rose, then the mist broke and drove in wreaths
across the horizon, and he rode back and forth greeting
the gathering huntsmen in glorious sunshine.

India walked down to the stables with Preston. Tall
and easy in young Wade's "pinks," her hair securely
hidden under a tall silk hat, she moved along with the
men and boys in complete unself-consciousness.

Her mare was kept with the Hampton horses and she
went into the horse box poorly lighted by a small window. In the dim light India, without thinking, took in at
a glance the main points of her darling. Tracing back
in tail-female to Delphine, the dam of the great Monarch bought by the second Wade Hampton, the Colo-

nel, from the royal stud at Hampton Court in 1835, she had many of the characteristics of her famous ancestor. She was small-boned all over and though her chest was prominent in front it was narrow. Her hindquarters sloped and while her hind legs were extremely fine, there was a noticeable curve in her front ones. The muscles in both her hind and front legs were not particularly thick but she was very broad across the shoulders and about her was that air of quality that only comes in thoroughbred stock. Her skin was soft as delicate satin and her sinews hard as bone. In all her figure and especially her head there was a feeling of power and at the same time of softness. She was picking at some fresh straw with her hoofs but as India approached she started and shifted nervously from one leg to the other.

"Stallion's been whistling all night. Flossie in season. Better leave off riding her this day," said the Negro groom.

The closer India came the more excited Flossie grew. But as India patted the mare's strong neck, and straightened over her low withers a stray lock of mane that had fallen on the other side she became quieter for a moment. But the stallion kept up his beseeching and Flossie snorted out through her dilated nostrils, pricked up her crescent-shaped ears and bit at India, restlessly stamping her shapely legs one after the other.

"Hush, baby, hush!" India said, patting her and going out of the stall. The stallion's calling and the mare's excitement had agitated India. She felt her heart throbbing and suddenly thought of the way the muscles were laid in the back of Maximilian Allan's golden neck. And she felt that, like Flossie, she would like to bite and move. It was a bad feeling and wonderful.

When the groom led Flossie out she was fretting at the heavier saddle than the velvet one she had borne yesterday. India walked up to Flossie. The mare rolled her eyes sideways at India, showing the whites, and she slanted her ears back wickedly.

"Get up: you won't be nervous then," Preston had come up on Bay Monarch.

India looked all around hoping to see Maximilian Allan, knowing that they two must surely meet somewhere along the hunt.

"All right, all right," she said crossly to Preston, and firmly seated herself in the saddle. She smoothed the double reins, as she always did, between her strong fingers, and the groom let Flossie go.

At first Flossie tried to shake India off, pulling at the reins with her long neck. India tried to quiet her but Flossie kept dragging at the reins all the way from the yard up to the lawn where the hunt was gathering.

And as the horsemen came together, in their scarlet coats and shiny black hats and caps, on the soft bright green grass framed by the rows of gleaming white cottages, they paraded and saluted the porches filled with ladies looking like human bouquets in their embroidered muslins and organdies and lawns and filmy challis, their scarves of gauze and silk fluttering like pennants, their tiny hats bobbing with bows and flowers, birds and blonde.

The ladies waved at the gallants on horseback or flirted with the dandies in blue swallow-tailed coats gathered on the paths to accompany them in the cabriolets, landaus, hacks, gigs, and berlins pulled up and waiting all around the sylvan amphitheater. They were having a wonderful time imagining themselves Elizabethans on Holy-Rood Day, on a journey from one castle to another, transported into an age of chivalry they adored and emulated, a time of hawkers and mummers, flowing capes and stags at eve.

Flossie hated it all. She backed into Wade Hampton's gray and kicked him viciously. Hampton whirled about and recognizing India said seriously,

"Please don't come, my dear. I had no right to agree to this thing. Promise you'll pull out if you catch Turner Ashby's notice. He's helping me keep everybody straight and I wouldn't have him know for the world."

"Yes, sir." India's set wayward face, clean-boned and sharp with her hair pulled tightly back under her tall hat, gave no indication that she would do any such thing. She guided Flossie into a mass of horses stamping and nipping restlessly at each other, finally stopping beside a rather dull iron-gray Irish hunter backed by a lawyer from Delaware with long white hair flowing over his velvet collar.

"Your mare seems hot," he said, eying Flossie dubiously as she mashed her teeth up and down trying to crush her bit.

Then everything became quiet except the happy noise of bird songs coming from all the trees softly but full-throated with summer. Quiet. Waiting quiet. Eager quiet. Everybody quietly watching a thin Virginian riding up alone from the kennels and centering himself on the green, lifting a silver-mounted horn and blowing a full clear call that climbed high and was lost as the Negro keepers opened the gates and forty couples of famished hounds came tearing, giving full tongue, onto the lawn where everybody could see and hear their frantic excitement and catch it too.

Wade Hampton moved out first and Turner Ashby, the Black Knight of Hiawatha, his jet beard and hair thick as tar against his black velvet coat and cap, pushed his white stallion hard on Hampton's heels. India kept looking back and to the side for Maximilian Allan and his Lovely Lulu but the first galloping was so sudden and Flossie so hot that she could not guide her at all.

Trees, faces, horse tails, wind, flashed past. She sawed back and forth at Flossie's mouth, standing in the stirrups, to slow her before the first barrier that led out onto the hard rutty road.

Meanwhile the hunters were fanning out, settling down for a long go, close on the traces of the eighty hounds running, their noses keen, along the road. They picked up the stag in a fold of the mountain, exactly where Hampton had arranged for the gamekeeper to turn him loose and then it was across stream and over meadow as the stag bounded away seeking sanctuary.

Preston wasn't interested in a race so he cut out and made for Bedford's meadow to watch India pass through. Hampton and Turner Ashby had disappeared over a peak. Others galloped up and down various trails, yet heading in one direction following the hounds whose deep-throated music filled the whole area. India turned Flossie up a little gully catching a glimpse of houndhide cross in front of her when suddenly the stag himself leaped across the road and flashed close enough to Flossie to graze her side. Wheeling, India held Flossie in a minute, pushing up a piece of hair that had straggled from her hat, and was overtaken by a lean beautiful mare, lifting up her graceful, rather long pasterns as though borne on springs. The strong exquisite perfectly correct lines of the black mare with her superb hindquarters caused India to frown angrily but the gay laughing face of the rider, Maximilian Allan, agitated her.

Flossie had been troublesome all morning and, as the strange mare galloped past, exciting her further, she started into a rough gallop bumping India up and down. Max was now ahead of India as the stag bounded back with a group of hounds hitting at his heels and headed for the big meadow. This was perfect racing terrain and Flossie, outraged at the rear view of Lovely Lulu, bolted. Up the wide stream between the trail and the meadow it took all India's strength to hang onto the reins.

Lulu rose above the stream and flew across to the other side; Flossie darted after her. Once over the stream India gained some control of her mare and began bringing her in, intending to cross the rock wall behind Lulu and to try and overtake her in the fairly clear ground of the big meadow. Hampton and the whole assemblage of vehicles had pulled in and were watching as the two leading riders approached the solid fence. India was aware of hundreds of eyes fastened upon her from all sides; she felt a tendril of long hair whip across her nose, but she saw nothing except Flossie's ears and neck, the green ground flying under her, and Lovely Lulu's legs beating time swiftly before her and always keeping the same distance ahead. Lulu rose, with no sound of hoofs scraping on wood and with a frisk of her black tail was gone on the other side.

At the same instant, India saw the palings of the barrier right before her. Without the slightest change of pace Flossie flew over it; there was a splintering crash and the top rail vanished, grazing Flossie's hind hoofs. But she kept going at the same clip. Other huntsmen were not far behind them now. The stag had passed through the meadow once and backed on his tracks and was making another complete circle. The next time he came through the meadow Hampton and Turner Ashby would gallop in and run him back into the fold of the mountain, the kill taking place off stage to spare the tenderhearted creatures in the carriages who always called for mercy and hid their curl-framed faces.

Lulu was turning into the fold of the mountain close on the hounds and India thought that now was the time to overtake and pass; Flossie had the same idea and without a touch of the whip began gaining ground, getting alongside Lulu. It was uphill now and both mares were slowing considerably. Flossie came level with Lulu on the inside of the road but Max would not let her pass on that side. India had not thought of passing on the outside, remembering the pointed rocks and loose shale but Flossie shifted her stride and began to force the pass on the outside. For a few lengths they moved evenly. India dared not look over at Max. She held her breath hearing him breathing heavily. All would be well if—she caught a glimpse of his horrified face as Flossie leaped aside to escape being impaled on a pointed rock at the bend in the road. India's position shifted and she knew that something awful had happened. She just had time to free her leg when Flossie fell heavily on one side and rolled into a thick clump of rhododendron.

At that moment India must have hit her head for the next thing she knew, strong arms were holding her and her head was cradled against a thumping chest. A trembling hand touched her throat and she felt fingers fan out and run the length of her hair. Open her eyes she dared not but buried her nose further into the heavenly chest thudding so beautifully against her ears.

"Ah—you have some color in your face. For a minute I thought you were dead lying in that pool of black hair like a woman drowned."

Now she had to open her eyes and she saw his face

from the side. He had a high forehead and a large
straight nose that jutted trianglelike from his face and
was finely thin about the quivering nostrils—making
her think of a restless stallion. He was looking out
through a break in the trees and the hounds were coming closer and the sound of galloping horses was on the
ridge above them. She did not know how long she had
lain there in his arms but at a Halloo! from the meadow
below she sat up. Flossie was standing, head hanging,
beside her and Lulu was whistling and stamping restlessly, the reins of both caught in Max's hand.

"Don't tell anybody I rode on the hunt and fell off
Flossie. Promise you won't tell anybody!" Almost crying she clutched the lapels of his pink coat and tried
to shake him. It was like trying to move the mountain
itself.

"I won't. Why in the name of God did you cut so
near the road's edge? You would at least have had a
chance to pass me when we hit the meadow. Here—
see if you can stand. I've still got a chance to reach the
kill first without you to worry about."

She could stand up all right. It was her heart that
had gone wrong; beating so crazily at the very feel of
him. Even when he lifted her into the saddle it was her
heart's thumping that caused her to sway and the
trees to slant the opposite direction from the way they
did yesterday.

"Go home," he said sharply. "You'd no business on
a rough hunt like this in any event." And with a careless wave of his hand he galloped off toward the meadow.

India weakly kicked Flossie, completely spent now
from the shock of her fall. The mare hesitantly began
to walk forward and didn't even back her ears when
Turner Ashby rushed by, his wild black beard and
hair blowing fiercely, his cap lost somewhere along the
way, crying,

"Hurry, son, the kill is almost on. Everything has
gone perfectly." And was gone—without even noticing
India's hair hanging like a sooty veil down to her waist.

CHAPTER VI

LIGHTED CHINESE LANTERNS of every color were strung all over the grounds, glowing in the old oaks and maples like festival moons of green and red, yellow, blue and orange, casting their fairy light on the formally dressed ladies and gentlemen hastening along the graveled paths from the cottages to the main hotel as they heard the careful distinct notes of the fiddles and the thin sad horns tuning up for the first waltz.

The ball was only just beginning as India and her father walked down the long carpeted hallway flooded with gaslight and lined with flowers and yellow-skinned Negroes patting their feet and offering to take canes and capes, slipper bags and scarves into the dressing rooms. From the ballroom came a constant steady droning and the rustle of movement.

Edmund Ruffin, old and thin, stumbled against them and leered obviously, coveting India, whom he had met two days before.

"He pinched me," she whispered angrily to her father, "right on my hip! Oh, how unpleasant!"

"Scandalous and disgraceful," Guy spoke loudly; "the one thing to be dreaded is meeting professional Southerners on a holiday."

"Good evening, Miss India." A fair-bearded young man from Norfolk, one of the young gentlemen inhabiting Wolf's Row, in an emerald satin waistcoat, prinking out the ruffles of his starched shirt as he went, bowed to them, and after running by came back to ask India for the lancers. But as the lancers had already been given to Preston, she had to promise him the Virginia reel. George Peabody, the Yankee-born millionaire from London, stood aside to let them pass and, twirling his mustaches, admired the darkly pale girl.

Although the Duchess and India had spent hours with her dress, her petticoats, her hair-do, sewing her feet into soft white satin ballet slippers so that they would fit without a wrinkle, she walked into the ballroom as though she had been born in the white organdy and lace, her hair done like a tiara in braids interwoven with fresh white flowers.

She walked light and erect, her every movement smooth and graceful with a hint of sensuousness, even abandon, underlying the controlled delicacy of step and gesture. The filmy organdy dress was made in the newest mode from Paris, the skirt falling in long half-revealing folds from the high waistline to the tips of her satin slippers. Across the low décolletage, hiding the smooth ivory of her breasts, was a bertha of rare old rosepoint lace almost the exact color of her flesh and a scarlet sash tightly bound the slender roundness of her waist.

There was only one scraped place on her left elbow and a swollen egg behind her right ear to testify to her escapade of the morning. Her eyes that had been so boyishly wild racing over the meadow after Max Allan were now completely female, shining with the excitement of seeking him tonight. Tonight, her heart kept time to the word itself—tonight!

She saw the ballroom vivid with silken dresses and giving off a sweet sharp odor of flowers and bourbon whisky and perfumed beards and freshly sprinkled floor wax, and mingled with these another scent, the mysterious tingling scent of love. Hands touched white-gloved hands as the waltz sang; the rich-colored gowns and the ruffled shirt bosoms swayed together and glances held as the hands trembled a little, borne too swiftly along by the "Voices of Spring." There were a hundred couples dipping and whirling in the great new room that was larger than the Château de Fleur or the Jardin Marbile in Paris. A hundred magic puppets turning, turning, but where oh, where was Max Allan?

She had scarcely entered the ballroom on her father's arm and gone over to the group of ladies, all illusion, crinoline, fans, and flowers, waiting to be asked to dance, when Mr. Burke of North Carolina, the director of dances at the resort, flew up to her with that peculiar easy glide which is confined to directors of dances. Without even asking her if the first waltz was promised, he put out his arm to encircle her waist, and her feet in their fragile silken slippers began swiftly, lightly to move across the slippery floor.

"How nice that you came early. It starts the evening so well to waltz with you. Puts me in a good humor for the chores I have to do later on. With you the waltz is a—rest. Even to turn and turn like this—" Mr. Burke turned her so many times that people stopped dancing to watch. No one at the White could keep up with a man like India St. Julien! The intoxication of the motion possessed her now, even with professional Mr. Burke; her eyes glittered, she threw her head back, her lips parted a little so that breathing was easy. But when he stopped turning her and began to dip and glide, she continued to look about the room over his shoulder.

In the left corner a phrenologist was standing behind a gilt ballroom chair carefully exploring the mysteries of the skull of the Honorable James Chestnut, Jr. of Camden, South Carolina, while his wife, the caustic Mary, one white long feather swirled across her smooth dark head, watched the dancers, nodding intimately at those she considered important people.

In the far right corner India saw the cream of society gathered together. There, outrageously naked, was the snobbish dowager from New York City entertaining Commodore Matthew Fontaine Maury; there was the Carroll heiress from Baltimore with her older brother; there shone the theatrical shoulder-length hair of Mr. James Louis Petigru, he looking like an overindulgent actor, possibly Roman, who has lived too well, arguing with young rich Judge Perkins of Louisiana, the disunionist; there, too, she saw the aging beau, Horst Adams, his dyed hair black as jet, always to be found where the best people were; and there was lovely Sally Ward, the pride of Kentucky, flirting with Mr. Johnston of Hayes. Mary Hampton was there adoring her big husband and there she saw the pinkish head of Irene Allan. And *he* was there! Laughing with four crinolined, silly girls! India knew him at once and was aware that he recognized her.

"Another bit of turning?"

Heavens! Was she still dancing with the flimsy Mr. Burke?

"No. Take me over to the corner where the Hamptons are standing."

"Wherever you command. What a superb dancer you are!" Mr. Burke said with a sigh of relief wondering how any supposed lady could breathe so evenly at the pace he had set for India. He could feel sweat running down his legs, he knew his shirt front had come apart, and the whole room was awhirl from his last go-round.

Waltzing straight toward the group in the far corner intoning, "Pardon, sir, pardon, madame," and expertly steering her through the river of illusion, crinoline, tulle, and ribbon and not touching a feather, he turned her sharply so that her slender ankles in thin white French lisle stockings could be well seen and her dress foamed around his knees.

The group in the corner applauded the final cleverly executed turn and Mr. Burke bowed with pleasure giving India his arm to conduct her over to the Hamptons. But Wade Hampton, magnificent in black broadcloth and white ruffles, a length of pale blue satin for a tie, came to meet them saying,

"I'll take her with me, Mr. Burke, there are some folks I want to present to her."

"Thank you, Miss India," Mr. Burke bowed once more, wiping the perspiration from his face with a square of linen. "Miss India is a great help in making the balls gay and successful, Mr. Hampton."

"Yes. And now, India, would you like a turn with me before I introduce you to the young Allans?"

India flushed and caught a freesia that had come loose from her hair and fallen into the hollow of her throat.

"Let's rest a minute. I'm all out of breath," she said, a pulse under the thread of pearls circling her well-cut strong neck beginning to throb as Max Allan left the round-eyed girls and came forward to her.

Unaware of the sudden tension in India, Hampton leaned over and whispered in her ear,

"What about my hat?"

"Papa sent a letter to London this afternoon ordering it made in just your size. Henry gave him the measurements."

Max was staring at her, smiling oddly, his tawny eyes gleaming speculatively.

"May I present Mr. Maximilian Allan of Edgefield to the lovely Miss St. Julien of Charleston—"

"I think we have met before," Max said. "Shall we waltz and decide, Miss St. Julien?"

"She's too tired, Max; let me introduce her to your sister."

"No—she must dance the rest of this waltz with me. It won't be long. I'll bring her straight back here when it's over."

Preston came up just as India stepped into the circle of Max's arms. A lock of soft curly hair had fallen over his forehead and he watched India who with every instant was dancing farther and farther away from him, a growing pang at his heart. How excited she looks, he thought. She's never looked like that at me. Not even when she let me kiss her. And it isn't just the ball that has excited her but one person. And that person is Max Allan. And she's never seen him until yesterday. How can she look at him like that?

Every time Max spoke to India a joyous light leaped into her eyes and a happy smile curved her red lips. She made no effort to hide her intoxication. Signs of her delight in Max flushed her face. And Max, too, the daredevil carelessness gone, bent his head almost humbly to catch what she was saying.

Preston, watching, thought from their expressions that they were making the most ardent love to each other right on the dance floor, but what they were actually saying was how ridiculous old Mrs. Prim looked flirting so boldly with the young dandy less than half her age, and how the Carroll girl surely couldn't be planning to marry the old roué who was courting her and—

"How old are you?" Max asked suddenly.

"Sixteen—and you?"

"Twenty. I'm glad you're only sixteen. You must not dance with anyone but me the rest of the evening."

"I must dance the lancers with Preston and I've promised the Virginia reel to Harry Norton and the cotillion to Reid Randolph and the quadrille to—"

"With Preston you may dance the lancers but for all the others you must excuse yourself. I refuse to share you with anybody—ever." They laughed, he turning her swiftly around and around the room.

And so they danced, danced for hours to the waltzes, the reels, the quadrilles, and the polkas of the thin-toned orchestra. They were aware—they had to be—of the curious eyes upon them. But neither of them cared. This that was between them was too new to both. They wove in and out among the other couples, losing themselves as much as possible in the crowd, avoiding the corner where Irene Allan, stiff and sharp, angrily snapped open and shut her black lace fan with its mother-of-pearl sticks, avoiding the punch table where Guy St. Julien clutched his skinny hands helplessly around a claret cup, avoiding the walls where the dowagers sat and the wall-flowers leaned looking at them disapprovingly, nodding and whispering behind their lacy, feathery fans.

They went in together to supper and filled plates with rosy ham and chilled pheasant, quivery jellies, and lady fingers which they left untouched in a window seat. They returned together to the ballroom. Everyone watched them, no one saw them go, yet when Guy went to fetch her shawl the little perky maid told him India had left already.

It was after midnight and the magic lanterns in the trees had turned into ragged shreds of scorched paper. Max and India stood hand in hand knowing that it was time for her to go home. Behind them the darkened ballroom was hushed: a few late ones wandered up and down the paths arm in arm singing, but the majority of the resort had gone to rest. From the far side of the green, loud singing could be heard from a stag party just beginning on Wolf's Row: "Hock, give us Hock, Sparkling Hock from the Rhine."

"Where could I have laid my shawl?" India whispered. Max put his arm about her waist and drew his cape round them both. Close-pressed to one another they walked toward her cottage.

A lingering breath of the day's warm resiny scents, deadened and damp with the chill of dew, met them there. The half-moon had set and the night was very dark, the sky overcast, with murky gray clouds close down upon the pine and spruce. They came to the steps and he turned her in his cape until she was facing him in the darkness. Close in the close night. Her breathing was very young as he pulled her to him—young and eager and exciting. Her mouth was almost on a level with his and he only had to bend his head a little as she lifted her face to take his kiss.

He held her head between his hands—it was so sweet to feel his fingers sink into her hair, loosening her fragrant flowers—she felt she must repay him for such joy and so she clasped his golden head and tried to kiss him as he had kissed her.

When he put his hands upon her breast, she felt as though he touched all the way in to her heart; he pulled down the lace of her bertha and kissed between her rounded firm pointed breasts—it sent a throbbing wanting into her soul.

"I have never seen a girl like you," he was trembling and his voice was very deep and low. "Will you still let me kiss you when I come home from China?"

"Yes," said India, "I will. But never another so long as I live."

"Ah, so you say. But you are just sixteen and only beginning to be a woman. Suppose another comes more exciting to you than I?"

She threw herself into his arms again, knowing that this was madness yet whispering softly—and not caring what she whispered.

And then she was wholly in his arms and he was holding her tight against him and kissing her deep in the mouth and she was pressing her breasts against his chest, happier than she had ever been and he said, "You darling. You sweet. Promise me that you will not kiss anyone like that while I am gone."

"Don't go away. Why do you want to go to China? Nobody goes to China."

He put her from him gently saying, "Your father is standing in the window. I just saw the lighted end of a cigar."

"But the house is all dark. He hasn't come from the hotel yet. Or perhaps he has gone with Mr. Petigru to talk politics or—"

"No," Max spoke softly to her, steadying her with his hand, feeling her shiver and rubbing the long cool length of her firm arm with his hand, letting his fingers rest for an instant in the warm hollow of her underarm where the roundness of her breasts began. She gasped, feeling that she could not bear it, it was too sweet to bear, and then he was kissing her hand on the palm side letting the tip of his tongue lightly trace her life-line.

"India!" It was her father calling and the door was open and he had lit a candle and was holding it but it was all right for him to see a young man kissing her hand. All young men did that. It was part of the etiquette by which they lived.

"Coming, Papa. Good night, Max."

"Good night."

As she came onto the porch she saw Guy's face in the round spot of light from the candle. He did not look as she had ever remembered him. She saw at once that he had had too much to drink. He reeled in his walk and held to the back of a chair while she came in and closed the front door.

"Why are you looking at me so strangely?" she said much frightened. "I left word with the little maid at the hotel that I was being properly escorted to the cottage."

"Oh, I got the word all right," he said with a little laugh. "I wanted to be here to welcome you. Tomorrow we are going home." He sat himself in the chair, still holding the candle, rocking back and forth, laughing a little.

India breathed freer thinking that perhaps her father had not seen Max kissing her. She made as if to go in her room; but Guy caught her by the hand.

"I have more to say. I might have held my tongue about the miserable behavior of yours at the dance—breaking your engagements for every single dance—but to see you kissing that Up-Country farmer—that—that—scoundrel—"

India had been standing with arms hanging down and bent head. She looked up now into her father's face. She moved her lips, but no sound came out loud enough to be heard.

Guy looked away from his daughter's eyes; he struck out sideways with his hand.

"You must never see him again. Never."

"Oh yes, I'll see him again."

"Not in my house. Who but a rascal would kiss a child as he did you the first night he even met her?"

India stood a minute, breathing heavily.

"Then I will meet him elsewhere."

"Go to your bed. It is not good for us to talk any more tonight," Guy said with anguish in his voice. "Watching you dancing so bold and free in the ballroom like a wanton woman has shamed me beyond endurance. And this that you did with Maximilian Allan —this disgusting kissing. Wait—don't go!"

He held out his hand toward her; but she would not see it and ran sobbing, slamming her door as hard as she could manage.

There was no lamp lit in her room and no Duchess waiting to undress her. She was glad, for within her was a fierce joy and a panic and she wanted to tear off her dress and lay her body long and smoothly naked on the linen sheets in the dark and alone if—oh! if *he* couldn't lie beside her in the dark!

It was almost dawn when she was awakened by the plaintive notes of a guitar close under her window and the sound of a man singing in a true sweet tenor:

"And it's we have met, and it's we have met,
  And it's we have met," says he.
"And I'll return from the salt water sea;
  All for love of thee,
  All for love of thee.

"I could have married the king's daughter dear
  She said she'd marry me;
But I refused great crowns of gold;
  Waiting for love of thee,
  Waiting for love of thee.

"You will whirl yourself all in your room,
  And wear a crown of filigree.
And shine as bright as the morning star
  As you walk the streets to me,
  As you walk the streets to me.

"Come love, come love, my sweet little love,
  And go along with me,
I'll take you where the grass grows green
  In my far-off Up Country.
  In my Far-off Up Country.

The singing hushed and a sleepy bird twittered re-
sentfully. India lay stiff and still, hearing her father
pacing back and forth in the next room; not daring
even to peep through the curtains; knowing that this
serenade was a song of farewell. Tomorrow morning
whoever was singing the "Daemon Lover" under her
window would be gone. It was the code of the Springs—
the incognito farewell serenade.

"Get up. My God! It's ten o'clock with you lying in
bed bare as a whore and it raining." Duchess was wearing a bright yellow gingham dress and had pinned a
crimson dahlia in the center of her knob of hair making
the top of her almost brush the low ceiling of the cottage bedroom.

India sat up in the hard narrow bed glaring crossly
at the Negro woman who looked as though she felt better than any woman in the world.

"I won't get up. Hand me a shawl. I'm chilly. You
needn't break my shoulder putting it around me. Where
were you anyway when I came in last night?"

"I was out. What did you do—tear your dress off
and throw it on the floor? At least you might have
hung it over a chair."

"You're supposed to do that. Who were you out
with?"

"Chance, Mr. Allan's coachman. Lord defend me if he isn't the most man I've ever run across."

"You needn't act like a pleased pussy cat just because you finally found a man big enough for you."

"I am pleased and I pleased him too. You don't look like you pleased anybody. What did Mr. Guy say when you came in so late last night? He's drunk a whole bottle of brandy this morning and I've sent for the doctor. You have to get up and receive him."

"Is Papa asleep?"

"Like the dead."

"Then leave him alone. He was very angry with me last night. You should have been here. I've never seen him so unreasonable."

"He ought to have beaten you. Kissing a young man you never saw before in your life!"

"What about you and Chance?"

"Nobody saw us. And I don't often find a man a whole head taller than I. Plenty of pretty boys with yellow hair come courting you."

"Papa said last night we were going to leave today. Are we?"

"He won't be able today. Perhaps tomorrow and I don't care. Not with Chance gone."

"There's an epidemic of yellow fever in Charleston. We'll have to stay on the island with Aunt Childs."

"That will be better for you than here after last night. People were talking about you in the dining room this morning. There's not a man at the White will ask you to dance tonight. Not even the Hampton boy."

India looked out of the window at the slanting rain.

"You say Chance has gone. Does that mean that the Allans have left the Springs?"

Duchess raised a yellow-sleeved arm and yawned, stretching herself all the way to the ceiling. "At daybreak—in the rain; his sister wasn't happy over your making a fool of her baby brother at the ball last night. She was waiting up for him when he got to the Colonnade but she wasn't as gentle with him as Mr. Guy was with you. She had already packed his clothes and was ready to leave in the middle of the night. He argued with her for an hour then agreed to go at daylight.

Chance says she has always led him around by the nose. Do you think he'll ever come back and court you?"

"Do you?"

"I hope so. I'd like to have that Chance again. Mr. Max probably will come back. Wasn't that what he was saying in that song he sang?"

PART TWO

*Secession
Charleston,
December, 1860*

CHAPTER VII

DURING 1858 and part of 1859, it appeared as if the moderates had a chance to win over the radicals in South Carolina, but John Brown's raid in October of 1859 made secession an inevitability by consolidating the various factions of the state. At the start Rhett! Middleton! Burt! Bonham! Miles!; then came the moderates to stand beside them—Orr! Gist! Hammond! Chestnut! Magrath! Pickens! Bonham! Secede, they cried! Preserve our States' Rights! Protect our women! Hold on to our slave property! Down with the tariff! To hell with a national bank! We've argued for thirty years—it's time now to dare! So—good-by, dear old Union—we intend to go peaceably but don't try and stop us—we'll fight you if you do!

When the news of Mr. Lincoln's election arrived November 7, 1860, there was great rejoicing throughout the state. In Charleston large crowds broke into cheers for the Southern Confederacy. Stores were closed and a general celebration staged. "The tea has been thrown overboard—the revolution of 1860 has been initiated," crowed Mr. Barnwell Rhett's powerful *Mercury* the next day.

The Secession Convention met in Columbia on December 17, 1860, but rumor had it that rags and clothes from a small-pox-infected precinct of New York had been deliberately shipped to Columbia for the specific purpose of contaminating members of the convention and the legislature; and there being twenty-eight sudden cases in two days, Governor Pickens took an infatuated look at his wife's pretty little nose and promptly had a resolution passed to adjourn to Charleston immediately.

Salvos of artillery welcomed the delegates on their arrival in Charleston the next day and crowds of enthusiastic people swarmed about the delegates' hacks and buggies welcoming them with song and shouting. It seemed hardly possible, after all these years of quarreling, of debate, of dislike, that South Carolina was on her way to being an independent commonwealth; yet here was the Convention itself determinedly entering Charleston to proclaim States' Rights and to secede formally from the Union.

That afternoon the delegates reconvened in St. Andrews Hall in Broad Street, the scene of so many beautiful entertainments. Here the grave and venerable men, selected from every pursuit in life—lawyers, planters, scholars, doctors, and just plain gentlemen—sat themselves down in secret session on the hard, gilt, velvet-covered chairs sacred to the bottoms of the chaperones of the St. Cecilia; and the president, Mr. Jamison of Barnwell, stood on the dais below the beautiful young Victoria in her coronation robes painted from life by Sully for the faithful Scotchmen, and prayed that the Lord would direct the procedure to his liking. For two days in the midst of intense agitation they deliberated, and then on the morning of December 20, word ran throughout the state that the Ordinance was to be passed sometime that day.

At daylight the streets were packed with people though the convention was not to assemble until noon in St. Andrew's Hall. As noon approached the noise everywhere was so overwhelming that Guy closed his law office after having carefully locked the heavy mahogany cases holding his most valuable books and went home by a back street far removed from St. Andrew's Hall.

India was trying on hats in front of a long gold-leaf pier glass in her bedroom surrounded by mountains of white tissue paper.

As always, the sight of his daughter filled Guy with such a surging possessive love that he had to force himself not to run over and crush her in his old man's arms. Holding on to the china doorknob he said casually, masking his agitation,

"Honey, let's take a house in London until this affair blows over. The whole city has gone completely mad."

"It just goes to show how the people feel."

"They don't know how they feel. This is pure hysteria; all this hooray for Dixie! There was a notice in the London *Times* two weeks ago of a lovely house on Berkeley Square. You can buy a shooting box in Scotland and be presented to the Queen. We'll have a wonderful time. I can't bear confusion. The streets are so crowded with people not even pushcarts can go about their business."

"I wouldn't miss a day of this excitement; not even a minute. Everybody is planning parties and picnics and the whole town is packed with interesting people. Help me select a bonnet to wear; Preston Hampton was here this morning. He had just gotten in from the South Carolina College on the train with his Uncle Frank and is taking me to tea at the Mills House."

"Be sure and give him his father's hat. I never thought it would take a hatter two years to make a plain oversized beaver. Wade probably thinks you've forgotten your wager. Where are the Hamptons staying?"

"With relatives. Mr. Wade didn't come. Preston says he doesn't approve of Governor Pickens' Secessionist policy nor does he respect his judgment. Preston is here to report on the Convention to his father."

"Humph, more Up Country coxcombry. As a state senator, Wade himself should be here. Rather, none of them should be in Charleston—they'd no right to bring their germs here," Guy fumed, picking up a blue velvet imperial with a black lace veil and a branch of long slender velvet leaves from which descended pale blue feather tassels. "I like this one. Try it on."

India perched the hat on top of her heavy hair, tilted it up then down, snatched it off and fished a black velvet toque with a broad border of scarlet velvet covered with scarlet feathers from the crisp paper.

"I like that even better. Don't go out. I'll be here all alone."

"Oh, Papa, think how wonderful it is to have Secession signed in Charleston! You aren't patriotic any more. You used to be. For years state politics were all you talked about. Look! This darling red velvet Garibaldi hat! Duchess, have you finished the blue cockade?"

Duchess, sitting by the windows, lifted up a shirred blue satin cockade with a bit of palmetto piercing it.

"Ah," she said, coming over and fastening the cockade on the side of the red velvet cap, "perfect. You must wear your scarlet velvet cloak with the white ermine collar and carry your mother's gold bouquet holder with the Neapolitan cameos and the curved gold handle." Rummaging in the heavy wardrobe behind the door, her voice sounded faraway and thick, "I've made you a nosegay of Alba Plena and Mathotiana Rubra camellias. There were beauties on the bushes by the summerhouse. And I—I shall wear my green cape and the wide yellow velvet hat you had last winter. Where did I put the black ostrich plumes that Madame sent atop the box?"

India and Guy laughed at The Duchess, big as a cobra, now rustling through the tissue as fussily as a mouse.

"But you aren't going. I don't need a nurse. Preston can look after me."

"It's proper for you to have a chaperon. I am going."

Guy laughed again but nervously. Since the dreadful night at White Sulphur when he had almost quarreled with his daughter, both he and India had made every effort to be gentle and careful with each other. The Up Countryman had disappeared the next morning, thank heaven, and hadn't been heard of since. And here in Charleston she had grown into a perfect belle with dozens of suitors and in the good graces of everyone. Even Aunt Childs was satisfied though she kept her fingers crossed; saying, "It'll not last. She's up to something. I had a filly like her once. Ate out of my hand like a little lamb; then one day when I turned to look at something or other she kicked me as hard as she could right on my backsides."

"Does Duchess have to go, Papa?"

"Why do you think you should chaperon Miss India and Mr. Preston, Duchess? Do you have a reason?" His eyes darted sideways pretending to watch something out the window.

"I want to see the Catherine wheels and hear the guns," Duchess said quickly.

"What guns?"

In the silence of the big house India grew aware of a rising clamor on the street outside. Their voices alone no longer filled the room. And now waves of sound rolled in. Guy glanced at the two women and slowly rose. His mouth was a thin gray line with an outer band of bluish shadow as he followed them onto the second-floor piazza.

India and Duchess were leaning against the banisters looking over the immaculate brick paths of the garden, over the iron fence at the people rushing into the street. The clock in the hall chimed the quarter hour after one. And before the last chime echoed away every church bell in the city rang out as wildly triumphant as if it were Easter. Artillery salutes thundered from the Citadel. Windows flew up and people waved the red flag of Secession. Volunteers in makeshift uniforms galloped horses fast and on every corner little newsboys appeared as though they had been waiting all morning under the cobblestones, crying: "Extry! Extry! Read the Ordinance of Secession passed unanimously just five minutes ago in St. Andrew's Hall! Read it in full in the *Mercury!*"

India ran down to buy a paper. The house slaves had gathered whispering and giggling out by the little summerhouse leading to the street. Suddenly she saw them with a new feeling. They were what all this was about! Did they know? Were they aware of their importance? As she passed them the giggling stopped and they turned blank eyes to meet her curious stare. It was as though an invisible curtain had dropped down between them and her. Whatever they knew they'd never let on that they knew. She bet they'd even pretend there wasn't any war when fighting started.

Back up on the piazza Guy turned desperately to the Negro woman who had reared his child and ruled his house, "Can you buy me some laudanum? Ever since that summer at White Sulphur I've dreaded this day. War is now inevitable and that means some young hot-

head will persuade India to marry him before he rides
away to battle. I'd better try and sleep through it all.
I won't be a part of this evil day. Not even by listening
to the rolling of the drums."

CHAPTER VIII

AT NINE O'CLOCK that night Preston and India pushed
into the street from Institute Hall after the two-hour
ceremony of signing the Ordinance of Secession, screaming and cheering with the rest of the usually gentle
folk who had packed and jammed the galleries of the
hall. A single rocket trailing a comet tail of fire shot
into the sky and thousands of eyes watched it burst into blue and red stars high in the Carolina sky.

Secession! the people screamed; Secession!

The sky came alive with bursting rockets. Throughout the city cannon went into action, booming the
thunder of reality over the massed people. Then the
church bells, all the church bells of the city, began
clanging at once. The elderly bell ringers were swing-
ing on the ropes in unrestrained glee oblivious to the
chaos of sound from the sacred steeples.

Houses were suddenly illuminated with every candle;
the bonnie blue flag unfurled and whipped into the air,
bugles blew and bands played Hurrah! Hurrah! for
Southern Rights—hurrah!; military companies standing
in readiness stepped out in clean formation, their uniforms slashing gaily in the crowd. Here an aristocratic
old man in a Revolutionary uniform and a three-cor-
nered hat rubbed shoulders with a wild-haired Irish
bricklayer in greasy working clothes. Barbers, nuns,
tradesmen, vendors, children, slaves, and free persons
of color waved flags of every description except the
national colors with the same look of destiny as the
tall, thin, fine-faced planters in their blue swallow-
tailed coats bound at the waist with flaming scarlet
sashes.

Nannie Rutledge in white cassimere, a green wool

mantle over her shoulders, her brown hair parted in the middle, arranged in rich bandeaux then wound around her head in a double plait forming a diadem in the Imperative style brought from Russia by the Governor's wife, defied the chill air to show the charms of her Regency-style dress, tripping over the cobblestones in her dancing slippers, trying to avoid the soldiers who now were everywhere.

"Here we are, Nannie," India called and Nannie wriggled through the crowd, clutching Preston's free arm when she reached him, looking helplessly up into his pretty eyes.

But her beau, Eddie Prioleau, a saber clanking smartly at his thigh, in the uniform of the Charleston Light Dragoons was right behind Nannie and coolly pulled her arm from Preston's tucking it into the crook of his.

"Let's hurry to the Charleston Hotel. The companies are going to pass down Meeting Street in review before the Governor. Follow me—I'll make way." He charged into the crowd, like a happy bull, lifting Nannie off the ground in his exultation.

Preston tried to guard India from personal contacts with the yelling, waving men and women, thrusting his bulky shoulders sideways like a shield before her. But India reveled in the mob, wanting to be a part of it. I should have been a street woman during the French Revolution, she thought; how I would have shoved and cheered on the Place de la Concorde, and shouted like a Fury through the broken Bastille. Right now I'd give anything for a burning torch, give anything to howl and caper like those women over there. A big red face laughed into hers and her answering greeting was blown away on the shouting all around her. Mr. Hurley lurched past and in the opening his thick body left for an instant in the crowd, India saw the Duchess, her plumes flying like an avenger's crest topped by a black head that towered over everybody else's. I can't stand it, India thought wildly. That's Chance and if he is here, why then, *he* is here! Duchess must have known it all the time. I wondered why she insisted on chaperoning me then disappeared as soon as we reached the Mills House at teatime. Oh, how exciting this night is! How I love all these people! "Hooray! Hooray!"

"India, you mustn't holler like a field hand," Preston said and then—gentler— "You look like Christmas. In that red cloak you are holly and lighted candles and sugar candy all together."

"I thought I looked like Secession," she laughed, turning away from Preston's clear eyes to stare up at the canvas likenesses of celebrities suspended like big banners from one side of the street to the other blowing wildly back and forth in the high wind making the painted figures writhe like living ones: Judge Magrath tearing off his robes of office in rage at Lincoln's election; a gigantic Lincoln endeavoring to split a palmetto log; anticipated prosperity in Charleston, the wharves crowded with cotton bales and big-backed Negroes jumping and posturing against the fiery sky. Bonfires were now burning all over the city and shooting flames lightened the wintry night.

India could feel the thick human mass in the flickering glow of the pine torches swaying all around her like a running tide. The tide was flowing all over the city and the city would never be the same again. It couldn't be. There were people on Meeting Street this minute standing beside her who had never been out of an alley before. There were ladies who had never brushed the splintery planks of side streets, singing and cheering lustily. Men in elegant life were gravely shaking hands with poor whites from the country. There were slaves, confident for the first time in their lives that no "paterrollers" would hunt them into their rooms. And everybody keeping time to the rolling of the drums, the unfurling of the flags, the song—hurrah for the bonnie blue flag that bears a single star!

"Here we are," Preston said, breathing a sigh of relief. "I hope I never get caught in a maelstrom like this again."

They were on the corner of Meeting and Hayne and before them the Charleston Hotel was blazing with light. The handsome Greek colonnade across the second story was filled with men and women: stately John

Rutledge wrapped in a Scotch shawl against the risen wind; tall Mr. Wigfall of Texas and short Mr. Porcher Miles of Charleston; ex-Governor Manning with a saber and a scarlet sash; serious Mr. Jamison; oily Moses, secretary to the Governor, and yes—there was the Governor!

"Old Pick has a new wig," India whispered to Nannie.

"I guess Lucy snatched the other off on her wedding night," Nannie giggled back.

The Governor, a stout man with a big head and large important-looking face, watery eyes and flabby features, was looking very military in a full-dress uniform loaded down with gilt braid and lace, gleaming tassels and buttons. But the one who caught India's eye was the fascinating young wife of the Governor leaning on the arm of an enchanted young man looking at her alone with brilliant blue eyes fringed with stubby crow-black lashes. Behind them stood an arrogant-looking Negro woman holding a small girl child dressed in a Russian ermine coat and cap. This was the god-daughter of the Tsar, born in the Imperial Palace and christened Olga Francesca Eugenie Neva but called by her godfather, Douschka, his Little Soul! The child was a berry-brown impish-looking little thing with lots of ginger-colored hair but the mother was beautiful. She was dressed in yellow. A yellow velvet trimmed with little orange ostrich feathers and cut daringly low in the French fashion. Across her shoulders she had tossed a rich Russian sable cape and a black lace veil was tied over her face and around her heavy titian hair. India could tell that many in the street knew her by sight. She could feel their approval of their governor's lady who waved at them and sang, laughing gaily up at her handsome escort.

"That's her stepson-in-law, Matthew Calbraith Butler, a lawyer from Edgefield," Nannie joggled India's elbow. "He had dinner with us yesterday. Papa thinks he will be a general if we go to war, though he isn't twenty-five. Isn't Lady Pick lovely! They say that while the Governor was ambassador to Russia, she and the Tsar—"

"Stop gossiping; the Governor is speaking." Eddie frowned at Nannie; but only for a minute. The next he had caught her around the shoulders and was hugging her in front of everybody.

Governor Pickens had a most wonderful oratorical voice and his stirring, fiery words of personal fearlessness rang powerfully, spilling like glory cries across the crowd.

Then he had finished and the people's swelling roar surged through India. And she roared too, though she thought she was singing. Another speaker started to orate but now the parade was coming and the band music blotted out individuals.

Oh, I wish I was in Dixie—Hooray—Hooray—Hooray—Hooray! screamed the crowd.

The soldiers came marching—the 116th Regiment, of which only the officers were uniformed in gray frock coats and crimson sashes; the uniformed Volunteers; the Fire Engine Company; the Rifle Regiment, the Charleston Light Dragoons on their wild-eyed horses, and the German Hussars.

"Let's cut between the Hussars and go over to the hotel," Nannie called to Preston. "I'm hungry and Eddie says we can eat supper there."

"Yes, let's," said India, "I've never been so excited." Thinking: Maybe he's there. I know he is not here.

"Get ready then—we can cross now."

Within the hotel was the same crowded hysteria as there had been on the street. Christmas wreaths were waving in the arches, candles sputtered and dripped gleefully all over everything; blue flags and red flags hugged each other closely. The Ladies' Parlor was packed with well-corseted dowagers chattering, drinking coffee, running in and out to peep onto the street or to see who was in the hallway, giggling at the wolfish old beau with dyed hair and mustache, lounging against the arched doorway, leering at the occupants of the Ladies' Parlor.

"Hurry by, there're Aunt Childs and all my fussy cousins," India ducked behind Preston.

From the ballroom at the end of the lobby flooded in light by giant chandeliers and candelabra came the disorganized excited talking of the Secession delegates and hundreds of other people.

"Let's leave our wraps in the dressing room and see who all are in the ballroom," India's face was sparkling like the fireworks outside. Her Garibaldi cap had blown slightly sideways and bits of short hair had come loose curling against her temples.

"You look like the very spirit of revolt," Eddie said admiringly as Nannie blinked lizardlike at India and then turning to Eddie hooded her blue eyes at him in a soft way she had learned at thirteen, instantly fetching him back to her little satin heel.

"I promised Willie Preston and Nick Gaillard we'd eat supper with them. They've reserved a table here," Preston said. "Let's go in the dining room and sit down. I'm worn out. How can you girls endure all this? We've been on our feet for hours."

"Go on. I'll come in a minute. I want to peep in the ballroom at Lucy Pickens. Perhaps she will remember me and I can speak to her." India patted Preston's arm tenderly and the two boys hastened happily to order bottles of the most expensive champagne on the card for their sweet, sweet ladies.

Standing beside a fat round column at the ballroom door India hunted with her eyes for a golden head that her throbbing pulses told her must surely be in here along with all the pomp and show of Secession; along with the Governor and his lady at the far end of the room on a dais bowing and smiling as if crowns should have been on their heads instead of wigs and feathers. Then all at once she saw Maximilian Allan; he had stepped forward in front of Lucy Pickens and stood smiling while she spoke a few words to him. He had on a creamy beige broadcloth coat and tight breeches of the same fine pale color. He was kissing Lucy's hand, and the Governor, smiling importantly, waved him off with an indulgent gesture. Now he was coming straight toward her and people were making way to let him through.

India's whole body suddenly felt weak as though all her bones had melted away and her head seemed to have grown large and hollow. She noticed that his shapely legs bent a little outward when he walked. It was strange that she had not noticed this at White Sulphur—only that his legs were strong and his feet somewhat too large. In his hand was a length of thin red silk ribbon and trotting before him was a tiny long-haired dog with a flat pushed-in face and ears hanging like ragged flower petals, making music as he moved along from tinkling tiny silver bells fastened to his collar.

"Is it a monkey?"

"No, it's a cat!"

"No, no—a baby lion!"

"It's disguised as a dog—it's never a real one!"

"Move—he might bite you!"

And Max passed through the crowded room of sedate important people as unconcerned as though he were walking a blooded stallion past the judge's Stand.

"How ridiculous," a large bearded delegate sniffed to his wife; "what a show-off!"

"Ah, but such an engaging one!" his wife said.

Now Max was near India and she saw his goldish eyes were twinkling mischievously. He *was* showing off! She giggled at the lifted lorgnons and the high noses. Then he was really in the doorway and she stepped away from the fat column and the little dog barked shrilly and snapped at her toes.

"You!" Max said—"You!"

"Yes—India. Do you remember me?"

"Of course. You've spoiled no end of good times for me—remembering you. That's why I refused the King's daughter—to come back to you! I couldn't forget the perfume of the flowers in your hair and forgetting has always been very easy for me, even girls as lovely as you."

She was lovely in her clinging dress of white transparent tissue with narrow boyadere stripes crossed over her breasts and a double flowing skirt bordered with Napoleon silk stripes barred at intervals with red and blue.

"I think I'll kiss you right here in front of everybody."

"Oh, no. They don't approve of you anyway."

"How can you tell?"

"Men don't bring small strange animals into ballrooms and lead them around with ribbons. It's just not done."

"You mean in Charleston?"

"Yes."

"Then tomorrow I'll ride a stallion in here."

He was a little drunk. She could tell. And she—she was on fire. Yet she turned to go; not wanting to go but turning. He caught her hand.

"You can't leave me. Come—I'll take you home. I want to kiss you and I can do it in the calash."

"Oh—no, no—Preston Hampton is waiting in the dining room for me."

"Come over to the desk. Write a note and send it to Preston saying you had to go home suddenly."

"I couldn't do Preston like that."

"Couldn't you?"

They were face to face, so close that each could feel the other's breath. Their eyes met plumbing the depths of each other's will. Her eyes faltered first. She knew she would always do what he willed. Or rather will to do what he wanted.

CHAPTER IX

HE CAME to her house late the next afternoon while she was changing from her riding habit into a soft wool dress. Outside the noise was almost as clamoring as it had been yesterday.

Crowds of armed men still sang and promenaded up and down the streets; restaurants were full, clubrooms crowded and carousing was going on in taverns, private houses, tap-rooms, cabarets, and down narrow alleys in broad daylight. "Attack Fort Moultrie!" was the cry. "Prevent Anderson seizing Fort Sumter." Everywhere were lanky lads, clanking spurs and sabers, awkward squads marching to and fro, with drummers beating calls and ruffles and points of war; around them groups of grinning Negroes delighted with the glare and glitter, a holiday and a new idea for them

—Secession flags waving out of all the windows—little Irish boys shouting—"Extra! New Edition! Commissioners appointed by the Convention to go to Washington to treat with the President for the delivery of the forts and the public property within the state! Read it in the *Mercury!*"

"You're smart to wear red for him," Duchess herself, wider than the door in a forbidden hoop skirt, carefully buttoned the row of minute buttons down the tight bodice pinching India's waist into a slender circle. "Always look vivid and be gay with him. He'll never be one to catch with milk and honey."

"What kind is he? He's well born—wouldn't he want a lady?"

"He wants a lady all right but one who has sense enough to know when not to act like one."

"When is that?"

"Evidently you know. No lady would have walked out on a Hampton as you did last night. They say poor little Preston borrowed a horse and went galloping away down the road to Columbia within twenty minutes after he got your note at the hotel. That wasn't very smart of you. He was your best chance."

"You mean my richest one."

"Being responsible for you, I have to say—your best one. Mr. Allan will flirt with hundreds of pretty girls before he's done. He'll break any woman's heart who marries him."

"Not mine—if I marry him."

"Has he asked you?"

"I think he will."

"Wait until he does before you make up your bed."

"Duchess! You have no right to speak to me like that."

"Who has?"

"No one but Papa."

"Pooh! You aren't flesh and blood to him. You're a dream. I've always been responsible for you. And I don't hide my eyes from the fact that you're as hot a one as the next—lady or no. There—for God's sake—I never saw so many buttons! Go on—he's in the drawing room. Bring me a cigar from the box when you

come out. Mr. Guy counted them carefully yesterday
and if he counts again today I want to be able to swear
truthfully that I never touched a one."

Max wasn't in the drawing room but had gone out
onto the upstairs piazza. The flowers in the walled
courtyard were blooming with a last wild profusion of
color before a killing frost withered them away. Red
Jacqueminot roses, milk and wine lilies, ageratum,
coral vine, yellow chrysanthemums. He was looking beyond the garden to Fort Sumter out in the bay, the little
dog lying at his feet breathing snuffily. Max was dressed
today in a rich brown frock coat with fawn-colored
breeches and a cape of some dark brown material hung
loosely over his shoulders. The sunset, the light from
the sea, the towering fort in the distance cast so strange
a radiance upon his golden head and pale olive face
as he stood looking out at the sea that to India, breathless in the French window, he seemed like some messenger from another world. Out in the bay a line of
boats was passing, the slaves singing as they rowed.
These boats were so far off that they looked like a
covey of small birds afloat on the choppy water. With
the sound of oars was subtly blended the crying of
gulls, each searcher's lament swiftly matched by the
voice of his close-following mate. Max raised his hand
as though pointing at a particularly swift gull. As he
did so the golden hairs on his wrist gleamed against
the leaf-brown wool of his cape.

"Max," she called, and her voice was as soft as
brook water.

"The rustle of the palmettos sounds like rain," he
said, still looking toward the bay; "in the Up Country
the pines sound like the sea—on winter nights you
might think you were far out in the middle of the ocean.
It is a lonely sounding."

"Oh," she said, not knowing what to say. Last night
she had not cared what she said. She had wondered
how he would be today. And he was talking quite
matter-of-factly almost as if she had not lain heart to
heart with him—for how long? She had no idea.
Whatever his mood she would try to be a part of it.

The sunset was bright but there were black clouds

banked beneath the color and the sea. At the moment
the glossy harbor dazzled the gulls that, gleaming, flew
into the sunset. A last wasp glimmered on the grape-
vine hanging on the piazza but all the grapes were
gone. The wasp buzzed weakly and fell onto the floor
kicking his thin impotent legs feebly as the little dog
which had been lying quietly at Max's feet jumped up
and began worrying it with his hairy paws.

"Tomorrow it is going to rain. Winter will begin. I
should go home. I didn't tell you last night but I only
landed in Charleston yesterday on the clipper from
China." He sounded sad and suddenly she wanted to
do anything to make sure he was never sad again. He
must always be happy, always. Stooping she patted the
little dog's head and the dog jumped up and down gaily
licking between her fingers as if she belonged to him.

"What kind of a dog is he?"

"He comes from Pekin. I went into Pekin right behind the British Army with the Russian and American
ministers. We reached the Emperor's Palace just after
it was sacked."

"Was it a pretty palace?"

"It was in shambles when I saw it. Strewn with rolls
of silk and fans, broken ornamental latticework,
crushed jade screens, and magnificent Louis Quatorze
vases smashed to bits. The French soldiers were going
through the place with sticks breaking mirrors, screens,
and panels. They found a treasury of gold ingots and
sycee silver which they divided with the British. They
all had tied satin and crepe cummerbunds and pug-
garees around their waists and legs. I found Mr. Wu
in the ladies' apartments. Don't raise those black eyebrows! The ladies had all fled and left hundreds of
these pet dogs behind. They were running around the
palace in a completely distracted state. This little fellow was attacking an English sergeant who insisted on
tying one of his mistress's robes of silver and gold
thread around his waist. I thought Mr. Wu was worth
having so I put him in my sack along with a few odd
bits of jade and silk."

"Was the sergeant angry?"

"I let him take an English presentation sword with a

coat of arms of antiquity, studded with gems, that I had my eye on. He was going to murder little Mr. Wu."

"It sounds dreadful—"

"But exciting! I had a grand time all over the world. I shall hate to settle down and grow cotton. I won't if war comes."

"Do you think it is coming?"

"See those two steamers lying close to Fort Sumter?"

"Yes—one is the *Nina*—I don't recognize the other."

"The Governor has ordered them to stand by Fort Sumter to make sure Major Anderson doesn't move to occupy the Fort."

"What's wrong with the boats being there?"

"If Major Anderson considers the placing of those boats in the harbor an act of aggression, as he has a perfect right to do, he may fire on them; *ergo*—war!"

"Will it be an exciting war or a tearing-up war?"

"A tearing-up one. The North will win eventually. We have enough men but they have enough machines."

"You sound so cold-blooded—don't let's talk about it any more." Her breath began to choke her. "When are you going home?" She forced herself to say it.

"As soon as Lucy Pickens makes up the Governor's mind whether we will have war. Calbraith Butler and I are planning to go home together."

"I hope she doesn't make it up too soon."

"I, too, when I am with you. Your teeth are chattering!"

"I'm cold. I'll get a wrap if you'd like to stay out here—or shall we go into the drawing room?"

"Either that you wish," he answered and followed her through the French doors into the big room.

There were hundreds of him now inside the room. From each big mirror on every panel he went on and on and on. But never enough of him, she thought wildly. And the moment that she had shut the double doors behind them she was in his arms. . . .

CHAPTER X

THE NIGHT after Christmas was a crisp cold night with frost twinkling along the withered flower gardens and a half-moon bright as a spotlight on Charleston harbor.

Lucy Pickens smoothed the snowy ermine bands bordering the low décolletage of her white uncut-velvet gown and fingered the brilliant necklace of diamonds the Tsar had given her caressing her perfect neck. Strains of the new waltz, "Olga," drifted above the animated conversations of her entirely successful ball. She lifted her proud head a little more imperiously and the egret feathers in her titian hair, plaited high like a crown, danced in the warm air perfumed with flowers and beards, excellent food and the pungent odor of Russian tea.

The intimate dinner before the ball given by her and the Governor for forty of the most important men in the state, and their wives, of course, had gone like a perfectly wound clock, marred by only one refusal— the Wade Hamptons. It was unfortunate that the Governor and Wade Hampton were at odds. Unfortunate that Moses had told the Governor Wade Hampton had been heard to call him a fool. The situation would have been easy to remedy if Wade Hampton had come to-night and under the spell of her perfectly hostessed dinner let her soothe his peace-loving soul.

At eight o'clock dinner had been served in her private apartments. The heavy silver dish covers had reflected the wax candles in the massive Russian silver candelabrum, the Bohemian crystal goblets covered with light mist from the chilled wine reflected from one to the other their rainbow rays; camellias and roses had been strewn in a row down the whole length of the banquet tables draped in extravagant Italian linens; and in the gold-bordered Sèvres plates each heavily embroidered napkin, folded like a bishop's miter, had held a roll in the European fashion. Bowls of Russian caviar had nestled in blocks of carven ice; rich oyster stew thick with cream and redolent of mace and Spanish sherry had been ladled from the three-foot-wide solid silver tureen that the Tsar had publicly presented to her on leaving; there had been wild turkeys in their iridescent plumage and venison basted in the finest port; smoke had risen from the crab soufflé; aspics had quivered; jellies had shaken properly; Jerusalem artichokes fried to a crackling crisp had surrounded sweet potatoes drowning in melted butter; ducks from the forest and fish from the river: it all sounded like a song to long remember. In white court wigs and the gold-embroidered livery she had bought in St. Petersburg her Negro butlers and footmen, grave as judges, had offered white wine that sparkled and red wine that glowed as the courses followed each other to the ices and hothouse fruits piled high in silver baskets on beds of soft gray moss.

After supper she had served Russian tea from a samovar. Little Moses, behind the scenes, had seen that all progressed smoothly. Success was the word tonight. A great success!

The Pickens were on their way. War? War was always exciting. After Paris and the years at court in St. Petersburg, a beautiful woman needed an exciting life. Confederacy? If so—why not her own brilliant Mr. Pickens as the president and herself as its first lady? No one could doubt after tonight that she was capable of gracing a White House!

And to think that the Governor had almost made her call the party off! After Mr. Williams Middleton and Barnwell Rhett had warned him this afternoon that they had heard from a friend in Washington that tonight, under cover of the festivities, Major Anderson was planning to evacuate Fort Moultrie and move his men and arms to Fort Sumter. They had urged the Governor to postpone his ball and concentrate everything on securing Sumter. It had taken all her wiles and tears to persuade the Governor that Mr. Middleton was an old fuddy-duddy and if they never did anything on account of rumors she would be oh! so unhappy! Besides there had already been a thousand rumors. And what had happened? Nothing at all.

And now she was so happy! The orchestra Little Moses had arranged to hire from Philadelphia was enchanting. Look at the way everybody was enjoying themselves—the Langdon Cheves, the brilliant Trescots, the Rutledges, all of them, even the youngest belle, Nannie, with her infatuated Prioleau boy, ex-Governor Means, Dr. Gibbes, the Rivers, judge Whitener, the Frosts, the Haynes, the Lowndes, the Izards, Chancellor Carroll, Robert Gourdin, all the nice, sweet, fresh, pure-looking Pringle girls beaming on their clever brother Edward, waltzing with beautiful Mrs. Joe Heyward, in mauve satin that dulled her skin, and there, too, was the sarcastic Mrs. Chestnut in need of a new white feather for her pretty hair. Porcher Miles waving a freesia at her, and Senator Wigfall from her own loved Texas, a little drunk and untidy but with a face of fire not to be forgotten!

The ball was in full swing. Everyone had come; with the exception of the Hamptons, of course. And someone else—who was it she was missing? She had an infallible gift for knowing exactly what was going on in every part of a crowded room—of knowing which one out of a hundred had not taken her hand in the receiving line. Who could it be that she missed? Tapping her good white teeth with a French lace fan she remembered—Max! Her bad boy! How amusing he was. But so naughty! He had got into quite a snarl in St. Petersburg with one of the Grand Duke's daughters and Mr. Pickens had had to get him away to China quite hurriedly.

She was delighted he was here in Charleston because being near her age, he relaxed her with his gay vitality after too many of the Governor's contemporaries. Moses had spared no words describing Max's violent flirtation with a little Charleston girl of one of the best families—India St. Julien. India must be as wild a one as Max from Moses' tales: decking their horses in Christmas wreaths and satin bows on Christmas Eve and riding all over town in the pouring rain singing at the top of their lungs; kissing behind the portieres at Mrs. Smith's soiree; laughing consistently at the wrong time at the performances of George Christy's Minstrels at the Dock Street Theatre; being driven by that outrageous Chance, after balls and suppers, along the sea wall in a calash with the curtains hooked tight and fast until all hours of the night!

If Max brought India this evening she would drop a word of caution in the little girl's ear. She remembered the dark child from the summer at the White when, brokenhearted at her lover's death, she had agreed to go to Russia with dull old—no, not even in the privacy of her thoughts must she say that word—with powerful Governor F. W. Pickens who would someday be president of the Confederacy!

"Will you dance?" handsome John Manning was bowing to her and light as a willow she took his hand skipping swiftly to a polka up and down the crowded, animated room. Once as they neared the door a flurry of people seemed clustered around a new arrival. She signaled to John Manning to stop.

"A latecomer," she said. Perhaps the Hamptons had reconsidered!

It was India and Max looking the very essence of this whole Secession picture—wild, headstrong, thoroughbred, defiant, and glorious!

As she stepped into the room all the hundreds of dripping candles from chandelier and candelabrum seemed to waver toward India trailing endless ruffles of foaming sea-green silk that brought out the blue highlights in her heavy hair and the whiteness of her vivid face and swanlike throat. There was a world of daring in the smile that curved her mouth and all the wishing in the world glistening in her eyes.

To Lucy, seeing her for the first time grown up, India's beauty was almost a shock. Warn this girl? No fool she. She'd better see that her aging husband's eyes didn't light on her. Lucy turned her face up to John Manning as if for reassurance, looking love with her big blue eyes into his eager face.

"What beautiful dancers you Low Countrymen are," she purred, and he nodded fatuously, forgetting that he was from the Up Country!

At midnight supper was served by the gold-liveried Negroes—still grave but sweating mightily—truffles, *pâté de foie gras,* salad, biscuit glacé, and iced champagne. Mr. Wigfall got up to deliver a suitable toast to his beauteous fellow Texan, the Governor's Lady, but as he opened his mouth to speak, the reverberations of a cannon swept across the room. Everybody rushed to the windows and into the street to find out what was going on. All except two happy gentlemen. Barnwell Rhett, his white beard trimmed like a dagger, his blue-gray eyes triumphant in his flushed face, lifted a glass of champagne to William Middleton who lightly clicked it with another. They drank deep then Rhett impulsively threw his empty glass over his shoulder, saying, "The Governor took our advice. He has occupied Fort Sumter. What a clever man he is!"

But the shattering crystal and his words were muffled by the shrieks and shouts pouring in through the windows which had been hastily thrown up: "Anderson has just set off a cannon to announce that he has moved his entire force into Fort Sumter! He has spiked the guns at Moultrie. It is an act of aggression. War! Yipee—ee—ee—ee—ee! Hooray—Hooray—I'll take my stand and live and die—for Dixie!"

Someone lurched into Max and India pushing them against a post of the Planter's Hotel where Max had rooms. As on Secession night the city was wildly clamoring with inflamed, war-wishing Carolinians.

"God help me, India," said Max, "I cannot go to Edgefield without you and this means that I must go at once."

India shook—it must be because her heart beat so, she thought—her hands were cold and clammy though she had slipped on her velvet cloak. As Max kissed her vehemently, unmindful of the hot-eyed people everywhere, she weakly tried to push him from her. He lifted his face a moment and she thought of a hawk suddenly loosed from a chained perch.

"We'll find a minister and get married now—tonight—" he said hoarsely. She sank forward on his breast and gladly let him lead her where he would.

CHAPTER XI

ON NEW YEAR'S EVE, India and Max stopped to change their clothes at Burt Hart's house in the town of Edgefield just as a rising moon was struggling with the last gleam of day.

Burt, a cousin of Max, was a big jovial man full of exuberance and buttered rum. His short round wife, Anna, took immediate charge of the half-frozen, journey-pale bride, and in no time India was lying stretched out in a tin bath in front of a hot pine fire in Anna Hart's best company room, an eggnog soothing her tired stomach, while Mr. Wu stood on his hind legs whining and scratching at the side of the high tub that had swallowed his beloved new mistress.

"I'll take your party dress down for the girls to freshen. My, it's pretty! You just lie in that warm water and relax for a while. Cousin Emmy has invited the whole countryside to meet you tonight and you'll need your nerves quiet. Don't you want me to take the dog out so you can doze?"

"No, let him stay. How kind you are, Cousin Anna. Tell me—does Max's mother mind his—his—being married?"

"Lord, child, Cousin Emmy is delighted. Your mother was a relative of hers. She knows all about you. You'll love Max's mother."

Fat mother-henny Anna Hart carefully folded India's dress over her arm, blew out the candles and tiptoed from the darkening room leaving it lit only by the blazing fire.

India stretched herself gratefully in the warm soapy water giving herself up to thoughts of her father. Hurting thoughts. Wondering ones. Guy had refused to see her and Max when they went home the next morning after Dr. Bachman had married them so late at night. He had locked the street gates and shuttered all the blinds. Duchess, enraged, had leaned from an upstairs window and thrown down a few of her finest French

costumes and her sealskin cape to Chance who had
climbed the spike-topped iron fence cruelly tearing his
arms and legs. Duchess herself had attempted to jump
from the window and run away with them but Guy had
struck her with a whip shouting loud enough for loiter-
ers on the street and curious neighbors peeping from
behind blinds to hear: "You are my slave—not India's.
I forbid you to accompany her and that scoundrel to
the Up Country."

Duchess's cries—"My God! My God! A slave, he
says. A slave! My God!"—had echoed after India as
she had climbed back into the calash with Max and
driven away from Charleston toward Columbia where
the Hamptons had welcomed the two elopers as if they
were their own flesh and blood. Even Preston had
been sweet to her though Max had said he treated him
with noticeable coolness.

India sighed, feeling very hurt and lonely. A part of
her life had ended abruptly the moment she had rung
the bell of the little pavilion by the gate and Beverly
had whispered through the wrought grille: "Lawsamussy, Miss India! Mr. Guy fit to be tied. He say nurr
you nurr Mr. Allan to set foot inside dis gate urr he
gwine hoss-whup you bofe. Lawsamussy, Miss India!
And de Duchess maddern him. Her eyes as raid as
pomegrannies. Gawd bless you, Miss India, git on away
frum here but come back someday."

She didn't want to go back. Heavy as was the remembering of having displeased her father enough to
make him act so badly—heavenly was the knowing
that though her whole body ached with the wonder
that the ill thing sung in all the songs was thus—since
it was with Max that she did it, she felt herself grown
so wholly his that she could never live without him any
more.

A knock at the door: "Come in!" She was half-
asleep, warmed by the water and soothed by the crackling fire. Half-opening her eyes she looked up and
there was Max—his hair damp around the edges from
his bathing, his face flushed with the heat of the house
after the long day's driving in the winter air, wearing
the creamy beige swallow-tailed coat and skin-tight

trousers that became him so elegantly. Tonight he had added a silk brocade wedding vest across which he had fastened a carved coral watch chain with miniature coral charms dangling from it: a coral boat with diamond sails, a gold and coral pistol, a coral lady's hand with a pearl bracelet, a tiny gilded throne, a cat's face with emerald eyes. Max was staring down at her body half in and half out of the water, shining with wetness and curved so deliciously.

"Can you believe it!" he said joyfully. "Isn't it marvelous to be on our way home to our wedding feast. This is our true bridal night. You will sleep in my arms in my own bed and I will love you all night long."

India rose from the water and the flames cast licking shadows up and down her long slim legs and tipped her nipples with a hot crimson color.

"All you need is a shell to stand on," he said, "and your hair flowing." She took out the tortoise-shell combs holding up her hair and it unrolled down her back like ebon silk. "Now pick it up and hold it in front of you —with your left hand, there—right there—let your other hand cover your breast—spread your fingers a little—that's it—perfect! Botticelli made a great mistake. Venus was never a blonde—never!"

India held the pose a moment then she reached out her arms to Max but he just kissed her wet finger tips saying that she must hurry because they had miles to go and a group of his friends were downstairs, waiting to ride as escort with them to Shepherd's Grove. His mother had sent the coach to carry them to their home in style.

Anna knocked at the door and Max turned to leave. "We will have a proper wedding after all," he whispered as Anna entered, her cheeks burning. To think that wild-spirited Max had seen his own wife naked as a jay bird! She'd not tell Burt. It might give him ideas. And now it was too late. Six years too late.

Two Negro girls followed their mistress carrying the dress as tenderly as a precious child. Anna helped India tie on her drawers of finest mull edged with Valenciennes lace threaded with sky-blue ribbons, her ruffled petticoats of starched cambric to hold the dress out full, and then the girls slipped the dress over India's head letting it suddenly transform her into a great lady.

The dress was a fine white grenadine made with three flounces of scarlet uncut velvet. The sleeves were wide open to the shoulder lined with white silk and decorated with a narrow border of the red velvet edged with a fall of *point de gaz* on the outside and on the inside with a white satin ruche. With it, Madame had sent, just because she had seen a picture by Raphael in somebody's house, an Italian cap of white velvet edged with curling tiny white ostrich feathers. Anna brushed India's hair out to all sides then caught it in a heavy white silken snood so that it fell softly like a dark fan from the cap onto her neck.

"Now look at yourself, India," said Anna, and India caught a glimpse of her own face framed by the exquisite cap in the heavy mahogany mirror over the marble-topped bureau. Round about many shadows, bright and dark, were stirring in the mirror—but she saw that she had never looked so well nor had her eyes ever had so deep a lustre.

"Come ride with us," she said impulsively catching Anna's warm friendly hand. "I am afraid. I need someone with me. I won't know any of the proper things to do or say."

"You'll know. You've already made me feel close to you. You don't need anyone with Maximilian proud as he is of you."

Anna wrapped India's red velvet cloak around her shoulders and, followed by Mr. Wu they went down to where talk and laughter spilled from the cold dark hall into the dining room.

India thought she had never seen so many big noisy men in all her life. They all shouted greetings and congratulated Max and had another drink for the road and then she was going out into the night and people on the street called that the coach was waiting.

In the hard clay street was a tossing mass of horses and Negroes and drawn up at the gate was the magnificent scarlet coach she had seen that day when she and Preston Hampton had gone up the mountain to spy on

the nabob. The six bay horses seemed even glossier tonight in the torchlights. Each one wore a waving white
plume on his head and they pranced and tossed their
plumes like trained performers. The gilded cherubs
at the corners were decorated with white satin bows
and shiny magnolia leaves, the lamps were lit and
sparkling like crystal stars. Suddenly India wondered if
the pinkish sour sister was hiding inside but when the
door was opened the soft gray silk lining gleamed
emptily. She was tired again and nervous and she stumbled getting into the coach and almost fell but Max
caught her around the waist and whispered, "You are
the loveliest bride in all the world." And she was on the
inside of the scarlet coach looking out and it was very
cold.

The big men in their fine clothes, long flowing
capes billowing behind them in the wind, carrying
lighted torches aloft, mounted their horses and the wedding procession moved off through the moonlit timber-
lands with song and laughter for the bridal music.

The ground sounded hollow under the horses' hoofs,
for the earth was hard as iron with a black frost. Max
kept calling from the window to one and then another
of his friends; his face glowing from the biting wind
and from the whisky he had drunk at Burt's house.
Youth and gladness seemed to shine out of him and joy
and wantonness welled out in the tones of his sweet
mellow voice as he sat beside her shouting and laughing amid his friends and kinsmen.

India's heart began to tremble strangely. A girl should
have some of her own family at her wedding. Ah, but
this was not her wedding! Her wedding had been in a
chill, matting-covered parlor of the Lutheran parish
house standing beside a black horsehair sofa while the
disapproving Dr. Bachman pronounced them man and
wife. Suddenly she felt somewhere deep down a spot of
anger with Max that he had caused her to do these
things. And yet seeing his boyish pride and sparkling
happiness at bringing her home as his wife she felt
the spot of anger disappear.

"Do you catch the scent of the Up Country?" Max
asked her putting his hand inside her ermine muff and

warmly pressing her chilly fingers. India became aware of a strange strong odor of wild aromatic plants. "That is the scent of the Up Country. She is an unpredictable woman and that is her perfume."

They were traveling a broad trail of red clay between tall pale-barked sycamore trees saturated with milky moonlight. A nighthawk whistled shrilly, "wheeOO!" with a liquid tang and after one glance back at the silvered road they turned into the thick forest which seemed by contrast of inky blackness relieved by the road ahead which showed as does a candle ray between closed eyelids.

"It is weirdly beautiful," Max said, "I had forgotten just how beautiful."

"It is unearthly and unreal," India shivered and he put his arm around her and kissed her on the cheek. "It is like being in an empty house with all the lamps blown out." She turned and moved his lips from her cheek onto her mouth. Her pulse throbbed and the silence for a time was as perfect as breathlessness.

"It is a magic not seen in your city streets emaciated and shattered by gas lamps. Listen and look: there is color even in this darkness," he whispered, holding her very close.

She looked out of the window and saw the green of leaves great and small showing as a rich dark olive. Afternoon rain and new frost had left each leaf and bough filmed with ice and this struck back the moonlight as polished silver.

Behind them the road was like a dark aisle with only scattered stabs of light from the men's torches. Somewhere an owl was calling like a lonely soul. The cry started as a high trembling wail the final cry being lost in the depths of whispered woe. India hid her face in Max's shoulder and he laughed at her despair as five minutes later the owl called far, far away as if from a lower rung of purgatory.

"I am afraid," India moaned. "What sort of place is this I am coming to?"

At that moment there was a sudden tearing rush and ripping of vines and shrubs mingled with deep hoarse snorts and a big buck followed by a doe and dappled twin fawns leaped across the road just ahead of the horses, re-entering the forest in a momentary shiver of leaves like lost moon shadows.

"How beautiful," she cried, forgetting fear. Nearing the creek swamp a mist rose tarnishing the silver of the night and intensifying the myriad and bewildering smells of resin, crushed leaves, and decaying wood: acrid, sweet, spicy, and suffocating.

Then all at once the forest lessened, bare trees scratched the sky, the moonlight turned green pastures into silver lakes and a flock of wild geese passed overhead like a giant arrowhead, piercing the shining moon. For the last mile to the house brilliant bonfires every hundred yards lit up the woods. At each bonfire Negroes in old wool hats, shapeless bagging clothes, and clumping brogans jumped and jigged up and down singing and waving—

"Welcome, Mista Maxi—pretty missis! Yi-ee-yi-ee!" Africa glowed hotly in their eyes in the red glare of fire, and as the formal lawn of the Grove itself showed up ahead, dozens of little Negro boys ran to meet them with blazing torches. The horses' hoofs rang on the round flagstone-paved turnaround in front of the house, outlined with lighted Japanese lanterns strung about the tall dark pines and cedars. Max squeezed her fingers tight saying with a thrill in his voice,

"This is our home, India. May you be happy here."

India was not enough herself to see much of the house. Only that it was very large and white, that two molded lions crouched beside the steps, and that a gargantuan wisteria vine writhed like a snake thing from the ground up to the second-floor piazza. The plantation bell was ringing and hundreds of Negroes swarmed across the broad open fields with cries of greeting. The young men who had formed their escort waved their torches and yelled—and with a great clattering and the thunder of hoofs on the flagged paving and joyous uproar the scarlet coach came to a stop at Shepherd's Grove in a blaze of varicolored glow.

Max got out and handed India down with a flourish. The front doors burst open and people spilled onto the cold piazza crying: "Welcome! Welcome Home!"

The sister, wispy as the moonlight in a dress of beige illusion dotted with pearls, reached them first. Max snatched her in his arms hugging her gaily. India had not realized how thin and high-waisted the sister was, nor remembered how fish-cold were the light oblique eyes that now slid over her, tearing away the warm red cloak—the velvet flounces of her dress, the cambric petticoats, the frivolous mull drawers, and shivering in dislike at what she visualized.

Seeing the people crowding to meet India, Irene managed a simpering smile holding out her hand to Max's wife. India took Irene's hand and with a shock realized that this undersized bit of bone and skin belonged to a grown person! She had never touched so little a hand, nor one so unfriendly. She had an impulse to squeeze the fingers and feel them crush to bony bits.

"I—" She was going to say, I am so glad to be here, but Mr. Wu after a tentative sniff at Irene's skirts began barking and growling, tearing the tulle with his underslung teeth.

"Aieee—she's brought a cat! Bubba—Bubba—you know how I hate cats!"

Max caught up Mr. Wu while India ran from the cold night through the open double doors into a hall as big as any Charleston ballroom with a coved ceiling of carved wood from which suspended two mammoth Waterford chandeliers rainbow-bright from dozens of burning wax candles. The floor was made of wide polished heart-pine boards sweet and slippery now with powdered wax.

Someone took off her cloak and an elegant white-haired lady straightened her cap. Max smiled at the lady and she stepped back as Anna Hart smoothed the back of India's skirt where the cloak had crumpled it. Max asked Anna how she and Burt had got here ahead of them. Anna said they had taken the short cut through the swamp so that they could be on hand to see how Emmy greeted her daughter-in-law.

"No need to worry about that," he said looking down at India. His face as he looked was beautiful and India felt her heart sing with love for him. He bowed her into

the parlor motioning toward a carved Flemish chair by
a full-sized Viennese pedal harp where a dark-haired
woman, draped in seemingly endless folds of mauve
chiffon, was sitting but now rising with the aid of a
stout cane.

"This is my mother," Max took India by the hand
and led her straight toward Emmy Allan who watched
India as she approached, amid the greetings and happy
laughter of the guests, with no malice or reserve, just
an expression of warm pleasure and gaiety. Emmy Allan had a broad face with wide-spaced, long, light
brown eyes, a thick nose, and a wide generous mouth
that was smiling now:

"What a lovely mistress you have brought to Shepherd's Grove!" Then Max was in his mother's arms,
and after, she, too, was smothered in the soft, violet-
scented chiffon, and suddenly she wanted to stay there
and never go from the ineffable comfort of this woman.
But Emmy pushed her away and held her a minute,
looking full into her face saying, "Dear child, you are
very beautiful. Maximilian's two years about the world
have made him quite selective. You and I will be good
friends as well as the blood kin that we are. I hear
Lucy Pickens gave a ball in Charleston. She served fig
preserves and hot biscuits to the Tsar in St. Petersburg.
What did she serve the Charlestonians?"

"Caviar and champagne!" India answered, Emmy's
eyes twinkled as if she were going to tell India a good
story but remembering that this was India's introduction
to the Up Country she said,

"Go now and meet my friends who are here to honor
you. We'll talk tomorrow."

Max took India from room to room and she greeted
the people who to her surprise looked much as people
she would have seen at a Charleston reception. And,
as in Charleston, all talking of Secession; the failure of
the Governor's Commissioners in Washington because
of their highhandedness with Mr. Buchanan; their personal "infallible" plan for reducing Fort Sumter; Governor Pickens's bold seizure of the Custom House and
arsenal; the outrageous New York *Tribune* calling South
Carolina a "mob"; the excitement of the cotton market

with cotton at twelve cents a pound; are you going to join the cavalry?

They chatted and moved their chairs, the men gathered about the punch bowl singing old mellow songs, the string orchestra played polkas and waltzes, the women drank wine and fluttered their fans; all of which made such a confusing noise and wild medley of sound that India's head was spinning. What she had expected she was not sure, but that the ladies would be so fashionably dressed, the house so big and grand, the music smooth and true, the flowers fresh in spite of wintertime—these things she had not looked for.

It seemed she had not come so far away as she had thought back in the forest—and she lost all knowledge of time; hours and the pictures of her brain seemed strangely to float about loosely, mingled with each other.

At midnight they cut the wedding cake with Max's grandfather's jewel-handled rapier. The dining table covered in Brussels lace had been placed in the shape of a cross and in the center was a five-foot-high gilt candelabrum, each branch bearing a lighted white candle, and over the whole was thrown a network of spun candy filmy as a bride's veil.

"This is like in church," India whispered to Max, looking at the cross and the burning candles through the mystic veil.

"Bless you, my dear," he said and his hand closed firmly over hers as together they pressed the shining blade through the frosted cake.

There were groups of Negroes singing in the yard and dancing around big bonfires. They called out that the bride and bridegroom must greet them too and then she was dancing a reel with Max in the center of a ring of them on the crisp frosty grass. She seemed to come to a little in the cold air and her laugh rang out merrily as a tall, skinny, loose-legged Negro with a long scrawny neck sang, picking a guitar to the time of their dancing:

Way down yonder in Issaqueena
Where de wite folks sit in de shade

Dere I met my big black Verbena
De sweetest gal ever wuz made;
Her face so black dat we wite folks can't see her
When she rambled 'round in de dark
But I know she is dere
From de puffume of her hair
And de way my coon dogs bark.
Yippy-i-ee-i-ee-i-ee
Yippy-i-ee-i-o!

When the song ended Max led her out of the ring
and crushed her to him in the darkness of the cedars.

"It's been hours since I have had a chance to tell
you—you are beautiful—so beautiful and sweet everybody loves you."

"But I am tired, so tired," she whispered back.

"Soon we will go and sleep," answered her bridegroom looking out into the darkness where a wreath of
white fog floated above the wide open fields. The
moon had traveled far since they had entered the scarlet coach. "This is your first night in your home. It
must be your first completely happy one—the happiest
one of all."

India threw her arms about him. She had a sweet
wild feeling that now and always life would be wonderful. She did not see Irene standing on the lighted
piazza peering left and right directing Chance to search
for them.

It was a good thing, for Max lifted India's face a
moment, looked into her clear fine eyes and drew his
hand down over her face and body with a strange haste
and roughness.

"Let's not go back in the house. We've done our de-
voir. We can climb up the wisteria vine. My room
opens on the piazza. There is a fire burning—I see the
flames. Can you climb if I show you the way?"

She was hesitant as she followed Max to the great
vine but her whole body throbbed and quivered as
he put his arm around her waist and lifted her to find
the first big branch for a good foothold.

Too soon it was dawn. As the pines soughed softly
in the first day wind, the sky paled. A thrush sang de-

spite the chilly air; brogened feet crunched under the window blackening the rime thrown like a film across the crusty lawn; the plantation bell clanged; and roosters crowed, arrogant as the rising sun.

Max lifted himself on his elbow and looked down into India's radiant, proud face—at her red mouth slightly swollen from his kissing.

From the edge of a grain field came the cry of quails. Max whispered, soft and sleepy as the quails, "such is my joy!"

CHAPTER XII

EDGEFIELD, lying along the Savannah River, was settled before the Revolution by discontented Virginians who had ancestors but who wanted more land and different laws. Buffalo and bear still roamed the piney woods when they arrived in their wagons full of furniture, family, and a few slaves. Some were, as some always were, discouraged and went back; but those who thrilled to the calling of the wild turkeys and heard the majestic music of the cathedral pines on the night wind, cleared homeplaces and developed a peculiar society of elusive habits, intense and fiery, that made them different from most of the rural counties.

As cultivated as the gentlemen of Camden and the Old Cheraws, they drank more, gambled less, rode harder, hunted bolder, were more enterprising, and became masterly politicians.

King Cotton brought them great wealth and there grew up in the district a planter-lawyer aristocracy that was to the Up Country and the edges of the Back Country what the St. Andrew's Society was to the Charleston group.

To this district had come and stayed one Gomillion Shepherd whose father was a Virginia judge. By 1789, Gomillion had prospered so in the rolling piney land that he was able to build a homeplace finer than the one he'd come from in Virginia.

Shepherd's Grove was built of cypress on a brick basement, the weatherboarding cut to look like blocks of stone, with the front door directly at the head of three stone steps. The lines of the house were good and solid but Gomillion was mainly concerned with the interior which was paneled and carefully finished, particularly the hall, running down the whole center of the house, designed after the picture gallery of his grandfather's estate in Kent. The front doorway with its tall glass sidelights was flanked by four engaged fluted columns surmounted by a fanlight spread wide like a peacock's tail, letting the light strike obliquely on Gomillion's "folly," as his neighbors called the enormous drafty picture hall.

Gomillion's son, Kent, caring nothing for the fine paintings, concentrated on planting the new crop, cotton, and in 1809 added four Corinthian columns and upper and lower piazzas so well designed, fitting so well the style of the house, that they seemed a part of the original plan and gave no feeling of being an afterthought.

While the craftsmen were carving and fluting columns and pilasters, Kent's son, Nichol, graduated in law at Harvard, fetched home from his "grand tour" four marble statues representing hunting, music, dancing, and love which the workers set in green-painted niches cut from the thickness of the outer walls along the front of the house.

Nichol, who was the intellectual Shepherd, also brought home boxes of books purchased from the Duke of Devonshire's private sale and built an octagonal little house to hold them, in a grove of pine trees, reached from the big house by a graveled path edged with pink brick and bordered with dwarf boxwoods. French doors in the library opened in summer to give the room the look of an airy pavilion and in winter, closed, let the sunlight make russet tapestry of the book-studded walls.

There was a fireplace in the library inlaid around the chimney with glazed French tiles painted with forest scenes; its lofty mantelpiece upheld on either side of the big tile-framed cavity by perfectly carved pine trees of heart pine polished and waxed to a mellow amber sheen. On the wide mantel shelf was a pair of Rockingham pheasants and in the center a gilded clock with a hunter atop it and various hares, doves, foxes and deer worked in the gilt around it.

Over the mantel Nichol's daughter, Emmy, his only child, had hung a portrait by Scarborough of her golden-haired husband, Cantelou Allan, who had been able to prognosticate the cotton market so fortunately that today, twenty years after his unfortunate death, Shepherd's Grove, even under Emmy's lackadaisical stewardship, still brought in a yearly income that Messrs. Robertson and Blacklock, factors in Charleston, gasped at.

A chill wind was blowing at eight o'clock the next morning after their homecoming and the heavy sound of its voice was loud in the pine grove. Someone was in the bedroom. India was conscious with her first waking breath that a new fire was crackling on the hearth and peeping over Max's shoulder saw a fine-looking old Negro man, waited on by two bright-skinned girls in high blue caps, setting silver-covered dishes on a Queen Anne drop-leaf table in front of the fire. She pretended to be asleep as the man came over and touched Max's bare shoulder.

"Time to git up, Mista Maxi—you gotter go fox hunting wid Mr. Gary and dem in a hour. Yo' brekkus is all here fuh you and yo' missy! Sausage and hominy and fry aiggs and apples and a whole wild duck whut fell off his laigs yestiddy."

Max sat up in the bed—instantly alert.

"Happy New Year, Steeben!" he shouted. Steeben laughed and from a chair by the fire came a thin ancient cackle.

India looked over the mound of blue eiderdown and saw sitting on a stool a tiny old Negro woman with a face like a moldy prune. She had on several layers of green, red, blue, and ochre sacques, gray balmoral skirts, and a purple bandanna of such lofty proportions that it resembled a steeple. Her chin was crumpled and drawn into withered lines, her jaw sunken, the teeth gone, but her eyes were beetle-bright and her hickory-stick shanks brought her over to the bedside with cricket swiftness.

"My fine fat gold baby!" she crooned, catching Max in her arms and rocking him gently. "I been setting a hour watching you and dat lil dolly."

"How do you like my dolly, Mammy?" Max pushed the old woman gently away and started to get up. "India, this is Mauma Sangua. She used to be my nurse but now she is a witch."

Sangua nodded and folded her arms studying India's face critically.

"You're right peart looking even if you is got so mucha black hair," she said grudgingly. "Scuse me fer not being mo' mannerly but I cyant kerchy lukka useter. Me knee cripple but I wanter shek hands wid Massa' Missy."

India felt the chill claw grab her hand and wring it sharply.

"Go on out now, Mammy. I've got to get up and I haven't got on any nightshirt," Max said.

"Lawdy, git on up. I ain't keeping you frum."

"I told you I didn't have on my nightshirt."

"Whut diffunce dat mek? Law, boy, I seen you befo' you seen yo'self!" Laughing bawdily she darted out. India heard the tiny feet tapping down the stairs like marbles and for a minute Max lay back under the covers and held her close and tight in his arms rubbing his chin against her head and she felt his compact, powerful body warm and hard against her and she knew that she loved him above all the world and he was all of life there was.

"I would like to go hunting too," she said.

"Just the men go on New Year's but when you get to the Witherspoons' with Sister I will be waiting on the steps like a properly anxious bridegroom. Here, don't be so serious."

"Isn't your mother coming?"

"No—she hasn't driven that far in years. Sister will take care of you. Um—um—that duck smells divine. I'm going to get up."

He rolled himself like a cocoon in the eiderdown

and lay down on the floor, resting his head on the puffy fireside wing chair while India, having put on a pink cashmere kimono, lifted the dish covers.

"I love the feel of silk against my skin," he said, "sometimes I almost wish I were a woman so that I wouldn't have to wear cold fine linen and scratchy wool."

"You sound very wicked." India pulled a wing off the crusty brown duck and handed it to Max to eat while he warmed his big bare toes at the blazing logs, telling her just how much butter to put in his hominy and exactly how long to stir it before mashing two links of hot sausage carefully over all. She trembled with joy at looking after him and while his hominy cooled seated herself in the chair and Max half-reclined against her.

"Let's not eat yet—"

The entry of one of the Negro girls with a plate of hot batter cakes interrupted him. After India directed her where to put the cakes the lovers were silent. Nothing could be heard except the snap of the fire and the low wind and the hissing of a goose in the garden that mistook Mr. Wu for a pussy cat.

"Max, your breakfast is getting cold."

"No, no, India. I'm too happy to eat." He jumped up and stood before her, the eiderdown falling open and showing his chest, smooth and hard as a gilded shield. Putting his hand on her forehead he pushed back her hair. "Are you hungry?" He bent over her as he asked, forcing her neck against the wing of the chair. She felt the sweet breath of his mouth on her eyelids and made no effort to free herself from the hand that strained at her forehead and hair.

After he had gone, Mr. Wu ran in with Steeben when he returned for the dishes and she talked to the little dog as though he were a child. This was the first time she had been alone and she felt very lonely, first for Max, then for the Duchess; and sweet Flossie—who was exercising her? And oh! how she wished that her papa and Aunt Childs had seen the beautiful wedding cake!

Tears gathered in her eyes and to divert herself from sadness she went out onto the upstairs piazza to inspect the magic vine she had climbed so easily in the dark last night.

Someone was standing on the lower piazza. It was Irene. Irene was demanding that Chance hitch the two matched Messenger grays to the barouche and drive her immediately to the Witherspoons'.

"Dis de New Year day," Chance's tone was sullen.

"And I'm am going to a party. Hurry. Don't you see I'm all dressed and waiting?"

"Mista Maxi say I have holiday dis day and tomorrow. Big Dick to drive de family. Mista Maxi gin me t'ree beeves and six hawgs to passel out to de slaves. Sego turning em right now in de barbecue pit. Mista Maxi gin us fo' hawgsheads of rum and 'mission to stay up all night to celebrate his wedding. Why you so hurried to go? Where Miss India?"

"You are impudent. Fetch the barouche instantly. No one else wants to come."

"I tell Miss Emmy on you. I tell um right now. I bet you planning to go to de party widout even asting Miss India."

India heard Chance's heavy boots striking the stone steps and the front door shutting with a harsh thud.

She leaned against the rail trying to get a glimpse of Irene but evidently Irene was standing close to the house because there was no living thing on the green-rye-grass lawn but two peacocks running awkwardly dragging their gaudy feathers and a pert peahen tripping lightly ahead of them—her little head thrust forward like a snake. Chance's boots again hit the steps.

"Miss Emmy say I don' hatter go nowhere I don' wanter dis day."

Irene's slamming of the front door almost shattered India's eardrums. How did Chance dare to speak so to a white woman? Sharp sobs and screams came from the parlor and bitter ugly searing words, then Irene came running up the stairs—banged her bedroom door and grated the key in the lock.

From the parlor came the harmonious strumming of

a harp and, though faint, the sweet singing of "The first day of Christmas my true love sent to me a partridge in a pear tree."

Partridges are quails, India thought dreamily, lying back on the soft featherbed; my true love gave to me— ah—everything—everything! She noticed that the night before Max had thrown her silk stockings in the wood basket, her frivolous beribboned drawers on the mantelpiece, and her white feather cap on a Dresden Shepherdess, hiding the porcelain figure so that only the dainty feet and legs showed ridiculously small and unjoined. She smiled at this evidence of their abandonment and half-closed her great shining eyes in complete tranquillity.

She had lost her hair combs somewhere in the vastness of the feather bed and couldn't find them anywhere. So she smoothed the tendrils of hair about her face with one of Max's golden-backed brushes on his high shaving stand and carefully replaited her heavy hair. The little mirror told her she was as pleased looking as Duchess had been that long-ago morning at White Sulphur and she gaily threw over her head her best velvet afternoon dress. It was violet blue, deeply cut out at the bosom, with long slashed sleeves edged with black satin ruching and Chantilly lace. She drew on her French hose and laced up around her ankles the soft purple-blue slippers that Duchess, by good luck, had thrown from the window that day of commotion. Then she pulled her big plait over her shoulder, fitted on her head the blue imperial with the little lace veil and the fall of pale blue feather tassels, threw a black sealskin cape over her shoulders, and ventured forth to greet her mother-in-law.

The stairway was simple and perfectly balanced with a waves-of-the-Nile design on each riser. She had not noticed anything but voices and faces last night but this morning the house itself spoke to her and she wanted to see everything about this place that was her home now for all of her life. The freezing cavernous hall was empty and evidently had been gone over lightly this morning for it still had an "after the ball" look. Wouldn't Duchess scold the lazy maids! She crumbled a

twist of smilax crisp and shriveled between her fingers
and picked up a piece of cake from the bottom step.
The hothouse roses had shattered, dropping white petals
on the crimson Turkey carpet; the heavy smell of nar-
cissi filled the air. Fans were lying about and an egret
feather lost from a lady's hair drooped lifelessly on one
of the tall gilt candleholders. From the walls Italian
madonnas, French landscapes, English squires
mounted on handsome hunters, and quiet families in
neat tiled Dutch houses followed India with their mag-
nificently painted moods. Why, they all are glad I
am here, she thought, and the singing from the parlor is
warm and gay.

Opening from the hall on the east side were two sets
of double doors, both open. Through one set India
saw the billiard room—a snarl of scattered cues, balls,
and crushed cigars; the other doors led into the dining
room—last night so beautiful, now not even properly
swept—with shards of spun-candy baskets ground into
the carpet and sugared violets and rose petals scattered like sea stones in all the corners.

I won't go in there, she thought, turning back. The
doors on the other side of the hall were closed. One
set she knew led into Emmy's big bedroom; the other
to the parlor.

She opened the parlor door very gently not to disturb
the singer and saw her mother-in-law seated in the
comfortable carved Dutch chair at the gilt harp, her profile to the door, oblivious to the untidy house and
her daughter's temper. There were no loose-hinged
parts in Emmy's face—no weakness anywhere, only an
unfathomable mixture of radiance and shadow as
though instead of letting Irene anger her she was making the unpleasantness an occasion to develop the tranquillity of her soul.

"The eighth day of Christmas my true love sent to me
eight maids amilking, seven swans aswimming, six geese
alaying, five gold rings, four calling birds, three French
hens, two turtledoves, and a partridge in a pear tree!"
she sang, with no impatience or any discord of harmony in her husky contralto voice.

"Happy Eighth Day of Christmas!" sang Emmy,

catching a glimpse of the tall, dark girl in a Chinese Chippendale mirror framed with delicately molded gold-leaf birds and scrolls hanging over a rosewood cabinet with a marble top and petit-point doors.

To India, the room with its biscuit colored walls and soft brown velvet draperies was as harmonious as Emmy's song. In each window was a recessed seat covered with rosy tan cushions and on either side of the fireplace a pair of unusually long Duncan Phyfe sofas with cane seats and backs fitted with squabs of faded wine silk. Through the windows sunlight spurted in a golden jet onto the Aubusson carpet woven with a pattern of leaves and flowers in cream and green and red and blue.

"Happy New Year! I love that song. What a pretty room! And such a good likeness of you." India stepped in front of the marble mantel over which hung a picture that made the fine Meissen branched candlesticks and pair of dancing figures on the mantel shelf seem colorless and silly.

"That's not Emmy Allan." Emmy pushed the harp upright and her long eyes twinkled.

"It has to be you. Those are your hands—your eyes, your mouth—it *is* you."

"That's a copy of a painting by Frans Hals—Vrouw Bodolphe. Maximilan sent it to me from Europe last year. It's a fine copy. Maximilian thought it looked like me. I've always refused to have my portrait taken so he declares that he foxed me and will tell all of his children that Vrouw Bodolphe is their grandmother. I've had a cap made like the one the Vrouw is wearing and—don't tell Maximilian, he's too cocky as it is—I *do* look like her in it. But wouldn't Vrouw have disapproved of my chiffon apparel and this frivolous plaid shawl? She in her good Hollander's Sunday silk!"

"No, she'd love you," India said, looking at the seemingly endless brown chiffon engulfing Emmy today.

"You're wondering why I wear this chiffon?" Emmy asked. India nodded, completely unself-conscious. She would have been a fine actress with the quality of unself-consciousness so dominant.

"Yes, Mrs. Allan."

"Call me Miss Emmy. All my friends do. It will be more comfortable to you than trying to say Mother. I wear it because I was burned in an accident many years ago and corsets torture the scar tissue that was left. Without stays I bulge in the wrong places. It is more soothing to me and everybody to dress this way. This shawl keeps me warm and I rarely go outdoors in winter. Now—that's behind us. Let's get acquainted. Do you always wear your hair in a schoolgirl plait in the morning?"

The lack of malice in Emmy's attitude made it easy to say simply, "I lost my combs and pins last night. As Max probably told you, papa refused to receive us so I have only the few things my nurse threw from a window. Can you lend me some pins and combs?"

"Of course, but I'm glad Irene didn't see you. I can tell you a thousand times not to mind her sharp tongue, nor her absorption in her brother, nor the jealousy she is sure to show you—but you will mind. I mind."

"You don't seem to mind. Not like Irene minded you. She is upstairs crying, I could hear her from our room, and you're singing."

"She's crying because she gave rein to ugliness and I didn't. Let her cry for a while. Then she will take some tincture of opium and go to sleep. I've told Chance to bring up the barouche. We'll have a much better opportunity to get acquainted by ourselves."

"I thought you weren't going!"

"I am going today for two reasons. I want to show the Courthouse Cluster of Edgefield how important I think you are; and I want to find out about the war."

"Miss Emmy, do you think we're really going to have a war?"

"My dear—how can you ask that—and you Guy St. Julien's daughter? I expected *you* to tell *me*. Certainly war is coming. It's been coming ever since a hot summer day in 1832 when Mr. Calhoun rattled into Old Edgefield, hitched his horse in front of George McDuffie's law office on the village square, and he and McDuffie settled the Nullification Issue to their satisfaction. They chose young F. W. Pickens—he was

twenty-five at the time, and already a brilliant orator—
to carry out their dreams in South Carolina. By teach-
ing him to say States' Rights, States' Rights over and
over until he thought he was its creator, this whole
Secession picture was outlined. They baptized the
young Pickens with the idea that the state was supreme and sent him to the Senate, convincing him that
he was dedicated to keep our state more important than
our country. Didn't you notice his kingly attitude in
Charleston? It was this quality in him that won Lucy
Holcombe and compensated for too many years'
difference in their ages. If we have a Confederacy, wait
and see, she will be its queen—crowned or uncrowned.
I wish she were here today. Her fine airs delight and
refresh me. She's smart as they come, is lovely Lucy."

Chance knocked at the door and entered dressed in
his best gray livery.

"Ready, Miss Emmy?"

"You don't have to come, Chance. Mr. Maximilian
gave you a holiday. Let Big Dick drive us."

"Miss Emmy, I wouldn't miss taking you fer nothing. I'm proud to be going."

"Thank you, Chance. Call Ida and Steeben to get
my wraps and help me into the barouche. India, dear,
run in my room and you'll find hairpins and combs in
a tin box under my bed. Take the tortoise combs with
the sapphire stones. They will match your dress."

Emmy's bedroom was higher ceilinged than the other rooms and had a finely worked plaster medallion in
designs of flowers and birds. Originally intended for a
ballroom, Cantelou Allan had insisted on making it his
nuptial chamber and Emmy had dwelt therein ever
since. The room was crammed with furniture, and
ornaments jostled one another on the mantelpiece, on
the tops of several chests, over small satinwood and
mahogany tables which had been fitted into any vacant
space that offered. Nothing matched, Emmy having
crammed into the room every piece that took her fancy.
A red lacquer Chippendale *Chinois* cabinet stood between two repulsive plant stands full of ferns and plants
of tropical greenery. Flanking the fireplace were two
enormous Sèvres vases, on odd consoles. In one corner

stood a marble-topped modern washstand not hidden
by a lovely Chinese screen which showed one snow-
laden pine branch in the upper corner on a grayish
white ground and a laughing monkey in the lower corner. Close to this on the wall opposite the fireplace
was a Queen Anne highboy squeezed between the
screen and the fourposter bed that could easily accommodate five restless sleepers and was covered by a blaze
of color in the form of a patchwork quilt sewn in multi-
colored hexagons of satin, velvet, and brocade.

India looked under the high bed and discovered several japanned boxes with designs of flowers and fruits
painted on the tops. In one was a dark rich brandy-
soaked Christmas cake, a bowl of tipsy squire, and half
of a chocolate layer cake; in another, newspaper clip-
pings and bundles of letters; and in a third, a jumble
of necklaces, keys, earrings, and odd pieces of jewelry
that twinkled and winked at India as if to say: Who
cares?

India found the combs and some hairpins banded in
gold. Carefully she wound her hair into a glossy chig-
non low on her neck and the cut sapphires were no
more sparkling than the highlights of her blue-black
hair.

It took the three Negroes and India to get Emmy inside the barouche, but when Chance tucked the wool
angora robe over their knees and straightened the
brick-heated sheepskin under their feet, the three of
them laughed carefree as children as they drove away
leaving the drugged Irene alone in the plantation house
while around the yard and down the street hundreds of
Negroes sang and capered and filled themselves with
meat and warm strong rum. Occasionally one of them
would look at the big shiny house and through his
head would run the strain—Yankee Doodle keep it up
—keep it up! But not many of them bothered about the
word Secession. Nor did the name of Mr. Lincoln ring
any sort of bell for them at all. Not yet anyway.

CHAPTER XIII

ALL THE WAY to the Witherspoons' Emmy regaled India with funny stories about the people she would meet this day. It was over seven miles but with the Messenger grays trotting briskly in time to Chance's happy singing they were at the gate by two o'clock. A half mile farther a bevy of brightly dressed laughing darky children swung open a second pair of beautifully designed gates opening onto a twenty-acre lawn dotted with shaggy sheep cropping the short sweet grass. Now they could see the house, a Doric-columned mansion with sweeping galleries set in a group of cedar trees and so newly painted white that it gleamed ice-blue against the dark green foliage.

As the Allan barouche drew up at the front steps India saw girls in rich winter dresses of velvet and soft French wool belled out with crinolines and hoops, colorful as birds, running up and down the galleries, stopping to lean over the banisters and waving at young men in pink coats who galloped past toward the race track, sweeping off their hunting caps and beavers, bowing low and calling, "Howdy, mam, howdy! Come watch the games and be my love!"

"There's our host, St. John Witherspoon," Emmy pointed to an erect silver-haired man on the piazza. "Now give me a push when Chance starts to pull."

St. John Witherspoon composed of the quiet charm and graciousness of his daily life, motioned to his wife, the white-haired lady who had straightened India's cap the night before when she came into the hall at Shepherd's Grove, and who now was nodding her head like a happy Chinese Mandarin at the guests thronging her sunny front piazza. Seeing India and Emmy she forgot her dignity and ran down the steps to meet them as lightly as a girl.

"Miss Emmy! Miss Emmy!"

If Emmy had been Queen Victoria the importance of her arrival would not have been as great.

The whole district was at the Witherspoons'. India searched the guests for Max while she made small talk with the girls and young matrons who were exclaiming over her dress and the little feather tassels of her hat. She and Emmy were each the center of a circle of voices that rose higher and higher, and while Emmy let herself be piloted into the warm house to sit with the older women and men, India, hearing the call of a hunting horn found herself running across the lawn through the rose garden to the clay race track where the horses and huntsmen were gathered.

Hetty Witherspoon, a tall languishing-looking girl, moving along with the freedom of a deer in her rustling taffeta hoop skirt, while the other girls giggled and minced over the graveled paths, giving helpless little shrieks of alarm as briars from the roses snared their shawls and scarves, caught up with India and took her hand.

"We have a tournament here every New Year's Day. Do you have them in the Low Country?"

"In the spring at Pineville—but I know this one will be better. Perhaps it's because I'm in love—perhaps it's the sunshine. Anyway I know this will be better."

"What a frank person you are. I didn't think married women ever admitted they were in love."

"Heavens yes. Wait till you marry your sweetheart. Which one is your sweetheart?"

"Philip Abney, the one with black hair over by my brother, Toney. We're going to be married in April if war doesn't come before that. Papa has promised that if war comes earlier Philip and I can be married on a day's notice."

"I couldn't bear to have Max go away to war." India shivered catching sight of Max's shining head in the mass of men and horses just ahead of them.

"However did you manage to tame Max Allan?" Hetty asked, her green eyes twinkling mischievously.

"I ran away with him," India said, liking Hetty. "But he isn't 'tamed' by any means."

Nor did he look tamed as she and Hetty crowded up to the post-and-rail fence bordering the track. He was sitting his big bay carelessly, his pink coat buttoned with a set of big pearl buttons engraved with hunting scenes. He was talking to Calbraith Butler who was surely the handsomest man in the world and to another man she had noticed especially last night for the wild look in his brilliant eyes—Martin Gary. There, too, were all the various Nicholsons and good-looking Simkins, the Hugheses, the Abney boys and gentle Toney Witherspoon, the Blocker twins and all of the thick Calverts on tremendous horses, wearing argumentative "we stick together" looks on their dark arrogant faces. They had polished their horses' coats with whisky and now lunged around the crowd exuding from within and without the strong sweet smell of spirits.

There were at least forty horsemen milling around the open space where from a gallowslike contraption the Rigg was suspended holding the rings.

The judges' stand beside the Rigg was decorated with cedar garlands, pine boughs, and trails of scarlet berries, and when the ladies and the gentlemen who had not hunted plus countless children, black and white, were lined along the fence the Master, Kevin Marshall, marched in attended by the spectacular Chance and a tiny mulatto man only about four feet tall in a Moor's costume whose duty it was to pick up the ring where it fell and hand it up to Chance to replace on the Rigg.

The huntsmen lined up and rode past the stand to salute the judges. Then the Master handed a horn to the Mulatto who blew a sweet true call on it. The ladies fluttered and waved scarves and flowers as Martin Gary's horse leaped forward first racing at great speed toward the Rigg. India glanced at the gilt ring hanging from the crossarm. It seemed such a tiny thing—no more than an inch and a half in diameter—to capture at the speed Gary was riding. But the eagle eyes were keen and steady and Gary flashed past bearing the gilt ring on the end of his thin polished pole.

Bringing his horse to a stop before the Master he extended his lancelike pole. The Master removed the ring, handed it to Chance who replaced it on the hook of the crossarm as Gary now took his place at the end of the line to await his next turn.

Again the little Mulatto man blew the horn and Max's bay was at once in full career. Max, riding with seeming indifference that was the essence of skill, evincing no evident concentration of his faculties on the small gilt circle, waved gaily at India as he passed her and galloped away bearing the ring high on his pole.

One by one, turn by turn the others rode and at every miss the rider was immediately tooted off the field by three sharp laughing blasts of the horn until only Max and Fant Calvert had taken the ring six times in succession and had to ride until one or the other faulted.

"Hurrah for Max," the ladies clapped. And it was very obvious that the men felt the same way about the two as Fant, a scowl on his darkly powerful face, raised his arm to signal that he wanted to run the course first. Max was wiping his face with an embroidered linen handkerchief and his horse almost jumped from under him as the little man blew a terrifying blast on the before now gentle-toned horn.

There was a gasp from the ladies. Fant's black horse, frightened by the big noise, was standing on his hind legs and Fant, half out of the saddle, was jerking on the reins with all of his weight while the animal frantically pawed the air with his front hoofs desperately trying not to fall over backward. In a moment Fant was firmly in his seat again, beating the horse on the side of the head with a knotted fist while the animal plunged and reared.

There were cries and much creaking of saddle leather as the men shifted in their stirrups in protest at the unnecessary brutality. But Fant finally got his horse in hand and wheeled him back into the line.

"Let Max take it first," he called to the Master. But Mr. Marshall shook his head and signaled Fant to keep going.

Fant kicked the black viciously and the frantic horse, his nostrils dilated and his rolling eyes red as blood, bounded forward but swerved aside just as Fant had the point of the lance almost inside the ring.

"The Mulatto frightened the horse. He rattled something—it sounded like bones," India whispered to Hetty.

"Shh-h—" Hetty dug her nails into India's hand,

"don't even whisper that. Fant would kill Quasha. Just pray that no one else was as close as we and heard."

Fant galloped out of the enclosure as a derisive toot-toot-toot of the horn cried his failure and the other three brothers closed around the furious Fant, glancing unpleasantly at Kevin Marshall.

The crowd was silent now, breathless. There was a lovely mellow sounding of the horn from the curious yellow man's thick mouth. "Come away—ee—away—ee—away—ee" it seemed to say to Max and at the high, clear, flawlessly pure notes Max lowered the pole, couched it, carefully, deliberately.

"That's good," Hetty said to India. "Quasha is talking to him. Quieting him. I was afraid Max might have gotten nervous. He never liked Fant and he always hated for anybody to hurt a horse. Even as a little boy he would cry if any of us whipped our ponies."

Hetty's observation ceased, her fingers responded to India's gripping. The horn was still. Max's horse jumped forward. India saw that Max was pushing him as hard as he would go and that he was fully extended and breathing hard. This made the piercing of the ring much more difficult. As large and powerful as Fant's black, the bay was wildly excited and Max gave him his head.

As he passed India realized that Maximilian Allan was not riding carelessly this time. He was crouched forward in the saddle, his face pale and strained, his full lips tight. For a moment there was no sound but the thudding of hoofs and India's heart, then the Master let out a yell: Yip—eeee—eee—ee—and everybody clapped and shrieked, "Yip—ee—ee—ee— Hurrah— Max did it!" The ugly moment had gone like a cloud and Max, taking the white plume from Mr. Marshall, cantered his lathered bay over to where India and Hetty were standing, bent low and placed the plume on top of India's foolish little tasseled hat, then taking her hand pulled her to a pillion seat behind him and rode up and down the fence to show her off while everybody laughed and shouted good will and fellowship to all throughout 1861!

Afterward came the tilting with sabers at leather heads fastened on poles and other horseback games, but Max rode away into a little holly woods while India kept saying how wonderful he was and how everybody had wanted him to win; then she noticed his silence and peeping around his neck saw that tears were on his cheeks.

"I can't get the sound of Fant's fist against Sombrero's skull out of my ears. I'd like to go back and horsewhip Fant. I would if we were anywhere but at the Witherspoons'. I hate to see a man take advantage of a horse. I hate it worse than anything in the world."

He bent his head and kissed her wrist so passionately that the tired horse gave a lunge beneath them.

Damask-covered tables were placed all over the house. In the parlor, the library, the sitting room, and up and down the drafty center hall. In the dining room cedar garlands from Christmas festooned the mantel and the cornices, and holly crowned dark family portraits; the crystal chandelier was twined with smilax and in the center of the huge food-loaded table was an enormous pumpkin scooped and cut like a basket filled with apples, precious oranges, bananas, grapes, sprays of swamp berries; and around the basket half-shucked ears of red corn and yellow corn, polished yams and white cotton bolls, gourds of green and gold, and chinquapins, pecans and raisins. And at each end of the table reared a roasted peacock served in all its gaudy plumage!

India had never seen so much food in all her life. Here was no city feast of lobster tails and ramekins of crab and sherry oysters but silver waiters of roasted geese and wild turkeys, rosy brown Carolina hams, chicken and brain croquettes, a whole barbecued pig crusty brown and vinegary fragrant, roast quails stuffed with rice, barons of beef, saddles of mutton, candied sweet potatoes, rich macaroni-cheese pies, creamed green peas, buttered asparagus, potato salad, apple salad, tomato aspic, artichoke pickle, peach pickle, and, because it was New Year's Day and for good luck, a great mound of black-eyed peas and hog jowl!

A bowl of West Indian shrub, of rum, orange juice, and French brandy was filled and emptied and filled again. People helped their own plates and found seats at tables though there were Negroes everywhere to pass hot biscuits and corn muffins, pour wine, wrap shawls about the old men, fan the flushed middle-aged ladies, amuse riotous children, jiggle babies, and wait on any whims the courting ones might concoct.

India and Max, avoiding the hall where the Calverts had noisily ensconced themselves, sat by the poet, Paul Hayne, and his fragile Mary at a long inlaid Hepplewhite table in the parlor. Across from them a gentleman in a blue coat with a carefully tied stock of creamy silk was talking of France with a pale young woman in pink velvet wearing her hair in puffs and curls like Marie Antoinette. India listened with one ear to them sharing enthusiasm with Max and the Haynes over the galleries of the Louvre, the midday sun seen through the stained-glass windows of Sainte Chapelle, the tiny restaurants on the Left Bank where the food was so divine, La Petite Trianon, the scarlet geraniums in the Tuileries, silvery chateaux on the Loire seen from the river by moonlight.

With her other ear India heard a group farther down the table acclaiming the man on her right, a handsome red-haired horseman from Virginia, a cousin of Kevin Marshall's, who had outdistanced two of the most famous horses in the country early in the fall and expected to win all the fattest purses in the South this coming spring. Then someone said that if Governor Pickens tried to root Major Anderson out of Sumter, war would be immediate and there would be no races except after Yankees; another that it would be worth a war to hunt the Yankees down like foxes; and still another said where would the South get ammunition and shoes— you can't win a war with hounds and horses and there are no ammunition or shoe factories in the South; and still another said this Madeira is old and wonderful— let us talk of love and not of war.

"Ah—love! We'll toast the new bride!" Catching India's eyes the poet lifted a goblet of wine, quoting,

" 'Thy hyacinth hair, thy classic face,' "

" 'Thy Naïad airs have brought me home,' " Max continued.

He's teasing me, India thought—I'll surprise him for once. She lifted her glass of wine and in her dramatic husky voice finished the verse:

" 'To the glory that was Greece
And the grandeur that was Rome.' "

"I say—that's not toasting you—that's almost like toasting the South," Hayne said but he drank with her while Max looked as though the heavens had fallen.

"I didn't think—" Max began but India interrupted him.

"You didn't think I could read but I can. I adore poetry. Poe is one of my favorites. And I love Keats and Shelley and Byron and Christina Rossetti. I like anything with rhythm. Just because I haven't read all about that old-fashioned Plato and his Golden Ass—"

"Apuleius!" Max blushed furiously, seeing the lady in pink lift her lorgnon to eye India.

"Well, if Plato had had one it would certainly have been golden, India," Hayne laughed until he hiccuped and the horseman on India's right who hadn't even noticed her before turned around and after one look at her long gray eyes deserted his admirers farther down the table.

"I say—I like poetry too," he said.

And Max said, "Excuse me. It's five o'clock and Mr. Witherspoon asked me to join him in the library for a little scheme he has."

After he had gone, though the atmosphere of the afternoon dinner was warm and mellow, it suddenly became heavy to India. Looking through the front windows she saw that the sun was down and wondered if later they would dance on the ballroom floor in a separate wing of the house built on springs that carried you up and down like waves. But sounds of fiddlers playing Donizetti's *"Salut à la France"* came from the lawn and the young ones excused themselves and left the tables.

"Have you read one of Tennyson's latest poems?" The Virginia horseman was rising holding out his hand,

" 'Come into the garden, Maude, for the black bat, night, has flown!' rather, I should say, 'fallen' not 'flown'—will you dance with me? That's a good tune."

There were three bonfires burning under the darkening cedars and magnolias; around them moved the many-colored chains of dancers. The Negro fiddlers sat on a hastily built platform and scraped their fiddles. Early winter dark had fallen and the night sky stretched clear and dark green above the magnolias. It was nearly moonrise and from where it was coming, sailed some small clouds, their lower edges shining like dark silver.

Reaching for her partner, India realized that the horseman had jumped a pair and was whirling the girl ahead of her. She moved back out of the ring and stood alone feeling as though she had stepped through a glass into another life as all the lights inside the house went out and suddenly the yard was a blaze of light from flaring fat pine torches held by costumed Negro men on shining horses followed by eight young men dressed like courtiers in white wigs and crimson velvet coats mounted on matched sorrel Kentucky-bred high-tailed saddle horses whose manes and tails were decorated with plumes and scarlet ribbons. The fiddlers struck up "The Lancers" and St. John Witherspoon's trained horses with their skillful riders went through the dance.

Sirius pierced the sky and then Orion winked through the blackened curtain. An edge of the moon showed across the open fields—red as blood and full of portent.

"Aren't they extraordinary?" The horseman realizing that he'd taken the wrong jump had come back to claim her.

But India was so moved by the beauty of the night and the music and the quality of the men and the horses dancing on the lawn, and in particular Max's face—brushed with the fire of the torchlight, that she only nodded, for she feared that if she said a single word out loud all this would vanish in an instant. The lawn would be burrs and weeds, the house a crumbled shell and windowless, the young men disappeared forever and here and now as though it had never been.

PART THREE

*War
Edgefield,
South Carolina, 1861*

CHAPTER XIV

IN THE STATE of Kentucky, between the months of June, 1808, and February, 1809, two boy babies were born within a hundred miles of each other yet neither boy was raised in Kentucky. One, the poor boy, went with his folks to Illinois; the other, of some privilege, to a cotton plantation in Mississippi. Many years later when the boys were men their paths crossed for the first time: the Mississippian, Lieutenant Jefferson Davis, graduate of West Point, mustering officer of the United States Army, swore in lanky, self-educated, witty Captain Lincoln and his company of Volunteers for the Black Hawk War. In neither of the two young soldiers was there any consciousness of the other: each was faceless. Unremembered fifteen years later on Saturday, February 16, 1861, when Jefferson Davis stood on the balcony of the Exchange Hotel in Montgomery, Alabama, and was presented to the cheering throngs that filled Fountain Square as President of the Confederacy by Mr. Yancey who shouted "The man and the hour have met"; and during the same moon Abraham Lincoln proudly met his hour, being sworn in as President of the United States in Washington on March 4.

After their inaugurals, Lincoln and Davis took each other's measure and Mr. Lincoln felt very well about the odds. He was head of a going concern; Mr. Davis of a government having nothing but a will for war as compulsive as a burning candle to a lunar moth.

So, as Buchanan had done, Lincoln waited for some hotheaded Southerner to fly at the candle and then on him and on his children forever would be the onus of starting civil war! Throughout March and on into April, Lincoln waited—watching General Beauregard charm the Charleston ladies and at the same time effectively close Charleston harbor, making it now a matter of major undertaking for him to relieve Major Anderson in Fort Sumter. Lincoln's cabinet advised him to forget

Fort Sumter and let it alone but the wily one realized that the fort was not merely a hungry little unimportant post but a symbol and an opportunity.

He ordered the fort reprovisioned but whispered in the commanding officer's ear not to be in too big a hurry actually to reach the fort. "Loom into view along the horizon. Wave the Stars and Stripes high until some zealot is so outraged by the sight of this flag continually on his sky line that he is impelled to open fire on it."

There is always such a one.

This one turned out to be the dictatorial, disappointed Governor of South Carolina who thought he should have stood in Davis' shoes and who took upon himself the sole responsibility for ordering the firing on of Fort Sumter April 11, 1861, and thus solidified the wavering and divided spirit of the North. The Confederacy had made a bad move in the game of war and the next day, shouting Emergency! Self-defense! Mr. Lincoln called for seventy-five thousand men.

This call of Lincoln's did for the South what the firing of Sumter did for the North—wiped away all peace parties.

Now the two men whose life lines had run so parallel in the element of timing, faced each other in the soft early summer breezes across the Mason-Dixon Line and met their destiny with unwavering eyes.

To India the days between January and May of 1861 followed each other with sharply etched highlights like one of the Chinese painted scrolls that Max brought to hang in the library.

There was the day in late February when the wagons loaded with Max's trunks and boxes arrived. All morning lines of gray plunging winter rain slanted across the whole world. Emmy sat in the parlor rocking and swaying as she touched the chords of her harp. Loud notes swelled and scattered through the house: Sa—Sa—like wind blowing the rain; then soft notes dying almost to nothing—Cheh—Cheh—like lamenting spirits; again Siu—Siu—bitter as a she-fox cry. Her strong fingers followed no fixed pattern but went up and down the tonic, dominant, and superdominant tones as though she herself were the rain and free for an hour of her chiffon and heavy flesh.

"For heaven's sake, Bubba, can't you make Mother stop that dreadful twanging? She hasn't played a single tune all day." Irene, sitting by a mahogany sewing table draped with pleated rose silk, angrily snapped a length of blue thread and poking it irritably through a needle's eye, jerked it back and forth in a piece of sheer pink India muslin cut to form a bertha.

Max, leaning on the billiard table, carefully lined up his shot and sent India's ball out of the pocket's range. "That is a very famous song Mother is playing. I heard it sung by the Castrati in Milan."

"You could have sung it when you were a little boy. What a shame you lost your lovely lyric soprano voice."

"You wouldn't by any chance have wanted me to be one of the Castrati would you, Sister dear?"

India interrupted Irene's answer, "What are the Castrati, Max?"

"A cult of singers usually found through Spain and Italy who are willing to sacrifice their manhood in order to retain their high boyish soprano voices. They are very famous, highly paid, and quite respected."

"How horrible!"

"Not at all," said Irene, "you're just unsophisticated besides not knowing anything about music."

"Instinctively she knows more than either you or I," Max said.

"At least I know I prefer Max's tenor voice to a soprano one."

"You never heard his soprano. Nothing has ever been so beautiful as his singing 'Ave Maria' in the Church on Christmas night when he was nine years old."

"I heard him sing 'The Daemon Lover' that summer we met at the White." India smiled at Max but he seemed unaware of anything but the fact that he had put her in a bad spot in their game of billiards.

"The wagons should arrive today if they aren't mired down along the Ridge," he said.

"I hope you brought me a pretty roll of silk to make

a ball dress as I directed you." Irene covered her ears
against the high harp sounds.

India whacked Max's ball and, looking up, laughed
into his eyes.

"Pretty thing," he said, "put on your habit and let's
ride toward town to meet the wagons. I'll sing to you
all the way."

"I'll go too," Irene said. "It's stopped raining."

Max rode his bay, and Irene, who was an adequate
horsewoman, demanded Lulu though India had been
riding the mare every day since New Year's and now
considered Lulu all her own.

"Who ordered Bella Lee saddled? She's no horse for
a lady." Settling Irene on Lulu, Max looked anxiously
at India.

Irene said, "I told Dick to fetch her. India claims she
can ride anything."

Bella Lee was an iron-mouthed steeplechaser, fretful
and troublesome but too well bred to be disposed of.
India put her black satin boot on the groom's bent
back and was in the saddle before Max could give her a
hand. She hit Bella on the rump and the gray mare in her
surprise at being urged to run clattered across the flagged
turnaround down the forest road forgetting the ghost in
the magnolia and the booger behind the biggest holly.

"Let her cool off her temper," India heard Irene call
to Max so she kicked the mare into a faster gallop and
was at the highroad long before Max and Irene were
halfway through the parklike woods.

How can I bear to live in the same house with that
Irene? India thought furiously, walking and sliding Bella in and out of a steep slick ditch to keep the big nervous mare occupied. Half-closing her eyes India
conjured up Irene's image and never had the thirty-
four-year-old spinster appeared so unattractive. She'll
never get a man, India thought to herself, never. And
in the thinking felt a satisfaction of revenge. Irene was
really in love with Max, only she didn't know it. Or did
she know it? It didn't matter. She, India, had all his
love. Irene would never taste, never know, such a joy of
loving—such passion, ecstasy, and delirium as she
shared with Max!

Her anger disappeared as she thought of her love and now she wanted Max and Irene to hasten and be with her so they could have a good gallop along the big road. All of the dominant tones of this newly washed clay region were distinct and incisive in the winter afternoon sunlight. Clear-cut silhouettes of buzzards and black crows were hunched on sodden haystacks and fence posts. As if the rain had dissolved and washed away every mixed color she only noticed the few bright splashes: the wet-shiny red hills of Meeting Street Road; flocks of crows, black as witches; a single blackbird with a shining scarlet head; vivid cardinals.

Like the colors the sounds were sharp: the violent cries of jays cut the sunlit air; hawks with bright ginger and cream plumage hurled crisp piercing screams at a covey of bee martins waiting to attack them from their nesting limbs; the shrill going-home song of a Negro woman carrying a bundle of fat lightwood on her head, the needled shadows of the roadside pines playing over her glistening black cheeks like living lace.

As the brother and sister trotted onto the highroad, India waved her whip gaily and Max grinned sheepishly but admiringly at her.

She was charming on horseback: upright, with her slender waist, her knee bent on Bella's black mane, her face flushed by the fresh chilly air of the afternoon.

As they joined her she made Bella prance in the road. Irene yanked at Lulu's reins saying,

"Don't get Lulu excited. She isn't as easy to handle as old Bella."

Then the wagons showed over the slippery hill and Irene changed and was pleasant but her good mood didn't last through the giving out of the presents Max had fetched from his long trip.

First he opened a carved ivory box and showed them a little figure of a man which was a root. He called it ginseng and he had paid a large sum of money for it in Peking.

"It looks like you!" India marveled, caressing the miniature image, cradling it in her hand.

"Even to its slightly bowed legs," Emmy said.

And Irene said, "How silly. Fetishes are so primitive. I'm amazed at you, Bubba."

"I value it highly. It will preserve my identity," he said gaily, carefully replacing the brownish figure in its nest of soft silken floss.

"Foot! You mean maintain your manly powers!" Emmy struck a full bass note on the harp and Irene blushed deep into the roots of her carefully ringleted hair.

He had a Chinese fan for Emmy of ivory carved so exquisitely it appeared to be the finest lace with a scene of a temple garden painted in the center; for Irene a bouquet holder of solid gold and blue enamel set with pearls with a tapered mother-of-pearl handle and a patch box to match; for India a filigree silver cardcase with blue enamel flowers and a tiny French gold hand mirror; for Emmy a Chinese bracelet of soft tan carved peach stones set in yellow gold and then from the pile of presents still heaped on the rug Max unrolled a piece of silk the color of apple jade in candlelight.

Mr. Wu sniffed the scented silk, wagging his tail and barking delightedly at the familiar odor.

"How lovely for India with her black hair!" Emmy cried.

Max threw the silk at India as though it were an armful of soft green sea water.

"Oh, no—you must give that to me, Bubba. It's just my shade of green! See—see!" Irene snatched the silk to hold up against her face but India grabbed the other end and like two fishwives they jerked at the precious stuff—twisting it roughly as a hempen rope, while Emmy dragged her fingers dissonantly along all the strings of the harp and Max looked helplessly from his sister to his wife: from his wife to his sister.

"Cut the silk in half, Maximilian, since both claim it for their own," said Emmy.

"No, indeed, I won't cut it. I almost killed a man to get that bolt of silk. I'm sure it belonged to the Empress herself. It was in one of her chests. I've got my heart set on having it fashioned into a beautiful gown."

Seeing Max's face not eager any more, hearing his unlively voice, India dropped her end of the silk and picked up a carved perfume bottle of satiny white jade.

"I'd rather have this scent bottle. Give Irene the silk," she said lightly, wondering how in the world in such a short time she had learned so much control. Her fingers trembled to rake Irene's strawberry-cream cheeks and tear the reddish hair out by the roots. Yet she stroked the stone cold jade and removed the jeweled stopper to smell the musky sweetness.

"Smart girl!" Emmy laughed merrily and Max, laughing too, threw his arms around India and kissed her so vehemently right in front of Emmy and Irene that Irene had to sit down quickly in a chair hugging her prize greedily to her sparse bosom, quarreling at the homesick little dog, pretending not to see the lovers kissing in the firelight.

Just before they went to sleep Max made an effort to explain the way he felt about Irene.

"She was good to me when I was a little boy. Always ready to play or read or tell me stories. She was twelve when I was born and just after, Papa, whom Irene adored, was killed; so she concentrated on loving me. Try and not mind when she is jealous of you. Eventually she'll like you. She'll have to. Who could help it? My sweet—my long lovely love—"

India wanted to say—she'll never like or love me; nor will she ever let you go from her influence. But instead of saying this she put her arms up around his neck and he held her too and his lips were against hers firm and hard and pressing and the room was very quiet except for their loving, but outside in sudden gale the wind came blowing across the open fields sounding in the pines as though the waves of the sea were breaking over the rooftop.

Awake for some time after, India refrained from moving. Cheek on folded arm, she tried to guess the hour. The moon had risen and showed softly through the filmy curtains at the windows.

Lifting herself on her elbow she looked down at Max. Stroking the thick gold eyebrows which she loved she lifted Max's hair from his forehead. Lying so still and with his hair scattered over his temples, he looked as if he had been blown down by the furious wind.

What a strange husband I have chosen, she thought, he is twenty-two years old but he behaves like a mischievous boy. But he could be grand and powerful if he chose.

In the months she had been here he had showed her fox holes, possum hollows, rabbit burrows, turkey trots, dove and duck feeding places, broom sedge from which partridges flew, coverts for deer, and pools for darting fish, as though these were the all-important things in an Up Country planter's life. But she had heard one word from him calm a drove of angry buck Negroes complaining of Suggs forcing them beyond their task. She had seen him spontaneously point out the merest curve in a plowed furrow where cotton was to grow; she had watched while he read a statement sheet from the factor, in a glance understanding every point of it. Oh, he could be such a big man if he tried such a little!

As if from a far-off world he felt the force of her even considering regimenting him into a different mold, the gold head moved on the pillow and Max moaned in a dream. With a quick arm India snatched him from his nightmare and rocked him so soothingly that he burrowed his head into her soft armpit and sank into happiness without dreams, a sleep which was black and thick and which was guarded for him on all sides.

There was the trip to Columbia the first of March to order a fancy uniform for Max, and dance at the Dessassures' Ball. Boarding the train at Trenton, they were in Columbia within two hours. The car was strangely empty but on reaching Columbia they stepped down into a great tumult of voices and feet coming toward the cars heralded by blasts of music.

There were children and men and women of all ages following a line of marching gray uniformed college boys. The women were singing and throwing flowers, the older men calling, and the children getting in everybody's way. Negroes ran up and down with big waiters of fried chicken and tea cakes and ham. The band played the Southern Marsellaise and The Secession March.

The boys in gray boarded the train and instantly the

windows were full of heads and waving arms; families called—Good-by, Johnny—Shoot the Yankees right between the eyes—Good-by . . . Hurry back—Don't get your feet wet—Write to me every Sunday—Have you got your Bible? Your blankets? Your oilcloth?—Good-by—Get Anderson out of Sumter and come marching home!

The whistle shrilled. The train began to creep forward. As the last car passed, Preston Hampton in a beautifully tailored uniform leaned out of a window, shouting, "India—India—I'm going to Sullivan's Island with the Richland boys—write to me—"

He was waving a pair of new yellow kid gloves and he had never looked so boyishly huge and so manly handsome. Remembering the time she had let him kiss her for thinking of the day when he might go away to war, India ran along beside the train calling good-by. Preston leaned far out and their hands touched for a moment. The train gathered speed and the whistle shrilled. India kept waving as long as she could see the cars. Then Max took her by the arm and said,

"Mr. Wade and Mary McDuffie are here seeing Preston off. They want to speak to you. Smile; for heaven's sake wipe away those silly tears."

Wade Hampton kissed India heartily and thin Mary McDuffie, heavy with her second child, nervously whisked a puff of soot from India's white velvet collar.

"I'm so glad you got to tell Mr. Hampton's favorite boy good-by," Mary said, letting her light eyes slide toward her own frail little son, McDuffie, firmly held against the ample bosom of a fine-faced brown-skinned woman.

"He looked well, didn't he?" Hampton asked, staring after the train.

"He looked wonderful. But why is he going to the Island?"

"He's afraid the war will be over before he gets in. Wade, Jr. is going too, but later. Where is my hat you owe me?"

"Oh, Mr. Wade, I've forgotten it again. I'll write Papa to send it right away."

"I'm sailing by steamer for Mississippi tomorrow. I'll

collect it when I return. You young people must pay up your wages. Max, did your plantation in Mississippi make money last year?"

"Oh, yes, Mr. Burney is a fine overseer. I wish old Suggs at the Grove were half as good."

"Have you any cotton stored in Mississippi or here?"

"No sir, Mr. Robertson sold our last during the winter."

"A pity. I think the new government should send all available cotton to England immediately before we get blockaded so we can finance a war from there if things get too tight here. That's one reason I'm on my way to Wild Woods. To send my cotton to England to be held for me."

"What if war starts and you aren't here?" India asked.

"I don't believe even F. W. Pickens would dare open fire on an entire nation. This Sumter affair isn't necessarily serious though our old bore of the Springs, Edmund Ruffin, is, I understand, in Charleston at the present threatening to fire a cannon at the Fort with his own hands. What are you all doing up in Edgefield, Max?"

"Cavalry practicing at Lanham Springs twice a week to the tune of Dixie; playing at war with Calbraith Butler as our captain. We annihilate thousands of Yankees each afternoon then dance with the ladies in the pavilion, eat barbecue and drink punch in the evening. Suppose war does start while you're away, sir?"

"If it does I'll go immediately to Montgomery and get permission from my neighbor, Jeff Davis, to raise and completely equip a Legion; then hurry home and eat crow for a commission from our Governor Pickens. Tell Calbraith and Martin Gary not to rush off to war, even if it is declared, until I return. I'll want you Edgefield Hussars for my number one cavalry outfit in my Legion."

There was Aunt Childs' letter to Emmy:

"Charleston, S. C.
March 6, 1861

Dear Emmy,

I remember you most vividly from a visit you
paid my cousin, Anna Taliaferro, back in 1826
when you were fifteen years old. What a dainty,
petite brunette you were with rather large hands
and feet. D'Estaing Ravenal courted you and you
turned him down to return to Edgefield and marry
that yellow-haired Cantelou Allan. You should
have taken D'Estaing. He married silly Petty
Dubois and died in 'mania a potu' the year after,
leaving her rich. I am sure D'Estaing would have
been a less flirtatious husband than was Mr. Allan
from all the tales Guy has regaled me with since
India has deliberately turned her back on us.

"However she has treated us, I consider Guy's
behavior toward his only child shockingly cavalier
and this letter comes to you with much apprecia-
tion for your warm reception of my kinswoman
who arrived at your door with hardly a shimmy
to her back. Paul Hayne and his Mary Michel
called on me last week and described your enthusiastic sponsorship of India at the Witherspoons'
which, they say, is all the recommendation she
will need to take her proper place in Edgefield
society.

"Bid her send a van for her mare, her clothes,
and a chest of Rachel's linen, which her nurse, an
awful woman, who blows segar smoke in my very
eyes and is insolent, has managed to smuggle to
my house. The mare was sold by Guy to a Negro
pushcart peddler for a dollar but Cousin Alston,
seeing the lovely creature in a back alley hitched
to the cart with all her ribs showing, bought her
back for three dollars and she is at present fatten-
ing restfully in his comfortable stables.

"Are the people in your part of the state as
enthusiastic over Pickens's policy as we here in our
city by the sea? Porcher Miles said at a dinner at
Judge Huger's last evening that Pickens had better
quiet down, not having sufficient ammunition to
keep up a steady fire for more than three hours if
Mr. Lincoln should send a fleet to relieve Major
Anderson. I can't comprehend Porcher's lack of
patriotism in criticizing our Governor.

"One of your Up Country senators amused us very much at dinner. After Jack, Judge Huger's butler, had passed the wonderful river shad, your senator asked for the rice. To the first request Jack remained deaf but at the second he whispered in the senatorial ear. Your senator listed gravely, nodded his head, then, when Jack left the room, burst out laughing. 'Judge,' he said, 'you have a treasure. Jack has saved me from disgrace; he whispered, "That wouldn't do, sir, *we* never eat rice with fish!"'

"If all of you up there in Edgefield are so deliberately natural and unrestrained as is your senator I am sure India must feel much at home with you.

Yours,
Childs Turnbull"

Max sent Chance immediately to Charleston to fetch India's possessions. He just had time to arrive in the city when another letter arrived at the Grove from Aunt Childs:

"Charleston, S. C.
March 29, 1861

My dear India,
    Things have passed from bad to worse. Your father has been wearing your shoes ever since you ran away and his friends and colleagues have generously put it down to strained emotions but yesterday he appeared in court to try a very important case with your blue velvet capelet trimmed in yellow ball fringe around his shoulders and wearing the pair of high-heeled red satin pumps that went with the red bengaline you had last year for Easter! Naturally people are shocked but he seems utterly oblivious that there is anything strange in his wearing female attire publicly. Yet this is not the worst. On the day after I wrote your mother-in-law, thanking her on the part of your family for her courtesy to you, Beverly appeared at my door after ten o'clock in the evening begging me to come to your father at once. On reaching the summerhouse gate such was the

tumult in the night-dark city street, that people were rushing from their houses, fearful and curious, excited and afraid, wanting and dreading to know what was going òn in the St. Julien mansion. And, my dear—what *was* going on! Guy and the Duchess were screaming at each other like Furies, Guy demanding that she give him back the whip and she threatening to use it on him. And Lord have mercy but the police appeared and took the Dutchess to jail and now Guy has had it cried in the streets that she is to be put up for public auction, as though she were a wild bush Negro, on the block at the slave market one day next week. Perhaps you can come down by train and bid her in. Whatever I think of her, she was always good to you and your mother and in the Up Country she might fit in with no difficulty.

In distress,
Childs Turnbull"

India telegraphed Aunt Childs to bid Chance purchase the Duchess and bring her back in the van with him to Edgefield.

It was the night of April 12 when Chance returned to Shepherd's Grove. Emmy and Irene were sitting on the piazza in the dusk sipping Madeira, agreeing to discontinue their subscription to the *Atlantic Monthly* on account of its fiercely abolitionist articles; agreeing that they must not read any more of Ralph Waldo Emerson's essays since he had vilified the South in such infamous manner; agreeing that William Gilmore Simms was a fine writer, so long as you couldn't get a copy of Thackeray or Dickens from England hot off the press.

Max was with India leaning on one of the gateposts of the garden. The capitals of the brown brick pillars were of white marble, richly carved and surmounted by marble pineapples. Max had announced at supper that Chance should arrive tonight; having allowed him time to procure the Duchess, load the mare, and drive all the miles from Charleston back to the plantation.

He said to India, "Mother and Irene have never agreed on anything before. Tonight they are yessing each other continually. Listen at the harmony of their voices."

Looking toward the piazza where the giant wisteria vine was pouring out a wonderful delicate odor from a great burst of white blossoming heavy with sweetness, India said,

"It must be the wisteria vine. I've always thought it was magic."

"An evening like this makes me dread the idea of going to war—even for a month."

A chuck-will's-widow, the very essence of night, his wings edged with velvet silence, his feathers the mingled gray softness of moss and lichens and cobwebs, began calling from a greening crepe myrtle tree in the garden and some white pigeons cooed companionably from the top of the columns, joining in the conversation on the piazza. A tree frog clutching the leaves of a magnolia leaf with his vacuum-cupped toes bayed like a lonesome hound and from the duck pool at the foot of the garden two bullfrogs boomed in answer not like hounds, more like growling lions.

"Do you remember the night I first kissed you at the Springs?" Max asked softly, playing with her fingers.

India nodded and tried to smile. The air was so full of the heavy scent of wisteria and jessamine and tobacco plants and roses that she felt nauseated. Should she tell him tonight that she was sure now she was going to have a child? Or should she keep it a secret so that no one would try and make her stay at home or not dance all night long at parties or ride sweet Flossie with Max every day over the plantation and into the woods that already she knew as well as she had known the Charleston streets.

But she didn't tell him, for Irene came from the piazza and found them. Her narrow shadow swept down the steps, and crossing the flower beds swayed and came to a stop with her small head silhouetted against the magnolias. India pressed her handkerchief against her lips and ducked the whispering rush of a passing bat skimming close to her face. It was now quite dark. A group of Negroes piled up brush and lit a bonfire while pine torches flared here and there be-

tween the house and the quarters. Then they heard the
screaky sound of wheels and horses and India's sudden
nausea passed in her delight that now she would be
all right. Duchess was here and would look after her—
protect her from Irene.

The clumsy big van rumbled to a stop and Negroes
ran all over the grass and the road yelling to Chance.

"Duchess," India called, "Duchess darling—"

"De Duchess not in dere," said Chance, jumping
down from the driver's seat.

"Oh, but I telegraphed you to buy her and bring
her here!"

"I did, Miss India. I bought um and brung um back
to Edgefield."

"You rascal, you've played a trick," Max said, and
Chance, towering over them like a winter-black tree,
grinned.

"I sho' have, Mista Maxi."

"Didn't you get the word to buy her for me?" India
asked.

"Not exactly. I got a word to buy um and I buy um
fuh Chance's own." The tall Negro was serious now.
He turned to Max speaking with much dignity, "You
knows how I hankered atter dat 'oman ever since dat
summer to de Springs, Mista Maxi? I jest had to have
dat 'oman. So I gets a opportunity and I buys dat 'oman
fuh myself. You'll 'scuse Chance, won't you, Mista
Maxi?"

"Bubba, don't let a slave speak to you like that!"

"Chance is no slave, Sister, as you know very well.
He's a free man who works for me for wages. India,
the Duchess will be all right. Chance has a lucrative
blacksmith shop in the village square and is probably
as rich as I am. Where is Duchess, Chance?"

"I lef um in de room over de shop. She ain't in no
mood to speak civil to no white people. Dey treat um
mighty rough in dat jail. Say she too proud. Dey take
um down a piece. And all dey done is mek um so mad
dat now she's setting up on a pinnacle and nobody fit to
lace her shoes. Hit's jest 'cause she's hurted inside, Miss
India. She'll git over hit. But right now she don't even
want to see you, scusing me fuh being plain. But your

sweet little mare is here. Jest as shiny and fat as a partridge. Come look, Miss India, and let de Duchess sulk out her bad feelings fuh a while."

The next day an Extra of *The South Carolinian* rushed by train from Columbia announced that Edmund Ruffin, of Virginia, had had the honor of firing the first shot that started the battle of Fort Sumter! From then on there were no more sharply etched scenes but a blur of inflamed events that culminated in the Edgefield Hussars leaving for Columbia on the morning of June 6.

At dawn of that day it rained a fine rain that filled the needles of the pines around the house at Shepherd's Grove with a load of hanging pearls that glowed in the rising sunlight. India sat with Max in the library under the pines while he wrote instructions for her as to the handling of the Negroes and the plantation in general while he was away. Last night Emmy had insisted on this.

"India must be the mistress," Emmy had said, "not Irene. I am not able to continue in so much responsibility. Every day it is more difficult for me to walk about. We have seen how well she gets on with the house Negroes. You must give her this trust for the good of the son who will be born to you. It will keep her busy and she will be less restless if she is busy."

Now in the early morning watching him seriously filling page after page with his flowing educated script, India thought: Today did come though I was so sure it never would; it was too far away. I dreaded this day but it was only a dream on a vague horizon. Now I feel it near but I will greet this day however lonely I feel inside, for only one thing matters—how I meet it. He is going away from me. He is eager to go. I know what a mood that eagerness is. If I were a man I would have it too. It is an adventure—riding off in the morning in a new uniform full of exciting strangeness!

Today the world is going to end and yet everything is the same as it was yesterday. The watermelon soufflés of the crepe myrtles have not fallen, the thrush nest with its three speckled brownish eggs is still safe on that low branch of the magnolia and the blue jay is still after it but dares not come too close with the scarlet tanager helping the thrashers guard their eggs. Irene is in the house crying. I heard her when we came downstairs. But I will not cry. Miss Emmy will not cry either. After he is gone she will probably play sad songs on the harp and then I can cry if I like, pretending it is the sad song. Now he is putting his pen back into the bowl of crystals. He has finished.

"Your eyes are as big as saucers," Max said.

"I need my breakfast," she answered lightly. "I never did feel very optimistic before a cup of coffee. This morning with Julius Caesar jumping around so vigorously I am doubly greedy."

"Promise me that you will write your accounts in here at my desk," he said. "I want to think of you, full and round with my child, wearing the same sort of long soft white muslin dress you have on now, sitting here in my chair in this room that I love best of all at Shepherd's Grove."

"Yes, I'll sit there. But I never could add two and two. Do you suppose Mr. Suggs will help me?"

"Suggs isn't much good. Write the Messrs. Robertson, Blacklock in Charleston if you get in difficulties. Or talk to Chance, he knows our business and he is very loyal."

"But he doesn't work here any more."

"He will always be available to any of the family. I trust him above anybody. Now be quiet while I finish this last paragraph."

Outside the opened French doors two yellow butterflies were circling each other, flying faster and faster, closer and closer, until they appeared as a golden spindle whirling over a Maréchal Niel rose bush. India reached from where she was sitting and took down one of the old books richly bound in leather. She could almost feel the velvet and lace of the sleeve which had once touched it. Some far-off day would her son have any intimation that a muslin ruffle from her sleeve too, had fallen over the worn green leather, that her fingers had traced the gold letters of the title? Looking at the title she laughed. Max raised his eyes questioningly. She held up the book and he laughed too.

"Dear old Apuleius," he said, "why don't you tackle him while I am away? He really is delightful."

"Perhaps I shall. Would you like me to become an intellectual like Irene?"

"No!" Rising, he came over and taking the soft volume, replaced it in its proper place. "I'll send you some new books of poetry when I get to Richmond. I prefer you as you are."

"Mista Maxi," Steeben's grandson Mozart, called Moze for short, a mealy-mouthed black boy with one blue and one brown eye, was at the French doors, "breakfast ready. Pa say hurry 'fore the sliced white peaches turns brown and the cream sours."

Max and India walked slowly arm in arm over the green lawn back to the house. Mr. Wu ran from a boxwood bush and sniffed the unfamiliar odor of Max's new gray trousers. Not liking what he smelled he pretended to see a mouse scampering through the hollyhocks and giving full cry, made a dash after the imaginary monster.

It was going to be a warm clear day. To the left in a lane by the garden the cows were being driven to the big meadow to graze and Negro children, boys and girls, were walking by the herd. A brown bull in a fenced pen bellowed wooingly and struck the ground with his hard forefeet. A sanguillah sang in a pear tree and warblers were singing everywhere in the air, above, below, around.

After breakfast India put on a wide flat leghorn hat with a wreath of fresh red roses pinned around the crown and Max lifted her into the open victoria beside Irene whose cheeks were pinker than her pink taffeta bonnet trimmed with French lilacs and tied under her sharp chin with pink ribbons wider than her hand.

Chance had appeared in the Allan livery this morning and insisted on driving the horses though Big Dick was now head coachman. Max's bay stallion was restlessly throwing his powerful head up and down in annoyance at the yellow flies buzzing in and out of his soft furry ears and he reared a few times to let his master know it was time to leave this place.

Emmy, in a low-necked lavender mull dress, was sitting in the green grove apart from the house stirring her peacock fan. She took off her green chiffon scarf and hung it on a myrtle branch; a hot wind from the pine trees trickled on her bared head as she kissed Max and held him against her for an instant.

"Good-by, son," she said, and it sounded almost as though she were singing. But a sad song, not a happy one. "Write often to India. She will be very lonely in this big house with just the Allan women for company."

Max kissed her hand and, coming back to the front steps, said a few bantering words to the solemn-faced Negroes who had massed themselves in the yard. Just as Max put his foot in the stirrup old Sangua ran out from behind a tree and threw a handful of some dust-like substance on him.

"Good-by, Gold Baby," she shrieked, hooking her crooked fingers into a Voodoo sign.

"Is this a love potion, Mauma Sangua?" He settled in the saddle and tried to flick the powder off his new tight gray frock coat that fitted his strong rhythmic body like another skin.

"Naw—hit's to mek yuh brave!" Holding up the sack from which the powder had come she screeched, "Gawdamighty Jesus—dat wuz de powder to mek Hez-zie Lundy fuhgit chicken Mary. Bresh hit off, Gold Baby— Bresh hit off!"

Max laughed with the others at Sangua and, spurring the bay, was off with the victoria rolling along beside him so smoothly oiled and polished that there was hardly a sound except of hoofs and running feet as the Negroes followed their master all the way to the park, throwing flowers and singing as he rode away.

Behind them rattled Max's body servant, Danny, one of Chance's numerous tall sons by various temporary wives, in a spanking new Dearborn wagon piled with Max's baggage: a trunk of clothes, one of soft white wool bankets and linen sheets, one full of his favorite books, hampers of Madeira and Port, baskets of cooked turkeys and hams, sides of bacon, cakes, pies, and baked bread to sustain him on the long trip to Camp Hampton at Rocketts east of Richmond.

By now it was eight o'clock and the sun was very hot. The little rain of the dawn had turned to steam. In the fields on either side of the highroad, asparagus and beans were curling in the heat and the young cotton plants and peas were wilting; corn leaves had turned in on themselves like rusty spikes but the wild grape and blue-flowered passion vine burgeoned greenly on the ditchbanks.

"I hope it rains tonight and cools off." Max, riding close to the victoria, touched India's cheek where a trickle of perspiration glistened.

Irene said, "How can you talk of tonight?"

And India asked why did people plant one stalk of corn in their flower gardens.

"That is a thanks offering to Ceres." Max was leaning forward in the saddle giving himself up to the motion of the slow canter. Then the Hughes's double victoria turned in from their driveway and the two vehicles drove abreast. The Hughes girls were carrying little ruffly parasols and had on ruffly organdy dresses and wide floppy leghorn hats. Half a mile further they overtook Hetty Witherspoon and Philip Abney riding hand in hand as though they were sweethearts and not married for two months already. More and more people were now on the road and soon they were in sight of the town.

The public square at Edgefield was like a fair. Flags and flowers dripped from trees and lampposts. The sidewalks were thronged with clusters of little girls dressed as little ladies in colored muslins and leghorn bonnets, waiting impatiently with bunches of flowers; they were to shower the heroes with flower petals. A brass band marched around and around the square playing military music; after it trailed Negroes and gangling white boys lighting firecrackers and throwing them at the squealing girls. The excitement was contagious. The wooden Indian in front of the Segar store wore a wreath of red lilies on top of his feather headdress; in the barber's window all the cupping glasses

were filled with roses and sweet peas; from every shop
flew the blue South Carolina flag. Stalls had sprung up
about the square and Negro women in bright red and
blue bandanas sold ham biscuits and peanuts, fresh
peach ice cream and cakes, lemonade and, secretly,
fermented corn whisky. An image man with a tray full
of plaster busts of Governor Pickens, Jefferson Davis,
General Beauregard, Lucy Pickens, Barnwell Rhett,
balanced on his head, did a big business; the gingerbread woman called "Hot spiced gingerbread"; the catfish woman sang "Catfish, buy any catfish"; the broom
man sauntered along with the "walking advertisement"
men; and an Italian organ grinder with a monkey in a
little red velvet suit and cap alternately played and
sold patriotic songs: "Dixie's Land," "The Grand Secession March," "Lorena," "The Rose of Allandale."

The lovely columns of the Greek-style pink brick
courthouse were draped with bunting and the high
stone steps leading to the courtroom on the second floor
were crowded with people waiting to see the boys off.

The miniature columned white two-room houses near
the courthouse which were lawyers' offices were decorated with flags and their porches packed; dogs, carriages, wagons, coaches, horses, children moved in and
out of the shade trees and sunshine like silhouetted
shadows.

Chance drove around the square to the Planters Hotel
and helped India and Irene to the sidewalk. Irene
snapped open a pink lace parasol and turned to speak
to Anna Hart who was patting the toe of Max's highly
polished Wellington boot and crying in a painted fan
with tortoise sticks. For a minute, standing so suddenly
on her feet after the long cramped drive, India thought
she was going to faint. The crowd whirled and the
band sounded farther and farther away. She reached
out blindly and a strong arm circled her waist. A familiar arm. The smell of a sweet strong cigar filled her
nostrils and then the sharp acrid odor of smelling salts
was held to her nose.

"Get hold of yourself. He's looking at you and you
must be smiling when you say good-by. Don't stand in
front of these Up Country people with your head low.

That's it! Hold it high. Paleness becomes you—makes your eyes look huge and dark as a well. There—smile—lift the corners of your mouth."

"Oh, Duchess, Duchess!" India wavered but Duchess's big arms kept her steady and as the bugles blew for the Hussars to form and for the people to clear the area in front of the hotel, India smiled up into Max's face and he jumped from his horse though he was leading his company and held her for a minute—held her sweetly and with love—held her and the child; and then he was back on the horse and shouting a command.

It was now a quarter past ten and by half-past the Hussars, in expensive gray uniforms bright with gilded buttons and braid, gold sashes around their waists, jaunty kepis and top-heavy shakos, formed in front of the Planters Hotel. A saber flashed in the sun, and above the cheers a bugler sounded a blast that opened the ceremony of departure. First, Captain Hammond, a former captain of the Hussars, made such a sentimental speech that many of the ladies and some of the older men wept noisily.

After he had finished, the new captain, Calbraith Butler, came forward in his fancy uniform and spoke briefly but well in the manner of his day, ending with "We will go to the tented fields in the defense of our homes and firesides against the invasion of the hireling foe, whose only desire is for beauty and booty, remembering that we are all Carolinians, and we will return as honored soldiers or fill a soldier's grave. It is ours to act, and not to speak. You will hear from us. Farewell!"

The band struck up "Dixie's Land." The Hussars wheeled their horses and cantered around the square and down Main Street scattering the people who had spilled from the sidewalks, shouting at the top of their voices: Good-by! Good-by! There was a final rush after the horses, a good-natured scurrying and pushing. The little girls threw their flower petals and were jostled by the rude little boys, while the wives and mothers shook their heads in disbelief that their men were actually off to join Hampton's Legion in Columbia and from there depart at once by train to whip the Yankees in Virginia.

When the last horse had vanished in the dust, India spoke for the first time:

"Come home with me, Duchess. I can't go back to Shepherd's Grove with Irene Allan."

"You made your bed, now lie in it." Duchess's voice was rough as she loosed her arm from India's waist and waved a gaudy feather fan back and forth in front of her white face. Several people near began to whisper in loud sentences about "that woman." Duchess tossed her beribboned red bonnet delightedly and pointed to the victoria close by.

"Don't be so cross, Duchess. Let me go to your house and rest a while. Chance can come back for me."

"Oh no. You go on and don't be thinking Chance is your servant. He's my husband. We got married in church last Sunday night. He's making money in his shop and we're building a big house on Macedonia Street with four white columns. When it's finished I'll invite you to come and drink tea in my parlor. I have three slaves to wait on me now but don't think I'll forget what the St. Juliens did to me. See my wrists"— she pulled back a lace sleeve ruffle; ugly scarred ridges jagged the muscular flesh—"handcuffs; and worse scars are on my ankles—I was chained to a stob right out in broad daylight for people to mock me. Me—a duchess, whose mother was a princess with a blue bead necklace and a gold ring in her nose!"

"Think how Papa has treated me! And I'm going to have a baby. Won't you even look after me then?"

"When you get in labor you can send Big Dick for me and if I'm in a good humor I might come. Chance— hurry home; Maria has fried you two chickens for dinner and made you a peach shortcake."

As Chance assisted India into the victoria, Duchess leaned over the side and blew a big puff of smoke into Irene's face.

Irene lifted her umbrella and cracked it hard on Duchess's head but before the surprised Negress could retaliate, Chance flicked the Messenger grays with the whip and the victoria shot into the dispersing crowd.

India waited for a diatribe against the Duchess but
Irene only said fatuously, "Wasn't he beautiful! People
rave about Calbraith Butler and the young Gary boy
but Max looks like King Harold himself. Did you see
the way he smiled at me when he galloped past?"

CHAPTER XV

ON THE AFTERNOON of October 31, India was sitting
at Max's desk out in the library trying to digest Mr.
Suggs's weekly report.

"Shepherd's Grove, 31 October, 1861

Abbys newborn baby died today October 30th

Sunday 20	—Give allowance of Grits potatoes and peas
Monday 21	—Rain Men ditching on the up land Mill going hands geathering corn women pict Burrs Sampit Ben's boy killed by lightning
Tuesday 22	—all hands picking peas Jobe sent to Stur Pen for stealing
Wednesday 23	—Men picking peas women hoing land for Rye
Thursday 24	—All peas picked Men cutting wood women leveling Rye ground Big Dick delivered to me today to send to town to Chance to mend the coach Harnas I sent most of the baled cotton to be stored in the big warehouse Hens bought from Chicken Mary 30 head and 6 dozen eggs also two tom Turkeys for Mis Irene Sary's Susen locked up two nights.
Friday 25	—all hands harvesting and grinding shugar cain
Saturday 26	—all hands harvesting and grinding shugar cain Billeys Lizzei shut up for bawdiness.

Sick Suckey 6 days, Hager 6, Rachel 6, Sary 6, Binah 4, Lit Solomon 4, Page 3, Sandey 4, Nelley 4, Scinda 4, Caty 4, Wrenche 4, Doctor 1, Tobey 2, many children got hooping cough and worm fever."

Sighing, she picked up the latest letter from Mr. Burney, the Overseer of the Mississippi Plantation. Max had told her that Mr. Burney was the smartest uneducated man of his acquaintance and this must be true, for the money Messrs. Robertson and Blacklock told her had come from Buccleigh last year made her feel exceedingly rich even though Max had insisted on investing the entire amount in Confederate Bonds. Mr. Burney had written:

"Buccleigh Hall, Oct. 3rd, 1861

Dear Mam—Yours of the 1st inst recd and have wrote Mr. Bell who is likely at Wild Woods, Mr. Hampton's place. Saw him last tuesday A.M. he said he was going and wished to see me before he left Mississippi. I am more than sorry to say that Hamaday our best Driver died Wednesday night, was taken Monday P.M. I saw him Tuesday A.M. and attended to him late that evening he said he felt better as I wrote you. Wednesday morning he was sitting on the piazza said he had no pain but felt weak, about one o'clock P.M. was called to him sent for the Dr but he died between 2 and 3 o'clock and before the doctor came. Beck's child girl 2 months died of consumption Old Violet of cholera Morbus and Abram's Maria of Lockjaw. So many deaths trouble me greatly but I cant help or stop deaths. Our new mill ginned all our cotton. Mr. Jonas sent me word he will send for it in a few days. Mr. Keziah sends me word the new circular saw will cost up of a 1000 dollars Mr. Eason of Charleston makes them all complete and ready to go up. We has got from him before and if you get one and wish Mr. Keziah will put it up and run it until the hands understand how to manage. I hope I have give satisfaction to you with your master gone to War. Next year I think business will keep good but must have a extra

hundred dollars salary. I hope and trust there will
be no mischief amongst our hands. It would be
very dreadful for our Enemies to get hold of stories
at this time. God be praised for his blessing on the
labors of the year.

> Yours Resptfully
> *Duncan Burney"*

Oh dear, I wish Mr. Burney were here at Shepherd's
Grove and Mr. Suggs at Buccleigh. Mr. Suggs has
started locking the Negroes in dark rooms because I
have forbidden him to whip them. I don't like Mr.
Suggs. My poor brain! Why did I ever think I could
understand the running of this dreadful plantation? It
never seemed to worry Max or Miss Emmy as it does
me. Miss Emmy is a darling and lets me talk to her for
hours on end whether she listens or dreams of melodies
and syllabub; but Irene just sits apart sewing baby
clothes. That little dress she finished last night was
beautiful! The mull as sheer as a cobweb. She insists that
it will be a girl but I hope not. Irene looked almost
pretty when she held the dainty dress up for me to see.
I haven't sewed anything for you, my baby, but oh,
how I will love you! I won't think of these overseers'
reports anymore today. I'll write to your father who is
far away in Virginia hunting a Yankee skin to wrap his
little baby in! How silly I am!

"Dear Max—where will you be tonight? Manassas
is over and you are safe; the typhoid epidemic at
Bacon Race Church where you are camped is
lessening and you write cheerfully that the Legion
has lost some of its parade ground manners and
become hard and hairy, brisk at drill and clever at
scouting and that the new boys who came to replace casualties seem elegant and soft. At home
we are all well and relatively happy. The slaves
don't even seem conscious that there is a war.
Mr. Witherspoon's cousin at Society Hill was
murdered by two of her house Negroes last week
so Irene now locks and bolts the doors at night
and I have to go down and let Cook Ida and
Steeben in at dawn. It would be easy for them

to break a pane of glass and unlock a window if they meant to harm us.

"Now don't laugh—I have read a book! Miss Emmy suggested it—La Martini's *Genevieve* telling about the fidelity of servants in Augustus Caesar's time and during the French Revolution. I guess she doesn't want Irene's fear to take hold of me—as if it could.

"Aunt Childs sent me a copy of Mr. Rhett's *Mercury* last week full of taunts and sneers at the Confederate Government. What a vicious man Mr. Rhett is! She also says Papa has closed his law office and roams the streets day and night talking to himself. I must go to Charleston before long and try to make peace with him and bring him here to live with me. Miss Emmy wouldn't mind. I don't care about Irene.

"This morning I came on Steeben sitting cross-legged on a marble bench in the rose garden embroidering a monogram on a linen napkin. I told him I didn't know he could sew and he gravely answered, 'I does all de darning and de mending fuh Miss Emmy. Dis is jest a leetle pleasuring.'

"The pomegranates are ripe. There is a bush full of them just out of the door with its orange-gold balls bursting open and showing the shiny purple fruit-seeds. The persimmons are ripe too. The tree in the big pasture, its leaves gone, looks as though someone has strung orange Japanese lanterns all over its jagged black branches for a Hallowe'en party.

"The lower fields are ready for the planting of rye and winter wheat. I have given word to Suggs to plough under the cotton stalks as they look like desiccated bones sticking from the raw red earth with all the lovely cotton picked and gone. Suggs was unpleasant about it and said there was no hurry, that he never bothered about it until March, but I bade him do as I said and all this week the men have been ploughing and the women carrying straw to the fields.

"I superintended the giving out of clothes for winter Monday though Suggs wanted to wait until a hard frost had fallen. Shoes were shared out and the blankets went to the women. Suggs says the children take next year. I wish they could have blankets too. Their legs are nothing but twigs and their poor little necks bits of black string. Most of the men got Pea Jackets. Aren't they funny looking? Oh yes, and I mixed some roach paste and made Cook Ida put it around in the kitchen and it worked! Ida was scandalized at the sight of me stirring a pint pot of phosphorus mixed with flour paste with a three-foot stick (on account of my size). She wouldn't even help me stir the lard in when it was cold. She said, 'Them roaches been here when you come and dey gwine be here when you gone,' but they devoured my concoction greedily, swole up and died in swarms. I must say Ida swept them out willingly enough and this morning grudgingly asked me to give her the recipe so she could make some and put in her cabin. Imagine— me fighting roaches as though they were the most important things in the world while you, sweet you, are so close to those dreadful Yankees that you can hear their band music at night!

"The ladies were here yesterday cutting out pants for the boys. When they were all nicely cut, Daught Legg (at first the ladies didn't want to let her come but when she drove up with a whole bolt of cloth we decided that her morals had nothing whatsoever to do with good gray flannel) was given the task of basting the legs together for our Negro tailors here at Shepherd's Grove to sew. Daught picked up two legs, held them together and shouted—'You ladies sho' have forgot how a man looks mighty quick.' All the legs were left legs! The Hughes girls volunteered to go on the train to Graniteville and beg some more cloth from Mr. Gregg so that our valiant boys might have plenty of room. Hetty Witherspoon said that Mrs. Shemmy Nicholson said that 'They' say Major Ripley sent Governor Pickens word he must either attend to his demands 'or abdicate.' Maria Pickens Butler puffed up like a turkey gobbler and left at once. She isn't as gay and charitable as Calbraith. Somebody also said that Martin Gary has written some bitter letters home complaining of his differences with Wade Hampton. Mrs. Dunovant calmed us down by telling us that there was enough quarreling among such people as General Beauregard and Jefferson Davis and between Hampton and the Governor without us behaving like schoolgirls. Mrs. Dunovant looks ill. Somebody said she waits hourly for news that General Dunovant has been killed.

"I am sitting at your desk and oh, I feel so big and strange! Julius Caesar is warning me that he is getting ready to cross the Rubicon or was it the Pee Dee River? There is no need to be anxious. By the time you read this I shall be sitting up, perhaps walking about scolding Suggs for shutting somebody in the dark and frightening them half to death. Anyway I will be thankful that the long waiting is over. Nothing in the world is so bad as waiting for it. Mulatto Abby lost her baby yesterday and Irene has moved her into the house to be ready to nurse our little one so that as soon as I am strong I can come on the cars to Richmond as you have ordered me to do. How lordly you write and say—do this—do that—and how I love your lordly ways!

> Your devoted wife,
> *India Allan*"

As she laid down the pen, she felt that the afternoon stillness and the hazy blue of late October at her window were trembling with anticipation. The sweet smell of bubbling sugar cane came floating from the quarters. Deep-throated dark men's laughter and the singing of their women making a holiday of the syrup boiling were commingled with the afternoon calling of thrushes and cardinals. Some skinny Negro children, chased by the old Scotch head gardener, ran yelling through the boxwood garden carrying pumpkin heads on sticks to frighten the witches and hobgoblins that would rise from their graves to chase after them this night. A feeling of loneliness descended on India and a desire to hear Emmy sing and see the lighted candles of the big house. She placed a paperweight on the written letter and clumsily moved out of the door into the darkening afternoon.

There was a three-quarter moon shining low in the sapphire sky but thick purplish clouds were huddling on the far horizon. Scraping their fiddles weakly in the shrubbery the locusts foretold with their spidery legs the chill of coming winter though the autumn coloring in the woods and fields was bright and cheerful. There was a tannish bronzy tone to the hazy horizon despite the gold of tulip poplars, the orange plum thickets, the crimson sumac and the salmon and flame of dogwood clumps draped with the yellow of honeysuckle and wild grape. Goldenrod stems had turned a rusty brown, cornstalks stacked in far fields waited like hooded figures for a gathering hand; the cedars along the pasture fence were a brownish green and under a group of them beside a brook she saw Flossie picking at the unaccustomed luxury of the heavy upland grass.

"Hi—Flossie," she called. Flossie came trotting to the fence whickering eagerly. India walked toward the mare with more difficulty than she had ever known in moving. She to whom swift motion and grace were as natural as breathing—could this be that India? Or was this heavy-bodied woman a stranger?

She talked to Flossie until Milt, the watch, came along with his lantern and offered to light her way across the rough stubble back into the garden path leading to the house, which was shimmering now in the leaping flames of the flares and the lighted yard fires.

At midnight, after broken dreams in which she was wandering in search of Max over a battlefield shaped like a tight black tunnel, strewn with bloody mutilated soldiers, she awoke, drenched with sweat, in a terror that seemed to be half nightmare and half real. When had it begun? How long could it last without breaking her in two? Fearing to move she picked at the sheet with trembling fingers while the pain seemed to be grinding through the flesh into the very marrow of her bones. Then suddenly it was over and she felt eased and almost drowsy. I'll send for Duchess in the morning, first thing in the morning. I was dreaming, she told herself. But do you ever feel so sharp a pang in a dream? Just as she was relaxing another knot of pain unrolled across her body in a long spiral of agony.

"Irene," she called, "Irene, are you awake?"

Immediately, it seemed, Irene, her hair tightly rolled in curl papers, the lemon and cream mask she wore at night to keep her skin bleached making her look like one of the Halloween specters risen from its sepulcher, was standing beside her with a lighted candle in her hand. "I'd just lain down," she whispered. "Ever since you came in looking so wild and pale this evening I've been worried. Are you sick? Nothing must happen to this baby."

"I'm all right." But the words ended in a gasping moan.

"Get up and walk about. I'll call Steeben to send Big Dick for Dr. Quattlebaum right away."

"Have him bring the Duchess too. She said she'd come."

"I certainly won't. I wouldn't think of letting that vulgar creature in this house. She's the scandal of Edgefield with her fancy house and those outrageous clothes she wears."

"Oh— Oh—"

"Are you afraid to stay by yourself while I run and wake up Abby and send her to get Cook and Sangua?"

"But Abby's sick too."

"No matter, she can go and at least unlock the door and call Cook to start boiling water. It may be hours yet before you're through."

"Tell Miss Emmy to come. And please, Irene, dear Irene, send Big Dick for Duchess."

"Mother I'll tell but she hasn't been upstairs since she was burned—that Negress I won't send for. Don't get upset—why are you crying? I'll stay with you till the baby comes."

She melted into the darkness and India waited in terror for the returning pain, shaped like a crouched tiger which the shadow of the filmy curtains formed on the wall. Would the doctor come before the pain seized and tore her again? Was she racing with pain? Dragging footsteps passed slowly through the hall and she knew that poor Abby had started down to call for help. A sense of dislike of her once lovely body, more vehement than actual nausea, rushed over her. Where could she, India, hide while her body was degraded and pulled apart on the grinding wheel of the rack. Now—she knew where she was! She was in the Tower of London and both her feet were fastened to a screw that pulled her legs farther and farther apart from the sockets of her hips. This is my punishment, this hideousness! This is Max's love, this horror! This screaming is love—not the soft before-dawn cry of quails. Then before the pain was done a cry burst from her lips, "Miss Emmy! Miss Emmy!"

Suddenly arms were about her. She was pressed to a bosom as soft as a heart and as stout as oak, as sustaining as courage. A hand, large, strong, calloused on the finger tips, healing, pushed the damp hair back from her forehead and looking up in the still dark room except for the pale watery moonlight sifting through the curtains, she saw Emmy's face bending over her.

"How did you get up here?" India whispered clutching at the frogs of Emmy's red merino peignoir.

"My dear, I crawled. Now hold tight to me, India. Hold tight as you can. I won't let you go."

"Miss Emmy! Oh, Miss Emmy!" The strength of the woman, the gentleness of her large face, the generations who had been born, loved and died in this house now gathered above, around, and underneath India. She could give up now. She was safe.

All through the night India saw familiar and unfamiliar figures moving through the flickering candlelight. Once she heard it thunder and once Emmy was singing. Emmy sitting in a chair by the bed stroked her forehead and let her clench and pull at her hands. Sangua was there. Irene's voice she heard but her face she did not see. She saw Dr. Quattlebaum come in the door, his face weary and sleepy. Sangua hopped about like a rabbit knotting sheets at the head of the bed or shrieking for Cook Ida or some of the maids to bring more kettles of hot water.

Once a strong sweetish odor filled her nostrils and she was snatched from pain and thrown on a lovely floating cloud that went flying blissfully from the airless room. I am going to Max—I am going to Max—I am going to Max!

"Take that chloroform away, Sangua. She's turning blue. A pity but I don't dare let her have any more for the sake of the baby. The heartbeat isn't too strong and she hasn't got the proper width between her hips to deliver without danger. Why in the devil do women ride horseback and make their hips slim as a boy's and their abdomen muscles so strong that having a baby is a major job? Give me a milk and sugar girl who has never done anything but sit on a cushion and embroider all her life. They drop their babies like cats."

So they took away the blessing and after that throughout the night the beast was there and tearing, gnawing, breaking her so that she would never again be anything but a mutilated mass of horrible flesh.

Dawn had lighted the room when Dr. Quattlebaum said to Emmy, "My dear, you and Irene go out. Sangua, send for four of the strongest wenches on the place to come in and hold Miss India down on the bed. The fetal heartbeat is almost gone. I'll have to use the irons. She'll never be able to have this baby by herself."

"I'll stay, Doctor. Hurry, Sangua. Go on out, Irene." Emmy's voice was calm and clear.

India tried to speak and tell them not to bring people in to hold her, that she could stand it. Oh, God, she had stood so much already. Had the beast ground her baby to bits between her own loins? "Doctor—" she croaked as the door opened and somebody new came in the room. A familiar smell came in the room. Pain came in the room.

"I can hold her," Duchess said crossly. "Why wasn't I sent for earlier? If Chance hadn't been called out to a shoe a man's horse, I'd never have known anything was wrong. India—good little girl—here, Doctor— I've got her legs—Miss Emmy, can you hold her shoulders— My God, what big irons!"

There was a long frantic shriek of anguish, then utter stillness. Then India screamed again—a high wild scream of lamentation unlike the mad inhuman animal cry that had just gone before and stared in deadly horror at something the doctor was holding in a piece of flannel—a raw blood-red mass—like the inside of the beast that had crouched on the wall all night.

Emmy drew India's head down onto the pillow.

"Precious child—you have a fine son—and he breathes—Thank God he breathes. Doctor, he does breathe?"

Even while she said the last word India saw the sodden lump of flesh move and turn into a quite small wine-red boy child with two feet and two arms—it struggled and gasped a little.

"He is so tiny—so tiny—" she whispered in a ravaged voice but the doctor was hurrying from her room to Irene's room where the cradle had been fixed with hot blankets and Abby's full breasts with aching nipples waited hungrily for a little mouth.

Many hours later India woke fully. She was lying on cool clean sheets. Duchess had taken off the dreadful sweat-drenched night rail and put on a soft clean one and a blessed sense of release and healing was streaming through her body. Duchess had laid small bags of warm dry salt at her feet and packed her in with soft down pillows. From a million miles away somewhere beyond life, beyond death, there was a whimpering. At first she thought it was the baby, then she realized that it was Mr. Wu who had managed to climb up the steps by the high bed and was nestled in the hollow of her arm.

"Duchess—" she called weakly.

Sangua rose from a chair by the hickory fire and came over to the bed.

"De Duchess gone. Say she be back later."

"Miss Emmy?"

"Took fo' bucks to carry um downstairs in a cheer. She wore out. Her and de Duchess sewed yuh up wid a high harp string atter de doctor lef'. I neber see nuttin so purty. Dat Duchess say she ain't go let yuh be lef' all tore up an' Miss Emmy crawlt down dem steps and

fotch a teensy piecea gut frum dat harp and dey bile hit
down and 'broider yuh lak a fancy piecea cloff."

"Can I see the baby?"

"Miss Irene say if yuh planning to suckle Cantelou
fuh good an' all fuh me to fetch um w'en yuh asts, but
if yuh still planning to wisit Gold Baby in Fuhginny to
leave um wid she an' Abby. She say he kinda weakly
an' de doctor say don' move um round twell tomorrow but Abby say he ain' seem weakly to she and dat
he sho do suck good. I think Gold Baby need yuh
wusser dan Leetle Baby. He been widout a 'oman
fuh fo' months and I speck dat's about all de time he
kin be widout. Whut yuh tink, honey? Lemme go
fetch yuh some beef broff. I know whut 'stocracy lub.
Meat. Dat's whut dey lub. Hit'll mek yuh strong enough
to be wid Gold Baby fore yuh knows hit."

India still didn't answer so Sangua tiptoed out muttering loudly, "Meat—dat's whut dey lub—hawg meat,
cow meat, mutton meat, 'oman meat."

India felt tears sting her sore eyelids. She heard the
singing of the wind in the pines—the deep note of the
north wind heavy with wetness. Rain was pouring on
the slate roof; there was the whisper of rain falling on
soft brown pine needles.

I am here and Max is not here and our son is not in
my arms, she was thinking. Part of me is lying on this
bed and part on a camp cot in Virginia and part in a
cradle in Irene's room. The beast has torn me into three
strange selves and now I must lead three lives. But
which is first? Which is first? And, as if in answer, she
felt a surge of longing for Max. A longing she thought
must have been torn out of her by the beast of the
previous pain smothering night, the longing in her
body and in her blood, was stirring now again, faintly
and feebly as about to waken from a winter's sleep. A
longing that widened out like rings in a pool until she
was covered with it.

But, oh—I would love to hold my baby—the tiny
one!

She tightened her arm around Mr. Wu and he licked
her cool flesh with his pink tongue trying to comfort
her with his warmth and his little love.

PART FOUR

Virginia, 1864

CHAPTER XVI

IN LATE OCTOBER of 1864 General Grant of the Union Army dispatched part of his Second, Fifth, and Ninth Corps, with 6,000 cavalry under General Gregg to turn the flank of General Lee's Confederates defending Petersburg, Virginia, destroy the Southside Railroad, and force Lee away from Richmond.

The night of October 27, General Hampton moved to meet this force and was waiting, his men dismounted, his artillery set up, at Burgess Mill on the Boydton plank road near Moncks-Neck Bridge.

There was the smell of ripened apples in the air and the false wet smell of hanging smoke that at home would have come from piles of burning leaves but here drifted from yesterday's fired guns in the autumn woods.

"Sleep, men, sleep," Calbraith Butler whispered, loosing his wooden leg from the stirrup iron and letting it hang. It was galling him cruelly. He had worn it too long this time without ease. He could even feel the blister, on the foot that wasn't there, rubbed by his first pair of tight shiny cavalry boots en route to Virginia three and a half years ago. He was looking for Max Allan and found him rolled up in an extensive gray shawl, burrowed down in a pile of sycamore leaves, sheltered by the low stone garden wall, in the half light his gold hair mingled with the yellow leaves. No one, thought the twenty-seven-year-old general, except one with no conscience or one with a witched luck could have come through the three and a half years of constant warfare untouched, gay, still excited over "Boots and Saddles," able to sleep like a he-fox in a pile of leaves while all around him hung the heavy expectancy of coming combat.

Now and again a blade of dry grass came to life for an instant beneath Max's hand against his cheek and quivered like a woman's eyelash. Everything was very still and quiet; the predawn sky, the apple trees were dumb. Speech seemed to have been torn from the far-flung brigades crouching nervously in the wraithy mist. Never had a silence been so breathless, so loud enough to wake one sleeping even as soundly as Max.

He woke suddenly stung by a splatter of chilly raindrops on his neck and wrapped a rag from his pocket around his throat. He thrust his fingers into the soft gray shawl he always slept upon because it was the gray of a pair of remembered eyes and because of her perfume that came from it in hours of warmth and sleep. He loved her so and he loved the big shawl she had knitted with the scent of her on it and he pressed it to him in the dawning. Then a wave of resentment swept over him toward all the ones back home th·· king of him. Why must they be safe and warm and he shabby and hungry and cold at this God-forsaken Virginia mill? Then he repented, and tenderness for India and the little black-haired boy he had seen but once came back. He called himself by his first name. His whole first name; Maximilian—Maximilian—and courage flowed back into him.

"Captain Allan!" Another captain of the brigade—a wide-faced man from Georgia of Swedish descent knelt and shook Max's shoulder.

At the first touch of his hand Max jumped up shouting, "Hello, Captain Knutsen— I'm awake!"

"General Butler tried to awaken you but your dreams must have been very compelling. He left you a message."

Knutsen gave Max General Butler's orders while Max picked up a stick and drew on the ground saying, "I'll gather my men and join you at this crossing of the Rowanty River."

"Good. I will report this at once to General Butler. He expects us to be there immediately."

Knutsen remounted his lean brown charger and waving his forage cap, trotted away in the direction of Hampton's headquarters.

The day was now lightening rapidly. Smoke still smothered the air but some of it was from little fires of Negroes and soldiers boiling coffee and bacon. Danny came up to Max with a tin cup of sweetened coffee and a soft hot slab of salt pork on a fat heavy biscuit.

"Eat, suh. I gotta feeling hit will be a long time 'fore you gits a chance to eat again."

"Thanks, Danny. Has the bay been fed?"

"Plenty fuh oncet. Dem Scoutses brung in a whole wagon full of oats and all de hosses done start prancing already."

"Fetch him up. I'm in a hurry."

While Danny was gone Max ate his breakfast and as the rain lessened he saw Preston Hampton sitting near him on the rock wall munching a raw turnip while Nat Butler, Calbraith Butler's younger brother, perched beside him writing a letter on a torn bit of foolscap.

Why the hell is Preston sitting there staring at me Max wondered uncomfortably. Why is he making such a show of eating that damned turnip? I'll wager Kit Goodwyn has already brought him a hot biscuit and coffee and now he's showing off. But has Preston ever been guilty of showing off? Why should I feel this wave of hostility toward him? What is the event in my past that he has taken part in to irritate me and prick my conscience? And suddenly a new unexpected memory from that time of carefree happiness came before him. He remembered India as he had seen her at the ball at White Sulphur in 1858, with her slender neck and arms and with her vivid face ready for rapture and love, and tenderness for her, stronger and more exciting than ever, flooded his soul. He now remembered why his conscience had been disturbed by the poetic-looking, rather dirty giant on the rock wall eating a chilly turnip, who was gazing at him with unfriendly eyes, and a pity and affection for Preston took possession of his heart.

He felt a compulsion to do something instantly to make up to Preston for the unhappiness he had caused him at that long-ago ball.

He approached the two lieutenants and, noticing how absurdly young Preston looked despite his new mustache and chin-tuft of soft brown, held out the cup of coffee to him.

"Drink this, Preston. I've had all I want and it's too precious to throw away."

"Drink it yourself."

Nat looked up in surprise. Preston was the best-humored young officer in the whole army. These were the first rude words he had ever heard from him. How was Nat to know that Preston had been sitting on the wall watching Maximilian Allan curled in his nest of sycamore leaves as comfortable and at home as a wild animal. Watching and resenting that it was Max— Max—who had come between him and India. Sweet, sweet India!

Nat knew none of these things and he dropped the bit of paper on which he had just written, "My dear beloved—" for Max's face had gone the color of parchment and his goldish eyes were glittering angrily.

"You won't, won't you?" Max was speaking roughly, "Well, look!" And he threw the tin cup away, far across the turnip patch into a clump of berry bushes and God alone knew what a tin cup of hot sweetened coffee meant to them this dreary morning.

"Throw it away, I don't care," Preston said coolly.

Then Max saw Preston's chin trembling as though his teeth were chattering from the cold and he jerked off the gray shawl with the smell of India on it and insisted on wrapping it around Preston's neck. But Preston knocked the shawl away and though he was far larger than Max, Max could hold his own. Particularly in the mood of this morning. And the two struggled with each other and the scarf. Preston hurt Max and then Max hurt Preston still more for Max could see tears in Preston's blue eyes. Then suddenly a cannon roared and Danny came running up with the bay and Nat and Preston were on their horses galloping away fast and Butler's brigade shouted and ran for their mounts, as Hampton's men charged Hancock's right from the woods into an open field.

Max was in the saddle and across the dam in an instant and nothing was left by the little rock garden wall but a piece of foolscap with the words, "My dear beloved," and a gray wool shawl that had been trampled to shreds by the rough soles of two pairs of worn-out cavalry boots.

After Hancock's corps forced a passage across the Rowanty River and drove in Butler's pickets, Hampton ordered General Butler to withdraw and take a position higher up the creek at Burgess Mill itself, and wait for the sound of General Wm. F. H. Lee's guns on his right to move forward.

For Max the early morning had passed quickly enough with him and Knutsen in charge of throwing up temporary breastworks of fence rails, old logs, and cane, but at midday Major Hart, who had been ordered by Hampton to defend the bridge across Gravelly Run at all hazards until Hampton could support him, was brought by with a leg smashed and the guns got louder and louder as Young's brigade arrived and saved the bridge. More and more men came stumbling from the battle. Max thought that by now he was hardened to anything but the guns sounded different today. The firing was continuous and the inactivity by the mill became unbearable as the wounded straggled back pleading for help and there could be no help, for Butler's brigade had dismounted and were in battle formation waiting for the first boom-boom of Wm. F. H. Lee's fire to move up on foot.

Once the heaven broke up and a shameless sun skipped from one pile of gray clouds to another, gilding the one on which it rested for the moment. Then the clouds swirled back together and more rain fell and from the big oaks around the pond shells brought down showers of brilliant red and yellow leaves. After came a lull and the tender touch of true autumn sifted more yellowing leaves gently one by one to the wet earth.

Max, pale now and gloomy as the rest, paced up and down from the end of the orchard to the edge of an open harvested field, with his head low and his arms behind his back. There was nothing for him to do now and no orders to give or carry out. Everything went on of itself.

A group of three, their arms entwined, struggled back from the creek bank, the most severely wounded man in the middle. They turned very slowly when someone called to them. Like Laocoön and his sons they seemed hampered and tormented by an invisible serpent. Two soldiers came laughing because the same bullet had wounded them both, one in the head, the other in the foot. "What in the deuce were you doing together?" someone called out. A bearded fellow came walking very slowly like a struck beast and fell full length on the ground, and Butler ordered two privates to break ranks and aid him but he was dead so they pulled him under an elm tree and a few crisp leaves fell on his bluish face. Then above all the groans, clearly heard from the open field, a loud cry rang out: a wounded man, unable to drag himself to sanctuary had been hit a second time and, in his imagination, Max saw a jet of fresh blood as the vivid scream died away into the whine of bullets. A big blond artilleryman appeared under an old apple tree that was only a dark tangle of branches, walking slowly and evenly amid the less seriously wounded and taking infinite care for he had a bullet in his lungs.

"Men!" Calbraith Butler was impatient now as the rest, "Don't crowd around—let the wounded through to the hut where the doctors are working."

Later the men waiting to charge shouted like boy children at a small gray fox which trotted in a pre-occupied manner in front of the ranks with its brush stiff and erect as a dog's tail till suddenly a shell fell close by, when it jumped into the air and streaked into its covert under the wall. Hoic! hoic! yi—ee—ee—ee! shrieked the brigade.

Across the open field Max saw Wade Hampton gallop out in front of his men and turning right re-enter the forest while bullets and shells burst around him. Alone Wade Hampton galloped—again and again—in and out of the forest. But where is his shadow? Where is Preston? Max asked himself in a frenzy. Did I hurt him when I tried to tie the shawl so roughly around his neck? Was I trying to hurt him?

Throughout the war whenever big Wade Hampton galloped ahead of his men, Preston had galloped as close behind him as he was able to hold his hot powerful charger. The father had invariably turned around and waved his son to the rear and for a full stride

Preston would saw back and forth on Bay Monarch's tough mouth then grinning and leaning forward would be right back in his father's shadow. But today—where was he? Where was he?

"Max, have you seen Nat?" Calbraith Butler rode by, a hard tired look straining his handsome face. Max shook his head. The young general began to cough.

The smoke was thick in the woods and over the dam as the men stayed at the edge of the field waiting for the signal to move out. Over the field the smoke drifted in gray disjointed fingers, hanging close to the damp stubbly grass. Max saw Mart Gary, a brigadier general now, on his skinny horse shouting at Calbraith that Nat was over there on the right playing hookey, riding with Lee's cavalry. The rain splattered on Mart Gary's bald head and Calbraith's wooden leg jerked back and forth in the stirrup as he cantered along the low garden wall.

Twenty minutes to three! Would they never charge? How Max had gloried in that word—Charge!—gloried in it since the afternoon he had followed Wade Hampton up the hill at First Manassas. To a man the fashionable Legion, in which even the privates had body servants and were gentlemen, had spurred their fine fat thoroughbreds after their leader, the Carolina millionaire sportsman, his wide becoming gray felt hat pulled low on his brow as if he were going fox hunting and, though he had never had a previous hour's military experience, led them unerringly to the hillside he had been ordered to hold in entirely strange terrain.

Followed him? Who wouldn't follow Hampton? just to see his big broad back out in the front made everything about this war fine and worth the fighting. When someone would start the cheer, "Hurrah for Hampton!", the men would automatically begin galloping forward in full career; the cry louder on their lips than any cannon.

Following him had been like following their own separate stars, their individual ideas and ideals of The Cause. Through Seven Pines with Hampton shot painfully in the foot, keeping his horse while the bullet was extracted, directing his men, staying with them to the battle's end. Eltham Forest; White Oak Swamp with Hampton emerging suddenly from a thicket, Preston at his side, to face Jackson, discouraged, sitting on a stump worrying how the deuce he was going to catch McClellan when the bridge over the river had been providentially washed away just as the last enemy had crossed over. Hampton explaining to Jackson how he and his son had explored the intriguing swamp and discovered where the enemy lay in waiting on hummocks of oak and pine so dense and thickly grown that no birds sang nor vines flowered; had crossed and recrossed the rain-swollen river in which nothing moved but thick brown moccasins and the tawny water and found a good crossing with a sandy bottom and firm approaches where a bridge could be easily thrown by his men. "Build the bridge" was Jackson's comment and it was done.

Through Maryland, riding around McClellan with Hampton, Fitz Lee, Rooney Lee, Grumble Jones, William Wickham, and Calbraith Butler, all following Jeb Stuart, gay as feudal lords, while the beautiful, golden Pelham rumbled along behind with the big guns—crossing rivers where no guns could cross. Followed Hampton on the wild ride all the way to Chambersburg, Pennsylvania—ninety miles in two days—capturing food, shoes, guns, and hundreds of big Pennsylvania work horses with their collars on, fortunately, for there wasn't a horse collar in the whole Southland big enough to fit the smallest horse. Followed him on winter raids where his stalking skill was so daring and successful that even Stuart, strumming his guitar and singing a ballad or a sweet old hymn, decided to come along himself on the next good go. Followed him to Kelly's Ford where Stuart had leaned on his horse's neck weeping for Pelham lying by a wicket gate, his gold hair red with blood.

Paraded after him in Stuart's Grand Military Review the first of June, 1863, to show Robert E. Lee his five cavalry brigades with their elegant officers. And then the next day at Brandy Station they had been all worn out and hadn't fought well. All of them except Wade

Hampton, and he, though ten to twenty years older than most of the cavalry men or officers, did as clever a bit of woods fighting as had taken place during the entire war. Followed him to Gettysburg where he cursed in the hearing of his men for the only time, Fitz Lee having presumed to give an order to his brigade to charge while he was talking with Stuart. Remained at Gettysburg and seen Hampton borne from the field, a wound in his head and a shrapnel wound in his body. Cheered when Fitz Lee and Hampton were made Stuart's two major generals and twenty-seven-year-old Calbraith Butler was given Hampton's command. Had caught from him the grim discouragement of the Wilderness and seen the degeneration of the soldiers' spirits. Followed him in May, '64, when Stuart, the brightest flower of them all, lay dead in the scorching heat of Yellow Tavern. To Louisa Courthouse where Hampton still sat his horse after two entire days and nights in the saddle while he, Max Allan, and the younger officers and men lay sleeping in the lush fragrant clover; Hampton continuing to scout through the third night collecting enough information about the enemy's movements to put on the brilliant show at Trevilian the next day when he closed in on Sheridan. How proud they had been when Hampton was appointed Stuart's successor. But then had come the battle of Samaria; the nightmare heat of the Crater in July of '64; the frustrations of this autumn. Yet he was still ready to follow Hampton to the end they all now realized must come before long. Yes, he was still ready to follow Hampton though today for the first time he had no eagerness for the following. Was he, too, catching the disease called Dying Hope? Was it because they all knew that Lee had warned the Secretary of War that Richmond might be captured unless they sent him— men—men—men? Was it on account of Hood's evacuation of Atlanta, the decimated ranks of the officers— the sick—the thousands deserting—the thought of the future looming larger than the thought of the Cause? Was it because there was now no longer a great battle any day but a small fight every day? Was he upset over his quarrel with Hampton's son, Preston? Was he tired?

Or was he just taking a cold? Or was it this waiting? The guns? The—

"At the double-quick, forward—hawoh!" Butler shouted, standing in his stirrups, soft hat in hand, halloaing his men away—"Hoic together, hoic!" and the men rushed eagerly to Calbraith's voice.

Max bounded over the breastworks he and Knutsen had supervised, and advanced, firing; Knutsen was about four paces to his right, his face set. A shell exploded near him and the flash from it shone goldly on his day's growth of light tough beard.

The whole long line was advancing, stretched all the way from the orchard to the mill, into the open field. Their artillery covered them well, firing over their heads with rapidity and skill. Old men were in the line who had replaced younger ones side by side with beardless boys who wore their dead brothers' shoes. They were breathing hard and stumbling every now and then —but they kept up. Max's own breath was cold and he looked up at the little brow of a hill just beyond a thicket out of view of the battlefield where the enemy had set up their artillery. The cannon began blasting and around him the ground shook and smoke billowed from the right end of the line and someone shouted that Colonel Jeffords had been killed. Then there was a line of blue in front and Calbraith Butler, jabbing his horse with his wooden leg, galloped ahead, shouting, toward the action. Max felt a wave of anger at Calbraith. Why had he ordered his cavalry to fight on foot? This he hated. This was not the kind of war he had bargained for. This was the infantry's job. A rock thudded into the soft earth in front of him and something whistled over his head.

Beside him Captain Knutsen was singing a Viking song in his soft Georgia drawl and he heard shouts and saw Preston Hampton and Nat Butler riding in the midst of the line of advancing men, waving their hats and cheering them on. Thank God, he thought, there's Preston. It's an omen—now I'll be all right again. Preston and Nat were about a hundred yards on his left and through the smoke he saw Calbraith Butler signaling his younger brother. Nat obediently spurred his

horse toward the garden and Preston headed toward
the right rear for his father's headquarters and as he
turned in one direction and Nat in the other, he called
out, "Hurrah, Nat!" but Nat never heard him for his
horse fell heavily, shot through the neck. By now
Preston's charger was almost directly beside Max and
the eyes of the two cavalrymen met. For a moment
Preston hesitated and as he hesitated, Bay Monarch
missed a stride making a perfect target for a Yankee
sharpshooter. Max saw Preston pitch forward shot in
the groin and Bay Monarch screamed in agony, crashing on his back, thrashing wildly with his feet.

"Watch out, Mr. Allan, that there hoss is gonna kick
ye," a passing corporal, young and grim, from Lick-
skillet near Edgefield, jerked Max back a pace.

A bullet tore through Max's hat—he could feel the
hotness and hear the evil of it.

"Come on, suh," said the corporal.

But Max just stood on the damp slippery earth while
butternut and homespun soldiers pushed him, cursed
him, called him to move along.

I can't see to move, he wanted to explain.

All he could see was big Wade Hampton kneeling
down on the battlefield with bullets and shells spattering
up geysers of dirt all around, cradling Preston in his
arms. A lock of hair had fallen on Preston's forehead.
Hampton was tucking it back in place whispering in
Preston's ear as he smoothed the soft brown hair. Preston quivered and as he quivered once and was still
Wade Hampton cried above the guns and cannons,
"My son—my son!"

"Git out the way of that hoss, captain, git on. No
call fer you to spy on folks' grief." The grim young
corporal had returned for Max—

"Go to the devil, Fallaw. Look—there's young
Wade with them now. Oh God—no—young Wade has
been shot in the back! They're aiming at General Hampton now—the fiends—"

"Make way—make way!" Calbraith Butler had
found a wagon and come to remove the Hampton boys
from the field.

"Don't! Don't!" Max moaned, seeing the face of

Wade Hampton, tears running over his heavy beard and glistening the tarnished buttons of his frock coat. Hampton was lifting, alone lifting his son and for a moment he stood on the battlefield holding Preston in his arms as though he were a very tiny boy and only sleeping—tired sleeping.

"Hand him to me, Wade." Dr. Taylor was standing in the wagon and Hampton held up Preston. Preston's head fell back showing a red welt under his chin.

I did that, Max thought horrified, fascinated. I did it with India's shawl. I must tell Wade Hampton I hurt Preston. But where is he going? Why doesn't he ride along with the wagon?

Wade Hampton had remounted and was riding hard in the opposite direction from the wagon to a portion of the field where Lieutenant Bamberg of Hart's battery was engaged with two guns in an artillery duel with the Yankee batteries on the hill in the rear of the pine thicket. There Wade Hampton took his position and directed the fire giving particular instructions as to the number of seconds' fuse and the elevation of each gun at each discharge. And every crash exploded a Yankee caisson or blew up a horse or a group of men. Not one shell missed its objective that afternoon. Not one.

As the wagon went rumbling away under incessant fire with Dr. Taylor supporting Preston's beautiful unmarred head on his breast, Max's shock began to pass and he looked up at the sky and emptied all the chambers of his cavalry .44 pistol at a heavy cloud as though he were taking dead aim at God himself.

As he began replacing the pistol to finish off Preston's horse, Max's right leg was broken by a Minnie ball and he collapsed with his head not a foot away from the wounded animal's jerking hind legs.

In spite of the pain his first instinct was to get off the field; out of the fire. He tried to stand up but as he did so the gray line retreated and a blue line flowed over the center of the field mowing him down like a scythe. Every now and then a Yankee soldier would jerk him up and remark on seeing his foot fall, "Damm him, we have winged him and will get him when we come back." Others spoke kindly to him and one knelt and gave him water. One took his pistol and another his sword belt and the papers in his pocket.

Then Max heard, in the woods from which he had charged a short time before, the Rebel Yell and saw the Confederates emerging from the woods in a straight line yelling as if they had again sighted the gray dog fox and this time, instead of being amused, were after him on the double and then another ball hit him and he heard himself screaming in agony.

The Yankees who had threatened to carry Max back did not linger and Max now lay between the fire of both armies in the open field. The Confederate line passed over him and he could only moan: Poor Preston—Poor Preston. He must have fainted at last for when he could see again it was getting dark and the firing was still going on. He was cold from loss of blood and someone was bending over him and a flask of brandy was held to his lips. He tried to swallow but there was so much blood inside his mouth he began to choke instead.

"Captain Allan—Captain Allan—"

Max tried to shout—I'm awake—but at that minute the world exploded right over him and there was no longer anybody giving him brandy. There was the heavy weight of Captain Knutsen smothering his wounded chest—the blood from one shattered chest mingling with the blood from the other. "Are you badly hurt, Knutsen?" Max whispered.

Knutsen groaned, "My leg is smashed—" and managed to roll off Max but in doing so he fell against the hard hind hoof of Preston's dying horse and with one last violent spasm Bay Monarch lunged out kicking both Max and Knutsen wickedly and killingly on their heads and faces.

CHAPTER XVII

Richmond, Virginia
November 3rd, 1964

Dear India,

On the 27th of October my Brigade was engaged in a fierce battle at Burgess Mill on Hatcher's Run immediately to the west of the old Boydton plank road. I am sure the sad details of Preston Hampton's death at this place are by now known to you. I hope there was room for him to be buried beside his lovely mother in Columbia. The battle was a success for the Confederacy even with our thin lines stretched to the breaking point from Richmond to Petersburg and on south. Now the cavalry is planning a little rest as the Virginia roads have become well-nigh impassable and we have gone into our winter quarters.

About an hour after General Hampton's sons were shot, one of the cannoneers of Hart's battery reported to me that a captain was lying in the center of the field badly wounded. I at once sent out some scouts in search of him, but they returned unsuccessful. Later I went myself and found a wounded and dead captain lying beside Preston Hampton's horse. The dead captain had evidently been kicked in the face by the horse in his death struggle and was identifiable only by his bright gold hair. The wounded captain, also gold-haired, was brought to a little hut and as Dr. Taylor cut away his coat it was discovered that the Yankees had rifled all his papers and personal possessions. The captain's face is badly marred, his head is swollen and battered, his chest torn and his leg injured. Though seemingly conscious he refuses to answer any questions and the doctor says he is suffering from a disease known as loss of memory in addition to his wounds.

This must sound cruel and heartless to you, but even I, who have known Max intimately since boyhood, cannot say for a certainty whether he lives or is dead. That is for you to declare and immediately.

Danny refuses to discuss who he is waiting on so faithfully in the hospital. But he nurses his patient tenderly and today before I came he had managed to conjure up some sweet soap and given the man a bath. The doctors have shaved his head

to attend the abrasion from the horse's hoof and
say if lockjaw doesn't set in he has a good chance
to survive whether he recovers his wits or not.

Take the train from Columbia to Charlotte, to
Greensboro, N.C., to Danville, Va.; but beyond
there you will have to try and secure a ride in a
government ambulance or some other such con-
veyance, the railroad being presently disrupted at
Burkeville Junction, and get to Richmond as soon
as providence will allow you—probably three days
—perhaps two and a half.

God bless you, my dear, and give you strength
to bear death or affliction whichever may be your
lot at this sad time.

Extend my esteem to Miss Emmy and Miss
Irene.

Ever your friend,
Matthew Calbraith Butler

CHAPTER XVIII

IN RICHMOND India was fortunate enough to secure
a room at the Spotswood Hotel. She pulled off the in-
digo-dyed flour-sack blouse she had worn on the train
and through the jolting journey by ambulance to the
city and put on a green velvet suit Duchess had sent to
the Grove just before she left and which she seemed to
have remembered her mother wearing one autumn day
in the gloomy Charleston cemetery. What was Duchess
doing with one of her mother's costumes. She'd ask
when she got back home. Duchess had been wonderful when the baby came but since had shown little interest or affection. How nice though to have this suit.
It was decidely old-fashioned, but what was fashion
nowadays.

Winter was here in Virginia early—a somber damp
November winter with the sound of guns rumbling
down the river, church bells clanging for funerals,
wounded wagons bumping over the streets, and shuffling Negroes going somewhere to work singing tune-
lessly. The hack she had hired was topless and di-

lapidated and the emaciated horse looked as though only the shafts were holding him upright. Where were the coaches, the gigs, the phaetons? And the wind shrieked in answer—where—ooh—ooh! They drove toward the hospital down Main Street dotted with the red flags of auction sales fluttering in the November gale. Most of the men crowding the street were too shrewd and sleek, looking at her, in the topless hack, boldly, as if wondering who in all Richmond had still a sealskin hat and muff—a lustrous velvet jacket— enough money for a hack? There were wounded soldiers on the street and they made way for these smooth-faced men with their gold canes who went in and out of the auction houses, jaunty as crows in a new planted cornfield.

The hack bumped on down by the river and over the treeless streets of Rocketts where Max had spent his first summer weeks encamped with the Hampton Legion, writing as though war were one gay ball and parade after another. What a dreadful part of the city for the Legion to have camped even a few weeks!

The poor hack horse stumbled and heaved climbing Chimborazo Heights but finally the rough board shacks of the hospital loomed gruesomely and she felt a drop of blood trickling in her mouth and realized that she had cut through her bottom lip with her top teeth and that she was trembling with cold and fear and love and a desire to jump out of the hack and run as fast as she was able down the hill away from this dreadful ugly place.

He was lying in somebody's grandfather's old ruffled cambric night-rail on a narrow camp cot covered with a patchwork quilt. He was the color of ashes. In one dirty-nailed hand he held a chrysanthemum of gold that matched the hairs on the back of his hand; with the other hand he picked at a bloodstained bandage covering his head and most of his face. One reddened eye stared at her as she entered.

"Max!" she cried and a flood of love words—their love words—broke from her and she was weeping and kneeling by the cot.

But he pushed at her with his hands and shook his

head and she saw clearly that nothing she had said meant anything to him. She tightened all her muscles and restrained her thoughts for the benefit of a few words that seemed to come from the center of her being: He is there, before my eyes. See, he is still there. He's not out of reach as I dreaded every minute of the train journey. But—but—is that really he still there before my eyes?

At once a great inner conviction replaced the seeking words. Oh—it is you—my beloved—her sobs rose higher and higher in her throat as she more and more convinced herself—if the nose were not so swollen it could be his; if they had not shaved his head surely his hair would be the color of that chrysanthemum he has torn to pieces; if his mouth were not so strained— his uncovered eye so bloodshot. In a frenzy she unbuttoned the ruffled night-rail to see the curved hard golden shield of his chest. His chest—this torn matted thing covered with rags—his chest? She looked up in desperation and on seeing his face and meeting his unblinking raw-looking eye, felt her tears dry up and her sobs ceased. She suddenly felt guilty looking at his naked throat and grew timid catching the expression of his mouth and eye.

In his deep gaze that seemed to look not outwards there was an almost hostile expression as he slowly fumbled to close the opening she had made in the gown.

"What do you want?"

Had he shrieked in torment, that shriek would not have undone India as the tone of his voice.

"I—I am India and have come to take you home. Would you like to go home?"

"That, Madame, you must ask the doctor."

"But—you are Max and I am India. Don't you want to come home to Shepherd's Grove?"

"No."

India clasped his hand. Ah—it was his hand. She would know the shape—the texture of his flesh, if even a hundred blindfolds were on her eyes.

"Oh darling—your hands feel so wonderful." The contact made him wince. He turned his head slowly away from her and she did not know what more to say but continued to stroke the limp fingers and try to make them warm and clutching again.

"You tink him he?" Danny was standing in the doorway with a cup of arrowroot custard.

"Oh yes, Danny— Don't you?"

"Miss, 'fore Gawd, I dunno. But jest in case tis he I gwine wait on him best I kin. Hit don't ack vigorous like Mista Maxi but I'd sho hate to tink it was Mista Maxi and we let somebody else come and fetch him fer off from us. Lemme help you up. Cunel Marshall waiting to see you, out in de hall wid de book. He say fuh you to go talk wid him a minute."

Colonel Marshall turned out to be the red-haired horseman from Virginia by whom she had sat at the Witherspoons' New Year's Day party when she was a bride.

"India Allan!" He held out a hand with three fingers gone and she was as glad to see him as though he had been her lifelong best friend. And because she had known him once, though that for only a few hours, he seemed like a friend and she let herself cry in her handkerchief and he comforted her saying, "Poor dear. I am so sorry. So sorry. General Butler asked me to be responsible for this captain until your arrival. He is laid up with an abscess on his bad leg from wearing his artificial limb too long in this last engagement. What an ordeal for you!"

"How long will he be able to remain here?"

"Who?"

"Why, my husband of course."

"Not but a few days more. There isn't a vacant bed or pallet anywhere and the wounded are still pouring in from field stations. Now that his injuries have stopped bleeding and he is somewhat patched up we'll have to move him over to the asylum if you don't positively identify him."

"I do identify him. Of course I identify him. How did he happen to be in here alone?"

"Mrs. Phoebe Pember put him in here and is responsible for his fashionable attire. At first he was in the ward but he was so restless she moved her desk out of her office. This is her office. She shaved off his hair and wanted to keep it for either his wife or mother but a mouse made a nest in it and one of the orderlies threw it out."

Down the hall some soldier was picking a banjo and singing, "It's been long since we've met, Lorena."

"Let's go in and see if he remembers me from yesterday." Colonel Marshall bowed India ahead of him into the narrow dingy room. "Good afternoon, Captain, you look much better today."

"Much better."

"Do you know who I am?"

"No."

"But I was here with you yesterday."

"Were you?"

In his words, his tone, and especially in that dull almost antagonistic look, India could feel a wall between him and everything in his past, terrible in one who is living.

"Did he recognize you, Mrs. Allan?"

"No, Colonel Marshall."

"Can you say whether he is Max Allen or Erik Knutsen?"

Danny's wonderful words—"jest in case—jest in case"—beat in her brain. But she really didn't need Danny's words. Her own physical response to the man on the cot was answer enough for her.

"I told you at once."

"You must be very, very sure. General Butler ordered me to tell you there must be no supposition. You must swear he is or is not your husband. I saw Max as he went into battle that day. There was a Captain Knutsen with him. The two were evidently together when they were shot and, my dear, I examined them both and I feel quite positive that *this* is Knutsen."

"Ridiculous. I'd know Max's hands anywhere, Danny—let me see his feet—his toes I'd know. His big toe is unusually large and round at the end."

Danny uncovered one strong hairy foot.

"I'm sure that's his foot."

Ervin Marshall looked pityingly at her.

"Don't force a reality, Mrs. Allan. Hands and feet can be very similar. Isn't there some definite mark— a mole—a scar?"

Oh, dear—looking down India saw on the upper arm of the wounded man a big vaccination scar. Had Max ever been vaccinated?

"Yes—" she said boldly, "Max had a vaccination scar on his upper left arm."

"So has almost everybody," Ervin Marshall said dryly.

"Colonel Marshall"—India faced her fence and gathered herself well—"I positively identify the man on the bed as my husband, Maximilian Allan." She had cleared the barrier without a tick. Her voice was as clear and true as a church bell.

"So be it," Ervin Marshall sighed, opening the account book and with his thumb and little finger awkwardly gripping a stub of pencil making a bold check after the name "Allan" and drawing a line through "Knutsen."

"Come and drive me back to the hotel. This poor fellow is exhausted with the strain of us. I saw your hack outside and since I can't afford one myself and buy you a proper supper I'll let you share this part of the evening. I am anxious to hear of Edgefield and my cousin Kevin. He is the only family I have left in all the world. I'll help you arrange a place for the captain in the government ambulance bound for Danville one day next week."

"I can't leave him. I'll stay here. You take the hack."

"You'll have to come along and personally make the application. There are hundreds waiting and the sooner you get yours in the quicker you can take him to your home."

"His home, Colonel Marshall. Good-by until to-morrow, Max." India bent to kiss the man on the cot. He smiled oddly and India who knew Max's face so well saw with horror that he did not smile as Max had smiled, with gaiety or affection or even cynicism, but with a grim toothy irony because he thought she was trying what she believed to be the last means of arousing him.

CHAPTER XIX

AT THE SUNSET HOUR Emmy sat on an Italian marble bench in the middle of the boxwood garden laid out by a Frenchman who had come to this country to design some gardens along the Ashley River near Charleston. She loved this spot by the round fish pool where a fountain played melodically.

Two yellow leaves from a tulip tree fell into the pool and goldfish darted in the citron water, in and out of the whirling yellow leaves. Delighted with the scene Emmy suddenly longed for someone with whom she might share this pleasure; not necessarily someone who loved such things as she did but one who at least responded to them in an ordinary way. There would be no use to say to Irene—see the lovely sunset. Irene never saw sunsets.

She was happy that India was coming back this evening. She had missed India more than she had ever missed anyone at all before. She felt more kinship with India than she ever had with either of her own children.

The sky had never seemed so red and golden before. Above the pines lay a great cloud; it was shaped like a gigantic scarecrow and around it were numerous wisps of gray clouds like ragged birds scattering to all sides. Here in the little fish pool the sky was mirrored with the scarecrow and the birds around it; it seemed as though it were from down there in the water that the burning glow streamed up to tinge all that lay around her. Little orange wisps like bits of straw loosed themselves from the cloud figure and suddenly the shape changed and was itself a big bird, glowing within like clear burning amber.

Just such a burning amber had been the pine fire that had destroyed her loveliness.

Had her husband pushed her or had the edge of her pale blue eiderdown wrapper brushed the leaping flames?

169

Cantelou came home from Columbia in the middle of a stormy December night. The wind had been alternately moaning and thundering in the treetops for hours. Their child, nine-year-old Irene, was feverish and upset and she was sitting up by the fire waiting for Sangua to come and tell her that her daughter slept and was not seriously ill. She knew Cantelou had been with the woman he kept in a little house on a back street in Columbia. Once she had followed him and had seen the house. It had yellow scrim curtains at the windows and dozens of red rose bushes in the tiny yard.

She heard him slam the front door and heard Steeben soothing him, suggesting that he sleep on a soft pallet he'd fixed in the billiard room and not wake Miss Emmy. Po' little Miss Emmy.

But Cantelou said ugly things to Steeben and came straight to her room. His gold hair was tousled but oh, so shiny in the firelight. His beautiful, small, weak mouth shaped love words when he saw her—her dark hair hanging against her tiny waist—the beribboned blue wrapper pulled protectingly across her soft full breasts.

He lurched over and caught her hard against him but she pushed him down into one of the big chairs. He was drunk and he pulled her down on his lap tangling his long nervous fingers in her hair.

She looked at him. Scorning him. Not hating him. She had never hated him. Not even knowing that he kept a mistress who buoyed up his self-esteem and flattered him into good humors. Probably the woman was impressed with his elegant clothes, his shrewd money-making mind, his colossal self-interest. At fifteen she, too, had been impressed with golden Cantelou Allan who had moved with the careless easy grace of a wild animal, had shown such an interest in the orphaned girl's cotton plantation and been willing to relieve her of all responsibility of it. But at twenty-five he no longer impressed her. He just bored her.

"I won't let you sleep in here tonight," she told him and he ran upstairs and brought Irene down and fondled her on his knee by the fire muttering,

"Your mother is cruel to me. Your mother doesn't love your father."

Irene sat smugly on Cantelou's knee sliding her light oblique eyes around at her mother and saying, "I love you, Papa. I love you best."

Then she made the mistake, seeing the two light ones smirking at her in the firelight, of saying sharply to Irene, "Go back to your bed. I hear Sangua calling you. Go at once."

Cantelou set Irene down and, before she realized what he was doing, seized Emmy in his arms and was bending her back—back—roughly running his hands over her small lovely body crying, "Love me, Emmy —love me—" right in front of the child. She pushed against him and he pushed her too. In the end had he pushed her or had her wrapper brushed too near the flames?

Oh—no—no—Don't remember that!

She was back in the quiet afternoon garden. Cantelou was gone from her life forever. She had not been sorry when he died. There had never been between them the thing that was between Maximilian and India. That was a frightening kind of love. A love that transcended the impossible. A love her harp might be able to express but which she had not.

The sun shot forth through the cloud, rested on the pine crests and sent its light out over acre after acre of harvested crops. The evening was so clear—the light showed up starkly the rows of Negro cabins far back behind the barns among the picked cotton fields; she could see Mr. Suggs's house and his patch of collards gleaming blue green in the low land beside it.

The plantation bell began its tolling. Emmy sat bowed over her folded hands till the last of the big clangs died away on the air.

Now the sun was hidden in the dark pines, the golden radiance grew paler and the red more rosy and soft. After the old bell had ceased ringing, the wind in the pines seemed to rise a little and spread. The noise from the fountain tinkled louder on the ear. From the path beyond the garden, outside of the shrubbery border of holly and tea olive, came the soft clank-clanking bells

of the cattle being brought home. Her head still bowed
she sent up a prayer for the one whom India was
bringing with her to Shepherd's Grove. For the sake
of the great love between them—let it be Maximilian,
she prayed.

Somewhere in the distance a rain crow made a dole-
ful melancholy noise: it's–gonna–rain–rain–rain! Above
the house, by the barns, the outbuildings, the quarters, in the shrubbery, behind the orchards, and all
around in the orchards the songbirds were trilling:
We're–going–south–we're–going–south! A chuck-will's-
widow was calling to his love: Meet–me–tomorrow–
meet–me–tomorrow! The last of the frogs were bursting with farewell and you could distinctly hear their
words: Drink–er–up–jug–er–rum! The crickets scraped
their tuneless fiddles. What a noise there was. It seemed
as if all the creatures had stayed over or out a few
extra days to cry and sing on purpose so that Max
might remember them. Every one of them, even the
least important frog which was sitting bug-eyed on the
big wisteria vine obvious to the wildly barking Pekingese on the grass beneath.

There was so much going on in the underworld and
brush that she almost missed Chance's far-carrying hal-
loooo! But the others had heard and in no time she was
joined by Irene with little Cantelou dressed in a white
kilt holding a rock in one hand and a bunch of the
last Malmaison roses in the other. She hoped he wasn't
going to be naughty. Irene had spoiled him shamefully.
Sangua was there and Steeben, tears running down his
face—Mr. Suggs, the rascal—and hundreds of the Negroes, their eyes strange and wild.

"Run meet him," Emmy called to the slaves.

"Git and meet yer master," Suggs ordered and as the
calash came flying up, the black men and women and
children ran to meet the travelers. Silently ran—not
singing or shouting—just running. For a minute Emmy
thought from the looks of their heels that they were
going to keep right on running—away from here toward the freedom that with every Northern victory
came nearer and realer. But they stopped when they
reached the calash and followed it back to the house,

kicking at pine cones and jostling each other. But none singing; none shouting "Welcome, Mista Maxi—"

Emmy, usually so slow and cumbersome, was the first one to meet the calash. She reached in and grasped one hand of the man at India's side. He was very pale. His head had been shaved and his scalp showed white against the dull yellow of his face; there were hollows beneath his eyes. At her touch he shivered. Then a little color came into his cheeks—he managed a smile. It was as though sap and life might again well up.

"Maximilian Allan," he said weakly.

India's eyes met hers; daring her.

"Yes, thank God you've come home." Emmy stepped back for India to get out. India seemed so strong and supple as she stood there on the step, turned a little from the hips and looked over her shoulder.

"Let the men lift you, Max," India said, "don't try to help yourself. Your cheek has started bleeding again. My, it's hot!" She pulled off the fur hat that had been so admired by the riffraff in Richmond.

Emmy noticed that she had dressed her hair in a new way, piled high on her head in a big lustrous coil showing her rather large ears. It made her look unusually beautiful. And her eyes shone like stars.

"Mama! Mama!" Cantelou tried to climb in the calash to give the roses to his father. Max's cheek was now bleeding very much and the child threw the rock at him instead but Chance caught the rock before it hit Max and India jerked Cantelou off the step and hugged him saying,

"This is your father, baby, you wouldn't hurt your father." But the child struggled away from her, picked up another rock and ran to throw it at the Pekingese.

"Come speak to your brother, Irene," India called to her sister-in-law standing on the piazza looking as if she were on the edge of unconsciousness.

Irene had put on her new one-hundred-dollar pair of shoes and the two-hundred-dollar black and pink flounced calico that had come through the blockade. Her face was dreadfully white and she was breathing shallowly as she reluctantly came to the calash.

"Go away," Max said fretfully to Irene. "Stop staring at me."

Irene recoiled in amazement at this hostility, then she screeched like a pinched owl.

"Why that's no more Bubba than it is General Grant. What are you trying to do—rob Cantelou of his inheritance?"

India turned abruptly to Chance and Big Dick and Danny and the others who were waiting, expressionless as ever when they wanted to pretend not to know what was going on.

"Bring Mr. Maxi in the house. Which room is prepared for him, Miss Emmy?"

"The billiard room so that he needn't be dragged up and down the stairs." Emmy pulled the rather tattered ends of her rose chiffon as close around her as she could. Had he heard their futile ugly conversation? Had he recognized the indecision in her eyes when she leaned into the calash and took his hand?

As Chance gently lifted the poor thin body from the cushioned seat and held him carefully in his arms while Steeben and Danny balanced the injured leg so that it would not hang, Emmy glimpsed his face again and she saw through to his profound woundedness and something quivered inside her, flared up at the corners of her mouth and in her eyes.

"Don't be a fool, Irene," she said firmly and at the sight of her daughter's twisted bitter face she moved to put her arm about the small sloping shoulders but Irene hopped away from her.

"You would take India's side. Bubba was never your baby. He was always mine and I'll not accept this strawman in his place. Never—do you hear? Never." And ran sobbing around the house toward the now dark fruitless orchard.

CHAPTER XX

THERE WAS A HORSE on the lawn. A big speckled horse whereon sat an unattractive small-looking man with reddish hair and a long thin nose. Emmy and India and Max were under the wisteria vine on a bench, each with a varying reaction to the horse and rider but knowing that, familiar as was a horse and rider at Shepherd's Grove, this particular mounted man ended a way of life. It was not that he was the end of the war. With Hampton and Butler back in South Carolina desperately attempting to halt Sherman on his devastating march toward the shivering dwindling lines in the trenches outside of Petersburg, they yet realized that the end of the war must be soon and that they would be defeated. The defeat would belong to them all. But this man on horseback was a personal thing that was happening now this minute to each of them.

He was more real than the ones swarming like locusts in and out of the house and from the outbuildings carrying armfuls of clothes, carpets, bric-a-brac, chairs, food, chickens, geese, saddles, bridles, pigs, sheep, trunks, dishes, poles of hams from the smokehouse, tubs of lard, and links of sausage. Three of them came onto the piazza with Emmy's harp and started to cut the strings with a saber but at that moment Emmy called to the horseman, the first words exchanged:

"If you will order those ruffians to leave my harp alone, I will tell you where we have hidden the wine."

"Very well. It is a lovely instrument."

"The wine is buried directly under the spot your horse is standing on."

Emmy was rarely composed. For her, crises were stimulating—though she never knew it. Had her husband been living he could have told; he had watched her meet and rise above many he had caused.

"Now if you'll tell me where you have taken the paintings I came here especially to obtain, I'll call out my men and not burn your house."

"Oh no—that I can't do. I don't know where they were taken, to tell you the truth."

"And you—" he had at first insisted that Max was a deserter and tried to take him prisoner but seeing the condition of his still unhealed wounds and his bewilderment, he had left off bothering him.

"I don't know," Max said stiffly. "I don't even

know who I am. How could I know a thing as unimportant as that?"

"You?" He turned to India, unconsciously smoothing his drooping mustaches, but she shook her head vigorously. At that moment Mr. Suggs approached the man and pointed out Steeben who was quietly standing under the oak tree with Sangua and Moze and Ida.

Within three minutes after Steeben vigorously shook his wooly white head, he was strung up from a branch in the oak tree by his thumbs and left howling as loud as a hound dog caught in a bear trap.

Mingled with his howls were shrieks from Irene and screams from Cantelou. Irene had insisted on locking herself upstairs in her room and the raiders had evidently battered in the door.

"Stay here, Max." India and Emmy started into the house after the child but Max followed them limping painfully. In the hall the Union soldiers were tearing up the carpets; through the parlor door they saw two of them dancing on the piano and noticed that the mouth of Vrouw Bodolphe had been slashed by a saber. Cantelou was screaming louder and India dashed up the steep stairs. Emmy found it all she could do to take care of her cloud of drapery in the crowd and as it was caught on buttons and bayonets, with quiet dignity she unhooked herself.

Reaching the foot of the steps she saw India at the top.

"Is the child all right?"

"Yes. He just wants to come out and help the soldiers tear up the house. Irene is all right too. Not a man has entered her room. But oh—they've cut up all the mattresses and taken everything out of our chests and wardrobes!"

From the yard came the call of a bugle and the men began to leave the half-wrecked house. A tall skinny man ran from the attic wearing Emmy's beautiful rose-point wedding veil and carrying a blue silk parasol; another had Max's creamy beige trousers tied around his neck and the coat filled with sheets and dresses tied in a bundle by the sleeves.

Curiosity made Emmy follow the men to the piazza. A new man on horseback was now talking to the man on the speckled horse and he in turn called out to the two hundred odd soldiers spilling from the house and around it.

"Orders to join General Sherman at the Congaree bridge outside of Columbia by the day after tomorrow, February 17th! Fall in! Fall in! You'll have plenty of fun then."

"Ain't we go git to burn up Governor Pickens and his lady ner none of them Russian jewels?" a sergeant complained bitterly as the barouche flashed past the piazza piled high with soft white wool blankets and dozens of Coalport dishes; the calash with six drunken singing men and coffee skinned Billy's Lizzie draped gloriously in Emmy's colorful silken quilt; the little English buggy that had been Emmy's as a child; and the victoria with the handsome woman, who had appeared along with the man on the speckled horse, sitting in a nest of velvet draperies, cushions, and feathered hats.

As they had come, they were gone—suddenly. Max cut Steeben from the oak tree, the first act of his own volition since India had brought him home. Many Negroes went running down the road after the Yankees, foot-loose and fancy-free. Chicken Mary, fat and shaking, brought up the rear, every now and then stopping and jumping up and down and around and around hollering, "I'se free—I'se free—I'se free till I'se fool." Yet most of the slaves hovered around Steeben and at a cry from India from the back that the warehouse filled with all their cotton was burning, they ran to help her and to save for her and hers what they could.

"Miss Emmy!" Sangua crawled from under the house with Mr. Wu tightly buttoned in her bosom, his pink tongue hanging out, panting happily. Sangua was cackling with delight.

"Smokehouse burnt down."

"What else?" Emmy could afford to be disconsolate now. No one was looking.

"I lock dat ole snake, Suggs, in de smokehouse and when Yankee sojer come by wid de burning brand I say burn up de smokehouse, boy, so dem trashy white folks will all starve. And he say ain' somebody in dere? An' I say naw dat's ole Suggs—he's over yonder in de privy hollering wid piles."

"Don't tell me Suggs is locked in the smokehouse and it on fire. Not someone burning—" Emmy made an effort to run but Sangua caught her back.

"Honey, hit's been burnt down fuh a half hour by dis time. I done looked and couldn't find nuttin but a few knucklebones and dem charred crisk as hawg knuckles. What yuh tink? Sangua seen Suggs tell de Yankee on de speckle hawss dat Steeben been de one to cyarry away de treasure to de swamp wid us six hawsses what wuz lef' hitch to de scarlet coach. Sangua ain' go suffer none to treat ole Steeben so. Not Sangua."

Emmy sighed, but let Sangua pull her down onto the piazza steps. Suggs was dead now. She'd better not know any more about it. Nor could she face the inside of the house again just yet. The Yankees had taken all the exquisite small marble statues in the boxwood garden and torn up the boxwood bushes but they had left the four Graces along the front of the house and the wisteria vine was intact. She'd rather have the vine than the boxwoods anyway. Out by the warehouse she could hear India calling the Negroes to bring up water as if a few pails of water would affect the hundreds of bales of cotton which had been doused with turpentine and carefully fired. Over by the fence Emmy saw a group of Negroes coming home from running a ways after the Yankees. She lifted a hand and waved to them and some of them waved back. A wind had risen and from the peach orchard fluttered a shower of snow. A group from Massachusetts complaining of no snow in February had ripped up her linen sheets and tied them on the branches to simulate a snowstorm!

She leaned her head against the fluted column at her back, closing her eyes for a moment. Exhausted and soul-weary, she dropped off to sleep and was wakened a half hour later by Steeben bending over her saying, "You looks mighty white, Miss Emmy. Cook Ida done brewed up de las' of de coffee and sont yuh a cup.

Drink hit lak a good girl an' den I gwine tek yuh in de house and put yuh in yo' own nice sof' bed. Dey tuck two of yo' matridges but dere's still three lef' on de cords."

"Thank you, Steeben. Are you all right?"

"Sho. I hollered so loud dem Yankees thought dey done tied me by my thumbs but I had a holt of dat rope all de time and jest swung up dere in dat tree top as comfy and easy as a baby in a cradle."

Seeing the blood and bruises on his hands, the swollen thumbs, she knew this was not true but she let him think she believed him and drank the hot coffee, grateful that Irene had disappeared somewhere in the ruins and that at least her harp, her vine, and her bed were spared to her.

CHAPTER XXI

A MONTH LATER to the day, Wade Hampton stretched his big frame on a bench by the door of the Bennet House near Durham's Station and put his battered hat over his face.

There were soldiers passing constantly in and out of the house. He heard one of the soldiers, evidently a Vermonter, for his words twanged out nasally, say "Whaddyeeknow—Everybody's getting shot er shooting theirselves—Kilpatrick says the old Secessionist, Ruffin, what fired the first shot 'ginst Sumter, blowed his heart out with a silver-butted pistol yesterday."

Later a Yankee officer leaned over and asked Hampton if he would like a cup of coffee.

"Go away," he said calmly, wanting to shout, Our last hope and Defender has gone, you fool; don't you know that the world has ended? Abraham Lincoln lies dead in Washington leaving the South to the vengeance of fanatics. And you talk of coffee, not of corpses.

The news of the assassination of President Lincoln had just been read aloud by General Sherman to the group at the house. And a few minutes before that someone had whispered in Hampton's hairy ear, "Jefferson Davis is fleeing with the Confederate treasure train!"

The two stars had fallen from earthly glory in a single night!

But the one that Hampton was grieving over most at this moment was not *his* president but *their* president. Lincoln's death is the final death blow to the Confederacy, he was thinking. He would have given us defeat with honor. Now he is gone. Everything is gone. My sons are dead, my plantation ravaged beyond being a haven for vultures, I am loaded with debts. Every cent I possessed was in Confederate bonds. A million and a half dollars worth of cotton—all that was left me to start over with was burned last week in New Orleans to keep the Yankees from getting it; my Negroes have vanished; my command is going to be surrendered. Only I, myself, am left to me. I have told General Johnston not to include me in any surrender. Never. I didn't want war. I didn't want Secession. But now I will fight on in Texas or Mexico or from the trees so long as there is a damned Yankee left in the world to fight.

Wade Hampton didn't get to fight on. Johnston had aleady sent his name in with the surrendering officers when he received Hampton's note.

But I'll not be humiliated by a single one of them, Hampton was thinking as he trotted his big bay charger, Butler, the veteran of Gettysburg and Trevillian, slowly up to the Bennet House again a week later. His nephew, Wade Hampton Manning, rode glumly beside him, carrying the flag of truce, to join General Johnston and General Sherman in a final peace conference.

The flat and sandy fields all around lay under a haze of delicate pastel shadings of red and blue where sorrel and toadflax grew together. Massed spikes of blue lupines rose along the roadside; and beneath the longleaf pines, where giant cones and foot-long pine needles carpeted the ground, hound's-tooth violets and miniature flags lifted their gentle flowers. A wash of yellow above the violets and flags, thousands of biscuit-shaped flowers of pitcher plants nodded gracefully on slender stems. White dogwood lighted the forest edge. Purple wisteria and yellow jessamine dripped like garlands from rotting fences and greening trees.

Butler shied violently at an oak stump covered with a swarm of honeybees, parts of the cluster descending the stump like drippings of yellow candle wax. A little farther along he trotted through a great swirl of apple petals carried from a hillside orchard and all along the way larks and thrushes sang in the spring sunlight.

Under his breath Hampton hummed an old love song. He was thinking of Margaret Preston, the mother of his two sons who now lay dead beside her. *Nothing is left of Millwood, Margaret darling, except four broken columns. Four broken lives: yours, cut off so young; our lovely sons, little Wade and magnificent Preston; the fourth column is my broken heart. For what is my life without my loved ones? A burned-out house, a shell, a mocking memory of vanished loveliness. April was your favorite month. The month your roses began to bloom at Millwood—*

"General Hampton—"

Hampton turned in his saddle, arrogantly inclining his head toward the blue-uniformed man on the speckled horse.

"General Hampton, I received your challenge from pretty little Captain Lowndes to meet me on a field of combat with one thousand of your men armed with the saber alone against fifteen hundred of mine to settle the question as to which were the best men—Northerners or Southerners."

"That was in answer to your suggestion that our attack on your camp at Fayetteville was unfair and if we met you in proper battle the outcome would have been quite different."

"Let's settle the question personally, now. There are enough men of both sides as witnesses. I'll jump it off with you."

Hampton frowned disgustedly. He despised Kilpatrick and he considered such a childish exhibition beneath his dignity.

"Bold beyond arrogance," one of Kilpatrick's officers said loudly, catching Hampton's expression.

"I've heard he doesn't even know how to use that big sword he wears. It's just for show," another said.

"Insolent and vulgar—typical of his class which I hate with a perfect hatred," still another said.

The comments annoyed Hampton, who had trotted on past Kilpatrick. Reining in Butler, he gestured courteously for General Kilpatrick to jump the fence he had designated.

Kilpatrick spurred the speckled horse which rose to the fence but missed his stride and thumping the wood with his belly struggled across clumsily.

Wade Manning laughed, waving the flag of truce gaily.

Hampton himself smiled, then he gently twitched his bridle and put Butler over the fence like a bird with a foot of daylight to spare!

The remainder of the way to the Bennet House he trotted more briskly, singing now—

> Then hoe it down an' scratch your gravel
> To Dixie's Land I'm bound to travel.
> Look away—

Yes—look far away—far ahead away.

PART FIVE

The Day of Jubilee
South Carolina,
July, 1868

CHAPTER XXII

HER DRESS was salmon organdy, its full stiffened over-skirt caught here and there with big bows of black velvet. Her neck and shoulders, as close-textured and light tan still as if she were a young woman, were bare. She had pinned a pearl and diamond cluster, which held four tawny lilies, in her knob of oiled, jet hair and she stood now, splendidly, before the Columbia Hotel bedroom mirror not long enough to show her entire six feet plus the French heels and the lilies. She clasped a necklace of the same diamonds and pearls around her neck and again for a moment, surveyed herself in the mirror. She knew that she looked impressive. Quite as regal as Mrs. Witherspoon, who had pawned the jewels in Pushkin's new secondhand store in Edgefield and been unable to reclaim. I don't have to be white to look impressive, Duchess thought—I've never wanted to be white—a satisfying thought. Money, a husband bigger than she, a house with columns—what more could a white woman attain? Those things compared with being white, ah, she knew which she would always choose.

It was better not to be white now. The war being over, the outside pressure upon both political parties at the North being removed, they were snarling at each other over the policy of reconstruction in the South. The captured gray fox was lying passive on the sand, its proud brush matted with blood and grit while the dogs fought over the weary carcass. Thank the Lord for Charles Sumner who had had the guts to shake his fist in President Johnson's face and yell that without Negro suffrage the four years' war was a failure. And the lamb turned into a lion, Andrew Johnson, had answered that he despised a secessionist but he despised a fanatic still more. Enough of him. He had shielded the South for three years, stuck to Lincoln's plan for reconstruction with a welcoming hand held out to the

185

rebellious states, and insisted upon restricted suffrage for the Negro.

During those years she had pushed Chance into the wagon business, the real-estate business, the lumber business and got richer every day, biding her time. But when old Salmon Chase had come down to South Carolina to make his vitriolic hate-breeding radical speeches, and seen so many black faces massed before him, he had suddenly come to his senses—votes—these were not poor bewildered homeless human beings—they were Votes! And The Day of Jubilee had come! Grim Thad Stevens took up the chant: Votes! Votes! along with the obscene but powerful Stanton, Oliver P. Morton, Julian, Wendell Phillips, and Charles Sumner, still smarting under the sting of the youthful Preston Brooks's whip-line cane. They had finally broken Johnson even though they were unable to impeach him and convinced Grant that the day of the generous soldier was gone—the day of the politician was at the noon and he could be President if he came along with them. The Day of Jubilee had come! The Radicals ruled in Washington and Ulysses S. Grant would be elected President in November. They couldn't fail.

Not even for India did she feel a spark of compassion. Chance had insisted on helping India and her husband a little. He had seen to it that India protected the Allan property from the Negro militia and the Yankees and got the cotton picked, by offering a properly notarized contract to the field Negroes, to remain at Shepherd's Grove and work, with one-third of the crop as their freedmen's wages; for the house servants a wage of four dollars a month as soon as the war was ended. Chance had traded a practically new wagon to India for one of the old cane sofas in the parlor at the Grove which wasn't strong enough for him and her to sit on; which she in turn had sold to Pushkin for fifty dollars and he later sold up North for five hundred. Chance had told her to trade mules to India for the saddle horses and she had traded her good mules, or pretty good, for the old horses, or pretty old. He had even made her send out to Shepherd's Grove some of

India's mother's linen sheets, from the big chest she had brought from Charleston that she kept locked in her attic, when he heard about the raiders tearing up all Miss Emmy's bed sheets for a snowstorm.

Who would have thought, in St. Philip's Church when she'd held the infant India on a satin cushion while the bishop signed her with a watery cross, that any turn of events would come wherein the St. Julien heiress, born with a gold spoon if any child ever had, would now be actually in the cotton field while she, the St. Julien slave, was wearing Paris frocks and had money to throw out of the window if she took a notion!

She had not wanted Chance to know just now much she had hated helping India. Except for the one weak moment when she'd gone to her when the boy was born, she never thought of the little girl baby she had nursed.

Thoughts of the baby India brought up memories of the hated Guy St. Julien. The high moment of her life had been the afternoon she called at the St. Julien house the past January in her new imported carriage with a coachman and footman; Chance, a delegate, having taken her to the Reconstruction Convention in Charleston.

On lifting the unpolished lizard knocker and having the gate opened to her by a bleary eyed Mr. Hurley, she had been surprised but not a mite sorry. Not even when Mr. Hurley had told her with relish how he had taken possession of the wrecked house the day after Sherman's men marched away leaving Guy St. Julien dead of a seizure, hanging by his arms from the jujube tree in the walled garden, dressed in an old dirty party dress that had belonged to India as a girl.

"Why did they hang him by his arms?" Duchess had asked, wishing it had been his neck and he had strangled not just died.

"Because he wouldn't tell them where he'd hidden the silver. They didn't intend to kill him."

"Where had he hidden it?"

"Nobody knows. That nigger who waited on him had run away and the old woman who lived with him hightailed it to a relative's when the Yankees smashed

all the mirrors in the drawing room. She may have told
Miss India. I hope she did. Miss India deserves the
silver, her with that pretty hair."

"Why did they chop up the stairway?" She eyed the
makeshift ladder, glad that the lovely spiral was destroyed.

"I don't know. All I know is that now this house
is mine by right of possession and paying taxes on it
for three years and I've got lots of other houses too, but
nobody knows. I'm letting niggers live in them now
to fool the Yankee soldiers. But they're mine all right.
I've paid taxes on them. My beautiful houses! Say—
would you like to stay here with me? Ain't you the
one used to—"

"I was the child's nurse. But I wouldn't spend a
night in this house for a million dollars. It's haunted."

"Ah, go on. T'ain't. I've been living here for three
years and not seen a ghost yet."

"You will!"

From there she had gone to the churchyard. Why—
she could never tell. Cows and goats were grazing
among the mossy headstones. The whole district
around here, burned in the dreadful fire of December,
1861, looked like a vast graveyard with broken walls
and blackened chimneys. And there Guy St. Julien lay
with a goat eating nettles off his grave. She shooed the
goat away. If the nettles were pulled up, wild violets
might come. Leave him lay among weeds and nettles.
The Day of Jubilee had come.

It had come indeed. The Reconstruction Convention
composed of seventy-six Negroes and forty-eight whites
had seen to that. The whites had all been carpetbaggers, adventurers, and Northern politicians; but what
did that matter? The Negroes would get rid of them in
time as they had ridded themselves of the aristocrats.
Henceforth this would be a Negro paradise and why
not the Duchess as its queen?

She had drawn on her long white gloves and fastened
over them on each large wrist a heavy gold bracelet
(one of a pair given by the Tsar to Lucy Pickens and
which she had lately sold to Pushkin) and had taken
up her black gauze shawl with the green silk fringe—

she loved fringe—when Chance and another man
walked into the sitting room of their suite. Chance
looked grand as a duke in his tailor-made black broadcloth frock coat carrying his high stovepipe hat in the
crook of his arm as she had taught him to do. He was
easy to teach being a born mimic. She wished he were
quicker to think for himself—like Prince Rivers, a
member of the House of Representatives from Edgefield, a big black Negro whose mind was as sharp as a
kitchen knife and who hated white people as she did.

Chance didn't hate anybody. No matter what form of
ridicule she used he still tipped his hat to white people
and spoke respectfully to ones whom he had driven in
the Allan scarlet coach in the days of his servitude.
Why he'd even gone up and congratulated General
Hampton on a speech he had made at a Democratic
rally last week urging peace and harmony between
the races! Urging the Negroes not to listen to the radical
shrieks of hate! steal! destroy! grind down the former
oppressors! But to let themselves be led down a per-
manent path to genuine freedom and prosperity.

"He's right, honey," Chance had said that afternoon. "You had me all mixed up; Mr. Hampton's
right."

Who wanted ultimate benefits? Not the Duchess.
She wanted her privilege now. Her full cup of privilege now today while the sap in her flowed strong
and lusty for the enjoyment of earthly pleasure. Down
with Wade Hampton and all his breed! Down—down—
down!

Striding grandly into the sitting room she greeted the
Mulatto with Chance. This was Francis Cardozo, Governor Scott's new Secretary of State. Born of a Negro
mother and a Jewish economist in Charleston, he had
graduated with highest honors from Glasgow University,
where he had been sent by his father.

"Your husband has accepted an important position with me in the State Department," Cardozo said,
taking Duchess's hand with much finesse.

"And you've been invited to dance at Governor
Scott's Inaugural Ball tomorrow night, honey. You look
mighty pretty but ain't—aren't—you too dressed up?

Would you like to go to Janney's Hall with us and
watch the session from the gallery this afternoon?"
Chance said carefully in his trained voice.

She had spent years with his diction and grammar.
Now he sounded better than any of the white ones in
the Legislature except Franklin Moses and T. J. Robertson. She had given him just the right British inflec-
tion to make them think that he had been educated
abroad. "From Edinburgh University," she had told
the wife of one of the haranguing common carpetbagger legislators who hadn't got out of lower school
herself. "Such a distinction, don't you think?" She had
blown cigar smoke at the pasty-faced creature who had
agreed quickly, excusing herself to go and lie down
with a headache. Frightened out of her wits by me,
Duchess thought grimly. Scared to death of Negroes.
And she'd better be. I might eat her up someday. I
might at that!

Looking down from the gallery onto the Assembly
was like looking down onto a field of varicolored glob-
ular fruits. The faces were of every color from the
unhealthy white of the new-come Northerner through
the creamy Octoroon, the tan Mulatto, to the deep blue-
black of the African Gullah.

They were dressed in every sort of garment: the
long narrow coat of the evangelist; the black frock
coat of the genteel serving man; blue broadcloth swallow-tailed coats hastily snatched from the closet of a
master fighting in the trenches around Petersburg; the
stub jackets and slouch hats of the laborer unable to
read or write, too poor to outfit himself, but now a
lawmaker of the state of South Carolina; some had tied
heavy mufflers, though it was July, around their necks
to hide the fact that they wore no shirt.

My God! thought Duchess—look at this!

To divert herself she thought of the dance she had
had with white little Franklin Moses a few nights before.

"Mrs. Devonshire—" (Neither the Duchess nor
chance had had a last name and when they registered
to vote she, suddenly remembering a copy of a painting she had once seen that India had told her was

called The Duchess of Devonshire, had said instantly, "Chance and Duchess Devonshire." A good name. Suitable.) "Mrs. Devonshire—"

She bent her head to catch the little man's words. "You remind me very much of a lady whose husband I used to work for before I changed my politics."

"Who was that?"

"Lucy Pickens."

The image of the titian-haired beauty rose before her. She said, "My God, however could that be?"

"You both are obsessed by the idea that dressing a man up in a frock coat and a stovepipe hat, telling him exactly what words to say on every occasion, you can, with a push here and a shove there, land him on any throne you think you yourself would ornament."

"Humph," she answered making herself so tall that he only came to her shoulder, looking high over his greasy head for the rest of the fast-jumping polka.

Now, listening to the fluency of debate or, to be frank, the endless chatter going on down there on the floor about ways to raise money, how many gold spittoons to place on order, how best to go about catching and punishing the Ku Klux, free schools, higher and higher taxes, numerous bond issues, the disarming of the whites, outlawing dueling, the arming and drilling of black militias, she almost wished she had gone for a drive in the carriage instead of coming here. Would there be no end to this gush and babble? It was more like a camp meeting than a debate and the new Governor from Massachusetts who was to be sworn in with great splendor tomorrow night was putting his head close to his Secretary of State, who looked as though the Governor's breath smelled bad, laughing and pointing derisively now at one and now at another hysterical, ignorant speaker.

The Negro in the Speaker's chair, unfamiliar with procedure, did not even try to suppress the loose debate where no one was allowed to speak over five minutes without someone else bellowing above the tattoo of the Speaker's hammer.

Chance was trying to say something and what was he saying? Everybody a fair deal Negro or white? Was he crazy? Evidently they thought so for someone howled him down with, "What about the Klu Kluck?"

Flies were buzzing and the heat and smell were unbearable. Duchess left her seat and wandered out past the bar at the head of the steps where whisky and boxes of expensive cigars were served at the state's expense.

"Send two boxes of champagne and a box of the best cigars to me at my hotel," she told the Irish bartender who knew her well. Then she went downstairs into the open air where a small late afternoon breeze was blowing over the blackened ruins of the desolated city. This was the first of the Revolution. She supposed all first stages were like this. She was more fortunate than most Negroes having always lived with quality and not only had an education but the wits to go with it. She could skip this stage.

She did not understand that underneath all the shocking burlesque upon legislative proceedings back there in the Hall there was something very real about the uncouth and ignorant multitude. They had a genuine earnestness and interest that shone bright in contrast to the Moses, the Scotts, the Chamberlains, the Whippers, the Mackeys, the T. J. Robertsons who thought they would fatten on the unsuspecting legislators. The Negroes in there, whatever their foolish clothes, had an earnest purpose, born of the knowledge that though they were up today they might be down again tomorrow. Their primitive shouts were at least sincere and important in their own minds as compared to the honeyed speeches of Moses. Three years ago they were hoeing cotton under the whip of a coarse overseer. They had now escaped from the darkness into the Jubilee. They were seeing God Almighty.

Across the street Duchess noticed a thin shabby woman leading two little girls by the hand. Looking up, the woman stared at her and after a minute's hesitation waved. It was Nannie Rutledge from Charleston who had married the big Prioleau boy. Duchess did not return Nannie's wave but, bowing haughtily, noticed the worn scuffly shoes of the children and the stringy crepe of Nannie's black widow's bonnet.

Smoothing her own expensive stiff salmon organdy, she felt very happy and well off. So well off that she let herself slouch a little against the bench as she took a long fragrant cigar from her silver case and licking the end deftly with her tongue, lit it and blew puffs of smoke up toward the summer sky.

CHAPTER XXIII

THAT SAME AFTERNOON India, in a faded blue homespun dress buttoned down the front with persimmon seeds, was sitting on Flossie's sweaty back in the middle of an open field of blooming cotton. She put on and took off as the breeze blew and ceased, a big hat woven of wheat straw fringed around the front of the brim with gaudy peacock feathers to keep away yellow flies and gnats. So long as she remained with them the Negro women worked adequately and this year the crop promised well enough to pull Shepherd's Grove outs of debt, pay the taxes, and start them on the road to recovery.

It was perfect cotton weather—hot days, hot nights, dry, the dust like powdered tobacco over all except the silky blue sky decorated with white goose-feather clouds. To her left, beyond the cotton were layers of tasseled corn and on her right a growth of virgin pine casting long and longer black fingers toward Flossie's restive feet. In front of the pines along the little wagon road big white mallows were blooming amid clumps of black-eyed-Susans and Queen Anne's lace, rabbit peas, bright orange butterfly weed, and the rampant blue-flowered passion vine.

A scarlet tanager sang high up in a pine tree. India could distinctly see the glowing scarlet and jet black of the jolly male bird ventriloquist in the tallest pine at the edge of the forest, yet his song sounded directly below her on a cotton blossom! The birds had been incredibly beautiful and full of song this whole summer on the plantation as if trying to make up for the drabness that had come into their lives. She watched

a wood duck drake, who had a nest in the orchard
near the deep woods, fly slowly past. He looked like an
oriental mosaic with his blue, green, purple, black,
white, red, chestnut, and buff feathers. He was crying,
peet! peet! and from a peach tree his lady whistled
plaintively in welcome, oo——eek! oo——eek!

Over all hung the heavy sweetness of wild grape and
bay blossoms and the women hoeing cotton were singing slowly in time to their truculent chop-chopping of
the bushy plants:

> Dis time anudder year
> I may be gone
> To Jubilee
> Oh Lord how long!
> My brudder broke de ice and gone
> Oh Lord how long
> My brudder broke de ice and gone
> Oh Lord how long!
>
> Befo' dis time and anudder year
> I may be gone
> To de land of glory
> Oh Lord how long!
> Mind my sister how you stride de row
> Oh Lord how long!
> Your right foot slip and y'ur los' y'ur hoe
> Oh Lord how long!
>
> One a dese mornings
> It won't be long
> De sun come up
> De moon be gone
> Gonter hitch on wings and sing a song
> Oh Lord how long
> And fly to freedom singing dat song
> Oh Lord how long!

Three rifle shots rang out from near the highroad.
Since July Fourth, guns and cannons had been fired all
during the day and night throughout the district in
celebration by the Yankees and Negroes of the Radical

governor's inauguration. Most of her Negro field hands
had stopped work to go to town and join in the frolics.
Everything was in disorder. Had been in disorder since
the black troops had been quartered all over the
country at the close of the war to insult and degrade
the whites and to instill into the minds of the quiet
and orderly-disposed rural population a bitter hostility,
now showing itself in acts of violence.

Aunt Childs had written from Cousin Tiphaine
Ware's at Pinopolis that two of her cousins, young
girls eighteen and twenty, had been made to walk naked
in front of a line of black militia in order to save
their father from being shot; at a church in Sumter
District armed uniformed Negroes had broken in and
chased the white-haired minister from the pulpit; there
had been mobs, riots and killings in Charleston;
churches everywhere had been robbed of the commun-
ion linen and silver; houses burned; cotton stolen. Here
in the Up Country no white woman dared appear alone
on the streets or roads; yet while the feeling against
these outrages was intense, it was directed more at the
Radicals in Washington, the carpetbaggers, the soldiers,
the scalawags, the instigators of this spirit, than against
the Negro himself.

Even more fantastic than the sudden freeing of the
thousands of Negroes to wander homelessly, hungrily
about the state had been the sudden evaporation of
everybody's money. The banks had failed, the rail-
roads were ruined, Confederate greenbacks were not
worth the paper they were printed on. Overnight, for-
tunes had disappeared and the only money anybody
had was what few gold or silver coins jingled at the
bottom of their shabby purses.

India shifted her weight on the worn velvet sidesaddle and looked over toward the library. Max was lying
on the shaded grass staring up at the treetops with
Steeben beside him in a low rocking chair sewing buttons on a suit he was making for his "boy." Mrs.
Gryder, a small farmer nearby, had spun and woven
some good white cotton cloth, in exchange for some
lespedeza seed she'd got from Mr. Ravenal in Aiken,

and Steeben had cut out a jaunty white frock coat and tight pants like the clothes Max had worn before the war.

What was Max thinking lying there on the cool grass looking up at the silky sky, doing nothing except threading old Steeben's needle every once in a while? Did he think? Did he care about anything? Was he lonely? As India looked over at the golden hair gleaming in a shaft of sunshine, she recalled the past four years, when night after night she had gone up to her big empty room to stand at the window watching the flicker of his candle out in the library, wondering how he could be so indifferent to the rush of desire his presence caused in her whenever they were near each other. He seemed to live spiritually wrapped in a magic cloak of invisibility, seeing slip by, uncounted, sunset after dawn, day after day; not noticing as foreshadowing the end of summers, that the chuck-will's-widow, the cardinal ceased their songs and the quails started their passionate calling in the sedge. The quails! Whenever she heard them she had to bury her face in the pillow and weep for all the ecstasy throbbing in that soft "Bob-white! bob-white!"

She recalled how after the end of the war Calbraith Butler had come almost every day telling this and that about the cavalry to bring a spark to Max's eyes but, while Max had been polite, he had drummed restlessly with his fingers until Calbraith at last came only occasionally with Maria and the children for a social call or to hear Miss Emmy play upon the harp. She remembered the August evening the first summer he was home when he had suddenly asked to have his bed carried from the billiard room into the library and in the dusk Danny had moved mattresses and necessaries to the octagonal little house in the pine grove and she had walked beside Max holding a lantern, not daring to touch him or to say "Why not our room, beloved"; how high under a veil of cloud had trembled a mockingbird filling the night with silver sounds, while above the pines, with a thick pompous flapping of wings a giant owl flew, hooting at the mockingbird.

She sighed deeply and the pines seemed to grieve

with her; the weeping of the little brook that ran through the forest sounded louder on her ear. One of the women called,

"Ain't hit time to quit?"

"Let's finish this field. You all can have tomorrow off for the big barbecue in town."

From the lane came the tinkle-clank of the home cows; a June bug zoomed halfway around her and was gone.

She looked over the land that belonged to Maximilian Allan. Thoughts of this land, cares for it, had filled her mind and kept her heart from breaking. She had worked and planned—somehow never till this minute had she realized how hard and desperately she had worked to keep up the plantation and the house—just in case, just in case, someday he might waken and cry, "I am I! Maximilian Allan!"

Would she never grow wise and strong and tough enough to live a day without craving that it be *the* day she could say, "See, I was right, he *has* remembered!" Would this longing for him always gnaw within her, this longing to be again his India of the wisteria vine.

In those days she had been willing to leave her father, her home, dare anything rather than lose him. To bind him to her she had given him everything: her love and her body, her honor and her father's honor, and his devotion to his only child. She had thrown away the heritage of her parents, let her father die alone and in terror, let the house in Charleston pass into alien hands, rather than leave him even for a night when he came home wounded and lost from the Battle of Burgess Mill. She had let Irene cradle and foster her precious son so that she might be free first to follow Max, later to care for him and his plantation. She had staked everything she had on Max's love. And she would not cease to fight for it. His body was lying over there in the shadows. It *was* his body. Otherwise her craving for this man would have dimmed. She had chosen him first in a very frenzy of love and she chose him again every day that passed. His wild reckless passion she missed as though someone had torn a

living part of her away leaving her screaming in an
agony of wanting. Yet now the fight was not alone for
his body, but for his mind and his soul. And she would
fight to regain him as long as there was breath in her
throat.

Max—Max—! When she first saw him at White
Sulphur, half-naked in the afternoon sunlight, the muscles at the back of his neck as compelling as a God's,
this love had taken possession of her. In the months
here at Shepherd's Grove before he went to war, life had
opened full and perfect around her. Then the strangeness of his injury had burst upon them like a mortar
shell and a deep dark crater lay between him and her.
Would she ever be able to leap across it? Would she?

Max, my love!

Out of the afternoon stillness came the hoofbeats of
three horses on the hard dry road.

India touched Flossie with her heel and Flossie, hating the sight and smell of a cotton field ever since the
day she had had the indignity of a plow forced on her
lovely hindquarters by the determined India, kicked at
one of the Negro women and received a jab with a
splintery hoe handle in return.

Here came Lucy Pickens, chic and cool-looking in a
cream-colored linen riding skirt, a tight jacket of the
same soft linen, and a brown linen cap held on by a
flesh-colored French veil tied over her face. With her
was her ten-year-old daughter, Douschka, on a fast
brown mare and little Cantelou Allan on the meanest
pony in the District, called the Little Tsar. The three
were laughing and calling Halloo! Halloo!

India joined them at the flagstone turnaround and by
the time they reached the piazza, Danny was waiting at
the block to take the horses to the well for water.
Emmy, looking rather like a fat priest in a baglike
cotton garment, was bringing a china pitcher of chilled
scuppernong wine, calling Steeben to put aside his sewing and fetch more refreshments. Mr. Wu came barking
and standing on his hind legs at the sound and smell of
little Cantelou.

"Hello, dears. Have you ever known such heat? Not

like White Sulphur used to be, is it?" Lucy perched on the joggling board, her divided skirt showing her brown soft calf boots and shapely ankles. Cantelou hugging the hot hairy dog in his arms climbed up as close beside Lucy as possible, looking as if she might disappear at any moment if he took his eyes off her.

"Don't crowd so close to Miss Lucy, Cantelou—you're hot and dirty."

"Don't scold Cantelou, India; after all, someday he'll be a man and a handsome one at that." Lucy gently pushed a lock of soft sooty black hair from Cantelou's wide intelligent forehead.

"Lady Pick likes me," Cantelou said stubbornly.

Emmy said, "Lucy, you've taken your exile here in the country better than I thought you could. Aren't you going anywhere at all this summer?"

"No; I'd love to go to Washington and see Joe Jefferson in *Rip Van Winkle* or hear dear old Fanny Kemble give some of her superdramatic readings from *Othello* interspersed with anecdotes of the days when she was in the clutches of a wicked Southerner. I miss the theater more than anything. I don't mind the heat nearly so much as the dullness of things."

"I would like to see the circus," Douschka said. "Papa told me last night that someday when we get rich and he is Governor again he would take me to see Dan Rice's circus and I could pet the elephants and the tigers if I chose."

"I'd rather pet Lady Pick," Cantelou said, laughing merrily along with the ladies.

India said, "I wanted to take Max to White Sulpher this summer. I thought something there might remind him of the past but we just couldn't scrape up the extra money."

"I wanted to go too but old Pick isn't strong enough and he's so cross and querulous they'd probably ask us to leave within a week. I wonder what it's like now with all the new rich crowding in?"

"I suppose it's gay and glamorous as ever. General Lee had everybody bowing to him the morning he and Mrs. Lee walked into the dining room at the White. I

wonder who is in the Colonnade this year?" India
flicked her hat at Mr. Wu and he snapped at the waving feathers.

Emmy said, "Mrs. Ball from Laurens was here last
week and she said that poor Mary McDuffie, like her
father, has gotten so horribly nervous that the doctors
told Wade he must take her to the Springs this summer
to avert a complete breakdown and they had to rent
rooms in the cheapest boardinghouse at the cheapest
most unfashionable Spring in Virginia, now that he's
lost his house in the Colonnade."

"Ten summers ago he was the King of White Sulpher. Any invitation from him, to the Colonnade, was
prized like a royal command. What happened to his
house there?" India said.

"What happened to your plantation in Mississippi?"
Lucy asked.

"We sold it to Mr. Burney for taxes. Where's Irene?"
India couldn't bear thinking of the Master of the Hunt
at a cheap boardinghouse so she turned to Cantelou,
"I thought you were with Irene, Cantelou."

And Emmy said, "Where'd you leave Sister, son?"

"She went to the ice-cream parlor with old Pushkin
and was acting so silly that when I saw Douschka and
Lady Pick I rode off with them."

Emmy frowned. India and Lucy looked at each
other, their mouths tight, lest they speak the disapproval they so plainly felt in front of the children.
Emmy did not seem scandalized, but she was annoyed.
Very coldly she said,

"Irene seems to be keeping rather strange company
lately. She hates being poor."

"We all do." Lucy pulled off a soft chamois gauntlet
and reached for a tea cake from the silver waiter that
Steeben was passing. "We hate being poor more than
we hated being defeated. I've had to sell some of my
favorite jewels. The reason Cantelou saw us in town
today—I was doing business with Sir Pushkin so that
I could have a ball tomorrow night."

India said to Lucy, "Oh, wonderful—Max will have
somewhere to wear his new suit! Only—"

"Only what!"

"Irene always makes him so self-conscious when I take him to parties or picnics that I have about given up trying to make him sociable. He never dances anyway. He says he doesn't know how. Perhaps we'd better not come."

"You've got to come. I stopped by the Marshalls' on the way here and Kevin's red-haired cousin from Virginia, Ervin, is visiting them. 'Will charming young Mrs. Allan be there?' and I told him of course you'd be there. Leave Irene at home. She never adds anything. Max does. He is our man of mystery and good for at least an hour's conversation. Everybody is utterly fascinated as to whether he is or isn't; whether you are living in or out of sin; whether—"

"Lucy—Lucy—you know he is Max. I didn't think anybody listened to Irene's shoddy tales," India said quickly.

"I thought it would be comforting to have our own ball in the real Governor's mansion while the barbarians revel in Columbia," Lucy went on airily.

"I hear Scott has invited many of the important people in Columbia to his ball. None bothered to refuse but have no idea of appearing." Emmy called to Steeben to pour some more scuppernong wine.

"No thanks," Lucy was rising and Douschka and Cantelou ran to tell Danny to fetch back the horses. "Isn't that Max lying over there on the grass?"

"Yes," India said.

"My dear, are you *really* sure that man is Max?"

"Of course, Lucy." India waved her homemade feathered hat impatiently at a mosquito.

"Well, I certainly agree. No one but Max would lie there comfortably in the shade while you spent the afternoon playing overseer to cotton choppers in the July sun."

Even India smiled but Lucy had spoken loudly. Max had heard. He jumped up and went running over to a field where a Negro man had just walked off, thoughtlessly leaving a mule hooked to a plow. Vehemently Max jerked up the plow handles, slapped the back of the mule with the wornout lines and, true as an arrow, made a perfect furrow.

The women watched from the piazza as he reached the end of the row, executed a quick neat turn and came back, straight, to the near end of the field. Again he turned and headed back, expertly. Emmy put a big hand on India's trembling arm, and after one glance at her drained face said,

"Maximilian never touched a plow handle in all his life, India."

Lucy said to India, "What difference does it make? He couldn't be handsomer. That scar, since it's healed, only adds to his charm. Be sure and bring him tomorrow night. I don't care whether Irene comes or not."

"I'll have an attack at the last minute and she'll have to stay at home with me," Emmy smiled widely. "I'll eat a whole bowl of *coeur flottant à la crème*—that is if India will let me be so extravagant."

"She will. It will be worth it. Look at Douschka!"

The little girl was galloping Bonny Belle down the avenue, standing upright first on one bare foot then on the other, her fat ginger-colored plait slapping up and down against her boy's trousers. Lucy mounted and settling gracefully in her sidesaddle caught up with the child at the entrance to the forest.

"Hurry back," Emmy called to Lucy.

India started over to the field but Emmy caught her wrist and said. "No, child, perhaps Maximilian is awakening. Leave him undisturbed."

India slumped down on the joggling board staring at the powerful graceful figure plodding in the open field and with only a small interest listened to little Cantelou's excited explanation of going to Edgewood from town with Lucy and Douschka before coming here.

"Granny, Lady Pick was up on the piazza combing her hair in the sunshine and it looked more like sunshine than the real sunshine. There were three peacocks roosting in the magnolia tree by the piazza with their long tails hanging down and Douschka and I each sat on one of the iron watch dogs by the steps and Miss Lucy held out a hair—just one hair, like the hair the younger son found the princess by—and she said, 'Isn't it beautiful!' "

CHAPTER XXIV

THE CLOCK on the mantelpiece showed nearly five o'clock. Its hot glitter gone from the day, the light was softer. For a moment, refreshed by her bath, India sat on the steps by the bed. She looked down at her hands. They were rough and sunburned and her arms right up to the elbows were brown and the muscles hard as wood. Her slim hips hadn't enough womanly curve, but looked as if they belonged to a supple boy, and her face that Duchess used to make her wash in cucumbers and milk every night so that its whiteness would be dazzling against her black hair, was as dark and flushed as a gypsy's. Only her hair was still the same: soft and sooty as ever, falling thickly about her shoulders.

Oh, what a horrible dream! She had lain down after the three o'clock dinner of chicken pilau and fried okra and fallen into a deep heavy sleep. Even in the high-ceilinged, shaded room the heat had been heavy. Max was by the window smiling as he had smiled that afternoon in the Richmond hospital: a smile full of irony, all of his strong white teeth gleaming in the afternoon sunlight. He threw back his head, smiling, showing his teeth and she struggled to tell him not to show his teeth when he smiled, to scream a warning to him that if he showed his teeth he would turn into a wounded stranger. But still he smiled while from the piazza below she heard Mr. Wu and a stray hound barking at a flock of pot-racking guineas. Her will, her body tossed desperately and she pushed her voice with her hands until she woke screaming, "Stop smiling like that— don't smile anymore—"

She was still troubled when she went to the armoire and took out her one good dress. Steeben had made it last Easter out of an old black silk apron. He had carefully picked the silk to pieces; mixed a little wool with it to make a nice filling for the long staple cotton warp, and woven a length of soft gray filmy stuff that looked almost like an iridescent gauzy India muslin. If only her skin weren't so sunburned, she thought, not realizing how vital she looked in the off-shoulder pale gown, the waistline tucked high under her full breasts, a poppy-red scarf with scalloped edges about her shoulders.

She went down the stairs into the wide hall in which the late afternoon light fretted through the millions of pine needles in the grove was like light at the bottom of the fountain in the boxwood garden.

She almost dreaded to see Max after the dream and the episode of his plowing. He had plowed again today but refused to discuss it when they all gathered at the dinner hour. He had reached a crisis. They had all been aware of it. His goldish eyes had darted from one to another of them oddly. Was he remembering something? Lucy Pickens's derision had been the first thing to pierce inside him as far as she could tell. Did she want a crisis to come? She stopped suddenly still, as abruptly as though she had come to a new wall. For a moment her face was twisted as though in pain. Then she mastered herself and, the scalloped edges of her scarf fluttering in the dim still air, went out onto the piazza.

She heard footsteps. Max was walking over the graveled path from the library toward the house. The white cotton suit Steeben had made fitted him closely and he had pulled a wide fine Panama hat down over his golden hair. From some unlooted trunk had come a ruffled shirt and a bit of thin brown satin for a tie. The midday sun had made his olive skin glow and when he saw her standing there in the last of the sunlight on the piazza he smiled. She whirled abruptly so that she would not see his smile, calling,

"Danny, are you coming with the horses?"

Flossie and Lulu set off at a trot. Long ferns and vines by the roadside flicked at them. A trail of honeysuckle caught in India's stirrup; Max leaned forward and removed it as they rode along. As he did so his knee brushed against her leg and she could feel a thrill run like a hot sword up her thighs.

They passed Cantelou and the Pekingese with three

Negro boys hunting for turtles in the muddy creek. Cantelou ran along beside her for a little way saying,

"You look pretty, Mama. Take me. Douschka said I could come. Take me."

"No, darling, not this time. Another time."

"Meanie!"

She looked back. He was standing in the road watching them, his black hair hanging like a fringe above his stormy eyes, and a pang gripped her heart. He must look like my brother, Norman, she thought. Suppose a wind should come up and hurt him tonight while Irene is waiting on Miss Emmy? It's so hot and still it feels like tornado weather. I can't leave him alone in the road like that. She was about to suggest they turn back when Max said,

"I'm glad to be getting away from that unpleasant old maid and her forked tongue. Let's move along faster."

India almost fell out of the saddle in amazement. But when Flossie jumped to get ahead of Lulu as Max kicked the black mare in the side, she gave herself up to the fast motion and remembering the hunt at the White cried out,

"I'll race you to the highroad."

She tried to hold Flossie back and let him win but the mare was hot and in fine condition. She passed Lulu quickly, hearing Max shout Bravo! after her.

At the highroad they pulled in to a walk. Lulu was blowing like a bellows.

"Let's trade her off for a good mule," he said with unusual animation. "The one I've been plowing is almost ready to drop dead with age. Your Duchess friend must have made quite a profit off that last deal with you. Didn't you swap the steeplechaser, Bella Lee, for him?"

"But Bella Lee wouldn't plow and her mouth had got so hard nobody could ride her. We've got to have two riding horses if we're ever going anywhere together."

"I can ride a good mule better than this old nag."

Ah, no, her heart cried—Max on a mule? By choice? She said to him, "Why don't you trade with Chance this time? He loves you and I know he won't take advantage of us."

The Meeting Street road was clogged with Negroes on their way to town to dance on the square and eat barbecue in honor of the inauguration of their Governor. On muleback, in fancy buggies, afoot and in wagons and oxcarts, they were traveling—orderly as yet, curiously quiet and purposeful-looking. They were moving as might sea gulls before a gale, in one direction; each with his dreams of riches or of vengeance or of merely a long night's frolicking at the Governor's expense. An old woman dressed in rags and driving a sleek pair of Kentucky horses might be the new madame who had bought the Wilson mansion and hung the windows with scarlet lamps; a group of young men had pistols bulging on their hips and shiny knives hidden in their tattered shirts. None moved to get out of the Allans' way. It was the Allans who turned out of the road. Most of the Negroes did not appear to glance at them; a great number scowled and muttered; one threw a clod of earth that fortunately went wide of its mark. India wondered how many of them would be looting and burning and cutting before moonrise.

"Why do they resent us so bitterly?" Max said. "This is the first time I've realized how alone we are at Shepherd's Grove."

Emmy had been explaining the War Between The States to him lately; India had heard her when she came in from the fields for dinner. Telling him, as though he were a foreigner, why South Carolina had seceded from the Union, why war had come, when and why it had ended, the tragedy of Lincoln's assassination, Johnson's amazing courage as President.

So India said: "After the war, President Johnson appointed B. F. Perry as our Governor and he was a good governor. At that time not even Sherman considered giving complete franchise to the Negroes. The next year Orr was elected Governor—Hampton would have been elected had he let them put his name on the ticket. Thousands voted for him anyway. Orr surrounded himself with old die-hards who foolishly passed the 'black code' insuring segregation of the races and no votes for the Negroes. In the meantime Francis Cardozo who, by the way, is a brilliant Negro, organized the Union League, a secret Negro society formed in New York, protected by the Yankee soldiers, and got the Negroes excited and unified. The 'black code' of Orr's administration gave the extremists of the Republican Party the platform they needed and the demagogues poured in with Governor Pickens's former secretary, that nasty little man from Sumter, Moses, as their leader. Don't you remember him at the Pickens's party the night Anderson moved in to Fort Sumter?"

Max shook his head. But he was listening closely to every word she said.

"At the bogus Constitutional Convention arranged by the Radicals last January, the delegates were chosen by all the people except the ones disqualified as voters who fought for the Confederacy or were worth as much as twenty thousand dollars in money or property before Fort Sumter."

"Oh—that was when you took me to vote and made me push all those Negroes out of the way?"

"You remember that?"

"Of course! What a dolt I was."

That was last November 20. She had borrowed the buggy that belonged to Mrs. Gryder, hitched Flossie to it and taken him to town to vote. He had taken the oath—they might let him vote. On the Meeting Street road they met Toney Witherspoon astride a lop-eared mule, going back home, saying wearily, "No use to go. They won't let you vote. They won't let you drive across Log Creek."

"Will you do what I tell you?" she asked Max.

"Yes."

She had hidden a pistol in her skirt and made up her mind to use it. When they got to the bridge across Log Creek, the Negro soldiers threw up their rifles yelling, "Halt!"

Flossie was feeling good that day. India took up the long buggy whip, let out a hunting cry and hit her hard. The infuriated mare leaped into the soldiers like a battering ram. They jumped and scrambled down the ditchbank out of the way but once across the creek there was a line of Negroes two deep blocking the whole road hollering, "Halt! Quit that! Git back!" waving hoes and hickory sticks. Flossie still had that damn-if-I-can-humor and, her eyes red and wild, her small head high and mighty, her hoofs hard and angry galloped straight through the crowd on into town.

In front of the courthouse on the square India saw Big Dick, who had left the plantation and gone into a little grocery business of his own and she asked him if he would hold Flossie. He begged her not to make Max try to vote. "Po' Mista Maxi," he kept saying. "Po' thing." But she was angry now and Max seemed oblivious of anything except the need to follow her like an obedient dog. She led him to the voting place but the strange white man there said, politely enough, "Take your place in the line." Grabbing Max by the arm she pulled him toward the end of the line and on the way passed Philip Abney and the two Calverts who had survived the war, Fant and Cato, sitting on a bench looking whipped and disgusted.

"Why aren't you voting?" she asked them.

"The line never gives out. As fast as one Negro votes he gets back in line ahead of us and goes back and votes again. We haven't a chance. They're hundreds to one against us."

"Get in behind Max. He'll get you there."

Fant Calvert said, "Sure—if he will go first and get his head cracked. 'Twon't make too much difference—for him, I mean."

Hating him, she curbed her tongue, saying, "Max, instead of getting in double rank, get in the middle of the line, and you all get right behind him, one at a time. Now, Max—" He stepped between two big Negroes and his brow was puckered as he looked over at her.

"Sling them right and left with your arms—that's it!"

And before the surprised Negroes knew what was going on, Max was at the box ready to vote. She sat down on the bench exhilarated and excited and when he came back to her she said:

"You were wonderful. That's one good Democratic vote."

"The man at the box told me I had to vote the straight Radical Republican ticket or I couldn't vote! You didn't tell me who to vote for—just to vote."

Philip Abney joined them and said he'd like to leave Edgefield and go to Texas and live. The only job he had been able to find was clerking in a grocery store twelve hours a day but since the Witherspoons' home had been burned he had to support them as well as Hetty and the children. The plantation was a wilderness of briars and scrub growth. Tony Witherspoon worked like a field hand and was barely able to keep from starving. How could a plantation go so to ruin in a few years? She asked him if he knew what Max had just done. Smiling his sweet defeated smile he patted Max gently on the shoulder.

"It doesn't matter, my friend. Our votes wouldn't have been counted anyway."

When they returned to the buggy the Negroes sitting around under the old oak trees on the square in little French gilt ballroom chairs and broken Louis Seize sofas dragged from Mr. Burgess's house, rolled their eyes big at her as though she were a wildcat. She cracked the buggy whip twice in the air. Let them think that. She needed some protection with no angry man on the plantation to look after three women and a little boy.

"Hurrah fuh Mista Linkum!"

"Watch out!" Max's shout interrupted her thoughts.

Two little Negro boys were squatting by the ditch-bank holding hard molded clay balls.

"If you throw one of those," Max rode Lulu up to the boys, "I'll thrash you."

The boys dropped the clods and scuttled into the ditch. Max trotted old Lulu back beside Flossie.

"I haven't had a new white suit in so long that I believe I would have killed those boys if they had messed me up. What have you been thinking of? You haven't said a word in over a mile."

"You," she smiled, "and how well you look tonight.

Here—we're right at the village—take the left road through the gates into the Edgewood park."

From the village square they heard shouts, brass horns and drums, songs and howls, shots and screams and whistling rockets mingled in a wild jungle cacophony of sound.

He said, "Listen to the army of occupation."

But within the gracious shadows of the beautifully wooded park, the jangled noise soon faded into unimportance.

Ahead of them was the Simkinses' victoria and Milledge Bonham's carriage, behind them Hetty and Philip Abney with old Mr. and Mrs. Witherspoon, sitting in spindly Sheraton chairs, rattled along in a one-horse wagon. The avenue of interlocking cedars was laid out in a serpentine leading to a park of primeval oak, hickory and pine strung with colored Japanese lanterns surrounding the house. African geese, spreadtailed peacocks, and gentle deer were wandering among the guests on the smooth soft turf and Mr. Bacon, swathed in his flowing cape, though it was so hot, one hand resting lightly on his hip, called, *"Darlings,* we've been *dying* for you to get here," as Flossie and Lulu trotted stylishly up to the block where Chimpanzee, Lucy's ugly efficient major-domo, sweaty and glorious in his Russian livery still covered with gold embroidery, greeted them with dignity, though Douschka's pet monkey was sitting on his shoulder pulling petulantly at his ear.

The house was a lengthy, beautifully ornamented one-story Greek temple-styled structure, built more than ten feet up from the ground. In the patio to the left a fountain splashed coolly and the air was sweetened with hundreds of blooming roses and deep-scented warm-leafed boxwood. The stone steps with gracefully carved railings led to a gallery over a hundred feet long onto which all of the rooms opened, full now of ladies and gentlemen in odd assortments of finery left over from more fortunate days: organdy and broadcloth, silk and linen, homespun and crinoline, calico and Confederate gray, feathers, fans, fresh flowers, and shabby shoes. They were here from Edgefield, Columbia, Augusta, Abbeville, Laurens, and the big plantations lying between these towns.

A group of trained Negro musicians were down by Log Creek in the summerhouse playing Viennese waltzes to the guests wandering up and down the formal boxwood-bordered walks leading to mounds surmounted by marble statues. Above all towered the great magnolia trees and the other semitropical trees which gave the whole garden a damp coolness and a stale sweetness so satisfying after the sun-scorched day.

Seeing Governor Pickens sitting under the big magnolia tree near the house, India took Max's arm and they went to speak to their host. He was saying to Armistead Burt of Abbeville, in a whiney voice,

"No. I never expect to appear in public again. Did you know that Lucy wrote to President Johnson over and over and he continually refused to pardon me! Why does everybody blame me for Fort Sumter after all these years?" He had the look of a man chronically ill, the winnowed look of someone who endures a special pain. It wasn't altogether a matter of a frail body, tallowish cheeks; it wasn't even the scratchy quality of his once sonorous voice. It was rather his self-pitying smile, his look of detachment. He was like paper which has burned away so slowly that the dead ash retains the shape of solidity yet actually is so flimsy that it will crumble to dust at the first touch.

"Good evening, Maximilian," he said. "You're acting more like yourself. Have you decided whether you are yourself? Oh look—"

Lucy Pickens was standing at the head of the gallery steps, the light from the hall shining through the open door behind her like an aureole. She was wearing a white antique satin dress with rose-point lace draped over the whole skirt and looped up on one side with fresh white roses and a wreath of the same white roses around her head. "That's what she wore when she was first presented to the Tsar. Count Tolstoy clapped his hands and cried, 'The Emperor!' And in he came with his mother on his arm. His eyes were as blue as hers and he had on a blue uniform. And do you know what he said? We all heard—I've never been so proud —he said, looking at Lucy, 'Isn't she beautiful!' "

When it was quite dark the orchestra moved from the terrace into the long parlor in which the Ordinance of Secession had been formulated and drawn up. The heat was as intense as it had been at midday and though all the doors and windows were open not a candle in the widespread glittering crystal chandelier or in the heavy gold candelabrum flickered but burned steadily in an upward fire.

Over the marble mantel Lucy had bought in France, hung a full-length portrait of Alexander the Second, Tsar of all the Russias, painted for her in his full-dress uniform with his tight trousers scandalously revealing. At either side of the mantel on black marble pedestals were Parian marble busts of Lucy and Francis done in Rome and on the mantel was an ornate gold clock loaded with amorous shepherds and shepherdesses, given to Lucy by Count Waleswki, Naopoleon's natural son. On the rosewood piano was another tremendous gold clock with a gold horse and rider that the Shah of Persia had sent, begging her to remember their friendship at all hours of the day and night! Against the exquisitely carved, paneled side walls were gold-leaf mirrors over marble and gilt tables loaded with treasures and gifts from admirers all over Europe and as Lucy stood under the sparkling chandelier calling the guests to come and dance, the Tsar's diamond necklace at her neck, long dripping diamond pendants at her ears, her fingers and arms covered with pear-shaped diamonds of fantastic size and brilliance, she looked like frozen fire in the blazing night.

A gold-liveried butler came up to her with two fragile crystal goblets on a silver waiter and taking one glass she lifted it high, saying,

"A toast to Robert Scott, by the grace of bayonets, Governor of South Carolina!"

A murmur of disapproval ran through the guests but Lucy laughed gaily, lifting the glass and instead of drinking, shattering it against the marble mantel under Alexander's admiring eyes. Three little Negro

boys dressed like tiny Moors were already cleaning up
the splinters when she reached for the second glass of
champagne. By now everybody was crowded in the hall
and parlor watching her and she lifted the glass first
to her old husband in his tangled dead brown wig, then
to Milledge Bonham who had succeeded him as war-
time Governor and she cried,

"To the flower of Governors!"

Servants went among the guests with silver waiters
of champagne glasses and punch cups and the people
drank and toasted: "To the Governor." Poor old Pick
wept while his daughter Maria wiped the tears from his
clayey cheeks and his beautiful young wife went waltzing away, with an infatuated major from Camden, over
the polished floor of her little palace.

"May I have this waltz?" Ervin Marshall was holding out his mangled hand for India's. She instinctively
turned to Max standing beside her looking like a hawk
which had suddenly hooded his yellow eyes against too
bright a light. He nodded, and she, animated as always by dance music, let Ervin lead her in a smooth
glissade onto the floor.

"You are the most beautiful woman here," Ervin
said, bending his red head close to hers, "and I refuse
to call you Mrs. Allan any longer. India—what a
good name for you—so dark, so mysterious—"

"I feel very drab in this poor homemade dress," she
said. "Look at Lucy Pickens."

"You could never be drab. Gray is your color, it
matches your eyes. I prefer summer moonlight to ice
and frost. And you dance so lightly. You are so lightly
made. Just as a woman should be."

A woman! So long since she had been a woman!
So long since a man had wooed her with such pretty
words.

The Danube is Blue—

But that had been so long ago—too long—

Letting herself glide along with the Virginian, the
mood of the music possessed her and instinctively
she threw her head back and laughed happily up at
him looking very young and very, very vulnerable.
Then she wasn't dancing with Ervin but with another

man. Strong arms were around her and she was on fire.
She missed a step but he was such a powerful leader
that she was back in step immediately and she dared
not look at him for fear he would be smiling and far—
too far—away.

So she whispered, when she could speak above the
clamor of her heart, "I thought you said you couldn't
dance."

"Did I?" he said, and now she knew that however
far away he pretended to be he was her love and all
the wanting in the world would never drive her into another's arms.

She tried to let herself droop against him but while
he was waltzing with complete assurance and perfection, he was holding her carefully at a distance and the
expression on his face was so strained that she hardly
dared breathe lest he drop her hand and go back to sit
with Calbraith Butler on the Duncan Phyfe sofa or
join the others who had been maimed by the war
standing outside on the gallery looking enviously
through the open windows at the dancers.

When the last throbbing of the fiddles was drowned
in applause, her partner bowed jerkily and ran from
her through the wide hot hall out into the lantern-lit
night leaving her so agitated and exhilarated that without thinking she let Ervin Marshall reclaim her for the
country dance that Lucy insisted they all take part in
except herself—she sitting like a queen on one of the
sofas by her handsome son-in-law, stroking his big
sensitive hand and every now and then looking sweetly
up into his eyes while he ecstatically thumped the
floor with his artificial leg.

And this time, unlike the square dance she'd had
with the red-haired horseman at the New Year's Day
party in 1861, he didn't jump ahead but could hardly
keep up with her so swiftly did she glide and whirl
along.

A tall Mulatto in an ambassadorial frock coat, a
white starched collar up to his ears, his pomaded hair
brushed back till it stood stiffly on end, fiddle under his
chin, called the dance. The guests lined up as he called,
while all the fiddles played, "Sharem, don' keer how

you sharem, jes so you sharem even. Oh! dat water-
million!"

> Git yo' pardners fust kwattillion!
> Stomp yo' feet and raise 'em high;
> Chune is: Oh! dat watermillion!
> Gwine to get home bime bye!
> S'lute yo' pardners! Scrape perlitely
> Don' be bumping gin de res'
> Balance all! Now, step out rightly
> Alluz dance yo' lebbel bes'
> Fo'ward, foah!—Whoop up!
> Back agin, Don't be so slow!
> Swing co'ners!—Mind de figgers!
> When I hollers, den yo' go!
> Top ladies cross ober
> Hol' till I takes a dram—
> Gemmen solo!—Yes, I'se sober—
> Can't say how de fiddle am.
> Hands around! hol' up yo' faces,
> Don' be looking at yo' feet!
> Swing yo' pardners to yo' places
> Dat's de way—dat's hard to beat.
> Sides fo'ward—when you'se ready
> Make a bow as low's yo' kin
> Swing acrost wid opp'side lady
> Now I'll let you swap agin.
> Ladies change! Shet up dat talking
> Do yo' talkin' arter while
> Right an' lef'! Don' want no walking—
> Make yo' steps and show yo' style!

"Sharem, don' keer how you sharem, jes so you sharem
even!"

The fiddles hushed, the gentlemen bowed to their
ladies as, timed to the second, Chimpanzee stood in the
double doors intoning like a bishop:

"Supper is served."

But no one heard him for out on the lawn a drum
was beating, and over the drum a song came howling—

> John Brown's body lies amould'ring in the grave,
> John Brown's body lies amould'ring in the grave,

John Brown's body lies amould'ring in the grave,
His soul goes marching on!
Glory, glory, hallelujah! Glory, glory, hallelujah.
Glory, glory, hallelujah! His soul is marching on.

Yi—eee—Yi—eee—Jesus—Glory!
Bum-bum-bum-bum-boom-boom-boom!
Onto the gallery crowded the people and out on the
law were hundreds of Negroes. The Japanese lanterns
shone hot in their eyes and flames seemed to flicker
and dart from their eyes and some of them jigged and
most of them howled and they were marching, crushing the roses and one hit a doe on the head with a
stick and one kicked at an African goose, and Moze,
old Steeben's grandson, slick and fancy in a new Yankee uniform with a sword and a pistol at his side, was
leading them, calling them, Hiya! Boomba! Glory—
Glory! They were drunk with rum and drunk with
their freedom and they crushed Lucy Pickens's roses
under their bare splayed toes and they jumped and
capered and some had sticks and more had guns.

And up on the gallery the people stared and the
gold-liveried servants and the women servants in blue
dresses and high caps came and stared, but nobody
said anything while the singing went on and it seemed
like hours but it couldn't have been long before they
finished and melted away into the dark of the deer
woods still singing and jumping and waving their clubs
and firearms and swords.

Lucy Pickens was standing at the head of the steps.
If any of the Negroes had wanted they could have hurt
her, outlined as she was by the light of the open door.
Ervin Marshall was the first to speak.

"How does your neck feel, Marie Antoinette?"

And she said, "They ruined my roses but they
wouldn't have hurt me. However, it was a rather pro-
phetic serenade."

Martin Gary, looking like a violated eagle said, "This
is an outrage—let's go after them and crack their
heads."

And Governor Bonham said, "This is no time for

bloodshed, General. We must organize ourselves as they have done."

"It is just the beginning," Calbraith Butler said. "They have arms and the vote. We haven't anything left—not even fighting spirit."

"Don't they realize we're all paupers?" Mrs. Witherspoon was weeping noisily in a lacy mull handkerchief made from an old baby dress of her father's.

"Why should they, with our hostess standing in the light looking like a living diamond?" Ervin Marshall squeezed India's hand that he still held in his.

And Lucy cried, "Chimpanzee says the Grand Marnier *soufflés* have fallen and the lemon sherbets have melted but we can always eat cake."

CHAPTER XXV

LATER INDIA tossed restlessly on her hot featherbed in the stifling room.

He is so near, she thought; just beyond the graveled path. Just a few quiet steps beyond the house. And he is almost himself. While we danced tonight he *was* himself. I was so sure he would come back and claim me again, but he didn't. And all the way home he never said a word, just rode along in the moonlight with his face as hard and inscrutable as an image on an old coin.

Why won't he take the love that I offer him? He could tell tonight when he touched me in the dance how hungry I am for his embrace. Is it because he is afraid that if he comes to my room and I open my arms to him that in the very moment of taking he will recover his identity and not be Max at all? Is the risk for him too great? Is it because he heard that vulgar Fant Calvert and his brother laughing about his having been moved into bachelor quarters in the yard away from me? How sordid! That is Irene's fault. Always saying, "He doesn't resemble Bubba in the least—not in the least."

I thought I would suffocate when he suddenly

snatched me from Ervin Marshall's arms. I could feel his heart thumping as wildly as my own. He was jealous and angry. His face was completely alive. Why did he run away after? I think sometimes the sight of me is a torment to him. He must be aware of the way I seek and look among the scattered stones of his lost soul for something—anything that may force the door at the edge of his memory open. I wish he would pretend to remember. Even pretending would give me a chance to show him how desperately I need him.

I say—"Do you remember the big buck that ran across the road the first night we came here? Do you like liver? Was Amy killed in Ivanhoe? What did good middling cotton bring in 1806? How long do we ferment our wine?" And he has begun to answer sometimes without thinking. A year ago he wouldn't have dared to answer. Now he answers often and always correctly. Yet neither Miss Emmy nor I can convince him *why* he knows these things. He even conjugated a Latin verb in all the tenses for Miss Emmy the other night and yesterday—ah, yesterday—he minded Lucy laughing at him! Oh—Max darling you are so nearly awake. So very near.

She heard a footfall on the graveled path. Getting up from the bed she went onto the upper balcony. The moon was setting and the last of its light was slanting on the path. She could see Max, moving along the path toward the house, start suddenly at the whirring of a partridge which rose out of a clump of grass close by. What had startled the partridge? Certainly *he* had not made enough sound to worry it? Near the house India saw a black limb of a tree had fallen across the path in a patch of moonlight. When had it fallen? It hadn't been there when they came home and she would have heard from her room if it had crashed later. Max was about to step across the limb when she saw that it had straightened slightly. She strained her eyes but could not, in the eerie light, tell head from tail of the big snake. She started to cry out a warning, but Max, too, had seen the barely perceptible motion and retreated a step. The snake moved slowly—its progress seemed no faster than the hour hand of a clock but India knew that it moved, yet so close to the gravel that the whole path seemed to move with it. It had come between her and Max. He was backing away. Had he been coming to—her? And now, now that there was an obstacle was he retreating to his safe sanctuary?

For minute after minute the snake was still and Max, hesitant, was still; then with a shudder India realized that it was two feet farther on the grass and roused birds were squawking and rustling the shrubbery leaves. She could see a thickening near the middle of the snake and knew it must have eaten lately and was slowly making its way to some hidden place. From where she watched on the balcony it was impossible to determine whether it was a king snake or a rattler.

If it goes away perhaps he will come on, she thought. Surely he has started to me. Surely. No— No —he is running away! Back to the library. Back to safety. He isn't any better after all!

Defeated tears ran down her face and she turned to go back into the house when she heard the library door slam and saw Max come running with the brass log roller from the chimney piece and beat the head off the snake. Beat and beat the threshing writhing evil thing that had crossed his path until there wasn't enough of it left even to make a black patch on the deep grass in the moonlight. She could almost hear his breathing. She knew it was as loud and frightened as her own. He threw down the log roller and quickly now—urgent now—he walked and was hidden from her in the dark tree shadows smothering the house.

She went and lay down on the bed. Her thin mull gown felt like flannel on her smooth long limbs. The dark roses of her breasts tightened stingingly. At first all she could hear was the chittering of late insects, then a floor board in the hall creaked and a pinprick of candlelight showed up the wide stair well. He had found her unlighted candle by the door and the matches she always left beside it!

The stairs were kind. Only the fifth one cried Stranger! Thief! Interloper! In the upper hall the doors were all shut except hers. He crossed the space quickly, quietly, and came into her room. The gauze curtains were limp and still, the big bed was pulled over by the window in case a breeze might rise. She was lying on her back—arms outflung, black hair neatly plaited and lying over her bare shoulder, her lashes brushing her soft cheeks like black butterflies. He shaded the candle with his hand so the glare did not fall directly on her face.

She opened her eyes and they were deep and dark with passion. She smiled at him and he bowed his head and knelt down by the bed. She took the candle from his trembling fingers and he buried his head against the side of the bed clutching at the rumpled linen sheet with a crest and "St. Julien" embroidered on it.

"Did I frighten you?" he whispered and she answered,

"No. Are you all right?"

And he said, "I saw a snake and killed it, then I noticed that you had left the front door unlocked. You must never leave the front door unlocked for these are bad times and we are only four white people here surrounded by hundreds of inflamed Negroes." Then he got up and she held out her hand and he took it and crushed it against his chest and looked down at her and she almost said what he wanted her to say, but then she didn't say it for in the end he must be the one. She knew this thing because she felt he was more herself than she was; whatever stuff their separate souls were made of they were the same. And in her love for him she knew that to make it right for him he must be the one.

CHAPTER XXVI

MIMOSA BLOSSOMS are fragrant, they smell like pink honey, Emmy thought, looking at a crystal bowl of the feathery flowers the next morning. The whole family was already at the breakfast table when Max came in. India's face glowed with delight as he approached the table. She sprang up, took both his hands, and led him to his seat at the head.

Emmy beamed, Irene gasped, and little Cantelou stopped eating his hominy and a trickle of red ham gravy trailed down his sunburned chin. Seeing him in a shaft of the almost tropical sunlight Emmy was amazed at the transformation of Max. He sat jauntily erect, his face was bright and interested, holding none of the hesitation that had been there since Burgess Mill. Emmy's surprise exceeded Irene's. She didn't quite know how to speak to him. Max picked up his napkin ring and unrolled the crackling damask napkin looking at Emmy coolly till she chose to speak.

"Lucy must have had quite a party," Emmy said at length. "Now take your time and have some fried ham. The best we've cured in a long time. Some figs and cream? Yes, I insist—and then some waffles if you don't want ham and hominy. This is my birthday—I want everybody to be pleasant. I am fifty-seven years old and Irene is forty-one—you are thirty— Sit still and drink your tea. It is not necessary to rush off to the village as though you were going on a long journey. India has told me about your decision to exchange the old race horse for a good mule. How clever of you to think of it. Steeben—bring me a dish of clabber and the silver nutmeg grater."

"Silber nuttenegg grater gone."

"Then bring the tin one—fly now!"

Max smiled at everything Emmy said while India, sitting opposite him, kept her eyes on him as if she were afraid he might vanish if she looked anywhere else. He did not look at her often; just glanced at her quickly now and then but each time his eyes flashed more confidently the unmistakable delight he drank from hers. They were too much absorbed in their mutual joy to be embarrassed. Not so Irene: she turned red and then white as though she were sitting on thorns which pricked her annoyingly and finally became unbearable when India leaned forward and laughing like a person beside herself said,

"I dreamed of you last night. I dreamed that I saw

you and touched you and spoke to you for the first time in four years. Did you dream of me?"

Before he could answer, Irene said spitefully, "India, unless you want me to drink cold tea, please tend to to the kettle. The soldier will have a long hot day whatever foolishness he plans to unravel in the village; and I'm thirsty."

India turned down the flame under the kettle and poured boiling water into the china pot half full of strong steeped tea.

The rest of the meal hardly lasted ten minutes. India's teacup was never filled: she couldn't eat or drink. Irene merely made a slop in her saucer, and scarcely swallowed a bite. Only Emmy spooned her smooth cool cream-drenched clabber steadily and Max ate unexpectedly well—waffles, ham, tea, and at last a bowl of peeled brown turkey figs.

When he had finished he said to India, "Let the little boy ride his pony to the village with me."

"Can I, Sister?" Cantelou jumped up from the table and before Irene could say no, India pushed back her chair and grabbing Cantelou by the hand cried,

"Of course, and I'll ride Flossie along with you all to the road. There won't be a hand in the fields today. I heard them straggling home from the barbecue after daylight shouting and quarreling. I may even ride into the village with you. We three haven't ever gone anywhere together."

But Emmy called, "Stay here, India; let the men go by themselves. It's my birthday and you promised to make me a chocolate cake." When Max and Cantelou left she said, "Let him do this thing by himself. It's wisest for him to feel that you believe he is capable of doing things by himself. Come—help me tune my harp. I feel like singing all day long."

"I feel like screaming," Irene said. "You never dreamed he came to your room last night. I heard him in there. You are a shameless wanton woman."

"How can you call me shameless, you awful person?" cried India, furious at Irene for having heard and for her stupid words. "You are surely losing your mind. When have I ever been wanton?"

"Last night," sobbed Irene. "With him."

"Is it wanton for my husband to come into my room? You and that common carpetbagger, Pushkin, are far more wanton. Simpering at him because you are greedy and he gives you money to sit in the sweetshop with him. Soon you will probably invite him here to dinner if he pays you enough."

"You talk that way because you don't want me to have an admirer. Mr. Pushkin considers me highly intelligent. I have been helping him make out a brochure describing the health-giving miracles of the pines of Aiken. He has bought up some property there and intends to make it a resort, selling the pine lands to rich Northerners for a winter playground."

"Irene," Emmy said, almost choking as she said it, "does that carpetbag pawnbroker give you money? Have you ever taken money to sit publicly in the sweetshop with Pushkin?"

"No. Never. India loves to lie about me. He paid me for writing the brochure. Never to sit with him. He enjoys my conversation. India is jealous. She doesn't want anyone to be admired but herself."

India stared hard at Irene as she might stare at a chill hairy spider which she might be forced to step on in spite of the aversion to touching it with her foot.

"Control your tongue, Irene," Emmy said suddenly. "I have been thinking often lately that it might be well for you to take a room at Mrs. Dawson's boardinghouse in the village and teach at the Female Academy. You, as much as anything, have slowed Max's recovery."

"Faugh. You know that stranger is not Bubba. India is afraid of losing her power here if I can prove that he isn't Bubba. Bubba loved me more than anybody in the world. Don't you remember, India, that it was at me he smiled when the Hussars rode away to war?"

"Bubba or not," India said crossly, "he is Max and he hates you. Remember this, Irene, when his memory does return he will continue to hate you. I've talked to Dr. Quattlebaum and he says that when Max does remember his past it will be a continuous road backward from the instant things come clear. He will remember every day of these years that you have tormented him and made him feel uneasy and unwanted at Shepherd's Grove. Yes—he'll hate you. And I won't care—none of us will care."

During the late afternoon, in spite of the oppressive dry heat, after the sun began casting shadows and before the darkness made the roads unsafe for white people, the friends of Emmy Allan called at Shepherd's Grove to wish her a happy birthday. Steeben set the tea table out by the fountain in what had once been the boxwood garden but was now just a swept shady spot where the sound of the water splashing from the opened mouth of the marble faun into the round basin, greenish now with moss and age, gave an illusion of moist coolness.

A rich chocolate cake shared the table with the silver punch bowl full of smooth trifle. There was homemade scuppernong wine and blackberry shrub and minted tea. Danny carried out the harp and the Flemish chair and Emmy played the old sweet songs: "Believe Me If All Those Endearing Young Charms," "Come Back To Erin," "Auld Lang Syne," "The Hope That The Nearest." Everybody joined in the singing but nobody suggested "Dixie's Land" or "The Bonnie Blue Flag."

India was wearing the soft gray dress of the night before and she looked so radiant that Kevin Marshall, smoothing his pointed white beard, tremulously shook his old head as he thought of this beauty being wasted.

"I don't blame Ervin for admiring India so extravagantly, Emmy. You'd better keep your eye on her or he will carry her back to Virginia with him. My nephew is like a bird dog who will hold his point forever if he thinks he's spotted game. He refuses to believe that this Maximilian is *the* Maximilian. Ervin says he was there and is sure—"

"Foot! Kevin, you're in your dotage. Wouldn't I know my own son?"

"You know what you want to know, Emmy Allan. I remember how you used to wither poor Cantelou with a single word when he tried to put on airs about his financial success in the Cotton Exchange. And you knew he was right all the time."

"Cantelou had a disease known as 'love of money.' Withering him was the only treatment. Never a cure, Kevin—but a treatment."

Kevin looked toward the crowd of people rocking and strolling about the shady spot. "Ervin is wooing India this minute," he quavered.

Emmy turned to see Ervin Marshall, leaning indolently against one of the garden gateposts, smiling and talking to India. He had on a plaited brown linen riding jacket, buttoned trousers of the same material, and was fanning her with a large Panama hat of the finest and most beautiful texture in his crippled hand.

India was listening to him but her eyes were on the dusty road from the forest.

She is wild for Max to come home, Emmy thought, as during a sudden lull in the tinkle of thin Georgian spoons against old Worcester tea plates and the party chatter, she heard Ervin say, "Will you ride with me in the pair-jumping exhibition at the picnic at Lanham Springs Friday? You have the only mare which could possibly keep up with my Satan."

"I'd love that. How high are the jumps? Isn't that someone coming down the road?"

"Four to five feet—I'll come for you tomorrow morning at six before it gets too hot and we can take a practice round at Kevin's."

"All right. Oh, dear—it's that rough Cato Calvert and his poor little wife. They're so dull."

Later as the sun set hotter than it had risen and the toad frogs begged for rain, the guests rattled homeward in oxcarts, wagons, buggies, and on whatever horses or mules were left in their big empty barns, leaving the three Allan women sitting alone on the piazza in the murky afterglow.

"You should never have let Cantelou go off with that lunatic," Irene said to India.

Emmy was tired, and it seemed to her that Irene was eternally carping in this spiteful way about Maximilian. She cared for Irene, she supposed; but she did get tired of her constant ranting. She said, "He's better off with Maximilian than with you so much of the time."

"You're jealous now," said Irene, triumphant in ruffling her mother. "You and India are both jealous. I saw India looking at this new muslin dress all during the afternoon. She's sulking because I have a new pink dress and she had to wear the same old gray. Though that's not all the matter with her. I watched her flirting with Ervin Marshall after," Irene's assumed virtuous expression looked sly and ribald, "she claimed at breakfast she was so in love with her dear husband—never wanton—"

"Oh hush, Irene. I'm anxious for Max and Cantelou to come back. You know I wasn't flirting. Ervin asked me to take part in the riding exhibition at the picnic Friday. We're going to practice in the morning."

"Stop being unpleasant on my birthday," said Emmy to Irene. "You've no call to brag about your fine clothes. If you weren't so selfish perhaps India and I both could have a new afternoon gown."

Irene muttered, "As for you, I don't think an old woman should dress out of rag bags and go around looking like a shabby old monk at her birthday party. You could sell the Vermeer and buy a hundred dresses."

"Foot!" said Emmy in a fury—leaning toward Irene and actually shaking her fist— "I've heard enough from you for one day. Go to your room, miss."

The enraged woman and her spiteful daughter glared at each other and India, a displeased witness and tired too, was suddenly very angry.

"Stop speaking so rudely to Miss Emmy, Irene," she said, allowing dislike to sound cold in her voice.

"Nobody ever thinks of me," said Irene as one who disclaims any right to consideration. "Not since Papa died."

"Foot," said Emmy, like a bad child, "your papa!"

Irene uttered a choked sound of outrage, left the joggling board and ran quickly down the steps.

"Let her go," said Emmy.

Irene ran on, across the flagged turnaround toward

the darkening grove but on reaching the edge of the
forest cried, "Here they are!" and came running back.

A fine double-seated buggy with a yellow fringed
canopy drawn by a strong, sleek Morgan mare was
rolling toward the house. Behind the buggy came three
Negroes, riding mules, each leading another mule and
one leading two mules.

"What in the world?" exclaimed Emmy. "Law—
look at Chance in his long black coat! Howdy-do,
Chance! Have they made you an ambassador?"

Chance pumped her hand and kept saying, "Do
Lord, Miss Emmy! Fine and fat as a partridge! I am
glad to see you, Miss Emmy; very glad indeed to see
you."

Max was strutting, he was so proud and Cantelou
was screaming, "Look what Papa and me got. Lookit
what Chance swapped us for the old red coach out in
the coach house."

"Wonderful—wonderful—" India was stroking the
soft nose of the gentle, strong mare but looking long-
ingly at Max.

Emmy said happily, "Now I can go to the picnic
Friday and watch India jump. I'm glad to get rid of
the coach. It's no good to us anymore."

At that Irene screeched so shrilly that Emmy struck
her on the cheek. Irene sank onto the bottom step,
crying jerkily and they all had to stop being excited
and try to quiet her.

"The lunatic has ruined me after all," she kept re-
peating. "I knew he would. I've known it ever since
India fetched him here."

"What is she saying?" Max had turned white. "What
is she talking about, India? Does she mean me?"

"What will I ride in to my wedding? Every girl in
the family has driven in the scarlet coach as a bride.
Mother—do something to him."

But Emmy only said Foot and held a vial of smelling salts under Irene's nose, watching Chance driving
the scarlet coach, hitched to six big shaggy plow mules,
away from Shepherd's Grove toward the forest. It was
quite dark now and she could hear the coach creak
longer than she could see it. She had sat—fifteen and

trembling ike a captured bird—beside Cantelou Allan
in that coach on her wedding night. Now the coach
was gone. Nothing was left to remind her of Cantelou
Allan except Irene and the name of the little boy.
But the name didn't matter for the child was a combination of herself and Guy St. Julien, not reminding
her of *him* at all.

"I feel very rich with a horse and buggy again," she
said later to Max sitting on a bench on the piazza beside India. He was eating a ham biscuit and drinking
a glass of cool buttermilk.

On the tallest pine, like a great fruit, hung the
lemon-colored moon. Lightning bugs winked in and
out of the shrubbery like little fires. Everything was
very soft and peaceful; even the frogs had settled to a
low humming rhythm. Max closed his hand over India's saying, "Wait till you see the white mule Chance
let me have in addition to the buggy and mare. I'm
going to try to ride him before breakfast in the morning. Chance says he plows well but refuses to carry
a saddle. I hope"—turning to Emmy—"you didn't
mind too much about the coach?"

"No—I think in this day and time it will suit
Duchess Devonshire better than Emmy Allan. For a
few years anyway. You men will rise up and reclaim
our state when you have licked your wounds in private
a little longer. I'm not worried about the future."

The night was so dreadfully still and hot that
Emmy stayed awake, while the clock struck hour after
hour. She listened for the front door to open and the
fifth step of the stair to squeak as it had done last
night. A fly got under her mosquito netting. It buzzed
and buzzed trying to get out. She opened the net and
closed the net and finally lay back on the mound of
steamy feathers making up her mind that if she couldn't
get rid of the fly to learn to live with it and not hear it.
But that was the only noise that came from outside
into the house all night—the buzzing fly.

CHAPTER XXVII

As THE MOON TRAVELED from the top of the tall pine tree, one by one the lights went out in the house. All but one: Irene's. A low wind murmured and then fell in the pines and Max lay listening to that melancholy falling sound and wondering whether there could be any place where the stillness of summer was more overwhelming.

Would Irene never blow out her candle? He could imagine the moths and the night insects fluttering and scorching around the steady flame. He could imagine the little boy sunbrowned as a gypsy, restless under his mosquito net, tired from the long hot day of trying so hard to be a man. I will spend more time with him, Max thought. Whether I am sure in my mind of being his father or not. He needs a man to ride with and talk big with.

This has been my best day. India was pleased and proud of the Morgan mare and the fine buggy. Sunday I will drive her to church in the buggy—her and the little boy. In the morning she and the little boy will watch me saddle-break the white mule.

It seemed to Max that this was same old dream. He felt for a moment stronger and older than anyone. It was pleasant alone in this safe little house. The sheets of the bed held a trace of coolness. How still the night was. How still. Was she awake—waiting for him to come? Oh, yes—she would be awake. How soothing the silence was. How heavy—

Early the next morning Max awoke in anguish. His mind struggled for some seconds, tangled in the web of sleep like a thick fish writhing in a net, in desperate need to return to its natural element. At last it slipped into the water, dived and remained motionless in the unfamiliar, dark, hot pool.

As he had feared the dream of other nights had repeated itself. She was riding away from him—smiling at the faceless man whose hair shone redly in some unearthly light. Always away she rode, never looking back at him. Over and over he dreamed this dream.

He opened his eyes and the sun was rising like a copper moon. Or was it the moon rising like a copper sun? The atmosphere had a queer unreal quality. He looked down at his uncovered nakedness knowing that it was the sun and not the moon. That he had slept the night long. That he had not gone to her room at all!

Jumping up he ran over to the washstand behind a slatted wooden screen, poured water from the flowered porcelain pitcher into the basin and washed his face and neck. The water was tepid. The heat had come into everything. His brain felt as if it was wrapped in warm cobwebs. Pulling on a pair of faded homespun trousers he heard hoofbeats on the flagged turnaround. Looking at the gilded clock on the mantel he saw that it was six o'clock. Shirtless he went out onto the path to see who was coming here at this early hour. He saw India trotting from the rear of the house on Flossie, waving the peacock-fringed hat she wore to the fields. She had on a low-necked thin white blouse and a full skirt of some home-dyed red cotton stuff draped in the semblance of a riding skirt.

"You are on time to the minute," she called, low— but loud enough so he heard—to Ervin Marshall perfectly gotten up, looking very rich and prosperous in tailored linen breeches on a fat high-headed thoroughbred stallion.

India should have a nicer riding habit, Max thought irrelevantly. How gracefully she sits her mare—how vital she is.

"You knew I would be," Ervin answered. "How did you manage to slip out without waking anyone?"

"It was so hot last night I couldn't sleep."

Couldn't sleep? Then she *had* waited for him. Why —oh why—had he failed her—sleeping heavily like a worn-out fool?

"Are you sure you feel like going in this heat?"

"Oh yes—I want to go."

Want to—want to—want to go—where? Max felt the cobwebs tighten in his head, jealousy choke his breath. He started to call out to her but he didn't and they disappeared up the road that led to the forest. Max was left standing—deadly white of face. Suddenly he began to run. At the edge of the forest were some old mounds covered with a rare form of low-spreading juniper. Max ran up one of them; from there he could see India and Ervin yet a little way on, till they were swallowed up in the woods.

Max stood with his mouth half-open, the tears running down over his confused strained face, gathering in the ridges of his scarred cheek. He fell on his knees, then threw himself forward headlong on the scratchy tough juniper and lay sobbing, sobbing and tearing at the prostrate juniper with his long brown fingers.

CHAPTER XXVIII

IRENE FIDGETED on a singularly beautiful Carolinian day bed pulled from her room onto the upstairs piazza. She had thought the cane seat might be cooler than her featherbed but the squabs of worn mauve velvet against her back felt as though they were stuffed with hot ashes. A storm must be coming. It had to be coming. The corn and cotton fields seemed twice as brilliant green as yesterday against the odd metallic color of the flat sky; the pecan and peach trees loomed nearer than usual, heavy and dark; the pines looked a false green against a black cloud looming unexpectedly in the sky in the false colored sunlight. There was no freshness in the air, but a dead heavy stillness.

She had stayed awake most of the past night because of something India had said. Why should she ever worry over anything India might say? She was positive that the man who was leading the white mule out into the fenced pasture at this minute was not her brother. Her brother, wounded or not, would have reached out for her the minute he came home from the war. Her brother would not have pulled back from her, staring with hostile eyes, crying, Go away!

He was looking now toward the house and his face

was pale and terribly sad. He was naked to the waist and the scars on his chest stood out unusually livid— he was limping a little. The wisteria vine hung in front of her like a green screen through which she could see him but he could not see her.

The mule was a big ugly white with a mear head and powerful back legs and flanks. The man fussed with saddling him, talking quietly. She couldn't hear what he was saying but his lips moved and he patted the rough mane once or twice. He was a strong man. The mule kicked and bit at him while he tightened the cinch but the man easily buckled the straps and suddenly was in the saddle before the mule could jump aside.

Ah—he'll soon be on the ground, she thought, watching the mule go into action like a powerful machine —kick —jump —buck —hump —kick —jump — buck—hump! Then the pattern changed. Hump— hump—hump. The man's spine should be shattered by this time. The kick—jump—buck—kick—jump started again. Now he was galloping, bucking as he galloped, a big powerful killer mule, tireless as a machine, away to the far end of the pasture. Back again. Off again. Back again. Surely now the man would crumple and fall under the wicked hard hoofs—now surely—ah— nobody but Bubba could ride like that!

The world swam in front of her. The wisteria vine closed in on her. Her heart beat so fast that her breath wouldn't come. She tore at the vine to keep it from choking her; so that she could see him without the shadows blurring any part of him; the fine, graceful sun-tanned body, glistening with sweat—the flying hair like wind-ruffled wheat—the high head—the powerful neck. Bubba, she whimpered—Bubba!

She looked again. Now the scarred side of his profile showed and she ground her teeth triumphantly, muttering, What a fool I was. That is not Bubba.

But, persisted something inside her, suppose it *is* Bubba. You thought a minute ago it was Bubba. Nobody but Bubba could ride like that! Suppose he is about to remember the way you used to rock him when he could not sleep at night; remember you running beside him holding him on his first pony until his legs were long enough to grip its sides; remember your walks together in the spring woods to pick wild violets and shooting stars; the theater in Charleston and New York; his first glimpse of Paris with you beside him telling him the legends of the old castles, the cathedrals, the opera? Suppose—farfetched as it may seem—he is about to remember those things and also continues to remember the way you have shunned him, scorned him, scorned him, tried to humble him since he has come from the war a poor wreck of himself?

I won't suppose that. I would die if my sweet little Bubba ever looked at me, hating me. That was the reason I said, He is not Bubba, when he came home. I could see his instant aversion to me the very moment I looked at him and he said, Go away.

But suppose—suppose?

I won't suppose. I will do something. I must do something. For the end of the world would come if I admitted that this man who hates me is Bubba.

By the time she had jerked a black calico dress over her head and looking in the mirror had noticed that the pink of her cheeks had turned to purplish veins, that the locks of her hair crimped all night long on rags trailed about her ears like small dry pinkish worms, she had planned what she would do to save herself. She had at least an hour.

Cantelou was eating his breakfast when she reached the dining room. "Granny's sick. Sangua says she's full of wind. She got up in the night and ate all the cake and trifle left from the party. Can I hunt turtles with Ida's grandsons?"

He hadn't seen the man riding the mule! Evidently he had dressed himself while she was on the upstairs piazza trying to cool off.

"Yes, if you go right now. Out through the runway and the kitchen."

"Why?"

"It's cooler that way."

"I want some more biscuit and syrup."

"No. Go now. I have a headache. I'd like to eat quietly for once."

"Oh, all right. Your hair looks like fish bait."

"Don't be rude. Think how good to you I am. Think what you'll always owe me."

"There's a letter by Papa's plate." He was going away from her. Glad to be going. Last night he'd said he was tired of sleeping in the room with her and wanted to move out to the library with—with—

"He isn't your papa. How many times have I told you that?"

"I like him. I liked him yesterday and I'll like him today. Something's going to happen. Ida says none of the chickens will leave the chickenhouse. They're all huddled up on the roosts. Tell Papa to call me 'fore he rides that ole mule."

"I will."

The letter was sealed and lying under Max's silver napkin ring with the Shepherd coat of arms heavily engraved on its side. She didn't hesitate. She snatched the envelope and tore it open.

> Darling,
>   I've gone to practice a little entertainment for the Marshalls' picnic Friday. Don't ride the mule until I come come. It's too hot to ride him yet, anyway. Wait until late afternoon. I will be back home by eight or eight-thirty. Please miss me a little. I love you.
>
>   Your wife,
>   *India*

"Want some tea and peaches, Miss Irene?" Steeben was watching her read the letter. She hastily jabbed it into her pocket and said,

"I don't want any breakfast. It's too hot." And went out onto the piazza.

He was tying the mule to the iron horse-head hitching post. The mule was a dirty gray. Sweat was running off him and he stood with one of his back legs bent, heaving and breathing with difficulty.

"Oh! You!" she called, and her voice was hard. She had been afraid it might tremble but it didn't.

Max turned. His whole expression changed as he looked at her. His eyes narrowed with loathing and the scar on his cheek was red against his sudden angry pallor.

He does hate me, she thought. He would like to come and hurt me. I can see his hands flex to choke me.

"You!" She called again—contemptuously.

"I'm on my way to put on a shirt and some fresh trousers," he said, panting with heat, exertion, dislike of her. "I'll talk to you when I come in for breakfast."

"India isn't here," she said.

He said, "I know," and went along the path to the library.

Changed into a white homespun shirt and some tight trousers of thin old jeans cloth, he appeared surprised to find her still waiting when he came back to the house for his breakfast.

"What do you want?"

"Do you know where India has gone?"

"No."

"Ervin Marshall has received definite proof from Miss Pember in Richmond that you are not my brother. He has proof that my brother is dead and buried in Virginia. They have found his papers. A doctor had personally removed them from my brother's dead body. Ervin came for India this morning and they have gone to Calbraith Butler's law office to arrange to have you sent away after they read Bubba's will and prepare to execute it legally. All this property will then be mine and Cantelou's. Not hers."

"She would never send me away."

"Oh, no? Then why did she ask me to tell you all this? Why didn't she tell you herself. All of us have suspected you were a stranger for a long time. The Richmond doctors have now proved that my brother is dead."

"You are a witch to talk in that manner to me. I will not believe you," he said hotly.

She heard herself giving a sneering laugh that had nothing to do with amusement and she heard the lies fall from her lips as smoothly as ever truth had done.

"Yesterday at tea Ervin Marshall asked India to marry him. He is very rich, as you know, and she would have one of the finest homes in Virginia and a hundred silk dresses. How long do you suppose she intends to bury herself here in the country with a half-wit who has now been proven an imposter? If you have a grain of sense you will leave here before she returns, and make it easier for her. Little did I ever think I would be the one to be careful of your feelings, disliking you as I always have for attempting to impersonate my brother. Loss of memory! Faugh—We all know you're a lazy good-for-nothing."

He reddened deeply and clenched his fists.

Hot bitter tears of anger were pricking Irene's eyes but she forced them back and laughed with her mouth twisted awry:

"Anyone but a fool can see what a burden to India you have become."

"India does not make me feel as though I am a burden. She—she has seemed happier than usual lately. Has she said that I was a burden? That she would like —like to marry the Virginian?"

Irene's lips moved but before the piteous gaze in his eyes, she could not say another word.

"Answer—has she ever called me a burden? For if she has I will leave here immediately. Answer!" he said again with a pleading smile but she was so beside herself it merely embittered her more. A long shiver shook her thin body and she twined her child-size spidery fingers together, one hand gathering strength from the other.

"India is only being kind to you because she knows you will soon be sent away. You know how softhearted she is—even to chickens. Couldn't you see that she and Ervin Marshall had a secret this morning? Else why would she sneak away without telling you where she was going? To hide what they were up to from you— to keep from hurting you until time for you to leave here. You did see. I watched you running after them, half-naked like a savage. You know what I am saying is the truth and if you cared anything for her—which

of course you don't—you would go away now of your
own volition and give her this chance to make a better
life for herself without you to worry about."

"I didn't think you were ever so fond of India's
feelings," his face was sick with dread at the things she
was saying.

"I'm not; but she is young and beautiful and deserves a man who will cherish her and not make her
work in the fields like a nigger until she is dark-skinned
as they are: a rich man who could take her to White
Sulphur for the summers—to Newport, Paris, Rome.
She loves to dance, to be gay, to ride a fine horse, to wear
a velvet riding habit and a hat with a long silky plume."

Max stood a little. He turned pale and then red.
Then he turned and went wretchedly away from Irene
without another word.

The mule made no objection as he remounted and
the last Irene saw of him he was moving in and out of
the shadows of the forest road.

He had just passed from sight when India and
Ervin came cantering down the same road up which
he had gone.

"Irene," India called before she dismounted, "I
thought I saw Max coming along the road on the
white mule and then he seemed to disappear into the
forest. Ervin says I imagined it. Where is Max?"

"I haven't seen him," Irene answered shortly. "But
you'd better come on in the house. Look at those
lowered clouds and feel the unusual stillness of the
air. I shouldn't be surprised if a storm breaks any
minute. Mr. Marshall, Steeben is expecting you for
breakfast."

"That is a menacing cloud," Ervin said, "I think I
will come in. I should say that the atmosphere becomes
more oppressive every minute."

India followed Irene into the dining room. She looked
instantly at Max's plate and saw his napkin ring with
the unused napkin in it.

"Steeben," she called, "has Mr. Max eaten?"

"Nawm."

"Did he get the letter I left him?"

Steeben looked, surprised, at Irene. She glared back at him, daring him to tell he had seen her reading the letter.

"Mista Maxi ain't been in here, Miss India. Nobody but Miss Irene and de baby."

Irene's eyes dropped before India's and she said sullenly, "You know he'll be back in time for dinner. He wouldn't miss a meal—not he."

"Mama!" Cantelou was calling from the front lawn.

"Let him come in here and eat with us," Ervin said, following her to the piazza. "I like the child."

From across the fields they saw the wavering moving black column of the tornado.

"Cantelou," India screamed, "fly! Here comes a storm."

He came running with the Pekingese clutched against his chest. He was yelling above the now sucking wind, "I just saw Papa riding like he was crazy on the white mule through the woods. He was crying like a baby. Mama—Mama—"

India had started down the steps when a holly tree jerked from the earth and hurled flying through the air. Branches—sticks—a camellia bush were flung in her face. They were in a world of deafening sound.

Irene saw Ervin grab India by the arm and finally pick her up bodily and carry her into the house. It took all of them to close the door and they crouched in the hall as the huge roar of the storm drowned every other sound at Shepherd's Grove except the sound of India praying that Max might not be hurt.

Sheets of rain came rushing down, beating on the dry parched earth. The lightning began flashing like thrown fire. The cracking tearing sound of the thunder came simultaneously with each flash. Irene knew when the lightning struck the big chimney and the bricks came crashing down. She did not realize that India had slapped her until she saw that the letter had fallen from her pocket. It must have happened as she struggled to close the front door. But what did it matter? Bubba would never hate her now. No one could live in this providential stroke of nature. It was as though she herself, willing his destruction, had had the power to make this be.

CHAPTER XXIX

THE MINUTE the tornado passed over and the massive sound of the rain was a nearer sound than the dry roaring fury of the wind and there came a depth of echo into the thunder, a moment's pause between the lightning and the thunder, India flew through the front door into the living wall of plunging water. On the piazza the joggling board was blown up on end; two of the Graces from the niches along the house had toppled from their bases in the black mud of the ruined lawn. A six-inch board from the pigeon house had hurtled through the air and, unbroken, pierced a pine tree three feet in diameter like an arrow. Small trees and bushes were scattered everywhere. Tall pines and cedars had been uprooted and destroyed what remained of the formal garden.

India struggled, climbing over bushes and trees, to the library. The French doors had been left open and the room was a whirling pool of water with rare books floating on its surface like red and green leather boats. At once she knew he was not here. She knew that the tornado had swallowed him because he had turned into the forest at exactly the spot from which the tornado had come. She knew why he had turned into the forest. He had seen her with Ervin Marshall and had taken the short cut through the swamp to the village to evade them.

What had Irene told him? She had slapped and beat Irene until Ervin Marshall had pinioned her arms against her sides. She had clawed and struck at him. Finally Emmy said, when the wind lessened, "Let her go." And she jumped through the door onto the piazza. She would find Max. She would find him. Her mother had not gone after the little boys when the hurricane struck the Island. Rachel had cowered in her bed and let the wind blow her sons away. But she was not like her mother. The blood of the ancient Greeks was in her veins. She would find her lost one if she hunted for him till her life's end. And if he were dead she would have him. Dead or alive he was hers forever. In life and in death—in sickness and in health—where had she heard those words? Oh—in Dr. Bachman's parlor—

Suddenly she could see a streak of light through her veil of tears and the curtain of the rain. Somehow she had reached the creek. How had she reached the creek? She had no idea. The rain was lessening. How had she got down that bank raw with snags and jagged cypress knees? The rain was stopping and birds were wetly calling and whirring from their shelters. Black cuckoos —old witch birds—flew up like disheveled grackles, mockers flashed by, and shrieking jays glowed among the wet foliage. Jeering crowds and whining catbirds scolded her from sodden limbs. The tornado had not hit here, only the drenching rain, the smoking lightning. Wild ducks spattered up from the water's edge as she reached the trail's end and blue and white herons stood, S-shaped, like detached shadows of birds. The sun came out and steam rose in a fog from the soaking mold and underbrush. A tiny opossum with a single young one clinging tightly about her neck was marooned in the creek on a hollow log. India found a big stick and pulled the log close to the bank. The mother opossum scrambled to the shore but as she left the log the baby loosed its hold and fell into the muddy swirling water and was instantly snapped at and pulled under by a big fish. The mother opossum bared her teeth at India and slunk away into a clump of myrtles.

It was getting hotter and hotter; India took off and wrung out her dragging red cotton riding skirt, pulled her soaking blouse over her head and hung them on a bush to dry in the sunwhine. Crouched together with her wet feet drawn up under her briar-scratched thighs and her slender brown arms crossed upon her knees, she sat on the bank at the water's edge, grieving. Now and again her face quivered, but she did not weep aloud anymore. Not even when she saw the buzzards circling overhead and thought—*they* have found him!

But they hadn't found him. Nobody found him. For days the whole district hunted for him. Wherever vultures were noticed in the silken sky, Negroes and white people congregated to find his body. At the end of a week, every inch of the forest and the fields where the tornado passed having been gone over time and again, it became plain that Max had not been blown away or crushed by a falling tree.

He was gone but he was not dead. A storekeeper near Halfway Swamp told of seeing a yellow-haired man on a white mule pass by the day after the big storm ruined the crops, the ferryman at Chappel's Ferry told of carrying him across the Saluda River but he hadn't said anything the ferryman remembered. The mule had objected a little to the ferry and the man talked to him and quieted him. That was all.

PART SIX

Edgefield,
Autumn, 1876
Hurrah for Hampton!

CHAPTER XXX

Outside it was hot and dry, and the air was dusty.
India and Cantelou walked idly under the trees. The
ground of smooth red earth was stained with shadows
and sprinkled with sun. Through the foliage could be
glimpsed bits of the September sky, of a very bright
close-seeming blue. Under a pine stood a wagon, its
shafts fallen. Hanging between two fig trees near the
kitchen door were two fat purplish jelly bags. The dark
juice dripping, dripping, into an old smooth cypress
tub below them. The grape arbor was laden with fruit
and humming with iridescent June bugs and buzzy
brown bumblebees.

"The smokehouse used to be here," said India. She
stopped and pointed to the right of the first big tree.
"The Yankees burned it and they roasted our overseer
in it."

"Why?" He had heard the account of Kilpatrick's
raid a hundred times from Sangua and Emmy but his
mother was in one of her rarely talkative moods and
so he urged her to tell him the familiar tale.

"You know it backward and forward," India smiled
at her son who was as tall as a medium-sized man and
graceful as his father must have been at the same age.

"But I like to hear you tell about it, Mama. Were
we really as rich as Granny says or does she imagine
all the servants and balls and champagne suppers?"

They strolled on.

"You see that brick house there?" asked India, extending a hand. Cantelou nodded. "That was the gentlemen's retiring room. They used to come out here
and drink brandy and smoke cigars and talk politics
while the ladies prinked and powdered in your
Granny's room or in one of the upstairs bedrooms. I
turned it into a smokehouse, parquet floor and all, after the war."

"How could you do the things you did alone?"

"I didn't feel alone then—not ever until your father went away." India drew her heavy black brows together, stood an instant in reflective silence and then said: "I guess I felt like it was up to the women to save the world."

"You mean the Confederacy?"

"That wasn't the real reason, Cantelou—I'm just talking big. I did all those things to impress your father. To try and show him what a superior person he'd married." She laughed shakily and going over to the jelly bags lifted the net that hung over them and the buckets and gave them a quick twist. A spurt of sweet purple wild-grape juice poured into the half-full bucket.

"Keep fanning, Katydid," she told the little Negro girl who was waving a willow branch back and forth to shoo away flies and gnats.

"The building yonder was the coach house." She looked searchingly at him but no suspicion was in his long brown eyes. "Do you remember the scarlet coach? I thought I would die the night you and your papa came home with the pretty buggy. Sister had a screaming fit when she heard you all had swapped off the coach. When are you going to see her again? It might be a good idea to pick a few bushels of scuppernongs and take them to Aiken and sell them at Pushkin's shop. Irene would be tickled to have you stay with her. We mustn't worry too much about the cotton."

He thought of the last time he'd spent the night with Sister.

At sunset a Negro had passed in the Aiken street driving a flock of goats. He was singing a plaintive tune.

Sister said, "Listen at him talking to the goats in gullah to an air of Chopin's. Chopin wrote that soon after he realized he would die before he finished his greatest work. Listen and then come in the parlor and I'll play it on the harpsichord for you."

In the parlor the gas was lit throwing hard lines on Sister's portrait hanging over the mantel—a simpering faded figure with pink ringlets and drop pearls and a dress of amber colored silk.

Sister began to play the haunting little tune saying,

"This reminds me of the sadness of my life. I have had to leave my lovely home. The slaves who kept it to perfection have all gone away. It is a shabby home now. I don't ever want to see it again. I hate shabby things. My father is dead, who loved me. *He* would not have run away as your father did. He would have made money somehow and kept the plantation proud and beautiful. I was a lost little lady but now I have a fine house and rings on my fingers and Negroes to wait on me."

Her spidery fingers spun over the white keys of the early eighteenth-century rare harpsichord that had belonged to Philip Abney's grandmother and that Pushkin had bought from Hetty for the ridiculous price of fifteen dollars when her baby died. The unfamiliar twang of the instrument had a plaintive quality that went with the nostalgic character of the song. The sad song enveloped Cantelou who imagined the plantation in the days of its glory.

"There are so many wonderful cities in the world—so many trains to ride on, ships to sail in to places where there are theaters, circuses, bands of music. The two of us can go together if you promise to be my little boy and come to live with me and Mr. Pushkin. You don't want to spend your life on an isolated cotton plantation. Don't you want to see the ocean and London and Alexandria—don't you? We want you to come with us when we move from here next month. You can go to Princeton to college and wear soft linen shirts and have a thoroughbred horse to ride."

"No—I like Shepherd's Grove."

"Don't say that, Cantelou. The ocean is beautiful. Paris is full of trees and birds and men selling bright balloons. One day you will grow up and then you'll remember what I offered you but then it will be too late. Much too late. I will be dead. And you will be nothing but an ordinary dirt farmer."

His eyes still, Cantelou stared at the steady flame of the gas chandelier while a sadness rose from his bowels and struck through his chest and stuck in his throat painfully. He gulped and blinked away the tears. I must be a man, he thought, struggling not to cry. He had to cry a little but he did not let her see and the tears dried up soon in the bright gaslight though he continued to listen to the little music of Chopin tinkling from the harpsichord and the whining pleading of Sister to come away with her where it would not matter if the fields were weeds, if his Granny starved, if his mother was deserted by him as well as—the thought choked him—by his father.

Suddenly the room became intolerable and he wanted above all to see his warm dark mother and hear the full rich sounding of his Granny's harp. He jumped abruptly to his feet and almost ran toward the back door. But as he passed close to his aunt she caught his hand tightly in her tiny fingers, pulled him to her, pressed him against her flat dry breasts and whispered plaintive, embarrassing things.

"I'm so little and weak. You must come with me. You can't let me go alone to the North with a stranger even if he is my husband. I will die up there and you will forget me. Everybody will forget me and I have given my life for them. I always put you and your father first and now you must come and look after me."

Over her shoulder Cantelou eyed their combined shadow projected on the wall of the room. It looked like a dying snake. Sister was pressing him hard against her and he suddenly pushed her away, ran to the stable and saddled the Morgan mare, Bonny Jean, and rode all the way home.

It was very late when he crawled into bed with his mother and taking the thick black rope of her hair, wound it around his neck and felt safe and secure and comfortable again.

No, he would not sell grapes in Aiken. "I'd rather sell them in Edgefield," he said to India. She nodded and by her face he could tell that she understood he did not want to see his aunt so soon again after coming home in the middle of the night from there last week and getting in bed with her even though she was fourteen and a great big boy for his age.

Cantelou knew that India had not led him out here in the back yard to talk about scarlet coaches and smokehouses. This was the way she always acted when she wanted him to do something she knew he didn't want to do. She flattered him by making him feel very grown-up and very much a man and before he realized it he had done exactly what she had in mind for him to do. They reached the long scuppernong grape arbor next to which was the chicken house where a gaudy black and white cock with a scarlet crest perched rather imposingly on a stump, as though to watch superiorly over the hens around him.

India for some time observed the arrogant cock as if forgetful of Cantelou's presence. Nested on a box full of straw was a large black and white setting hen. Suddenly India said: "You know I've got to kill one of those hens but the old booger on the stump looks so fond of all of them I hate to deprive him of any pleasure."

"Don't kill a hen. I've made enough money selling the eggs to buy my winter's supply of shells. Let me go in the swamp and try for a wild turkey or some birds. Who is coming?"

"Oh—nobody. I just like to have food in the house."

He knew why she wanted to kill the hen. Since the Hamburg Riot in July, Shepherd's Grove had become a meeting place for various farmers, doctors, merchants, and lawyers because it was centrally located in the county and, no men living there, neither the Yankee soldiers nor the Radical Negroes suspected it of being a meeting place where the scheme to rejuvenate the Democratic clubs in the state and throw off Radical rule began with the eagle-eyed Martin Gary, the gentle handsome Calbraith Butler, and fearless brilliant womanish James Bacon. They were quiet meetings, yet Cantelou understood what was going on. Make no overt act that can draw attention to anything. Play possum. Take insults, threats of violence, injustice, but don't ever answer a Radical back. Not a word.

But from the time of the August convention in Columbia when Mr. Gary got Hampton to agree to run for Governor on a straight-out Democratic ticket against Chamberlain the Reformer, on a Fusion ticket, the hard riding had begun all over the Up Country.

Every white male from Cantelou's age up, went armed. Simultaneously the Red Shirts appeared and groups wearing them were coming into Edgefield at a gallop and cheering as they came. At first Shepherd's Grove was more or less crowded with men from all parts of the county and sometimes leading men from other counties were with them. At any hour, day or night, Red Shirts rode to the Grove, stabled their horses and mules, ate and slept in the house.

They were coming less frequently now that the county was more generally organized. The essence of the plan, as Cantelou understood it, was to make and sustain until the election should pass an unceasing demonstration that would intimidate and terrify the Negroes and carpetbaggers and scalawags without at any time doing actual violence that would bring the Yankee troops down on the Red Shirts. So the thunder of horses' hoofs was everlastingly on the high-roads and the echo of the Rebel yell never died in any corner of the Up Country. The echoes were underlined with pistol shots fired toward the sky and a song was on every lip: Hurrah for Hampton!

The Low Country was for "Reform with Chamberlain" at first but now even Dawson of the *News and Courier* was known to have cried on a public street corner while the band played "Dixie"—Hurrah for Hampton!

But Cantelou did wish they hadn't scared all the Negroes out of the cotton fields. They had a fine stand of cotton at the Grove but he and India certainly couldn't pick it all. A group of Radical Negro hep men had hauled Danny from his bed one night last week and beaten him with knotted ropes for hiring a gang of striking Negroes to come and pick cotton at the Grove, and now Danny didn't dare to help him pick. He thought getting the cotton out of the fields was a lot more important than spending so much time galloping over the country shouting Hurrah for Hampton! and wasting bullets aiming at the stars.

Thinking of these things Cantelou watched India go into the old coach house, come out with a pan of corn and sprinkle it about for the Dominicker ladies. She looked especially pretty this afternoon in a pale pink gingham dress with short ruffled sleeves and three flounces on the full skirt. He wondered why she didn't have beaux courting her all the time like Lady Pick since Old Pick had died.

The warm voice of India woke Cantelou from his reveries.

"There's going to be a Hampton rally in Laurens next week."

"Douschka told me."

"Would you like to go?"

In the chicken yard three hens were after one grain of corn, cackling and pecking the ground frenziedly. The black and white cock remained impassive.

"Mama, I don't think we ought to leave the plantation for two whole days. I could pick four hundred pounds of cotton in that time."

"But Cantelou—Hampton's going to make a major speech. I can't miss it and I promised Calbraith I wouldn't go anywhere without you or Danny to protect me."

"I can't see what's so magic about the name Hampton," Cantelou grumbled slapping at a mosquito. "You act like God Almighty had stepped down from his throne to condescend to be our Governor."

"I almost feel that he has. Hampton has become the symbol of our past to us. It doesn't matter whether his speeches are profound or not. Just the sight of him sets us wild with hope and courage. You wait and see how he affects you. I'll wager you'll begin cheering the minute you lay eyes on him. He's so vital and dynamic you won't be able to help it. You'll feel vital and dynamic as well. It is a power that he has as a man."

"I'll have to wear a red shirt."

"Not yet—why you won't be fifteen until the end of next month! You're too young."

"I'm not too young to belong to the mounted baseball club which everybody knows is an armed secret society. If I can carry a pistol why can't I wear a red shirt?"

"Did you ask Steeben to make you one?"

"He said he would but the only red flannel we have is one of Sister's old petticoats and Steeben says he won't touch it even with a needle."

"He'll make it. Come—I'll show you the cabbage plants Mrs. Gryder sent you."

Cantelou followed her without a word. Then he felt an irresistible urge to speak plainly.

"Why do you go to all these rallies? I think we do more than our share using the Grove as a meeting place." He said it and awaited an explosion. But India's voice was cool and calm.

"*He* may be there."

"Who?"

"Your father."

Cantelou lifted a hand to pick a fat brown grape and popped it into his mouth.

"Sister says he is definitely dead." Cantelou spat out the fragments of grape skin and seeds in his mouth.

"But I know he isn't!" Her gray eyes flashed fire and she turned on him laughing a little breathlessly, daring him to repeat the remark. "I'm going to Laurens hoping he'll be there. As long as I live I'll go anywhere he might be. He idolized Wade Hampton. Wherever he is—if he hears Hampton speak or sees him ride by—he'll follow him. Besides, I think this Red Shirt campaign is the most exciting thing I've ever known except Secession. I want to gallop all over the country with my hair flying loose behind me like wings, screaming at the top of my voice, Hurrah for Hampton! Imagine what it will be like to live in a town with no enemy soldiers spying on everything you do; where a white woman can walk alone on the street without being insulted or molested; where *you* can ride away from me and I know you'll come back with an unbroken head. Why, honey, Hurrah for Hampton means so many freedoms I can't even name them all: freedom from fear, freedom of opportunity, freedom for the Negroes to work if they want to, freedom for me to roam the whole world looking for Max. You're excited too—that's why you want to be a man all at once—isn't it?"

She roughed his dark silky hair and he grabbed her

around her slender waist thinking—how could Papa have gone from her and forgotten her? I wouldn't go away from her for all the money in the world.

CHAPTER XXXI

CANTELOU SET OFF for the swamp with his shotgun and when India, after twisting the jelly bags a few more times, went back into the house she heard someone moving about in the parlor. She was about to call, "Miss Emmy," when Emmy rose from a chair behind a painted screen in the hall and whispered,

"We've got a visitor."

"Who?"

"Look through the front door."

The Allan scarlet coach was drawn up and the fly-tortured cropped-tail horses were being held by a liveried Mulatto.

"It must be Duchess."

"She didn't knock. I was lying down and heard the doors to the cabinet in the parlor squeak. Evidently she's having a fine time. Nothing is in there, is it?"

"No—everything is in the coach house."

"Let's watch and see what she's up to when she comes out."

India tried not to breathe loudly as Duchess, walking silently for all her size, carrying a green fringed reticule, came from the parlor and looked carefully in the Chinese porcelain walking-stick jar by the front door; moved over into the billiard room and drew a breath of surprise at the pallets spread on the floor around the room.

India stepped from the screen.

"Good afternoon, Duchess."

Duchess smiled a queerly triumphant smile, then quickly sobered and said, "Many people must sleep in here."

"Cantelou is having a spend-the-night party for some of his young friends." This excuse had been planned long in advance.

"I was just passing by and happened in. Aren't you going to ask me to sit down?"

"Yes—come out on the piazza."

"Too many gnats—I prefer the parlor."

India felt the back of her neck prickle horridly.

"Come in the parlor then."

This was no social call. Duchess was here for something. Had she heard a rumor that the Red Shirts sometimes held their meetings here? Could someone have suspected that the boxes marked "Agricultural Implements" and "Shoemaker's Tools" shipped at Grant's directive from Washington to Edgefield to be distributed by the Yankee soldiers among the Negroes had been taken off the train by the Red Shirts before it reached Trenton and brought to the Grove by night and hidden under the floor in the old coach house?

"How is Chance?"

"Chance?" Duchess's yellowish slanted eyes were taking in every corner and nook as though she had not just come out of this same room.

"Yes—Chance. We haven't seen him lately."

"Well, neither have I. We're divorced. I'm living with the Justice—Prince Rivers. My God, he's a lot of man!"

"Why have you divorced Chance? I remember when you thought he was a lot of man."

"He isn't any more. I didn't have to divorce him. The Governor says we are forbidden by law to cohabit with Democrats. If our husband becomes a Democrat we are automatically divorced. Nothing to it at all. Chance is a turncoat. I always did hate wishy-washy people. After the Hamburg Riot he just folded up and resigned from everything, even the State Department. He's back shoeing horses in the village for a living, sleeping over the shop as he was in the beginning. Everything else—the wagon factory and all—belongs to me."

"You mean you divorced Chance for becoming a Democrat?"

"Isn't that reason enough? Why, my whole future hinges on this election. It would have been simple if you Edgefieldians hadn't nominated Wade Hampton. He's the only white man in the whole state who could possibly hurt us. Chance is not alone in being a turn-coat. Lots of fools are pledging to vote for Hampton not realizing that they're voting away their lifetime op-portunities. Moses, Whipper, Elliott, Nash, my black Prince and I have no idea of letting the Negroes con-tinue to go over to Hampton. It's high time they real-ized this is an election of race, not party. We've got to win. The Hamburg Riot was merely the beginning. Grant is behind us. He told Chamberlain so. We've just begun to fight you white people. Haiti was a simple ceremony compared to what we will accomplish here. We planned that Hamburg Riot especially to consoli-date the Negroes and we have other riots at strategic spots in the state prepared. Did you know McKie Meriweather?"

"Yes. He was a dear boy. His mother is one of my good friends."

"I shot him."

"Then you are responsible for the riot! Why are you telling me these things? What have you come here for?" A cold thought coiled and uncoiled in India's brain that Duchess had become her enemy. That the woman who had nursed her as a child, the woman who had come in the night to help her when her baby was born, had turned with the turning years and times into a dangerous foe to everything she valued and be-lieved in. "There's nothing here to interest you," In-dia said, suddenly sick of the sight of the big woman covered with diamonds and feathers and rustly taffeta that smelled of dark sweat in the close September air.

"You aren't very hospitable after I've driven such a long distance to call on you."

"You didn't come to call on me. You haven't been to see me since Cantelou was born. What do you want?"

"What do I want? You were always a rude high-headed child. Well, let me tell you. I don't want any-thing from you. But when you see your house burned down and your fields wasted for lack of labor to help you with your harvest; when your taxes force you to sell your land, don't come saying, 'Duchess, you cared for me and loved me once. Help me now.' For I won't help you. You don't even touch my heart any more. You just remind me of your father. Look at your cracked fingernails and those shabby shoes—your sunburned face and those big wild eyes!" Duchess spread her own long manicured, creamed fingers wide. She wrapped the feather boa fashionably around her damp hot neck and picking up the red taffeta of her skirts rustled like a snake in dry grass down the steps into the tufted new pink satin interior of the graceful coach, slamming the door after her as hard as her great strength could slam.

As the coach neared the forest India saw a dark form moving among the pines near the empty library. Her heart pounded irregularly. No doubt about it, it was a man; a black man. He was slipping like a thief mingling with the tree shadows but always moving in her direction. India felt the blood hammering hard at her temples. There was no one in the house but Miss Emmy to hear her if she screamed. Steeben was out in the kitchen with Ida getting ready to boil up the second batch of grape jelly, singing loudly of Jesus and his love. What help could Steeben be anyway, poor old thing? And Cantelou—she wondered if he could hear her. As if in answer two rapid shots came from far down in the swamp. Ducks, she thought, while watching the man come nearer to where she stood on the bottom step of the piazza beside one of the sleeping lions on its onyx base. Her pistol was in the cabinet in the parlor. Should she run for it? Sweat rolled down her forehead and her breath escaped from her half-opened mouth like the panting of a tired dog.

Shall I run for the pistol? I'd hate to kill a man. He's coming nearer. He's moving from behind the trees. He's peering out—he's coming toward me. Slowly, very slowly. He must think I don't see him. Now he's behind the magnolia. I must run. Quick, before he comes any closer. Run.

She backed up the steps and then the man stepped from behind the tree.

"Chance!"

Should she continue to run? Had Duchess been telling the truth or was *he* here after the guns?

"Miss India, don't look so frightened. Is the coach completely out of sight? Are you sure it is moving on or has it stopped? I can't seem to hear the wheels turning."

India strained her ears. Chance was no enemy. His tense sorrowful face told her that. The air about him told her. The smell of him was not enemy smell.

"Make like you're walking over to the pasture. Flossie is at the fence. Make like you're going to pet her. From the fence, if you climb up you can see if the coach has gone or if she has just pretended to go."

This was a nightmare. This was worse than Kilpatrick's raid. That had been open and in plain view. This was the sort of thing you dreamed might happen to you. And you would be alone. Always alone.

Her feet moved as heavy as in nightmare but they moved. "Flossie," she called hoarsely. "Pretty girl."

The old mare heard and took a stiff buck to prove that she *was* still a pretty girl. She gave a friendly whicker. India stooped and leisurely pulled a handful of sweet clover. How many more steps to the fence? Giant steps or lady steps or baby steps? How silly—that was a game she used to play in the small city garden of her childhood. No—not silly. It relaxed her. It steadied her. Lady steps. How many lady steps? Ten steps to the fence. But how many steps to the fear? Maybe five maybe nine. The day was hot but her hands were cold as ice. There was no sound of wheels or hoofs on the clay road. Come on, India, you've been bragging to Cantelou about how brave and fine you are. Ah—the fence. "Pretty Flossie—here's some clover for you. Good old lady. I can't ride you to Laurens next week for you are too old and stiff. You might stumble and spill me in the middle of the parade. Look at that bird flying over the forest! I declare, I believe it's a snow owl! Let me climb on the fence so that I can see it better—No—it's just a hawk—"

From the fence she could see the coach. It was pulled up and there were about forty mounted Negroes with rifles over their arms gathered around it. Duchess

was standing on the top step talking excitedly to them.
She turned at a warning from one and saw India on the
top fence rail staring at her. She raised a long red silk
arm and waved. India waved back and then the coach
went away and the Negroes rode silently along beside it.

As soon as the coach was well gone India ran back
to the house.

Chance wasn't in the yard but was in the parlor
talking to Emmy.

India said breathlessly, "She was there and she had
about forty armed militia with her but she went on
when she saw me."

"She'll be back. Mr. Gary told me he thought Prince
Rivers had an idea something was going on here. We'll
move the guns tonight so you all won't be in any danger
here at the Grove." Chance passed a big hand nervously over his harassed face.

"Isn't this a good place for them?" Emmy asked.

"The best, Miss Emmy, but you all might be frightened if they come hunting for them. They are getting
desperate since so many Negroes are pledging to vote
for Hampton. They'll stoop to anything to carry the
election for the Radicals."

"India and I don't scare easily," Emmy said. "I think
it's better to leave the guns where they are. They've
probably planted spies around and if we don't lead
them to the guns they certainly won't find them by
themselves. We can't risk losing them. How many are
there, Chance?".

"At least five thousand Enfield rifles, Miss Emmy."

"Good old Grant. I'll write and thank him when he
falls from his perch. As for now—we'll just go about
our business as though all we're interested in is getting
the cotton picked. Steeben nor Ida nor Cantelou have
any notion the guns are here so they won't have to put
on an act if anybody questions them. Danny does know
but he's so outraged at them for beating him in the
night last week I don't think he'd give us away."

Chance said, "Miss Emmy, you're a heading woman."

"Foot, Chance. It's exciting to have things happening at the Grove."

"I wish Mr. Maxi would come home. It would feel

like old times if he was here. Do you think he'll ever come back?"

India felt her neck and cheeks burn at the calling of his name. She turned so that Miss Emmy would not notice her agitation. It was so silly to blush like a young girl just hearing someone say "Maxi." Going over to the cabinet with the petit-point doors and looking in she said sharply, "There's nothing in here but the ivory box with Max's little man in it. The pistol's gone. Duchess must have taken it. I thought her reticule looked mighty heavy."

Chance had risen from the chair by the door and he said, "I'll bring you another one tonight. I've got to ride back to town and tell General Butler it's not necessary to send Red Shirts to move the guns. He'll be mighty proud of you folks."

CHAPTER XXXII

WADE HAMPTON SAT on the speaker's platform in a shady oak grove on the outskirts of Laurens watching the hundreds of mounted men in their red flannel shirts riding back and forth getting ready for the grand procession, yelling Hurrah for Hampton!

Since August 23, riots had been daily taking place on the Combahee rice plantations between Negro strikers and honest Negroes who wanted to gather the crops. Complete anarchy prevailed, for Governor Chamberlain hooded his eyes and refused to see or hear or speak against the evils.

It being a presidential election year made things doubly hard for Hampton in this campaign. He, personally, had no use for Tilden, the Democratic nominee, yet it was vital for South Carolina to oust the Republican carpetbaggers. For the past ten years legislatures, governors, and state officers had existed in name only for personal enrichment through plundering the state's resources. The courts were notoriously corrupt, crime unpunished, and pardons, like cotton, for sale to the highest bidder. Elections were a farce, the stuffed ballot boxes were fraudulently miscounted and now the white people found themselves pitted against the whole force of state and federal power in an election which the country thought was hopeless and yet which he felt confident of winning.

The ten years of corruption had not destroyed the spirit of the Carolinians, it had merely solidified them. Representative government was in the very lifeblood of his race. As a symbol, the thousands of his old cavalrymen, veterans of Gettysburg and The Wilderness and hundreds of other fights, were wearing their new uniforms, blood-colored shirts! They were mounted on thoroughbreds, mules, plow horses, ponies. For him this morning they had procured the most spirited horse in the county and the nag had groaned with pain when he gripped it gently with his knees. Oh, for one of his heroic monarchs in this campaign! He had worn out horses at the rate of three a week. He had worn out the gentlemen who accompanied him however young and tough they claimed to be. In his memory rose a picture of the powerful Bay Monarch and then a picture of Bay Monarch's rider. A picture not to be looked at except in a lonely room or by a dim campfire. Come back, Wade, he told himself sternly—back to here and now.

All of the area had turned out to acclaim him after days of preparation. Arches of flowers at intervals spanned all the five roads leading into the little town. Along the sidewalks were clusters of little girls dressed like angels with opened gauze wings. A band that knew two tunes—"The Bonnie Blue Flag" and "The Wearing Of The Green"—marched round and round the square and past the grove playing one tune and then the other. The enthusiasm was contagious. It was even hard for him to keep still. From all the churches flew the blue flag of the state, the stars and bars of the Confederacy and, yes—there it was on the Episcopal church —the stars and stripes! The balconied houses that faced the line of all this parading were decorated with flowers and bits of old bunting of red and blue.

In the crowd of more than five thousand people massed in front of him were many familiar faces. There

was the man who had told the tale of catching an
eight-pound bass with a rod and reel in little Pee Dee;
there was the man who'd promised him one of his big
liver-colored hounds. He would make a grand bear dog.
Ah—he had liked that hound; a fine head and a won-
drous bell in his deep chest. There was the one-eyed
Sergeant had fetched him the cool cup of tea in the very
middle of the scorching Crater. There was David Flen-
niken of Winnsboro, one of his best scouts and couriers,
who had saved his life at Gettysburg! And there was Fed,
his Negro jockey, who had ridden Lithgow to capture
the Jockey Club Purse at the Charleston races back in
1850, the day his friend Inigo Gaillard had been
kicked by Edisto. Stop remembering, Wade, this is a
new day and a new time, he told himself sternly. Look
at the people—bow, smile! There was the pretty widow
he had met last night. Howdy, mam—he bowed gravely to her in her wide flat hat with the long curling
plumes. She was a little obvious in her flirtation but she
was a fine figure of a woman. A mighty fine figure of a
woman.

He smoothed the lapels of his ill-fitting huge gray
suit, ordered out of a catalogue. It was a comfortable
suit, big enough for a giant. He liked it much better
than those tight broadcloth coats his London tailor
used to cram his muscle-bound shoulders in. And this
soft shirt with the loose collar—how much simpler
than those stocks and starched ruffles of by-gone days.
At fifty-eight, widowed, bankrupt, homeless, he was
deeply moved by these men who kept shouting, "We're
ready to storm hell with Hampton!" He felt very grati-
fied at the turnouts he was getting all over the state. The
campaign was purposely starting in the Up Country
which was hot for him and would end—hoping the heat
would gather momentum and travel—in Charleston.
This was in opposite rhythm to Secession which had
started in Charleston and forcibly swept the Up Country along with it.

At first he hadn't thought he had a chance to be
governor when Mart Gary, who had never liked him,
approached him. But when Calbraith Butler had nominated him he felt it was his duty to "pull out" the best

he could, as Rooney Lee used to say. So here he was.
Up front again. And it felt good to be up front again.
Yes, by God, it felt good. Though from the past occupants, the honor of the governorship did not hold the
same luster as it had when he was young and had
watched the brilliant McDuffie ride in his elegant berlin
up to the State House.

He thought of F. W. Pickens and his stupidity at fo-
menting Secession; defying the whole United States on
the insistence of a wife young enough to be his grand-
daughter.

Of Orr, who had gone over to the Radicals when he
saw that they would be the big power after first passing
the "black code," the *coup de grâce* of decent reconstruction.

Of Robert Scott drunkenly signing hundreds of thousands of dollars worth of fraudulent convertible state
bonds over to his big blonde in their illicit love nest in
the old St. James Hotel in New York.

Of the salon in Columbia where the Governor planned
his next big steal—the home of the brown Madame
Rollin and her lovely daughters, Euphrosyne, Marie
Louise, and Charlotte, where Scott and later Moses let
the Rollin ladies direct the destiny of South Carolina in
return for their pretty favors.

He remembered one day when Moses was the Governor of South Carolina seeing a handsome landau drawn
by a spanking pair of Kentucky horses containing that
outrageous Duchess and the Rollin girls, all dressed
in low-necked dresses, their bosoms and arms shining
with diamonds and rubies, pull up in front of a bar-
room on Main Street and out of the saloon stepped his
eminence the Governor of South Carolina, former secretary to Old Pick and Lovely Lucy, Franklin Moses,
accompanied by Elliott, the thief, and Whipper, the
degenerate, followed by a servant carrying a silver
waiter on which was champagne and glasses, and right
there in the public sidewalk had occurred a perfect
orgy of drinking and philandering and screaming laughter. Ugh! It sickened him even to think of it.

And this Chamberlain the Reformer, who had seen
the writing on the wall and was howling, I will be a

good boy and protect you white people from the
Radicals! This Chamberlain—a New Englander of
good birth, graduate of Yale University, a man who
should have known better—appointing Whipper and
Moses to be the Supreme Court judges of the prostrate
state; in his speeches to the Negroes leading them into
the sanctity of his wife's boudoir, to the very cradle of
his child. This man was worse than any for he was
brilliant, as slippery as an eel, making a promise one
day and breaking it on the next.

What a nest of vipers!

He was as mad as a hornet. Good. He'd make a
better speech today. Never an orator it was hard for
him to wave his arms and shout at the assembled
multitudes. But today he was mad. Ready to storm hell
to clean out the whole corrupt and festering black and
tan administration. It was just as easy to storm it as
live in it anyway.

At last—the program was beginning. And in the
usual way. In hobbled the black hag covered with
tattered rags. Up stepped Chancellor Ball and took her
by the hand, and as the cheer swelled and rolled
Hurrah for Hampton! Hampton rose from his chair as
a cherub with a pink sash ran up and touched the hag
with a wand. Rising from her crouching position, the
hag threw off her tatters, transformed into a golden-
haired maiden who welcomed her redeemer with radiant smiles. It was always the same, he thought, though
not all the girls were as handsome and full-bosomed
as this one!

Now came the procession. Company after mounted
company, some of them stretching hundreds of yards,
swept across the square into the grove and the yelling
and cheering never stopped, it only rose and fell in
waves of sound. From Edgefield, Laurens, Spartanburg,
Abbeville, Clinton, they came bearing banners reading,
"Let Us Have Peace" and "Tilden And Victory."
Humph—I don't care for Tilden. I hope Hayes is
elected. I'd rather work with him any day. Then came
the wagons with men holding up life-size cutouts of
Chamberlain and Hampton. The man who carried
Chamberlain shouted over and over in a high shrilly

voice: "I am going home." The man with Hampton
boomed in a husky bass: "I will be the Governor of the
whole people." Chamberlain: "Write me in care of my
law office in Boston on January 1, 1877." They sound
like frogs, Hampton thought, as transparencies in profusion followed. One showed a box of guns, with bayonets fixed, extending over the side with the President
of the United States above the box and a Negro reaching out to take one of the guns from the box marked
"Shoemaker's Tools." Another showed the public crib
represented by a large iron safe with Chamberlain
kneeling, his left hand filled with greenbacks which he
was placing in other hands stretched toward him while
with his right he was going for more and he was saying, "This is our last grab and we will have a big one."

And now a new band had arrived—the Greenville
Helicon Band and they could play "Dixie" and the
crowd went wild—screaming and howling with all the
pent-up emotions of the past eleven years of defeat and
humiliation which would soon be ended by the big man
up there on the platform.

The red shirts were not all plain red flannel, for many
of them were elaborately trimmed with blue and yellow
and the men wore sashes of red and blue and gold.
Here and there a marshal with a plumed hat and
clanking sword dashed from place to place while the
procession, three miles long, lasted over an hour. Hawkers cried balloons, rockets, Hampton badges, ice cream,
grapes, gingybread, boiled peanuts, lemonade, and wool
Hampton Hats guaranteed to fit any honest head. The
Negro Democrats in their red shirts rode side by side
with the white Red Shirts and they laughed and joked
together in good fellowship—glad to be going together
again. They had missed each other. It was better to be
marching together than hating each other. There was
room in the procession for all who wanted to get rid
of the dishonest men sitting in the high seats of government.

The day was dry, the dust was thick and choking.
The speaker's platform had HOME AND HAMPTON
worked in moss and ivy in an arch over it and the back
of the stage was elegantly set off with big green stars

made of soft fragrant cedar. Colonel Ball presided and he had his little boy with him on the stand.

Just before Hampton began to speak he turned to little Billy Ball sitting round-eyed on the platform with his aloof parent.

"Watch my hat, Billy," he said, laying his black stovepipe on the table. "If anybody should take a fancy to it for a souvenir I haven't got the money to buy a new one."

He began in his usual way by complimenting the ladies present and then calmly, as though he were their host and they were his honoured guests in the once priceless paneled library of his lovely Millwood, he told them exactly what was going on—exactly what they had to expect from Ulysses Grant and his robber barons.

"This is not a question of race as the Radicals are trying to tell you. This is a showdown between corruption and incorruption. The only way to bring about prosperity in this state is to bring the two races in friendly relation together. The Democratic party in South Carolina, of whom I am the exponent, has promised that every citizen of this state is to be the equal of all; he is to have every right given him by the Constitution of the United States and of this state. . . . And I pledge my faith, and I pledge it for those gentlemen who are on the ticket with me, that if we are elected, as far as in us lies, we will observe, protect, and defend the rights of the colored man as quickly as of any man in South Carolina. . . . If there is a white man in this assembly, who because he is a Democrat, or because he is a white man, believes that when I am elected governor, if I should be, that I will stand between him and the law, or grant him any privilege or immunity that shall not be granted to the colored man, he is mistaken. . . ."

He pointed to the record of Radical government in the state and asked the Radical leaders to explain how they proposed to accomplish the reforms that they promised. He reminded the Negroes that the whites of the state had tried to get good government by backing the reform element within the Republican Party at every election and he urged them to trust in politics the men whom they trusted in business and daily life. He said he was the first white man in the South, after the War Between The States, to advocate giving the Negroes the franchise. He promised peace and protection for all classes and he ended with his slogan: Reconciliation, Retrenchment, and Reform.

He had hardly finished his calm, dignified address when the Red Shirts at a signal from Mart Gary started the Rebel yell and in the ensuing frightening screaming excitement which was probably a much more convincing argument to the Radicals than his own heartfelt appeal, he reached for his hat to slip from the platform and rest a minute. But horrors! The scamp of a Ball child had disappeared and his hat was gone! On the table was a hat to be sure—but it sat on the top of his big head like a monkey cap. Well—he'd slip down anyway. He had to have one minute alone before he faced the handshaking and good wishes of the multitude. Yesterday he had ridden horseback over forty miles and tonight he had twenty more to go.

"Mr. Wade—if you're trying to get down—give Cantelou your hand and jump here in the shade."

"India St. Julien Allan! Hat! You two always go together. Where is the hat you wagered me a lifetime ago? I demand payment now. Did you see that someone stole mine up there on the platform? My—you look like this boy's sister not his mother. However do you manage it?"

"That was a wonderful speech, General." The boy with India was looking at him with such idolatry that Hampton almost blushed. Cantelou wasn't much like his devil-may-care father but appeared a sound young fellow. Sound.

"Thank you, son. You look like your grandfather St. Julien. India, have you heard from Maximilian lately?"

Heavens—was she going to faint?

She whispered, "Mr. Wade, I haven't heard a word from Max since he disappeared eight years ago. I keep

hoping that he will turn up behind you some place.
That's why I pushed here so close to the platform. I
keep hoping—"

"Gracious, I know where he is. I saw him last week
at the Hampton Rally in Walhalla. I've known where
he's been for years. Oh dear—why didn't someone tell
me you didn't know. Ouch—stop it—"

India was digging her fingernails in his big wrist and
trying to shake his arm. Her eyes looked like a wildcat's
which had almost clawed him one night on Williamson's Island near Darlington. Visiting the Ervins, he'd
been. Good people, the Ervins, fine hunters. Gentlemen.

"Where is Max? Tell me at once—at once—" Tears
soaked her sun-brown cheeks. "Tell me—"

"Honey—he's right up in the Smokies at Cashiers
Valley. He followed me up there one June eight years
ago. Stayed with me at High Hampton at first. He behaved rather strangely, crying and so forth, but he
calmed down in a few weeks and moved into a cabin
on the top of the mountain where he trades in roots
and herbs with the mountain women. I wondered why
you never came to see him. I thought you'd left him.
I've been in Mississippi so long I've gotten out of
touch with my friends here in the Up Country. Now—
now—don't cry so hard. Take the train to Walhalla
from Columbia and ask at the station for Rutledge
Bean. He used to be one of my slaves and he always
has a horse for rent and guides folks up the mountain.
It won't take you any time to find him. Everybody
knows who he is. The 'sangman' they call him. Maximilian was always a rascal. Oh—I'm coming, Mr.
Ball. Just resting a minute after my speech. It tires me
more than fifty miles' hard riding. Now—don't forget
my hat, India. You owe it to me. Especially since I've
located Maximilian for you."

CHAPTER XXXIII

RUTLEDGE BEAN was a lively cricket of a black man who sang as he straddled his piebald horse and kept calling back to India, dizzy and tense with her hopes and fears.

"Looka yonder, Missy! See dem! See dose! See dem udders! Watch out fuh pulling on Clingy. He know dis trail bettern you. Gib em mout' room and you'll get to de sangman. I know he up dere 'cause he come back frum de big Smokies las' week wid a wagonload of lettle sangmen."

The first twenty miles up from Walhalla had taken a day's winding. The second day's climbing looked to be steeper and rougher and there was a hard touch of frost in the air. The chill of it struck through to her bones, coming up as she had from the stifling heat of the cotton-belt September. A morning fog clung in a mile-high cloud all around. As they set out along the twisting trail through the dense mist she could hear the singing of winter wrens, in a long unwinding bird song, sweet and full in the core of the enveloping cloud.

The trail turned and wandered through a cloud forest of dim wet woods. Every leaf was dripping; every tree trunk was hoary with moss and lichens. The trees were trees of the North: maple, chestnut, spruce, white pine, fir, yellow birch, and beech. Beneath them was a thick plush carpet of russet-green moss and the horses moved up the cushioned trail as silent as the fog. She felt as though she were making her way into another planet. A realm that was half water, half land; half night, half day; half human beings, half animals. Snails and slugs and brown insects with yellow legs moved wet and shining over rocks and moldering trunks, hares and chipmunks scurried and hopped across the path. She herself felt like a hard-shelled beetle working through cotton batting and when the cloud began to break up she watched it tearing into long wind-blown shreds like loosened witches riding high and letting blue sky show. She found herself riding along a razorback ridge with stupendous views unfolding on either side and then the window in the sky slammed shut. The blue sky disappeared. The fog swirled back and the wind rose.

Around noon they stopped near a fallen tree, got off the horses, and ate the biscuits and ham that the mountain woman with whom they had spent the night had fixed for them. Standing still India realized that through the fog sound was clearer than it had been when the fog lifted and the wind blew.

"Hush," she said, "I hear somebody beating a drum. Could it be Indians?"

A series of muffled thumps were heard slow and measured at first then gradually accelerating into a smooth drum roll that slowed in time and faded into the wet stillness.

"Dat's a ruffle' grouse," said Rutledge. "Walk up to de end of de tree and maybe you see em. He sound like he up in de branch part."

She felt her way in the cloud following the dark twisted trunk, jagged in places where bears had clawed it, and saw the grouse dimly, his black neck and ruffs raised, his tail spread, beating out the drum notes of his song with his powerful wings.

She crept back to the trail through a tangle of fiddlehead ferns browned by early frost, growing thick and close under young birch trees whose silvery trunks vanished at her looking, like very ghosts into the ghostly fog. A giant brownish grasshopper leaped from under her feet and sailed past her like a wind-blown leaf. She jumped back and slipped in the droppings of a bear.

By now she felt as bewildered and strange as she had the first winter night driving in the scarlet coach through the Up Country forest to Shepherd's Grove. But then *he* had been with her. This time he might not even welcome her when she at long last reached the top cliff of the mountain where Rutledge said the sangman lived.

She still had five more miles and an ascent of a

thousand feet higher to climb. Fortunately the fog lifted a little and through it began to gleam the burning fire of the autumn maples—the chestnuts, the hickories, the scarlet-berried ashes, the beeches, the sumacs. As afternoon came, she forgot her fatigue and time ran swiftly. It cleared completely and the sun gilded the sheer cliffs with undulating waves of flaming color. She saw the little two-room log cabin as a mere brown dot in the spreading meadow of the bald around it. Along the meadow the wind that had boomed at her this morning on the razor ridge was booming still. The valley below was sinking into shadow.

"Want I should go to de cabin wid you?" Rutledge obviously was anxious to start back down the mountain before the sun got lower.

"No."

"When you want me to come back for you?"

"He'll bring me down to Walhalla."

"Well, keep old Clingy long's you want."

"Thank you. Good-by."

"Bime."

The wind from the mountain caught at her hair and swept chill and raw against her hot cheeks as she kicked old Clingy into a semblance of a trot through the waist-high dying grass of the bald. The sunlight gleamed on the wide timbers notched at the corners of the cabin but near it she could see no living thing, just a primitive wagon made of hand-cut boards. There was no smoke from the rock chimney, not even a dog to bark at her.

She unsaddled Clingy and led him to a water trough. She then took him into a lean-to against the cabin, the sun stabbing unkindly on the accumulated filth through a hole in the roof.

A black bearskin and two foxskins were stretched upon the cabin wall for drying. By now she refused to think or to hope and expected to find the house locked, but the ill-fitting door flew over the puncheon floor when she touched the heavy iron lock. Evidently he did not fear or expect visitors. A smell of animals and more drying skins and roots was in here. The first feeling that rushed over her as she stood within the

miserable little cabin was heartbreaking pity and re-
morse that he had been impelled to run from his home
to this. It seemed more like a bear's winter hole for
hibernation than a man's dwelling.

The room she entered was small and square. The
walls were unfinished but the ceiling was gracefully
supported by old hand-hewn beams from which hung
strings of dried apples and peppers and twists of tobacco. The wide fireplace was fashioned of lovely stones
with a solid slab of granite for a mantel. There were
two windows of tiny leaded panes. Some of the panes
had been broken and were stopped up with sacks. Dirt
was thick on the floor and there was a stumpy little
split-bottomed chair and a thin pine bench in front of
the hearth. Guns, skins, and old clothes lay all around;
the trestle table held a greasy pewter plate with the
remains of bacon and corn mush and a recent New
York newspaper on one end and on the other a granite
mortar with a heavy pestle pressing on some pungent
silvery dried leaves.

She saw a long bench in the corner and her heart
started thumping. Something was lying on the bench!
Entirely covered over with a ragged quilt. She knew it
was—it wasn't—it mustn't be—

She set her teeth and made herself go and lift the
edge of the Rose of Sharon patchwork quilt. There
was an array of roots that looked like little dried-up
people bedded in straw on the smooth board of the
bench reminding her of the funny charm Max had
fetched for himself from China long ago.

She looked over toward the low maple bedstead in
the other corner piled with rumpled covers and a fresh-
oiled saddle and bridle. How had he lived in this lonely
house? Slept in this dreadful bed? He must sleep
in that bed. Perhaps she herself would lie in that bed tonight. She went over to the bed—it hadn't been made
up for days. The shucks of the mattress had been lain
on till they were hard as stones. The chicken-feather
pillows smelled damp and fusty. Dust and trash rose
from the quilt when she shook it.

Max—who could never have enough luxury about
him; Max—who wanted soft silken underthings

against his bare skin and wrapped himself in a satin and down comforter, who didn't want her to put on a gingham dress in the mornings but always insisted that she go dressed in silk and lace as though she were receiving elegant company, who would scold the slave girls if so much as a tiny wrinkle was left in his fine bed sheets. And he had gone from Shepherd's Grove to this! To this—because of Irene? Or because of thinking she was in love with Ervin Marshall? Or because of some deep lacking in his wounded soul?

To keep back the tears, to bear it, she hung the saddle by a stirrup from one of the numerous dusty pegs along the wall and carefully smoothed the covers over the bed; looked for a broom but there wasn't a broom or a mop anywhere. She looked into the other room which was windowless and murky and now she saw why this room smelled so weird. He had probably brought his dog in here so that at night he would not be all alone atop the high rocky cliff that seemed to be at the very peak of his cloudy world. It smelled like dog and other hairy animals as well.

There were all manner of skins stretched and drying in here: foxes, deer, another bear, coons, and the most loathsome rattler hide, long and thick and diamond-marked. High piles of leaves, twigs, and roots lay neatly arranged in orderly fashion with labels written on cheap paper atop each pile. She looked up at the dark beams and as she did so she heard a dry rushing sound and a disturbed bat, like the shadow of a bat rather than a bat itself, dropped and wheeled squeaking about the room, then disappeared again onto a dusty timber.

As the sun was setting she heard him coming and ran to the window and looked out. From the forest by the same trail up which she had ridden came a huge white mule harnessed to a sled of firewood. Max walked by its side, driving. A long-eared hound dog sat on the top of the wood.

The white mule strained at his collar and dragged the sled forward, bumping it over the rocky ground. The hound jumped down and ran through the grass, barking. Max, who had begun unharnessing the mule, realized that the dog was aware of something. He took the axe from the pile of hickory logs and walked toward the cabin.

India shrank back from the window and stood trembling—waiting.

Max pushed the door wide open and the hound bounded after him and ran up to her, greeting her with his bell-like voice.

The first thing she saw was the wave of red blood that rushed over Max's face—the trembling of his fine wide mouth, the long gold eyes slanting under the shadow of his thick brows.

Just the sight of him took away her breath. She saw the healed scar, the unshaven stubble of light beard upon his lower face, she saw that his hair was clipped close to his skull like a snug-fitting gold and silver cap, but the color came and went in his olive face in waves, as when he was young—he still looked young and so handsome, it was as though none of this ugliness had had the power to touch him.

He was dressed like any poor mountaineer in a wool jacket, spotted and colorless, but fitting closely to his body's strong and graceful motions. His tight woolen trousers were torn at one knee and snagged behind the other. Yet never more than now had he looked the nabob, the aristocratic scion of an old and prideful family. He carried himself as he had done before his injury—easily and proudly; the hesitation of manner, the lowering of his head had disappeared entirely and he stood there, resting a little on one foot, a hand tucked in the belt about his slender waist, the other on the head of the tan and black hound, looking at her, saying nothing. Neither saying anything. At last he said in a voice that trembled a little,

"How did you find me? Why did you come?"

"Wade Hampton told me you where you were. I came to see you."

"And now you have seen the hall of the mountain king!" He cast his glance around the room. "You see in what style I live. Not comparable to your Virginia mansion but comfortable and clean. Don't stare at me so—what is wrong?"

"Nothing is wrong and you know quite well I have no Virginia mansion. I came here to beg you to come back to Shepherd's Grove where you belong. We need you dreadfully. We miss you, all of us—" She lowered her eyes.

"Didn't you marry the Virginian?"

"Heavens no. You had no right to believe anything Irene made up without asking me the truth." She was red now and a little angry. Almost very angry— seeing him there so well and fine and proud.

"I saw the way you looked at him that day. And when she said I was a burden to you—well—I rode away. I thought Mr. Hampton had probably told you I was here. I thought—but never mind what I thought. . . . You must be hungry."

He opened a cupboard and took out some corn bread and a jug of buttermilk and a platter of roasted grouse. India was hungry and thirsty but it was hard to eat, though Max ate quickly and was soon through.

He talked of himself for a while. Of his ginseng roots and herbs that the mountain women fetched and he sold to an importer out of Charleston. There was a family nearby who brought him milk and butter and a little food for firewood that he cut for them. Mostly he hunted and fished. However, he was getting tired of the loneliness and might himself take his roots to China the next time instead of selling them to a middle man.

"Ah, no, Max!"

He looked at her strangely but he had not replied to her when she had asked him to come home and now she was shy with him. Had he been the same as when he left her eight years ago, quiet, uncertain and lost, she could have said anything that was in her heart but this man was whole—proud—sure of himself and of what he wanted.

Dusk sifted into the room . . . her face glowed palely in the darkening light against the rough gray walls. Max rose and made a fire in the fireplace. Then he sat down on a bench across from her, looking at her, the flare of the fire flickering over his powerful body.

"Do you still not remember who you are?" she said suddenly.

"I am the sangman!" He smiled to himself, his eyes far off and mocking. "The people up here think I am a king or a witchman in disguise. They think as I appeared up here one windy day so will I disappear some windy day. They ask me no questions and I have not had to think of anything but what comes in my head. I can go and come as I like . . . and I sleep well. Better than in the pine-shrouded library of Shepherd's Grove. Here I don't have to try and wonder who was—or am. They have helped me. These years of solitude. Oh—I have missed you—never doubt that. I have wondered what you were doing and whether you *did* love the red-haired man and go away with him. I have started down the mountain to return to you a thousand nights but this is the better way—for you to come to me in my own kingdom. You must be tired after the long trip up the mountain. It is time for you to go to bed." Tense and stiff, she watched Max turn back the dirty quilt. "Not down or satin but, as someone I knew somewhere used to say: 'a poor thing but mine own'!"

"Max!" She twisted her fingers together under her breasts trying to know the right words to say. Oh—it was so important that this come out right. This was the last chance she would have to reclaim him. This she knew and she also knew that everything else that touched against her life was worthless without him to share it. He took up the dirty rose and green patterned quilt from the roots and flung it over his arm.

"Would you like me to leave the hound in here with you?"

India had risen and was standing in front of the hearth with the tongues of flames showing around her like living daggers.

"Where are you going, Max?"

"Out to the barn. The night is not too cold. I can gather an armful of grass from the meadow as I go."

"No—" Max stopped . . . he stood in front of her straight and strong and young in the glow of the burning fire. "I am afraid to sleep in here without you. Stay with me."

"Are you inviting me to share the bed with you?"

She saw the old devil-may-care smile curve his sensuous lips and familiar laughter glitter in his eyes. "It has been a long time since I have loved a woman. I might crush you to death. Remember—I don't have to pretend to be the gentlemanly Maximilian Allan up here in my mountain kingdom. I may be a witchman like my ginseng women think, for all you know." He spoke lightly but his eyes belied the lightness of his words.

In answer she held out her arms to him and a deep wild tremor went through her as he vehemently pressed his open lips upon her mouth.

Eight years? This was blessed enough to wait a lifetime for!

All night the wind buffeted the cabin. Gust-driven fog swirled over the roof like foaming clouds. They were in the heart of the sky and in the heart of the wind. The wind was still roaring when she awoke the next morning. The leaden colored fog grew slowly brighter in the early dawn. Through the wind a robin was singing and somewhere near she heard the same song that had come out of the mist yesterday—the long, sweet, unwinding song of a winter wren. Max was sleeping with his cropped head pushed hard into her armpit. She saw red marks on her breast and on her arms, thrilling again as memory after memory of the night flowed over her. She caught his head and pressed it hungrily against her breast.

Max awoke . . . leaned up on his elbow, looked wondering into her face. His eyes dark with sleep were at the first wild and then gentle and full of waking passion. "I was afraid—" he smiled as he used to smile, not showing his teeth at all but the corner of his red mouth curving sweetly and kissed her on the throat and she throbbed at the joy and the fear in his voice, "I was afraid I had been dreaming again. But you are here in my arms—India, my love!"

CHAPTER XXXIV

By afternoon the sun shone and cloud shadows lay long across the undulating waves of ancient ridges, relics of the early Paleozoic continent that flowed around the bald top of Max's mountain where, he said, the Nunnehi, a race of spirit folk, used to live. It had grown quite warm during the day and India was delighted with the unending sweep of peaks and sky around her. Almost naked rock slid downward from the bald into the chasm. Here and there some ancient wind-carved hemlock or spruce clung to a bit of rock. Over the crags a pair of dark ravens flapped past, calling hoarsely to each other across the empty spaces. At intervals one of the ravens would dive and twist wildly, sometimes even flying upside down to impress his mate.

Once as Max and India rounded a trail bend walking hand in hand noiselessly on the soft moss, there was a windy roar and two ruffled grouse whirred past them into the forest. Max carried his rifle and India moved by his side, slender, straight and supple as a girl. Her hair, plaited and wound around her head, shone blue-black in the sunlight. Her cheeks glowed and her mouth was as soft as red velvet from his kissing. Every time she looked at him he smiled at her and she almost sank onto the ground when she saw in his face how lovely she was.

She tried to tell him the way things were happening at home but he was anxious to show her where he bathed and so she followed him to the stream she had heard roaring with the wind last night, which slid like a thin foaming layer of lace down the face of successive shelves of gray rock. The sound of the falls was soft and murmurous. Red-gold sand formed a little bar at an edge of the pool and they took off their clothes and bathed in the cold clear water, splashing and playing like children until she forgot everything but the sunlight on his shiny olive body and the hardness of his wet lips burning down on hers.

Afterward, there was the sunset to watch from the top of the bald and night came swiftly in mid-September. The next day found her so outrageously happy that try as she might to remember Edgefield and Cantelou working desperately to get the cotton picked, the angry Duchess, the shouting Red Shirts, it was as though Max were truly the witchman he had joked about and had thrown poppy seeds across her brain and heart: as though she had climbed the wisteria vine straight to the top of his mountain into a world inhabited only by her and him.

At the end of a week the women came with the fall gathering of roots and herbs and she saw a different Max emerge. They were sitting in the sun on a big rock near a clump of Balm of Gilead trees watching for the women.

"There's something I want to tell you before the women come."

"What is it?" she asked lazily, leaning her back against his chest and feeling the wonder of his arms go around her waist. She could hear the little falls trilling and gurgling far below. Now and then Max kissed the back of her neck.

"I'm not poor as you might think from the little cabin. You won't have to sleep on corn shucks forever."

"Why did you ever sleep on them at all?"

"Because I discovered, like Diogenes at the country fair, 'Lord, how many things there be in this world of which Diogenes hath no need!' Now don't ask me where I heard about Diogenes. That is one of those jack-in-the-box things buried in my past that popped up suddenly from an unlabeled box. But not remembering doesn't worry and bedevil me any more. When I think of how harassed and astray I was at Shepherd's Grove with Irene constantly embarrassing and hurting me; with you so utterly desirable and I too bewildered to reach out and possess you, I wonder that I waited so long as I did to run away. I don't care whether my memory comes back now or not. I have the two things in the world I want: you and money to do as I please."

"How much money, Max?"

"I'll not tell you. You say I am all in life you desire.
I intend to let you prove it, my sweet, by staying here
with me, in my world. I will buy you a warm pair of
shoes and a heavy cloak and you can help me with my
business. Pay close attention to everything you hear
and see today. Be friendly with the women and don't
frown at their grammar. There will be a large, gaunt
woman with sharp black eyes from whom I will buy
you a cow and soon I will build you a barn and you
can raise a few pigs and chickens to keep you occupied."

India laughed and started to wind her thick plait
about her head to look tidy when the women came.

"How would Cantelou and Miss Emmy manage if I
deserted Shepherd's Grove? Then . . . there's you . . .
you would say . . . on the day your memory returns:
'Woman, why have you lost my plantation and delivered me up to the witches?' "

"Don't you like being delivered up to the witches?"

She said, "I like you." And then the women were on
the bald and Max made a great show of introducing his
wife who had blown up to him in the big wind of a
week ago. And the women stared at the gray and red
Balmoral skirt she wore and admiringly touched the
tip of her shabby old kidskin shoes and one asked
if she might hold the red Llama lace shawl she had
about her shoulders.

"Where is your son to help me weigh the herbs?" he
asked the gaunt woman from whom India was to have
her cow.

"Gone to see whar Bobby Tuttle's abeen horse
throwed down the clift and lying in a manner stone
dead."

"And where's Molly with the fattest roots?"

The women cackled raucously, "Had her front tooth
jumped out and Uncle Neddy Carter whut wuz to
jump hit missed the nail she wuz holding 'ginst hit and
mashed her nose with the hammer."

"Next time tell her to come and let me pull her
tooth," Max said. "Root season won't wait and a tooth
will. Come into the cabin and let's see what you've got
for me this time."

India followed, amazed at Max's ease with these women and the knowing way he appraised the heaps of dried ladyslipper roots, thick felty hare's-beard, fragrant sassafras bark, blackberry roots, treadsoftly berries split and dried; weighed them and handed out money from a leathern sack. Lastly he turned to the sharp-faced, black-eyed woman, chewing a twig of sweet birch dipped in snuff, who had not spread the contents of her sack onto the floor.

"All right, Rose Quilla, you look like a cat that has swallowed a bird . . . what do you have?"

"Sang!" the women cried.

India crowded close and there on the rough burlap lay a heap of little dried-up-people, roots like the ones she had uncovered on the bench the day she came.

"Why, that one looks just like Miss Emmy." India pointed to a short, fat, albeit graceful, brown root with thin fibrous hair and a hand extended in the very position Emmy took before striking her harp.

"Take it for her," Max said bending over the roots. He carefully picked the miniature folk up and turned them round and round, examining each part shrewdly. Finally he weighed the batch on his crude scales. There were ten pounds of the roots.

"A thousand dollars, Rose Quilla. These are perfect specimens. I've never seen finer."

The women gasped and loudly sucked their snuff sticks but none grudged Rose her good fortune and when Max counted out the money from his bag, leaving it by no means empty, they laughed some more and took their leave singing and calling to Rose Quilla good-naturedly.

As the line of shabby, old-young women threaded through the waist-high grass of the meadow of the bald, Rose Quilla turned and called, "I'll send you a extry good bait of victuals this evening by Susie. I kilt a hog yesterday and hit was good and ripe with the juiciest chitlins you ever seen."

Alone again Max met India's eyes coolly.

"You see now why I want to go personally to China with my roots. Especially fine roots like these bring as much as seven hundred dollars a pound in Manchuria where men set great store by their virility. I possess a fortune of them right here in this cabin. No one can say I am a burden now."

That night Max was exhilarated. He was always exhilarated after a day's bargaining; excited. He liked himself very much. He was glad she had seen the trading. It delighted him. He talked gaily of the places he and she would enjoy together, the wonders they would see, the elegant clothes they would wear—smooth and silken-soft and many colored. His manner which had been sad and insecure at Shepherd's Grove and shrewd with the ginseng gatherers was now exuberant. He was glad India was sitting across from him. He stroked her hand and the electric shock that always leaped from her fingers into his was intensified. Ah, there was so much for him to do with his life—so much he could be. With the money he had banked in Charleston and with the roots he had stored in the warehouse there and over a hundred pounds of them here in the cabin, he was a rich man now. Very rich, and that was just the beginning. He had definite plans for opening an importing business. Perhaps in Wilmington or Charleston or New York if that was indicated. As he talked he kept looking at India across the trestle table. His eyes that shone in the firelight with a tawny flare looked steadily at her under his long thick lashes. From time to time they lightened when a tongue of flame, high leaping, reflected in them, like a leopard's half-hidden in moonlight. The open neck of his green flannel shirt showed his throat like a lithe strong tree.

They both jumped when from the meadow came the high wailing hollering of Rutledge Bean:

"Ah—hoo—Mr. Sangman. Here be Rutledge Bean wid a message for Miz Allan, so don't be athinking I'm no hant and shooting me wid yo' silver bullets."

The message was a telegram from Miss Emmy:

Mr. and Mrs. Maximilian Allan
In care of Mr. Rutledge Bean
Walhalla, S. C.

Cantelou was shot today in the fields while picking cotton. Come home at once. His condition is
critical.

Emmy Allan

Max sat gazing at India while she cried a little and
insisted on going back down the mountain at once. At
last he spoke with a strange smile, baring his teeth a
little as he smiled.

"I didn't think you'd leave me for anyone. But since
it is your child I suppose you must go. However, you
can't ride down the mountain tonight. Rutledge can
sleep in the storeroom and I'll get you off by daylight."

During the night rain drove against the cabin and in
the morning the clouds enveloped the bald completely.
He went with her a half-day's riding down through the
clouds. She had not asked him to come nor had she
censured him for not coming. She was as one on the
edge of waking from a dream and he could not tell
what she was thinking. She clung tightly to him when
he turned to go back up the mountain. They sat, she
on Rutledge Bean's Clingy and he on the restless big
white mule, side by side and he kissed her over and
over and between the kisses he looked at her with ques-
tioning eyes.

"Please come with me," she broke down and said at
last.

His answer was a long kiss and then he told her to
be careful of Clingy's footing on the razor ridge and
he watched her as she went from his sight in and out of
the big trees seen dimly through the blanketing fog,
and he was tempted to kick the mule and ride home
with her but he could not leave his ginseng fortune un-
guarded in the cabin. Besides, now that she had found
the way to him she would come back. For she could not
live without him any more—nor he without her!

CHAPTER XXXV

FOR THE REST of her life this time until Election Day remained in India's mind as a vague but horrible nightmare. For a week Cantelou hovered between life and death, while in the hall men and women came and went, talking softly and slowly. India sat day after day by her son's bed and felt as though she were sitting far back in a cave. At a great distance and in a curiously blurred way, things went on happening outside the cave. There was a great and greater riding, more shooting, more Hurrahs for Hampton! more fear, more death, and destruction of property. But she had no part in them. She had run away from life.

Voices wove in and out of her unnatural composure in the big dim room.

"He can't live through tonight."

"Dr. Quattlebaum dug out the bullet but he left a big hole in his left lung."

"Mama! Mama! Don't let her—Mama!"

"Law, feel his forehead! He's burning with fever."

"Lemme stanch hit wid a spider web, Miss Emmy."

"He's so white!"

"Don't let her, Mama!"

At the end of a week he sucked a little beef tea through a reed and that evening India asked what she had not dared to know until she was sure whether Cantelou was going to live or not.

"Who shot Cantelou, Miss Emmy?"

"I've been wondering when you'd ask. The Duchess shot him. Steeben and I saw our old coach pull up along the woods road. Chance moved out here the day you left. Duchess had had his shop burned and all his blacksmith equipment torn up. He was picking cotton in the field with Cantelou and I'm pretty certain Duchess meant to shoot him and hit Cantelou by mistake. Calbraith Bulter swore out a warrant for her but she had six Negroes declare in court that she was in the Low Country that day. I even went into town and said

I saw her shoot the child but the Radical judge laughed and called me an old fuddled woman."

"Perhaps she meant to shoot them both. For the first time I can see that Cantelou looks like Papa, lying there with his eyes closed. She hated Papa."

Loud, loud the wind of autumn rolled tidally through the tops of the giant pines and cedars. India thought of a little girl held in a man's arms watching the foaming breakers boom and shatter into sun-specked foam along the sandy beach of Sullivan's Island. She thought of a little girl with a cropped head cantering proudly with the high spirit which was hers, through the shaded summer streets of Charleston. She thought of the man's love for his little girl, the little girl's happiness riding along the summer streets. Suddenly she knew, and poignantly, how little she had feared life in the soft sea-drenched air of the old city. Now looking at the dark-haired boy on the bed she knew painfully and accusingly. How illy had she repaid her father for all his love! The memory was cruel and terrible.

And her spine crept coldly as she thought of the big Negress with the slanting eyes coldly leveling a pistol and firing at Cantelou. The thought pounded into her vitals. She remembered the hostile expression on the woman's face when she caught her in the parlor three weeks ago. She had felt then that Duchess had become her enemy; someone to beware of. As she sat by Cantelou's bed listening to Emmy describe in detail the assault on the farmer's wife and little son near Ellenton by two Negroes and the consequent riot in which several white men were killed she heard without surprise Emmy say, "The whole affair was carefully planned in advance. The Negroes were armed and in battle formation to meet the white people before the woman had stopped screaming. And—to put the final punctuation mark—the red coach with the flamboyant Duchess was in Ellenton the night before the incident. She was also reported in the Low Country on the day before the Cainhoy Riot last week. Wherever she appears violence breaks out. Chamberlain must have

known about the Ellenton affair ahead of time for he
absented himself from the state so that he would not
be forced to aid the white people."

India looked down into the drained face of her son.
She seemed composed and thoughtful, gazing at him,
unaware of anyone's coming into the room, until
Chance softly spoke her name. Then she looked up
and Emmy saw her eyes, how tragically they looked at
Chance, and she cried, "Oh, darling—"

But India said, "I'm all right, Miss Emmy. I just
have a feeling that the Duchess knows the guns are at
Shepherd's Grove. I wish Max would come home. He
should be here with us but I don't love him any less
because he isn't; never misunderstand me. I can't ever
love him any less whatever he does or doesn't do and,
remember, he still has no memory that Cantelou is—is
—his too."

"But you look so sad, honey."

"I am sad but I'm more angry now than sad. I've
done so many things I shouldn't have done because I've
always wanted and put Max first above all. I should
never have left you and Cantelou alone here."

"Foot, you couldn't have hindered the Duchess. She
was shooting at you anyway, wasn't she, Chance?"

"I don't know, Miss Emmy." Chance had an ashen
color about his mouth. "Miss India, will you step into
the hall a minute?"

"Yes. Now, Cantelou, don't try and talk but tell
Mama by a flick of your eyelid—one flick, yes; two
flicks, no—whether or not you think she meant to shoot
you."

One flick! He was weak. So weak he couldn't move
his head but he was conscious. With a trembling hand
she closed his long nutmeg-colored eyes and went out.

"What is it?"

"Come on the piazza where our boy won't be
bothered."

India followed Chance. He said, "Miss India, do you
know what this is?"

India looked at the big old-fashioned trunk almost
indifferently. Her only sign of strain was tapping the

column where the paint was flecking off with her finger tips; her face was frozen in expressionlessness and she was staring at the trunk.

"That is my mother's trunk."

"And these?" Chance lifted one by one a pearl-inlaid mahogany lap desk, a silver christening cup of the time of George the First, a heavy silver inkstand, and a big hatbox with the name of a famous London hatter on the top.

"My desk, my brother Norman's cup, Papa's inkstand, and I don't recognize the box."

Chance opened the box. Within was a splendid, tall, satiny, black beaver hat. "Do Lord—what a big hat! It must have been made for a giant. It would even swallow my head. Don't cry—now, Miss India, don't cry—you haven't cried since you came home."

"That's the hat Papa ordered for Wade Hampton back in 1858 when I lost the race to Mr. Maxi at White Sulphur. Oh . . . I can't bear all this sadness . . . I can't bear feeling so guilty about Papa and Cantelou—"

Emmy was in the door, "Hush—hush—you're upsetting Cantelou. At least you can remember that you made Guy very happy for many years. He was not a strong man and nothing you could have done would have changed what finally happened to him. He went his way, not because of you, honey, but despite you. You could never have pleased him after he learned he had to share your love. He wanted all of your love like some men crave whisky or opium. It was his escape into the never-never land of security."

"What shall I do with these things, Miss India?"

India wiped the tears away with her hands. "Bring them up to my room. Where did you get them?"

"I brought them in the van when I fetched Flossie and the Duchess from Charleston in 1861. Duchess said they were her things but I knew then that Miss Childs meant them for you. Duchess has gone off somewhere and I slipped in the house on Macedonia Street this afternoon and carried them out of the attic. I intend to burn the house down and I thought you should have these."

"You can't burn a Radical's house. Mr. Wade says we mustn't do anything overt against them. Otherwise I would go after her at once. If the law won't punish her I intend to shoot her myself the minute the election is over."

Chance smiled. "I wasn't planning to burn the house until after the election either."

The next day India realized that there were prowlers constantly in and out of the yard; wandering back and forth from the coach house to the flagged turnaround. Negroes and hard-faced whites appeared and disappeared incessantly. Strange ones. In the big house no one dared say anything. None of them. Chance seemed to grow taller and grayer about the mouth. Danny went to bed with chills and fever. Sangua muttered and rocked the half-blind, half-deaf Pekingese tenderly as a baby on the porch of her tiny cabin. Steeben dropped one of the best and last Worcester cream jugs on the floor at dinner and even Emmy made mistakes in the chords she struck from her harp.

But when night fell, as if by magic, the yard was filled with men in red shirts and before midnight the Radical Negroes and carpetbaggers had faded into the woods or gone home and several men in the flaming flannel shirts took their seats in rocking chairs on the passageway between the kitchen and the dining room where they could keep their eyes on the coach house. Every now and then one of them would shoot his pistol or yell, "Hurrah for Hampton!" India curled up on a pallet by Cantelou's bed and slept soundly for the first time since she'd come down the mountain. She was fully awake from the dream; free now to will what she ought to do.

CHAPTER XXXVI

DAYS PASSED. Late October began and one afternoon Irene Pushkin paid a visit to Cantelou in company with her husband. Emmy entertained Mr. Pushkin, with the exaggerated politeness she reserved for people she par-

ticularly disdained, in the parlor while Irene sat by
Cantelou and examining his face attentively found
traces of his grandfather St. Julien, particularly the
black hair growing in a widow's peak on his high forehead and the long nose sharpened by suffering. She
shook her head sorrowfully, but said nothing. India walked back and forth telling Irene about Cantelou's being shot without warning in the cotton field.

"Cantelou," said Irene, looking at her nephew,
"won't you change your mind after this and move with
Mr. Pushkin and me to New York? We'll look after you
properly—never leave you alone where things like this
can happen to you."

Cantelou raised his eyes and fixed them on his mother, who dropped hers to her shoe tips.

"No, Sister, we're waiting for Papa. I want him to
find me here when he comes back."

Irene was rather disconcerted on hearing Max men-
tioned but managed to cover her embarrassment by a
dainty ladylike bit of choking. When she had drunk a
cup of water she said to India, "Pushkin tells me that
there isn't a chance for Wade Hampton to be elected
governor if he doesn't carry Edgefield County. The
odds throughout the rest of the state are about
even."

He had told her, too, that if the lost shipment of
guns could be recovered and the Radical Negroes
heavily armed, Red Shirts or not, they could keep
enough Democrats away from the polls to carry the
county. The key county, Pushkin had said, rubbing his
hands and pinching her thin arm fondly, the key county. She and Puskin got along well together. He loved
beautiful things and pretty music. And he appreciated
her and considered her a very superior person. She almost felt an urge to tell India what he had said about
the guns to fluster her but she knew which side her
bread was buttered on.

India said, "We'll carry Edgefield. Martin Gary and
the Red Shirts will see to that. It's reported that
General Ruger of the United States Army with five
companies of regular United States troops in addition to
the armed Negro militia is going to be sent to Edgefield

to keep order on Election Day. But even that won't hurt us."

"Suppose five thousand armed Radicals block every road into the town that day?"

India said positively, "They won't."

"Well—what about this—" Irene's face was pink with excitement. "I heard some men tell Mr. Pushkin last night that a warrant for the arrest of five hundred of the leading citizens of Edgefield County has already been signed as of Friday before the election and they will be kept in jail until too late to vote on Tuesday. Tell Mart Gary not to get too cocky."

India stared at Irene, mouth agape, breast heaving. This *would* hurt them. "What will become of us if this carpetbag rule continues? This crazy misrule."

Irene eyed her sister-in-law in a melancholy silence. She was embittered, had the feeling that something inside herself was beginning to rot. "Sometimes I almost hope they will continue to rule." She looked sourly at India who appeared very agitated. Her deep gray eyes glowed like moon fire. More so than usual.

"I suppose you do since you're one of them but they won't continue to rule, for we're going to have a little Thermopylae right here in Edgefield on November the seventh if it's necessary." India walked over to the mantel and picked up a pistol that was lying next to a chipped Rockingham cabbage. "It's time for Cantelou to be quiet. I'm sure he has enjoyed seeing you very much."

CHAPTER XXXVII

THE DUTIES of General Ruger, U.S.A. had always been clearly defined and he had never had any difficulty carrying them out. One would have thought that this assignment to take charge of the "State of Edgefield" (how stupid could orders get?) and remain until after Election Day would have seemed like a paltry affair to him. But much to the Radical Republican's annoyance Ruger was able, by his undoubted gift for lurid words, to express the way he felt about the unimportance of setting him down in a tiny village with twelve companies of soldiers to keep order. "That's not the point," his commanding officer had said. "If New York and Indiana go Democratic then South Carolina's vote could surely swing the Presidency and it is understood that the Up Country Edgefield total may well prove the deciding factor in that state. Little pieces are sometimes the most important of a whole puzzle, General Ruger . . . I expect you to fulfill your duty." William Tecumseh Sherman looked out of the window at a dull autumn drizzle wondering why Ruger didn't keep his mustaches clipped more neatly.

Ruger had wanted to tell General Sherman that his duties as a soldier were to command infantrymen in combat against other reasonably well-armed and outfitted soldiers, not against shabby, impoverished people with unpainted houses who sang and yelled as if they were crazy at all hours of the day and night.

Ruger's chagrin over recent scenes in Aiken: the dead bodies of the two fine-looking Germans; the big Negress in her feathered hat and silken dress laughing at the charge that she had been observed driving away from the gin of the father and son who had recently sent in a statement, signed by all the German settlers in Edgefield District, to a leading New York paper, protesting the lies being printed by Governor Chamberlain about the lawlessness of the white citizenry; the stone that had bounced off the skull of an elderly lady thrown by a carpetbagger from an upstairs window; the sounds and sights of popular contempt and hatred which had so signally marked his entry into the village, had completely unsettled him.

Contempt—even assumed contempt—had been a totally new experience to a man who had always prided himself on being a soldier who strictly adhered to the rules of professional warfare. He warmed his boots at the smoking wood fire of the Saluda House in Edgefield and wondered at the emotional tenseness which possessed him in this country town. He now felt and acted as though he were guilty of something, as if he had actually assumed the sins of Reconstruction personally. The clear denunciations of Hampton's voice as he had heard it Saturday night in Columbia rang more and more accusingly in his ears. Even though he had looked aside as his troops entered into the spirit of the occasion and helped the ladies and workmen string flower garlands up and down the street—helped roll out and direct the firing of the cannons of the Columbia Flying Artillery, describing itself as the Hampton and Tilden Musical Club with four twelve-pounder flutes, that hadn't salved his conscience, for after all—blood was thicker than water.

Perhaps the weather was responsible for his depression. It was raining outside, a drizzly chilly rain. He had a cold. Across the square the doors of Kearsey's saloon kept flapping open and shut—the sound of singing and shouting was continuous from the bar of the Palmetto Hotel and there was riding, riding, riding constantly. An officer of the day came in and breathlessly reported that hundreds of Red Shirts were pouring into the village with provision trains; transforming the courthouse and Masonic Hall into barracks, stacking their arms with military precision and reporting to General Martin Gary for orders.

The officer was a patriotic young man who had missed being in the war and he was terribly excited over the importance of his intelligence. He almost burst into tears when Ruger's reply was:

"Run over and buy me a bottle of Monogram rye whiskey from the Palmetto Bar and then go into that grocery store next door and fetch a pound of rock candy. I'm catching a dreadful cold."

The ugly little rain fell all during the day. It was November the sixth and the next day was the election. From his window Ruger watched campfires winking in the public square and big pails of hot rum being carried around to the men who had spent the rainy day in the saddle. As dark came, the Rebel yell greeted whining fiddles from the upstairs of the stores around the square. Ruger could almost see the public buildings quiver with the ecstasy of hobnailed boots and the ringing laughter of gay young girls. Where were his own soldiers in their safe blue jackets? Why, they were dancing with the village girls and swapping jokes with the Red Shirts! And that was good. The boys needed a little fun so far from home.

Ruger sipped his rock and rye and ate a stewed chicken and a plate of hot crusty biscuits that were brought for his supper. He was beginning to feel a great deal stronger. His appointment with Gary wasn't until dawn.

The officer of the day interrupted him before he finished his tasty stew.

"Sir, all day I've done as you ordered and refused to hear the Radicals and Negroes knocking at the door to see you but there are a couple out there now I don't dare ignore."

"Why not?"

"For one thing . . . he's a judge and she . . . well . . . she's terrifying."

"Bring them in."

In swept the Duchess and Prince Rivers. Duchess was livid.

"Why did you nullify the warrants for the five hundred arrests on Saturday? The town is swarming with lawbreakers. My God—anybody would think you'd been sent here by the Democrats."

Ruger was still smarting from the feeling of shame that had oppressed him since Saturday.

"Control yourself, woman," he barked. The rye was very helpful. It gave him confidence. Even before this dreadful-looking creature.

The big black man started to speak but the woman said, "Shut up. Let me do the talking. Ruger," she was so insolent that he wanted to slap her face, "unless you do something we're liable to lose this election and if we do I shall report you to the President of the United States. You don't know who I am. I am the most powerful Republican woman in South Carolina. I can do you great harm. There are five thousand guns stored in a coach house near here and unless you do your duty I am going to take matters into my own hands. With five thousand armed Radical Negroes we'll shoot your puny little twelve companies to hell and run the voting entirely to suit ourselves. Martin Gary thinks his five hundred Red Shirts are invincible but bullets go through those bits of flannel as easy as through your blue-coated boys grinning right this minute like jackasses at the village girls." Her eyes glittered and she seemed to uncoil taller than she already was. The gray velvet bonnet on top of her narrow head looked like the hood of a cobra. Her filed teeth were fangs ... they were, he could see them. ...

"Get out!" Ruger roared.

Deliberately she took out a long cigar, lit it and carefully blew the smoke right into his raw stopped-up nose.

He clawed at the pistol in his belt and leveled it at her. "Get the hell out of here!"

"Then you refuse to order your soldiers to instantly stop this Red Shirt terrorization?" Was she hissing or talking?

"Shut up!" It had been years since he'd bellowed so loud. Not since Second Manassas. The officer of the day and three others who were playing whist in the downstairs hall ran in and at a nod from their general forced the big man and woman out of the door. But not before two of them groaned in pain from jabs in tender places that the woman gave them.

Ruger stood in the window and watched the woman get into a magnificent scarlet coach, grand enough for royalty, and go tearing around the crowded square with no thought but to run down and kill man or beast foolish enough to trust the mercy of her horses' hoofs.

CHAPTER XXXVIII

AT OAKLEY PARK mounts were packed in the stables and overflowing into the grove, tethered to naked trees and dripping vines. Light streamed through the majestic columns which extended around two sides of Martin Gary's big square white house. Every window blazed a welcome, the massive double doors were flung wide and pretty girls were waiting with bowls of hot rum and coffee to greet the wet riders galloping down the long muddy lane. Hickory logs crackled in the fireplaces; from the balcony over the porch came the gay scraping of fiddles and the happy excited twanging of guitars and banjos. Two Negroes in red shirts beat the bones in the hall and every now and then someone would call a reel or a quadrille and the sound of boots and slippers sliding across the waxed floors kept time to the knocking bones.

Just before dawn someone new appeared in the doorway. He had on a red shirt of fine English flannel and had left his big white mule unhitched beside a bush. One of the men knocking the bones, Big Dick, started shouting, "Lawdy, Lawdy—hit's Mr. Maxi!" And because he was one of their own who had been a long way off, because the night was a night of strange happenings and events and there was not going to be any giving way to sleeping or tiredness or any lessening of excitement, this seemed entirely fitting and the men began shouting as though they were ready for a fresh charge and Philip Abney and some of Max's oldest friends picked him up on their shoulders and went waltzing around the room with him hollering, "Hurrah for Hampton!" and Max thought, This whole world is crazy. I wish I felt even a surge of remembering these men. I had hoped when I heard the music from the street that India would be here. I can't ride any further tonight. Everything is crazy but I'm staying through the election anyway and I know I'll see her at the polls tomorrow.

As the cold gray dawn came the news exploded at Oakley Park like a spatter of grapeshot. Three thousand Negroes were massing on the public square from all parts of the county to vote for the Radical Republican Governor. They had been sifting in all through the night and, unless something was done immediately, not a white person would be able to get even near the polls. People said that the red coach had stopped at every Radical's house in the county during the night. That the six horses had been changed four times. The Duchess had been heard screaming, threatening, commanding, finally promising a gun to every man to protect himself with and to kill a white man. People said that the Radicals were here to settle once and for all that it was going to be a carpetbagger state, not the kind of state Hampton wanted. Not a working combination of black and white.

The church bells tolled the alarm and for a while Edgefield looked like the end of the world. Women, children, and old folks who lived near the square, from which violence would probably come, run to houses in the farther part of town, taking refuge with their friends and kinsmen. Many women were weeping and wailing; others, outraged, cried out to give them a gun and let them fight and ride along with the men.

Ruger looked on the thousands of black faces filling up the public square like a rolling tide and Martin Gary, his Confederate greatcoat wrapped around his gaunt frame, his cavalry boots squeaking furiously, his fingers itching on the brace of pistols fastened to his belt, said, "General Ruger, I suggest that we set up two voting places in town. You can see that it is impossible for all these people to be handled at one box. Let the white folks vote at the courthouse and the colored people vote at Macedonia church."

"That's a bargain." General Ruger took the cold talons of General Gary into his warm steady hand. "And if that big Mulatto woman comes high-tailing it to town in the red coach to make trouble, I've already sworn out a warrant for her arrest."

Gary said, "She'll never show up on the scene itself. She's always behind the scenes. If I hadn't made sure she couldn't harm us, I tell you, I would be worried what she was up to."

As Gary remounted his skinny horse, he called out to Philip Abney, "Are you sure the Horse Creek boys are at the Allans'?"

And Philip said, "Those were the orders Fant Calvert took them last night."

Max, riding beside Philip, said, "Why do they need men at the Grove? If anything's wrong I'm going out there immediately."

"The five thousand guns intended to arm these Negroes are hidden there. Should Duchess and her gang find them we'd be in a sorry pickle. Don't look so

worried. The Horse Creek boys are guarding the Grove
and you know how tough they are. Aren't you supposed
to be on duty at the door of the courthouse?"

Max took up his station at the door of the courthouse together with a handsome red-shirted Mulatto
who had recently finished law at Harvard. As the day
finally broke fully into a chill foggy mist the voting pro-
ceeded briskly. Democrats, approaching the stairway to
the courtroom on the second floor, were lifted bodily
above the heads of the Radical Negroes waiting in line
to vote there, whether Ruger said this was the place for
them or no, and passed upward by powerful arms until they found solid footing near the ballot box. As soon
as they had voted they were passed back down, crying,
"I'm off to vote now at Good Hope—Bound Tree—
Liberty Hill—Horse Creek—Chestnut Hill—Spring-
field—Hurrah for Hampton." They left the square galloping toward other polling places singing, "We'll hang
Dan Chamberlain on a rotten apple tree."

As the Negroes refused to move from the courthouse
and go to the voting place that General Ruger had ordered them to use, the manner of the Red Shirts, black
and white, became truculent. They nagged these Negroes but nobody struck a blow. The Radical Negroes
were waiting for their guns. The Duchess had never
failed them yet. They were a patient race, used to
truculence and loud orders. Used to waiting, but at the
end the killing would come easy. Suddenly Cato and
Fant Calvert armed to the teeth started quarreling with
each other, drew their pistols and flourished them.
Their friends took sides. There was swaggering, shov-
ing, cursing; it looked like the white man's bloody riot.
The ruse drove many of the Radical Negroes back
from the steps. But not for long. They rolled back and
then the clatter of hoofs came from the northeast corner of the square. A splitting yell tore through the
gloom as thirty Red Shirts from Horse Creek galloped
almost onto the steps and pulled in their foam-flecked
horses so suddenly that they stood on their hind legs
and pawed the air. Then they galloped around the
courthouse yelling and firing their pistols and Martin
Gary thundered, "I thought they were at the Grove.

Fant Calvert, didn't you arrange for a guard at Shepherd's Grove?"

"Fant was in his cups last night," a young thin man with a pimply face guffawed. "He was visiting Daught Leg and they forgot to pull down the shades."

Fant drove his fist in the boy's face and the youth looked surprised as his nose burst open and his front teeth fell onto his chest. Surprised, and then he lay down quite gently on the steps.

Max hit Fant on the head with his pistol butt and Fant blinked a minute and came toward him, his head lowered, his body crouched with his weight well back on his heels. Max jumped for him but the Mulatto lawyer flattened Fant with a powerful blow behind his ear and said frantically to Max, "For God's sake take fifty men and get home quick. I thought something smelled with no sign of the Duchess having been here."

Mart Gary roared, "Fant Calvert has messed things up good. I thought the Horse Creek men were guarding the guns. This means India and Miss Emmy are out there all by themselves with nobody but Chance and the wounded boy to protect them. Leave Fant to me, Max, and get going. It'll be a long time before he's woman hungry again when I get through with him."

CHAPTER XXXIX

INDIA SLEPT FITFULLY wondering why the guard was so quiet on such a night; why there were no shots, no cheers, no shuffling footsteps as usual round and round the house. When first light came she got up, refreshed the low fire of hickory logs and tiptoed upstairs to dress. I'd better put on the old velvet suit of Mama's she thought. There will probably be comings and goings here all day and if it's possible I want to ride into town tonight to see the torchlight procession and the green velvet will easily serve as a riding habit without the hoop.

She had prayed last night; she would pray today, that Max would miraculously appear at the polls in Edgefield to vote for Hampton. But if he didn't, she must endure until she was free to go to him again. She brushed her hair and let it lie caressingly around her shoulders for a minute. It had been so long since she had worn it soft and unbraided. She hunted in her porcelain, velvet-lined jewel box and found enough tortoise-shell combs and pins to pile the blue-black lengths high on her head as she had learned to do that time in Richmond. She touched the fall of old lace at her round time-yellowed satin collar and nodded at herself in the mirror.

It was cold in here and she pulled a red and black Scotch plaid shawl around her shoulders as she went down through the wide dreary hall where the watery light showed the vacant places, lighter than the walls, where the paintings used to hang. The Vermeer was in the parlor now and the Gainsborough as well; the pair of Herrings in which red-coated gentlemen still bravely hunted russet foxes through autumn-tempered woods, waving hats and loosely sitting their long-necked hunters —these were the only remnants of the once famous collection that had so fortuitously saved Shepherd's Grove from the auctioneer's hammer.

This house had known so much of love and death, joy and misery. Held so many memories of the passion of death and the terror of love. She shivered and felt very sad for a moment. Then she mastered herself and, poking back a pin that slipped from her heavy hair, went through the back door toward the kitchen to make sure that Ida had the fire going, the sausage fried, and the big iron pots of coffee and hominy boiling for the Red Shirts.

She heard no sound except the disgruntled crowing of the black and white rooster. But he soon gave up and crept back into the sanctity of his chicken house with his broad fat wives.

The back yard was full of a stagnant gray cloud that seemed to have settled there from the big wind that had roared the night away in the giant pines. As she went down the steps onto the passageway, the beginning day darkened and drops of rain leaked through the low ceiling of cloud and wet her cheeks. An extra thick part of the dull cloud wrapped itself with funereal scarves of strangely shining mist around the big old coach house in the distance. It all looked very gloomy and like the illustrations in the book of Dante that Miss Emmy had been reading aloud to Cantelou these afternoons.

The kitchen was dark and cold; the fire completely out. This had never happened before in all her years at Shepherd's Grove. If Ida were ill there had been Steeben, or Sangua, or Danny, and lately there had been Chance again. On him, she could always depend. And the Red Shirts—where were they? And their horses? Suddenly she looked down at the ground. It had rained hard shortly after midnight and the wet surface of the ground was smooth as poured jelly. Not a hoof had passed over it. Not a boot. Nothing had moved anywhere near the house. It had stopped raining around two so she realized that there had been no Red Shirts guarding them the night long. Not unless they had quartered themselves within the barn or the coach house.

She stepped onto the slick unmarked ground wondering what in the world had happened to Ida and Steeben. Because of a pool of water and soft mud, she was forced to go out of her way from the house toward the barn and in a contemplative frame of mind, holding her skirt high and carefully placing her thinly shod toes on the least soggy spots, she took an unused bit of road that formerly was kept open between the barn and the house in the days when the stalls were full of high-mettled racers and this was a short cut to the training track where they were in the habit of jogging back and forth to loosen the horses up a bit on cold mornings. The short stretch of road had a set of wheel ruts in it. But not jog-cart ruts. They were made by firm broad tires like those of a heavy vehicle. A number of horses, at least six, she wonderingly noted . . . perhaps more . . . yes, definitely more—

She glanced up at the barn toward which she was heading. She saw the wheel tracks led straight around the barn. Her curiosity was aroused. This was very queer. She pulled the shawl close around her and threw an end of it over her head. On impulse she followed the old road around the barn and approaching the big opened doors saw that here the vehicle and six horses and other horses had gone inside.

For a minute she stood undecided wondering if the vehicle was still inside the barn, if Duchess was sitting inside the coach. She knew that she was looking at the trail of the scarlet coach, a trail that led fearsomely into the big dark barn.

It gave her the creeps to think of Duchess sitting inside the coach inside the barn. The Duchess, she knew it well, was bound on some dark mischief. With great caution, in order not to make a sound, to avoid giving the occupants of the barn any hint that she was about, she climbed a catalpa tree that grew right outside of a window opening on one of the big stalls. Inside the dimness she could see the coach in the wide runway between the stalls. Little Mulatto Quasha was holding the horses. They were standing with their heads hanging, waiting there in the shrouded darkness. She could see his thick lips quieting the horses. In various stalls were other horses—but nobody. Just Quasha. Where were *they?* And where were the Red Shirts? Chance? Was nobody here in this misty weird world but her and Quasha and the tired horses?

Yes . . . suddenly she realized that a group of Negro men were grouped in the stall beyond the window. She could just see them now that she was getting accustomed to the murky gloom. One of them coughed and another cautioned him to be quiet; another bumped against a feed box and someone swore at him in a low mellow voice.

A tattered scarf of mist detached itself from the edge of the opened barn door and unwinding slowly entered the barn and drifted silently through the dark open windows of the coach. While it did so, India balanced in the crotch of the tree spellbound.

Duchess was not in the coach. Had she been, the windows would be closed against this penetrating raw dampness. Since she was not in the coach, where was she? India could just make out the faces of the men in the stall. All were strange. All men.

Her attention came back to the old road. It didn't end at the barn. It wandered roughly on to the coach house. As her gaze followed the road, her stomach constricted and the breath of her lungs fought to come out of her mouth that felt as though someone had suddenly stuffed it full of old wool. Duchess was in the coach house! There were footsteps in the old road, all pointing that way. One set of footsteps.

She slithered out of the tree and crept along the old road, keeping low in the broom grass and weeds along the edges. She was almost at the corner of coach house when a cold bare hand gripped her arm. Looking down she saw enormous black fingers close about her elbow and wrench her off her feet into a low ditch. Instinctively she struck backwards with her free arm and opened her mouth to scream but he spoke in a low whisper: "It's Chance, Miss India. *She's* in there. I don't think she's discovered the guns yet but she's close. She's got a stick and is tapping every board. Did you bring your pistol?"

"No. I had just started to the kitchen to see if Ida had breakfast on for the Red Shirts."

"Something must have gone wrong. They didn't show up all night. Steeben is under the house with a shotgun ready to shoot anybody that approaches the steps. Danny is up in that chinaberry tree with a shotgun. He's got the door to the barn covered so that when she signals he can start shooting the men who come out of there. You go back to the house and wait but keep your pistol cocked. I'll get *her* before she finds the guns. Run . . . we haven't any time to lose. This is her last straw and she'll resort to any meanness to get those guns."

A black shiny spider had woven a web across a briar bush to the left of where she and Chance were crouching, without noise. And started a new pattern. She could hear the wet breath of the silence overhead amid the tangle of briars and crooked branches and the lattice of wild grapevines; amid the sharp-needled pine seedlings against the coach house from where the tap,

tap came. At longish intervals—so long that the spider finished the new pattern and sat a minute in the wetness of his diamond-studded trap.

It must be half-past six, thought India. Full daylight will soon be here and the Negroes will come from the barn and Danny will shoot one or two—then they will shoot Danny—

"Go on. Run for it, Miss India, but be quiet as you can—" Chance lifted her to the other side of the ditch. A yellow leaf fell on her nose. She brushed it off as she ran, slipping through the soft red mud.

The house was still dark. From Emmy's room came rhythmic snores of untroubled sleep. In the billiard room the fire she had made up earlier glowed cheerfully and cast a radiance on Cantelou's smooth young face buried in the pillows. The cover had slipped off his shoulder and she gently folded it back up under his chin. She tiptoed over to the mantel. Her finger tips were freezing and she held them to the low blaze for an instant before she firmly picked up the cold steel pistol from the mantel and glancing once more at her son made her way noiselessly out of the dry, seemingly safe house into the gray, shrouded morning where death was lurking in the misty trees and waiting in the dim cold empty buildings.

Chance was not in the ditch where she had left him. But it was easy to track him in the soft wet earth. She leaned low and was almost at the door of the coach house when her shawl caught on a blackberry briar and was jerked off her head taking most of her hairpins and combs along with it. She could feel her silky hair unrolling down her back. It gave her a feeling of comfort and security as the lengths of it wrapped around her body to the waist. She was close to the pasture fence and a dark unmistakable form came moving forward to her. The form whickered a greeting as she reached the coach house door. Flossie, she thought— oh dear! A bullet whistled over her head and Chance called loudly from within the coach house, "Drop down . . . get out of the light of the door."

Another report crashed through the silence and she heard a grunt and a dull thud and a raucous wild laughing as she darted through the door and was swallowed up in the sudden darkness within the building.

"Don't worry, my pet," Duchess was saying to Chance, "I'm not ready to let you go yet. I'll finish you off slowly later. It looks like I got you in the chest but it must have missed your heart. Strange. You always seemed more heart than brains. I would have expected your heart to fill up your chest. Now where did that white-faced ninny get to? She must have run. Did you think she'd come to your aid? Ha—ha—you probably did at that. Well, lie there and grunt all you please. I've found the guns."

India, wedged back in the shadows behind a barrel of nails, watched, sick with horror, as the Duchess raised an axe and splintered a broad pine board. She eased the blade under and with little effort pried up the heavy plank and gave a gasp of delight at the big wooden box marked "Shoemaker's Tools." Another board up—"Agricultural Implements"; another and another . . . There in front of her lay all that was needed to win this election. And the day had hardly begun. Hardly begun.

"Plenty of time to get to town," Duchess gloated. "Can you hear me, you tall no-account man?"

Chance groaned and coughed and the woman's demented laughter made India's heart empty itself of any pity and become dry and hard with hate. This woman had shot her son down with as little mercy as she had shot Chance. As she intended to shoot her. An accumulation of terror and trembling overcame her and she was forced for a moment to lay her head against the nail barrel. The dim light entering through the open door served only to heighten the distorted mask of Duchess's face and India saw her lean over Chance and kick him three times in the groin. This time he did not make a sound and his breathing could be heard rasping shallowly from the top of his lungs.

A low cry escaped her and she gasped. Instantly Duchess stiffened and got quickly away from the revealing light of the door.

"Where are you?" Duchess called. "Come out, India. I wouldn't hurt you. Are you over here? Over there?"

Like a snake uncoiling the big woman began to move carefully along the side walls.

She doesn't know I have a pistol, India thought. And if she did know she wouldn't care. She's sure I wouldn't use it.

Very carefully India peeped over the barrel. The room was long and it appeared that she was looking down a deep well with a moving black reptile at the far end. She put her foot a step back and started to move away from the approaching figure. For an instant, she was arrested by Duchess saying, "You know I wouldn't hurt you. My sweet. Come out and let Duchess talk to you a minute. Come now."

No mouse ever crept more stealthily back into the dark corner than India. Every honeyed word was a spider thread thrown out to circle her and pull her in. Oh—why didn't Danny come? He must have heard the shots. She must cock her pistol. The Duchess was coming nearer. She was not ten feet away from her. India could hear her breathing and see the glitter of her slanting eyes as they turned for a moment to face the door. She pulled back the hammer softly, scarcely able to stifle a scream. She even remembered to point it right between the two pin-point eyes that were coming closer, closer—not wavering—not, not wavering because they had found her there in the darkness of her corner.

The roar of the pistol in the coach house completely deafened her. She shut her eyes and breathed deep. Was she going to faint? She stared in front of her. The slanting eyes were gone. The Duchess was writhing and sobbing on the floor; jerking and twisting like a headless snake. And then the thing on the floor stopped moving and was getting up. Another shot shattered the silence and India screamed, dropping the pistol. Her hand was on fire. She lost all sense of anything except the intolerable pain that shot up her arms to her shoulders. From the direction of the barn came two blasts of Danny's shotgun and his shouting, "Here they come! Run fast, Miss India!"

Now there was more shooting and the thing was crawling toward the door to block her escape, but India holding her shattered arm with the other hand ran through the door and the fog was so thick that she managed to slip over to the pasture fence as the Negroes who had been waiting in the barn came rushing into the coach house.

"Find her," Duchess was shouting. Evidently she wasn't too badly wounded. "She can't have gone far. And some of you get up these guns and put them in the coach and take me to a doctor. My God, I think she's blown my leg clean off—the bitch."

And I thought I hit her right between the eyes! India feverishly balanced herself and painfully pulled herself up onto the post-and-rail fence. Weakly she whistled and from a pear tree nearby came a low "Bob White— Bob White."

Ah, quails! Oh Max, where are you? Darling . . . darling . . . Here comes Flossie. Good girl . . . come closer. No . . . turn around . . . closer . . . that's it. Now stand still. Oh, wait and let me put my arm inside my jacket and button it. Now—

She grasped Flossie by her wet mane and riding astride as she had done as a child, kicked her and though she herself could not see the fence except as a dim blur put Flossie at it. Old and stiff as she was the mare rose to the occasion nobly and cleared the top rail and was going away almost as soon as her feet touched the slippery clay ground.

"There she goes," yelled Duchess and there were more shots. One whistled over her head and another hit a tree she was passing. Her hair streamed behind her like a big wing that threatened to fly her over backward but Flossie was aware that this was a high day such as she had not been a part of for a long time. Once she had had a pulled thin mane, but now it was ragged and shaggy and easy for India to hold onto and guide her by. Her head showed gray hairs but there was a dangerous glitter in her eyes. She galloped hard in front of the house and was off down the woods road toward town.

"Thank you, Lord," India whispered, "thank you very much." But she had hardly breathed the second thank you when it seemed as if an army of Negroes mushroomed in front of her. They threw up their hands and two of them risked their heads to catch Flossie around the neck and hang onto her.

"Stop whey you at, Miss India."

It was Moze, Steeben's grandson, and in the mist he looked like a mean gnome with his blue eye and his brown eye fastened on her useless arm.

"Let me go!" India was almost screaming with pain and terror for she could hear behind her and in front of her the galloping of many horses and the rumbling of heavy wheels which could belong to nothing but the scarlet coach.

Flossie began to move restlessly and she tossed her fine small head high so that the foam flecks spattered her chest and shoulders and the frightened rider on her back.

"Don't let her git away. Keep aholt of dat hoss. Here comes de Duchess," Moze said. But India grasped Flossie's mane tightly and wheeled her half round.

Moze jumped in front of the mare. India said, "Get out of the way or I'll run you down."

Moze reached up for Flossie's nose to catch it between his cruel pinching fingers but India kicked him in the face and Flossie reared and struck out with her forefeet. The sound of many horses was coming nearer and nearer. The sound of shouts and cries and the whining screaking sound of brakes. And as she heard the horrid voice of the Duchess call, "Good God—turn quick and head back toward the bridge," she also heard a high sharp yell and on the mist a loved tenor voice crying, "Hurrah for Hampton!" She pressed her knee into the mare's side bending forward to take the lunge into a gallop but as Flossie leaped forward Moze struck her on the chest with a heavy axe and she fell forward neighing wild and shrilly so that the coming horses and in particular one big white mule answered.

"Kill her," India shrieked at the man in the red shirt who was jumping off the white mule coming toward her where she stood blinded by tears straddling the heaving animal. "Kill her," she pleaded, pointing to Flossie lying on her side frothing blood at the mouth and kicking with her hoofs. And as the shot reverberated, India pitched forward over the head of her old mare and lay on the wet shiny clay road in her soaking green velvet suit, her hair spread all around her like a dark fan.

She was unaware of the tide of Red Shirts flowing past her shouting and shooting at the fleeing coach and the mounted Radicals as they tore away from Shepherd's Grove into the swamp. The first thing she was aware of was being in Max's arms and hearing him say, "Oh, I *am* Maximilian Allan and you *are* my India. The curtain has rolled up. I see everything from the moment I held you like this at White Sulphur. Below us the hunt was going in full cry. I heard Turner Ashby calling from the top of the ridge and Wade Hampton—Hoick . . . Halloo—back to him. Oh—open your eyes and let me see if you still love me. Open—India, my sweet—my wife."

CHAPTER XL

INDIA, wrapped in shawls and banked with pillows, lay on a long leather couch pulled from Calbraith Butler's law office onto the little piazza facing the public square. The rain had stopped and a five o'clock misty dusk was falling in thick deep blue tones of shadow. An ominous silence gripped the people packed upon the plaza.

They had just learned that the Negroes were marching from Macedonia Church to take over the courthouse. They had not finished voting and there were too many left to be taken care of at the church before the poll closed. They were coming to capture the box at the courthouse. A courier had brought the word and Gary had sent immediately for Ruger to meet him on the square.

"Are you sure you feel strong enough to stay out here? Things may get unpleasant. Let Hetty and me help you inside the office to the fire. You're white as a ghost and you've been quite heroic enough for one day."

"No, Lucy," India's somber eyes were fastened on the powerful man with the gold and silver hair sitting the big white mule at the foot of the courthouse steps animatedly talking with the nice-looking Mulatto who, with him, was to make sure no Radical set foot on the bottom step. "Duchess may still have some devilish scheme in process."

"If she shows up, we'll attend to her."

The women nodded their bonneted and shawled heads grimly and Lucy Pickens smoothed the trailing plume of her elegant new Empress Eugénie riding hat and draped her velvet riding skirt around to a more becoming line as General Ruger in his long blue overcoat sauntered by the law office and touched his hat admiringly to the village ladies.

He took his time crossing the street, aware that the Negroes were almost at the square. Thousands of them. Infuriated. Did they have the guns? Was this going to be a fight; a massacre like Custer's a short week ago; a forlorn hope for Hampton after all?

Pine torches flaring in the hands of the Red Shirts made the sky above the dripping trees seem almost cobalt and very very close. A flying courier galloped onto the square and, spotting Gary, tore across the turf and said something to the Bald Eagle as he approached General Ruger from the opposite side of the square. Gary looked alarmed and spat out some crisp orders. Magically, marksmen, sharpshooters of his old brigade, appeared in all the upstairs windows hemming the plaza. Mounted Red Shirts closed in stirrup to stirrup barring the entrance to the stairs of the courthouse packed with members of Stonewall Jackson's foot cavalry. Rifles bristled out of the tall paned windows of the courtroom.

India leaned forward but she couldn't hear Ruger's voice as he and Gary came together and saluted punctiliously. Ruger pointed to the approaching mass of black men and Gary answered loudly, "You made the bargain this morning. You've got to stand by your word."

Then another courier galloped up and said something and Ruger slapped Gary on the back and Gary laughed and grasped his hand.

Ruger turned, shouting to his companies in battle

formation beyond the courthouse. "The Duchess has tailed it North. Those Radicals aren't armed at all!"

India looked at the first row of Negroes who had just reached the square. At Ruger's words, without saying anything to the ones behind them, they disintegrated and disappeared. That was all. Not a Radical ever set foot on the square after they heard Ruger telling how the Duchess in the end had deserted them. They just melted away, silently, into the deep blue shadows of the dusk.

And to everyone's amazement the band standing ready to lead the procession, if the dice rolled up that way, drowned the Rebel yell as the brass instruments blared "Oh Say Can You See." At first nobody sang except Ruger and his soldiers but at the close the whole square was singing the anthem at the top of their voices.

After "The Star-Spangled Banner," the band hurried quickly, happily, back to the beloved "Dixie." Then the shouting really rolled while the torchlight procession got into formation as the man with the largest voice in the county announced, "Edgefield gives Hampton a majority of over three thousand and there are still five boxes in Georgia to be heard from!"

Douschka Pickens in a red Garibaldi cap, a long red plume curling under her chin, a red velvet cape billowing behind her, led off on a white horse as though she had indeed been born a royal child, and behind her rode the Red Shirts, white and black, singing and yelling. Ruger's soldiers got in the parade, too, and the women who had been standing on the law office piazza and huddled in the darkened stores ran out waving their shawls and bonnets and howling as loud as the men. Even Lucy Pickens forgot her superiority and let a bearded old man from the backwoods pick her up and whirl her out into the street in a jerky reel.

India reached down and her fingers closed over the twine tied around the hatbox at her feet. She was getting very tired. The glare from the torches hurt her eyes, the shouts made her head spin. She leaned her head back against the pillows.

Max pulled his Rosinante out of the procession, dismounted and made his way over to Calbraith Butler's office. Calbraith was in the courthouse with some other men getting together the boxes to take on to Columbia. Max wished now that they hadn't asked him to go along. He never wanted to leave India again.

Oh, India darling! He whispered to himself, it's too fantastic the way everything has cleared and you are still the shining center of my life. You never stopped loving me . . . not an instant. I can't bear to leave you . . . even for this one night.

From the courthouse he saw Calbraith and the men coming. He must tell her good night. He ran over to where she was sitting, as alluring and intense as she had been that night of Secession when he had seen her suddenly in the old Charleston Hotel.

She was rising to meet him, her injured arm hanging in a sling. "Max—Max" India threw herself into his arms and clung closely and tightly to him. He stood with his arms tenderly around her so as not to hurt her. Then with a soft urgent whisper in his throat he crushed her to him.

When he left her she was standing where he could see her all the way to the head of Main Street. He lifted the hatbox high in farewell-until-tomorrow to her. She was silhouetted against a waving mass of burning torches and crimson shirts and deep blue twilight sky—tall —youthful—gallant. She was smiling at him, but her great gray eyes were wide and deep. They gazed across the surging throng. Her unhurt arm raised in a gesture of good night.

"Isn't she splendid?" Max cried, and Calbraith Butler who was riding beside him looked back and seeing India there, pale yet dauntless, saluted her admiringly.

Max turned his head and looked toward the West. The clouds were lifting and a red glow burned bright in the twilight sky, low on the horizon, with a promise that tomorrow would be fair and the road smooth and swift for him to come home again.

ABOUT THE AUTHOR

ELIZABETH BOATWRIGHT COKER was born in Darlington, South Carolina. Her marriage to James Coker in 1930 joined two of the oldest and most aristocratic families in the South. Mrs. Coker is the author of seven bestselling novels, including *Daughter of Strangers, India Allan, La Belle* and her most recent, *Blood Red Roses*, which are all set in the South of the Civil War. Her books were book club selections and have been translated into half a dozen foreign languages. She now lives in Hartsville, South Carolina, the seat of Coker College, established by her husband's grandfather.

RELAX!

SIT DOWN
and Catch Up On Your Reading!